STARSHIP LIBERATOR

DAVID VANDYKE

PLAGUE WARS: DECADE ONE

The Eden Plague	*Skull's Shadows*	*Apocalypse Austin*
Reaper's Run	*Eden's Exodus*	*Nearest Night*

PLAGUE WARS: ALIEN INVASION

The Demon Plagues	*The Orion Plague*	*Comes The Destroyer*
The Reaper Plague	*Cyborg Strike*	*Forge and Steel*

PLAGUE WARS: STELLAR CONQUEST

First Conquest	*Tactics of Conquest*	*Conquest and Empire*
Desolator	*Conquest of Earth*	

B.V. LARSON

STAR FORCE

Swarm	*Conquest*	*Annihilation*
Extinction	*Battle Station*	*Storm Assault*
Rebellion	*Empire*	*The Dead Sun*

with David VanDyke

Outcast	*Exile*	*Demon Star*

THE UNDYING MERCENARIES

Steel World	*Tech World*	*Death World*
Dust World	*Machine World*	*Home World*

GALACTIC LIBERATION BOOK 1

STARSHIP LIBERATOR

DAVID VANDYKE
B.V. LARSON

CASTALIA HOUSE

Starship Liberator

David VanDyke and B. V. Larson

Published by Castalia House
Kouvola, Finland
www.castaliahouse.com

All quotations from The History of Light Infantry: *The 4GW Counterforce* by William S. Lind and LtCol Gregory A. Thiele, USMC are used by permission from the authors.

Cover Art by Tom Edwards

The development of the mechsuit bridged the gap between light infantry and heavy armor, combining the best attributes of both. For a time it was able to decisively defeat any equivalent ground force. Yet by its very successes it bore within itself the seeds of its own destruction. Battles became narrowly focused on how to best employ, counter, or acquire this singular technology. Commanders soon forgot that victory depended not upon machines, but on men.

—*A History of Galactic Liberation,*
by Derek Barnes Straker, 2860 A.D.

Contents

Part III: Liberator

Part I: Mechsuiter

*Light infantry [is] a flexible force capable of operating in austere con-
ditions with few logistical requirements and employing tactics unlike
those of line or mechanized infantry.*

—The History of Light Infantry; *The 4GW Counterforce* by
William S. Lind and LtCol Gregory A. Thiele, USMC.

Chapter 1

Planet Corinth, in low orbit above the capital city of Helios. Present day (2817 A.D., Old Earth reckoning).

Assault Captain Derek Straker flexed his hands inside his fifty-ton Foehammer mechsuit, keeping his fingers limber. The gauntlets—and the rest of the suit—didn't move. It'd been locked down in pre-deployment mode next to its three companions within the open belly bay of the Marksman dropship. If it had been unlocked, any motion might have torn pieces out of the release mechanism.

Below them an alien world stretched out in an arc. A mist of hazy atmosphere was just beginning to cause friction as they descended toward the surface. The gray splotch directly below was the target—a city wreathed in smoke and flame.

A tiny crack left over from the last battle in the lower right corner of Straker's faceplate HUD caught his eye, but he didn't let it worry him. The crystal was tougher than diamond, and the optics were periscopic offsets anyway, ensuring even a lucky penetration wouldn't take him out.

"How you boys doing?" said Flight Lieutenant Carla Engels, the dropship's pilot, in her crisp contralto voice.

"Ready to kick some Hok ass!" came the snarling reply from three of the four armored mechsuiters.

"Glad to hear it," Engels replied, her voice deceptively light.

Only Straker held his tongue. He let his troops rave, pumping themselves up for combat. He had no need of such techniques. The icy hatred for the Hok that inhabited his heart fueled him like a mechsuit's power plant. He saved his enthusiasm for destroying the aliens as quickly and efficiently as possible.

The briefings had made clear that First Mechsuit Regiment was being thrown into battle as a fire brigade. It was a losing fight, no matter what the optimistic intelligence officers said. Veteran of many such operations, Straker could read the signs, and he didn't like them. He didn't like losing, either. In fact, he'd seldom lost an engagement, much less a full city siege like this one was shaping up to be.

For the first time in a decade of continuous campaigning he considered the possibility of bloody defeat. First Regiment had been assigned to reinforce the defenses surrounding the city of Helios, which was clearly about to fall to the Hok. The metropolis contained critical war industry, factories that the Hundred Worlds needed and the Hok wanted. With a population of more than twenty million, it was the largest concentration of people on the planet of Corinth.

More than twenty million potential slaves.

The Hok were fighting to capture the city, rather than simply bombarding it from orbit. Most ground actions were fought for exactly this reason: possession of valuable infrastructure, territory, and workers.

Like most Hok attacks, this one had come as a surprise. Sidespace jumps allowed task forces to appear in the outer reaches of any star system without warning. Fortunately, jumping ships had to transit out of sidespace far from gravity sources, so there was always a few hours warning. Strategically, only extreme vigilance and speed could counter their assaults, and like the elite light infantry formations of Old Earth, mechsuiters were always the ground element of choice.

Coexistence seemed impossible with the Hok. They were totally xenophobic, treating all others as lower life forms. Hok never stopped trying to conquer other species, never negotiated, never gave up.

In that sense, Straker understood them. He never gave up either.

"To defeat monsters, fight like a monster," he muttered to himself in a voice too low to trigger his brainchip network's smart systems, its comlinked semi-AI or SAI.

Flight Lieutenant Engels voice floated through Straker's comlink. "One minute to drop."

Adrenaline flowed through Straker's blood at the warning, and he figured the rest of his four-man unit was feeling the same surge.

Within their suits, First Squad—Straker, Paloco, Orset and Chen—hung from the Marksman's open underbelly bay as it power-dived toward the edge of the planet's atmosphere. Mechsuiters were sitting ducks while attached to their dropships, and Straker knew the Hok always reacted strongly to any insertion, sending every warship available to try to catch mechsuiters before they detached and became combat-effective.

But Engels never let them down. She was the Hundred Worlds' top dropship jockey, a perfect complement to Straker, since he knew he rated as the best mechsuiter alive. His First Squad, First Battalion, First Mechsuit Regiment was the finest unit in the Hundred Worlds.

First regiment was, itself, the premier military ground formation in the Hundred Worlds. Of course, it was also the *only* mechsuiter regiment, head and shoulders above the usual ground combat units.

Though expensive, more mechsuits could be built, but mechsuiters had to be genetically enhanced from conception and trained throughout childhood to use the brainlinks. There was no point in putting an inferior pilot into a costly weapons system he couldn't use properly.

"Tip of the spear, end of the shaft," said Loco, the eternal joker. "Bend over, boys, here it comes again."

"BOHICA," echoed Orset.

"What, you guys wanna live forever?" Straker replied, forcing himself to banter. The troops got nervous when he allowed his grim darkness to show.

Loco laughed. "I'll be lucky if I live to our next R&R."

"You'd better. You still owe me three rounds."

Engels broke in. "I've got incoming, gents. Have to let you go early or risk a lucky shot. Three, two, one… dropping now."

The dead thing Straker wore came to life as soon as the Marksman dropship let go of him. Gross and fine psychomotor movements combined with his linked brainchips and biofeedback to create the illusion that he not only occupied the seven-meter-tall construct, he *was* the suit.

Its sensors fed his optic, auditory and tactile nerves; he could see in multiple spectra, hear the chatter on the comm bands, feel the brush of the thinnest air against his skin. In combat, he could even smell the hot metal and taste dust mixed with smoke and explosive residue. Part of a mechsuiter's advantage over his enemies came from this oneness with the battlefield.

A mechsuiter didn't *control* his suit. He *became* his suit, a demigod of battle.

Above him Straker could see stars. Nearby, the flares and sparkles of other dropships and mechsuits matched with their IFF transponders. Below him, the capital of the friendly world of Corinth desperately tried to hold on until the cavalry arrived.

First Mechsuit Regiment was that cavalry, riders on—*in*, rather—the duralloy horses of their Foehammers.

"We'll be coming in above spec, so pulse your brakes as soon as you have enough atmo for control," Straker said. "Unless, of course, you *like* crisped feet." His squadmates acknowledged through their short-range comlinks.

When Straker felt the air bite and the soles of his feet begin to heat, he flared his airbrakes from his shoulders. The braking-wings roared with the buffeting of friction, but the heating spread out and stayed within easy tolerance. The random motion the pulsing imparted to his falling mechsuit also reduced his vulnerability to flak.

Speaking of flak…

"Go active," Straker ordered, and each Foehammer began transmitting multiphase sensor pulses, looking for incoming missiles, gunshells, or the telltale atmospheric sparkle of lasers.

His HUD showed the enemy spread out below him, a mechanized division consisting of a lethal mixture of heavy and light tanks, missile tracks and hovers, plus battlesuited infantry among the vehicles. Straker longed to angle his mechsuit toward the enemy headquarters, but even now, he could see missiles lifting from the surface, heading upward at the battalion's hundred and twenty-eight falling troopers.

Flak guns firing guided shells joined the party, and lasers as well. The heaviest concentration of firepower surrounded the Hok mobile HQ. Even if Straker disobeyed orders—took the initiative, as he could later claim—and went for it, he'd likely end up dead against that much weaponry. He was elite, not insane.

Not that kind of insane, anyway. This was shaping up to be a brutal fight, maybe the toughest he'd ever been in.

Straker waited until the threats got close and ordered countermeasures deployed. All around his squad, the others of the regiment followed suit.

Chaff balls were fired downward from strap-on pods. They exploded into formations of tiny darts that turned with gravity to fall straight down. Each trailed a cluster of fine filaments that slowed them slightly. These created a confusing blanket of reflections and false positives, hiding the mechsuiters from the radars of those below.

At the same time, flares streaked in all directions, tiny hot rockets that would decoy heat-seeking missiles or shells. The mechsuit drop pods also dumped pinwheels of fine nano-sand crystals. These were heavy enough to fall faster than the suits and numerous to form clouds that blocked and reflected lasers in a million directions—reducing the coherent light beams to a fraction of their original power.

Straker felt a beam strike, but the sand and his suit's reactive-reflective skin did its work. The laser stung him, but caused no damage. Several more sizzled nearby, but no more hit him.

He slipped sideways, cyber-enhanced reactions allowing him to spot and avoid a cluster of frag shells. The killer missile following in their wake worried him more; the chips in his head and the ones in his suit coordinated with his brain, aiming the integrated gatling in his left arm at the highest probability of the target's future location. He triggered short bursts that blew past the screen of shells and knocked the weapon out of the sky.

An alarm told him someone in Third Squad hadn't been so lucky.

No, let's be honest, he corrected himself. They'd screwed up. There was no excuse to getting killed during drop phase, but the Regiment had plenty of newbies assigned lately. Some said they had been pushed in before they were ready, and that the Regiment was losing its quality. But that wasn't Straker's problem. His men were all veterans.

Straker was focused on the landing zone below, but there was plenty of action overhead as well. Fleet had engaged the Hok's space squadrons above— the Marksman dropships were acting as gunships to support their mechsuits, firing railgun bullets accelerated to more than one thousand kilometers per second.

These streaks from above joined the countermeasures, aimed past the mech-suits at the enemy on the ground. Given that their range to target was less than one hundred kilometers away, firing and impact might as well be instantaneous, and each shot that found a target destroyed it with a duralloy penetrator that glowed white-hot as it passed through the atmosphere.

But each Marksman only carried one such railgun, and as awesome as this fire support was, the regiment had a mere thirty-two dropships while the targets below numbered in the thousands. With all the weapons, countermeasures and counter-countermeasures filling the air, getting a good sensor lock for the gunners was a bitch.

Over the following thirty seconds, a missile got close enough to deploy its warhead. A wheel-shaped net of molecular strands spun out, weighted with contact explosives. Straker snapshotted a burst of gatling fire but he was too far. As designed, the net wrapped itself around a descending mechsuiter from another dropship, its monofilaments cutting through the unarmored strap-on pods.

While the net couldn't damage the occupant, or even the underlying dural-loy hull, the multiple smart-charges swung inward by design, to slam into the armor. The repeated explosions blew through its overlapping conformal plating and superconductors. Fiery jets of molten metal found cracks and destroyed the suit's internals.

Even if the trooper survived, the systems damage had rendered the unit combat-ineffective. Wrapped tightly in the net, the whole mess would crash into the surface like an unpowered aerospace interceptor.

Straker watched the destruction in concern. If the mechsuiters won this fight, the pilot might be salvaged and rehabbed. Otherwise, he would no doubt be killed by the Hok. The equipment was a total loss no matter what happened.

As they closed in on their waypoint, Straker couldn't see much, so he jinked left and right, forward and back. These adjustments were done more by instinct than anything else, his subconscious mind moving him before his consciousness even knew what was happening, like a hand-to-hand fighter instinctively ducking a punch.

He double-checked his people and noted they remained in good formation, tight enough to ensure mutual support but loose enough not to make an easy target group. He saw Chen fire his force-cannon, the Foehammer's main anti-armor weapon. He nailed an enemy shell cluster, detonating all of them well below the squad, adding to the chaos.

Right now, chaos was a mechsuiter's friend.

Six minutes from drop to ground was all it took, but it always felt like a lifetime. Three minutes had passed. The regiment's sideward vector curved, turning the feet-first dive from its original lateral slant—imparted by orbital velocity—into a pure vertical fall directly above the city of Helios.

As the mechsuiters approached, a pitiful few friendly guns opened up to support the landing. Conventional forces depended on mass and, if they had it, precision weaponry to keep the enemy at bay. It looked like the militia below had neither. Scattered artillery shells and missiles flew toward the Hok divisions driving on the city from the east, but the enemy clawed them from the sky before they had a chance to become more than a nuisance.

Still, the distraction helped the mechsuiters. The garrison forces below had to know their city, their freedom, even their lives depended on First Regiment. Straker could see lines of refugees fleeing to the west, but there was no way the millions of civilians inside the battle zone would make it out in time.

If First Regiment couldn't stem the tide, the deaths of one hundred twenty-eight mechsuiters would be a drop in the bucket compared to the slaughter and slavery that awaited the inhabitants of Corinth.

"We've got to hold," Straker muttered as they fell. His SAI interpreted this as an order and so transmitted it to his squadmates.

"We will," said Orset, always the optimist.

"Remember, conserve your hard ammo. Time to access the resupply pods will be tight."

"Sure, boss, hog all the kills for yourself," said Paloco.

"Not my fault you can't match my single-shot hit percentage," Straker said. "Try to keep up this time, Loco."

"You always pick off the ones we engage, you selfish bastard!"

"That's the way it's supposed to work. You guys set 'em up, I knock 'em down. You're my wingmen, I'm the striker."

Chen grunted. "I think we'll have to revise the R&R rules. *Most* kills buys, instead of least. You haven't bought a round in…"

"Years," Straker admitted. "How about this? You three can combine your kills into one score. If you win, I buy."

"Now you're talking, boss!" Chen shouted. "Break out your credit stick!"

"One minute left," Straker warned them, his tone becoming deadly serious again. "Here comes the soup."

Crossing twenty kilometers in altitude meant the air started to thicken. Missiles slowed down but gained a lot more maneuverability. Unpowered shells came in faster, closer to the muzzles of the guns that fired them, and lasers hit harder.

Long ago on Old Earth, low atmosphere was the realm of fighter aircraft, but no one used the fragile things anymore unless they were expendable un-manned drones. Too easy to see and thus shoot down, they lacked the armor and countermeasures of either ground forces or true aerospace warships, neither of which had to fight gravity and use fuel just to stay in the air.

"Retract brakes and rotate," Straker said, and as one, the four mechsuits flipped head-down. Like falling divers now, they pointed their arms at the ground. This put the gatlings and force-cannons in their arms into the best po-sitions to fire at threats, and also maintained their high speed in the thickening air and made them more streamlined than the feet-down attitude.

When they needed extra velocity, a mechsuiter could also trigger foot thrusters for a short burst of speed. The trick was, of course, to retain the ability to shed that speed before slamming into the ground like a bullet. Even with the best genetic enhancements, there were only so many Gs a man could take.

"It's not the fall that kills you, it's the sudden stop at the end," Paloco said cheerfully.

"I heard it was poisoning," Chen replied.

"Poisoning?"

"Yeah. Dirt poisoning, concrete poisoning, seawater poisoning… whatever you impact gets right into your bloodstream. Hell on the kidneys."

"Hey, *I* do the jokes around here," Paloco complained.

"You mean you *are* the joke around here."

Indifferent to their chatter, Helios rushed toward them with gut-wrenching speed. Straker watched his radar altimeter until...

"Turn and burn, gents, *mark*," he ordered, and their head-down plunge flattened into a short-lived flight, aided by the airfoils and canards that sprouted from their mechsuits. This was less true flying and more of a controlled stalling fall, rather like the squirrel-suits of extreme skydivers, but it allowed them to roar in over the city low enough to use its ground clutter as cover.

Timing it perfectly, Straker and his men braked hard on blazing jets and landed on their feet in the suburbs, just beyond the line of skyscrapers that formed its heart. Behind them lay the prize, the industrial district, stretching along both sides of the south-flowing River Argos.

Friendly conventional forces already occupied the best dug-in cover positions, but mechsuiters were close-in fighters. Using their superior speed, skill and feel for combat, the finest men and technology of the Hundred Worlds always took the fight to the enemy, getting in among the Hok armor and infantry to destroy their cohesion and ability to operate.

Unfortunately, the Hok seemed immune to fear. They fought and died in droves, always attacking, never retreating, like organic machines.

The rest of the regiment joined the squad, landing to the left and right. Straker's unit held the very center, as befitted the best of the best. Two of the regiment's troopers had been KIA on the drop, not bad for a hot insertion, but it still fed his anger. He didn't even look at who they'd lost. Better not to know until later.

Undoubtedly, the toll would climb.

So be it. The Hok would pay. No matter how pessimistic the assessment, Straker knew in his bones he was invincible. Twenty-six years old and he'd never been seriously wounded in forty-four distinct actions. He'd seldom even lost a major suit system or ended a battle with more than heavy bruising. His teachers had told him he'd been blessed with the best genetic engineering known to mankind, his body purposely designed to link with a mechsuit.

Beyond that, the random genetic variables that nobody could control had favored him above all others. The dice had stopped while showing eleven, the cards had dealt him a royal flush, the slot machine of life had come up 7-7-7, and as the scientists had said, he'd hit the jackpot. He'd tested in the top one-thousandth percentile of human nerve-transmission and reaction.

No one else had even come close, not even other "physicals" who'd been genetically gifted with similar abilities. Add in the brainchips, the cyber-wetware that enhanced him even further, and he knew nothing could touch him.

When he was in kindergarten, he'd amused himself by holding two styluses like chopsticks and catching flies out of the air. In school, he'd dominated every sport that relied on coordination, such as racquetball or football, failing to win only contests of pure endurance, like distance swimming, running, or cycling.

Other children with differing genetic enhancements had won at those. Derek Straker didn't begrudge them. They weren't destined to become mechsuiters. Only those with supreme psychomotor skills wore mechsuits, because one mechsuit and its trooper cost as much as ten interceptors or a hundred tanks.

That meant a regiment of mechsuiters embodied the firepower of at least a division, with the logistical footprint of a mere battalion. Like elites throughout history, the Hundred Worlds used them—and used them up—when the job absolutely, positively had to get done, and done right, whatever the cost.

And today it was going to cost. Never in his memory did he have to fight at such a disadvantage, a mere one regiment against at least three Hok divisions, maybe four, with a city to defend. But as long as Fleet battled in orbit above, he would tie up the enemy, deny them the factories, and buy time for the civilians to flee.

"First Regiment, by the numbers, report," came the commander's voice over the net.

"One-one-one ready," Straker said. He heard echoes up and down the line, all squads reporting in. It was an unnecessary ritual, really, given the network that linked the regiment, but he appreciated it anyway.

Command technique, he told himself for the hundredth time. Makes everyone feel like part of the team. He resolved to use it once he moved up the ladder.

"First Regiment, engage," the commander continued. "Squad leaders, you're cleared for independent action."

Straker waved his men forward and into the teeth of the enemy.

Chapter 2

Seaburn City, Planet Oceanus. Thirteen years before the Battle for Corinth (2804 A.D., Old Earth reckoning).

Long before Derek Straker wore a mechsuit and killed his first Hok invader, he stood in his family's backyard and watched the lights streaking across the night sky. The man on the vidscreen inside said the aliens were attacking, and all personnel must report to their duty stations.

Derek didn't have a duty station yet. He was only thirteen, but he knew when he grew up he'd fight the Hok to defend the Hundred Worlds. The Hok were evil, and he'd be a crack mechsuiter.

Mechsuiters were awesome. Mechsuiters were the best.

This wasn't just a silly dream. He'd been genetically enhanced, and had been trained at a special school. On his tenth birthday he'd been brainchipped, which let him play VR Mechsuit Onslaught on the supernet. Someday he would pilot a mechsuit for real, better than *anyone*. Everyone said so, and he believed them.

He'd taken advanced martial arts classes and competed in lots of sports. He usually won, even against the other physicals. They said he couldn't go to the Hundred Worlds Olympics, though. It wouldn't be fair to the unenhanced people.

That was okay. The Olympics had nothing on mechsuit battle.

As he watched the invasion unfold in the skies above, his only wish was that he had a mechsuit now so he could fight the Hok.

By age sixteen, maybe before, he'd go to Academy Station, the Hundred Worlds' central officer training base. Until then, he played Onslaught, a game that made him feel like he was already a mechsuiter, it was so realistic.

"Derek, come inside, *now!*" his mother called in a shrill voice.

Her tone worried him. She was usually so calm. Was it because of the Hok above? Why was she afraid? Hundred Worlds mechsuiters *always* won. Hundred Worlds fleets usually won, too.

"Don't worry, Mom. The mechsuiters will beat the Hok," he said as he dutifully tramped into the house.

"Come here and help me pack," his mother called from inside his room. He had his own room because he was a special child, something he'd been told time and again.

His sister Mara was special and had her own room too. She was wicked smart. At school, the special school, they called the ones like her *mentals*, though the slang word was *brainiacs*. They called kids like Derek *physicals*.

That was the biggest social divide on Oceanus. Everyone worked at their own pace, though, and they were encouraged to see each other as complementary. Or was it complimentary? He could never remember. He was no brainiac.

His mom and dad got extra credits because of Derek's and Mara's genetic enhancements. Pre-enlisting in the military was lucrative for struggling families. The extra credits bought them a bigger dome house and nicer cars—all kinds of expensive stuff the average worker didn't get. The credits had bought him the best VR console on the market, so he could play Onslaught. That's what his parents said when they wanted to remind him to be good. That was fair. Be good, do his schoolwork and his chores, play Onslaught, be a mechsuiter. That was life, though sometimes he felt like he was only waiting for real life to start.

"What are we packing for, Mom?"

"You and Mara are going on a field trip, Derek. With your friends from school. It'll be fun." His mom's voice quavered and she didn't look happy, but that wasn't surprising. She usually worried when he had to go on a field trip, and he was used to that. Most mothers worried too much, but his father didn't seem to worry at all.

His father came into his room a moment later. He had Derek's field pack and spoke to his mother. "Put everything in here, so he can carry it easily."

"Why not a travel case?" she asked. "I can't get as much into a pack."

"This is better. Less likely to get lost. It has his name and our names stitched on it, it has a locator chip, a place for water and rations…" His father trailed off as he concentrated on stuffing things into the pack—underwear and socks, Youth Brigade uniform, shorts and a shirt. Derek's phonetab went into an outer pocket.

A horn blared from the street outside. "Oh, Cosmos. They're here for Derek already," his mother said.

"That was fast," replied his father, as if remarking on the weather, but didn't move. He stared at the wall, hands opening and closing on nothing.

"Can't you tell them to pick him up last?" Mother asked. "You're on the committee…"

"I asked, but they have a priority list. You know our kids are two of the best, so they've been selected to go early in the event of an emergency."

Derek put on the youth-sized backpack. "What emergency?" He smiled at his father. "We'll win, Dad. We always win."

"That's right!" his father said, patting him absently on the shoulder. His father's face stiffened, and he turned it toward his mom. "Honey, go help Mara finish. Her bus will be here soon, too."

His mother hurried to his sister's room. She was only six, but the little brainiac tried to act like a grownup, which was annoying.

Derek followed his mom. "Hey, pest," he said to Mara from the doorway as his mother threw little-girl stuff in a backpack.

"Shut up, neuro-typical simpleton," she said.

He laughed. "Don't forget your dollies."

Mara glared. "They're *Heroic Action Figures*."

"They'll make one of *me* someday."

"Your arrogance is exceeded only by your hubris."

"Whatever. See you later."

"Not if I see you first."

Derek smiled, and after a moment Mara smiled back. His sister had once told him matter-of-factly their sibling rivalry was only a veneer to hide their affection for each other. He thought that was weird. Most brainiacs were weird.

"Bye, Mara," he said. "Have fun on your field trip."

Mara moved forward and pushed him into the hallway, hissing, "Field trip, my butt. Field trips don't start at night. We're being evacuated. The Hok are pushing hard."

"I know that," he whispered back.

But he hadn't known. Not really. Evacuation? That word seemed extreme. The emergency his dad had spoken of must be serious after all. "That's why Mom's freaking."

"Yeah. Don't feed her anxiety, okay?" Mara smiled weakly. "The buses are honking. You have to go."

"Okay." He hugged her impulsively. "Don't worry. We'll kick their asses."

"If they have asses." She shoved him away. "Go on, moron."

"Better a moron than a more-off."

"That doesn't even make sense."

"Come on, Derek!" his father yelled. "You're holding up the others!"

In front of the house an armored bus waited, but it wasn't Derek's school bus and it wasn't driven by anyone he knew. The driver wore a Ground Forces uniform, though he was just a private. Derek knew all the rank insignia.

The faces of a couple of Derek's classmates could be seen peering out the tiny viewports at him.

"Hey, Derek!" called Johnny Paloco, his best friend. Everyone called him Loco. He was one year younger and smaller than Derek, with curly black hair and a bright, ready smile. He often played the class clown, unlike Derek and his earnestness, but like many of the physicals, he'd be a mechsuiter too when he grew up.

Derek waved. "Hey, Loco."

Loco got off the bus when the door opened, even though the driver yelled at him to get back on. Loco was always doing stuff like that, ignoring the grownups. Somehow he got away with it, by smiling and acting like he didn't hear, and then saying "sorry."

Derek took a step toward the bus when his mother grabbed him and hugged him fiercely. "Goodbye, Derek. I love you."

"Knock it off, Mom. It's only a field trip. I love you too." Derek waved at his father, who stood there with a strained look on his face.

"Bye, son."

His mother broke down sobbing, and he might have seen tears in his father's eyes too as he pulled Derek's mom away, back to the porch of the house.

Then he remembered the Hok. He'd seen explosions in the sky, flashes of weapons fire from warships, burning attack craft. Despite Mara's words, he wasn't worried. Hundred Worlds fleets would drive them off, and if not, the mechsuiters would fight them on the ground and kill them all. That's what always happened on the Mechsuiter Roundup showvid, anyway.

Derek grabbed Loco by the shoulder and muscled him onto the bus as the driver spat bad words at them. The door slammed behind them and the two made their way to the very back.

Out the rear window, Derek saw his parents waving from the front porch. They kept on waving and crying. For a moment, the feeling he would never see them again overwhelmed him.

It was a stupid thought. Of course he would come back home in a few days. Everything would be fine.

Before they'd made it two hundred meters down the road, a shudder shook the ground, followed by a blast of sound. Then another roar followed that. Bursts of light silhouetted the buildings on the next street over, and then Derek's house blew up, faster than in a war vid.

His father and mother vanished in the blast. He saw blood. Smoke and dust enveloped the armored bus and billowed into the open windows, making him cough at its acrid odor. An impact threw him out of the seat and onto the floor. The bus stopped.

Loco ran forward to look at the driver. "He's out," he said, shoving the unconscious man's face off the steering wheel.

"Open the door!"

Loco pushed the big button, and then grabbed the manual release. Together they pulled it open and scrambled off the bus.

Derek began to run back the way they'd come, pack thumping on his back. Loco ran after him. "Derek!"

How could this happen? People weren't supposed to blow up houses, not even in war. War was something between mechsuits and tanks and spaceships. It never happened in a neighborhood. Not on the showvids he watched, anyway.

Something knocked him flat from behind, a wall of air that shoved him forward, like being illegally hit in the back by another player in a football match. He found his mouth full of lawn and dirt, and his ears rang.

Loco yelled something.

"What?" he yelled right back.

"The bus! The bus!"

Derek turned to look back through the swirling haze. The bus was… well, it wasn't a bus anymore. Just a flat bottom and some wheels. He saw the driver's legs and torso sitting in the seat, but his arms and head had vanished. Blown off. On the combat vids that was cool. It wasn't nearly so cool now. A sudden urge to vomit came over him.

"Where are they?" Derek asked, already knowing the answer. There had been kids on the bus. His classmates.

"They're gone."

"How many kids got on?"

"Umm… three before me. Fack, Renny and Tina."

Derek put the bus aside in his mind. He couldn't do anything about that now. Staggering to his feet, pack still strapped on, he stumbled toward the ruins of his house.

Parts of it were on fire, sputtering flames. Water from broken pipes spurted. He could hear sirens, but his ears were ringing so badly he had no idea if they were close or far. Many of the streetlights were dark.

On what was left of the front porch he found his father and mother. Dad was wrapped around Mom. They looked peaceful, as if they were lying in bed. Derek reached out to check his dad's pulse, like he'd been taught in Emergency Medical Response class. He felt nothing. Then he saw that his father's neck twisted at a funny angle.

On his mother he found a pulse, and then it faded. He witnessed her take one last breath.

"Loco!" he screamed, suddenly energized, waking as if from a dream. "Loco, help!" He pushed his father's corpse aside and rolled his mother onto her back and began the steps of CPR as he'd been drilled in Youth Brigade.

Loco threw himself to his knees beside Derek, who compressed his mother's chest and tried not to think about what would happen.

"Come on, Mom," he muttered, over and over, and, "Please, somebody help." He had no idea who he was calling to. Maybe the Unknowable Creator the regimental chaplain always mentioned at the military funerals they showed on the vids.

Nobody answered.

When he got too tired, Loco spelled him. He felt helpless, wishing he had supplies and medical training and…

After an interminable time, he knew.

"She's gone," he said. A coldness settled on him like a blanket, a comforter that kept him numb.

"It's okay. I can keep going," said Loco.

"No. She's gone. She's dead." Derek turned to his friend. "Oh, Cosmos. *Mara*."

The two scrambled to their feet and began searching for Derek's sister. They couldn't find her, but they did find her burnt pack, and a bloody shoe. She couldn't have survived.

In a daze, he took Mara's Glory Girl figurine from the pack and dropped the rest. He wasn't sure why, but it seemed like the right thing to do. He felt numb, but he tried to think. Being a kid helped. He couldn't absorb all this shock at once—so he didn't bother. He became practical instead.

"What about *your* parents?" he asked Loco.

Loco's eyes widened. "I… I don't know…"

"We should find out."

"Why aren't you freaking? Aren't you sad?" Loco asked him. There were tears on his face.

Derek gazed at Loco, knowing he should be crying too. But he didn't feel it. Not yet. "I'll be sad later," he said.

"Me too." Loco wiped his eyes and put on a brave face. "Let's go. The Hok are coming. We have to see if my parents are okay. Then we have to hide somewhere until we find a way to fight back. Weapons or something." He stood up. "Come on."

"How do you know the Hok are coming?" Derek demanded as they jogged down the neighborhood street.

"Because that's what they do. They come and enslave everybody until the mechsuiters free them."

"That's just on vids." Derek slowed to a walk and glanced at his best friend, ignoring the devastation around them. A few people stumbled along or ran here and there. A fire truck sprayed foam on a burning dwelling. Dogs barked in pointless alarm.

"Jeez, Derek, you're always so gullible. You believe everything the teachers say and you think showvids are real. Don't you watch the news? The war reports?"

"Mom won't let me. She says it's too depressing. I just watch Mechsuit Roundup, and histories of Old Earth."

"That proves it," Loco said. "She doesn't want you to see. Mechsuits *don't* always win. Sometimes they lose and nobody gets freed."

"They do not!"

"If they always win, why haven't we won the war already?"

Derek felt more confident about that one. "The Hundred Worlds has a hundred systems. The Hok have thousands, but their tech isn't as good as ours. It's a big war."

Loco shook his head. "No. We don't always win."

"Mechsuiters do." Derek gave up on the argument as he felt his energy drain away, leaving him with barely enough to walk and look around. Many houses in the neighborhood had been smashed flat. "This was a surgical bombardment," he said. "Orbital smart spikes, no warheads."

"How do you know?" Loco demanded.

"Because I actually read all the schoolbooks and a lot of military texts instead of only watching showvids, dumbass. Warheads would have wiped out a dozen houses at a time, maybe hundreds. These zeroed in on structures and smashed them kinetically, one by one."

"Why civilians then?" asked Loco. "Why not armories and security stations?"

Derek chewed that one over. "Maybe they knew we're special, gonna be mechsuiters."

"How could they know?"

"Spies? Traitors? Intercepted intelligence?"

Loco grunted. "Why no warheads, then? Why not just nuke the city?"

Derek thought hard. He'd been trained on all things military—but he was still a kid.

"I don't know, mutual retaliation maybe. They don't want us to nuke their planets," he said. "Or they're limiting damage to stuff so they can take it and use it. Also, spikes are cheap. They can drop thousands, tens of thousands from orbit."

"So they're trying to capture Oceanus?" Loco wailed. "Our whole planet?"

"Yeah, probably. But it's okay. Mechsuiters will come."

"It's too late. Your family is dead!"

"I know." Derek wondered why he wasn't bawling with grief, but right now he felt nothing, as if his insides had been refrigerated. "There's your house."

Loco stopped in the front yard and stared in horror at the ruin, twin to Derek's. Then he ran into the wreckage, Derek following.

After five minutes of searching they found the bodies.

"They're dead too," Loco said, choking. "They said they'd be watching the news after I left, trying to get info on what's happening."

"Sorry, Loco."

They hugged, and Loco sobbed. Derek wondered why Loco could cry and he couldn't. He awkwardly patted his friend's shoulder. "Come on, man. We can't stay here."

Lights flared in the sky, missile launches from the ground reaching upward toward bright specks that fell. Lasers flashed red and orange and green, visible because of the haze rising from the damaged city. Flares appeared high above, like fireworks on Establishment Day.

"They're doing a combat drop," Derek said. "The Hok assault ships. They'll be here soon. We have to hide."

"Where?"

"Some of these houses are okay. Somebody will be home."

"The Rasheeds live right there. They'll take us in," Loco said. "Their kids are neuro-typicals. They go to a regular school."

"Wait. No. That won't work."

"Why not?"

"Because the Hok will look there first."

"At the Rasheeds?"

"At intact houses. They'll round everyone up and either kill them or put them to work in labor camps. We have to find a better place to hide until the mechsuiters come. Somewhere for a few days or weeks."

"Okay." Loco looked around. "Where then? The emergency shelter?"

"Same problem. The Hok will find them."

Loco snapped his fingers. "Food market."

"What?"

"Trust me. Let's go." Loco began to run, and Derek followed.

The food market was smashed as well, but the building was so large that much of it still stood, albeit half-wrecked.

"There's a basement for employees," Loco said. "It has bathrooms and a kitchen and stuff. We can take food down there and survive for a long time."

"We can't take the food! That would be stealing."

Loco grabbed a bag and began to fill it with cans and boxes. "This is war, Derek, my uptight friend. Real war. And we're going to be mechsuiters. You may know all the facts and statistics and stuff, but you're not thinking about what it all means. Peacetime rules don't apply. It's our duty to survive any way we can, so we can fight later."

"I guess we can keep track of it and report what we took…"

"Yeah." Loco laughed. "Maybe they'll take it out of our pay."

Derek didn't laugh. He'd never laughed all that much, anyway. Most of the time he let Loco laugh for him. He wondered if he'd ever laugh at anything again—or love anyone again. For the first time, Derek realized that loving someone meant they could be taken away from you, and that would hurt.

Everything seemed either far away, as if he viewed it from the wrong end of a telescope, or very close, as if through a magnifying glass, nothing in-between. To stave off the sense of unreality, he joined Loco in filling bags and carrying them down to the basement.

Other people showed up, looting the food market as well, but no one joined them in the cellar. The others all filled bags or carts and left, probably going back to their homes nearby or to the shelter. Derek wondered where the civil defense forces were. This was a Central World. The Hok weren't supposed to be able to reach this far, or get past the defenses if they did.

Half an hour and a dozen trips later, Derek noticed the other citizens had fled. An ominous silence descended over the nighttime gloom, and he could hear noises of pounding feet.

The noises were half-familiar, but wrong somehow, like a sound effect on a showvid.

"Loco, look!" he said, hiding behind a ruined wall and peering over it.

Loco joined him. "Battlesuiters. Ours or theirs?"

Derek studied the outlines he could see at a distance, humanoid shapes running and jumping through the streets like miniature mechsuiters. Antipersonnel guns chattered and a big electric cannon spoke with a whine and a crash. A building exploded. He saw one of the figures lift his weapon and gun down a fleeing woman, who fell and lay still.

"It's the Hok. Our forces wouldn't be blowing up houses and shooting civilians." He grabbed Loco. "Come on. We have to hide."

Chapter 3

Academy Station. 2804 A.D., Old Earth reckoning.

In another star system far from Oceanus, Cadet Second Class Carla Engels snapped to attention.

Major Soames, Academy's senior intelligence officer, had entered the auditorium. Around her, the other Seconds fell silent and stood tall when they spotted the major. The Firsts below soon did the same, along with the Thirds and Fourths above and behind them in the stadium seating. A smattering of alien cadets occupied end seats, but the Hundred Worlds was a human-dominated empire.

Sharp-faced, handsome and black as night, Soames had a resonant speaking voice. The man always reminded Carla of a vidfilm star, or maybe a newscaster. She'd had desultory fantasies about initiating a relationship once she'd graduated and was commissioned.

Too bad he was a brainiac. Brainiacs and physicals hardly ever related socially. Even in training, their roles had specific boundaries. They were simply too different. They were so different, in fact, the two types of cadets didn't even take classes together.

So, this assembly was made up entirely of physicals: Cadet Corps Alpha. Brainiac Bravo would be briefed separately… if they needed briefing at all. Rumor had it the brainiacs lived most of their lives in VR, or parked forever in front of holoscreens, only getting up to eat or do mandatory exercise. They were probably online right now, briefing themselves, or watching.

"Take your seats," Soames said when he arrived at his lectern.

The Corps Alpha assembly sat all at once, everyone no doubt wondering what this special briefing meant. Afternoon classes had been bumped, and the schedule reshuffled to make room. Engels sighed. They would probably lose their personal hour before lights-out to make up for the lost time.

As Soames spoke, a graphic appeared on the holoscreen above and behind him. "Four days ago, a Hok fleet consisting of five light and two medium squadrons initiated a raid on Oceanus, inflicting considerable damage to military and civilian targets. They then dropped suicide squads and fled before our reinforcements arrived. Our planetary defense forces fought valiantly and blunted their attack, but couldn't stop them entirely. Home Guard forces are still hunting down their suicidal lurkers."

A Firstie held out her fist, a request to speak. Soames motioned toward her and she stood. "Oceanus is a Central World, sir. How did they get past our orbital fortresses?"

"Excellent question. They overwhelmed one of the twelve orbitals with concentrated missile and kinetic strikes, followed up by an all-out attack on that sector. They lost nine ships, and six more as they extracted."

"For a *raid*, sir?" The Firstie's tone dripped incredulity. "That's a lot to pay. Why would they do that?"

"You tell me. Anyone?"

Fists leaped into the air, mostly from the Firsts and Seconds, the upperclassmen. Soames pointed at a boy.

"Something on Oceanus must be worth the loss and the resource expenditure, sir. The real question is: what was it?"

"Correct. Their targets were your future classmates. According to our preliminary information, schools for Specials were targeted, along with the homes of many of the students. As you know, Oceanus was one of two planets that host our genetically enhanced potentials. Suicide squads of Hok battlesuiters are rampaging through the capital city of Seaburn, murdering every child they find. Our mechsuiters have arrived, but it's too late to save most of them."

A collective gasp swept through the assembly, followed by angry murmuring.

"*Silence!*" Soames' amplified word quashed the noise like a flyswatter. "We have a right to be outraged, but this shouldn't surprise you. The Hok don't follow human standards in war."

A fist lifted. Soames nodded and the cadet stood. "If they commit these atrocities, why shouldn't we? I say hit them back. Bombard their cities. Wipe them out by the millions!"

The assembly held its breath, Engels along with many others, waited for Soames to slap down the questioner.

Instead, he shook his head with an air of sadness. "Ladies and gentlemen, the Hok are *not* our teachers." He paused to let that sink in. "We do not dishonor ourselves merely because the enemy does. We retaliate proportionally, to show them indiscriminate bombardment doesn't pay. And, as a practical matter, what do you think the result of the first total planetary genocide would be?" Soames pointed at another cadet, who stood to answer.

"They'd do it back to us, sir. Projections show that within a decade the Hundred Worlds would be devastated, along with a similar number of enemy planets. Keeping the war limited buys us time."

Carla Engels couldn't contain herself. She stuck out her fist and stood before Soames completed his nod to her.

"But sir," she asked, "how is that worse than losing slowly, getting ground down as we are now? Why not hit them back as hard as possible? Surprise them with massive asteroid bombardment strikes? The Hok are fighting against others too, alien multi-star nations and planets. Maybe our escalation will allow those others to counterattack and win."

Soames' tone remained even. "If this were a wargame, if we could coordinate an alliance of all the Hok's enemies, that might be the best strategy. Unfortunately, many of the aliens are xenophobic, and given that the fastest communication possible is via sidespace drone or courier, what you're suggesting is difficult. There's no way the Hundred Worlds will sacrifice itself only to have alien nations sit back and use the time we bought them to fortify. Besides," he gripped the lectern, "we remain ahead of the Hok, technologically. We have interior lines, and our rear systems, outward up the spiral arm, are relatively secure. Our analyses show that we should be able to hold them off for at least fifty more years, perhaps a hundred, and during that time, many things could happen. For example, a technological breakthrough."

"But we're still losing, sir," Engels said. "Right?"

"When your team is behind at halftime, do you give up the game, Cadet Engels?"

"No, sir!"

"And neither will we. Take your seat." Soames advanced to the next graphic, which depicted Cadet Corps Alpha's organizational chart. Across the bottom, below the Fourths, rows of hundreds of empty boxes had been added.

"We're still waiting for the results of the Oceanus raid, but Command has already set contingency plans in motion to evacuate all surviving Specials to Academy, where we will integrate these newbies into the Corps as sub-Fourthies. I know this is an enormous disruption in the middle of the school year, but we'll handle it professionally, and we will get through it. Think of it as a leadership opportunity. Apply your problem-solving processes as you've been taught, and show your cadre you're worthy to be Hundred Worlds officers!"

He gestured toward another officer waiting to the side. "Captain Yoshida, Education and Training Ops, will now brief you on the way forward."

* * *

Planet Oceanus, Seaburn City.

Derek and Loco pulled a tall display shelf against the food market's cellar door to cover it, squeezed past, and locked it behind them as they went down. They turned off all the lights and crawled behind stacks of boxes, waiting for the Hok to come down and find them.

But the Hok didn't find the hidden door. Not that night, or the next two after.

By the third morning, it became clear the enemy had passed through their neighborhood in a sweep, but afterward had left it to rot. Derek didn't know where the Hok had gone, but right then he didn't care. He was alive, he had his best friend, and they had a safe place to sleep, eat and even wash themselves. The power had gone out and with it the hot water, but the cold water flowed. They would survive.

As they sat up top, hidden by rubble, eating breakfast in the sunlight—for it was chill and dark in the basement, even in the daytime—Derek heard familiar sounds: a screaming whine, an explosion and the thumps of giant feet pounding across the ground. More such shrieks, rumbles and crashes followed.

"Mechsuiters!" he cried, running to peer out of the nearest opening. He scrambled from place to place, looking for the source of the noises. "There!"

Loco's eyes followed his pointing finger. They could see movement above the buildings to the south, away from the city center. Explosions and flashing energy discharges showed a battle was taking place, though it seemed localized.

"How do you know it's mechsuiters?" Loco asked.

"The sounds. They sound just like in Onslaught and on Mechsuit Roundup. It's their force-cannon and the sound of their feet hitting the ground. They must be counterattacking. See, I told you they'd show up and kick the Hok's asses."

"If they *have* asses."

Derek closed his eyes. "That's what Mara said, right before..."

Loco stayed silent for a moment. "Mechsuiters won't help my mom and dad. Not yours, either. They're never coming back."

Pain blossomed anew in Derek's stomach. He slugged Loco in the back of the head, hard. "Why'd you have to say that?"

"Ow, dammit. Stop being an asshole!" Loco turned and threw a punch, which Derek ducked easily. Everyone else, even Loco, who was also enhanced, seemed to move slower than he did.

"*You're* the asshole for saying that," Derek said.

"Ow." Loco probed his skull melodramatically. "Jeez... I'm gonna get you back for that. You gotta sleep sometime, Derek."

"I sleep light." He turned to look again. "What should we do?"

"Hide."

"Why? We're winning."

Loco ticked off reasons on his fingers. "One, we don't *know* we're winning. Two, even if we do, we don't know how long it will take to clear and secure the area. Three, a stray shell could kill us and that would be really stupid." He grabbed Derek's elbow. "And four, I'm still hungry. Let's go back to the basement and wait."

Reluctantly, Derek allowed Loco to drag him back down. As he sat in the dark, he tried his phonetab again, as he did every few hours, hoping for a signal. He didn't know how these things really worked, but maybe he could get something, anything.

Through the cellar walls they felt and heard the noises of combat build to a crescendo over the next hour, and then fade to nothing.

"Should we go look?" Loco asked.

"Yeah. Let's look."

As they climbed the stairs, the locked door at the top rattled.

"Shit." Loco began to back slowly down.

"It's our guys."

"How do you know?" he hissed.

Derek shrugged. "If not, we're dead anyway."

"We should hide. Maybe they'll miss us again."

His phonetab beeped. He looked at its display. "Huh."

"What?"

"It says, *Derek Barnes Straker, stand fast. Johannes Miguel Paloco, stand fast.*"

"That's weird."

Derek poked his friend with his index finger. "Johannes? Really?"

"Hey, I didn't pick it. My mom was an astronomer, remember? I'm named after Kepler. Or maybe her first boyfriend, I don't know."

The door abruptly swung open with a shriek of tearing metal and a crash as it was pulled off its hinges. In the light of day, Derek saw the wide faceplate of a Foehammer mechsuit peering down the stairs.

It spoke in a voice like thunder. "Come on out, boys. We're here to rescue you. Hurry."

In the street an armored bus like the one that had shown up at Derek's house waited. A mechsuiter squad of four stood guard, facing in all directions as the driver waved frantically for them to run and get on.

"How did they know where we were?" Loco asked once they'd taken their seats. The bus was otherwise empty. The driver began to steer like a maniac through the shattered city.

"My phonetab, I guess."

"But I didn't have mine. How did they know I was there too?"

Derek thought about it. "Our brainchips."

"Yeah, that must be it. Why didn't they tell us they could find us with them?"

"I'm starting to think there's a lot they didn't tell us."

Half an hour later, after picking up five more of his former classmates, Fleet ratings strapped them all into a real planetary shuttle, which lifted with a roar, rocketing for orbit. Everyone was in a hurry. There wasn't even a countdown.

Derek felt disappointed. There should have been a countdown.

As soon as the pressure eased, Derek unbuckled and crawled over to take an empty seat next to a viewport. He couldn't see much from this height. The ground was so far below that Seaburn and other nearby cities looked like glowing rashes connected by tiny strings of light.

More lights appeared, short-lived ones that glowed brightly for a moment before Inserting; a few at first, and then ten, twenty, a hundred.

"Explosions," Loco said from his elbow.

"Big ones, maybe even nukes," Derek replied, numbly speaking the first thing that came into his head. He'd seen lots of war vids. "Suicide charges from the Hok battlesuiters and dropped armor. Their usual last stands. Why now all of a sudden?"

"All us Specials are leaving," said Loco. "Their targets are gone."

Nothing seemed real. Again, the world had been wrapped in a thick blanket and pushed beyond arm's length.

"But we're winning, right? I mean… we got rescued."

Derek shrugged. "Fleet came back to pick us up. Hope for the future. Specials. And to take the planet back too."

Loco stared out the port. "Specials. I always thought that was just something they told us. You know, to make us try harder." He turned back to Derek. "What about everyone else on the planet?"

Derek sat back, suddenly unable to watch. Now he understood his mother's frantic hug, and his father's rare emotion. They'd known what was coming. What an attack meant. Not like on the showvids.

Why were his parents killed? Nobody but the Hok ever died on the war vids, except a few Hundred Worlds heroes that had to sacrifice themselves to win the battle sometimes. Never civilians. Why did they lie on the vids? Why did they tell kids things would be all right if it wasn't true?

Then he remembered one episode where the Hok had slaughtered everyone in a town, lining them up and shooting them in their heads. It was called an *atrocity*, he recalled. Something you shouldn't do. Something evil. The mechsuiters had hunted down the Hok unit and killed them to the last ugly, rough-skinned alien. It was the only time the Hok had seemed rational, when they bowed their heads in shame to be punished with death, only what they deserved. Their strange, scaly faces had almost looked human.

Well, maybe they did. Or maybe, like Loco said, Mechsuiter Roundup wasn't really... accurate. Showvids were different from newsvids, after all. Much better. Everything always worked out in showvids, but not in newsvids. Derek was starting to see the fundamental difference.

"I guess the Hok are scorching what they can, before Fleet drives them off," Derek said with sudden insight.

"That's insane! Good planets are hard to find. You don't scorch them, you conquer them!"

"You said it yourself. Maybe they don't tell us kids everything." Derek stared out the window. "The Hok are evil. I hate them."

He hadn't hated them before. They'd just been the bad guys, like in a VR game. Now, a dragon stirred in Derek's guts, making him feel hot and strong.

"I want to kill them all," he said in a flat tone.

Nancy Sinden, one of the brainiacs from his class, looked down her nose at Derek from across the aisle. "The Hok is an inimical alien humanoid species that seeks relentless expansion of its territory. They're not evil. They simply are the way they are. Like bugs. It's an instinct."

"Yeah, and it's my instinct to slap you, smartass," said Loco.

"Better than being a dumbass like you," Nancy replied.

"Shut up. Derek's right. If they killed our parents, they're evil," Loco insisted.

"You physicals are so retarded."

"You brainiacs are so stuck up, like you know everything."

Derek pried a pebble from the sole of his shoe and flicked it unerringly at Nancy's earlobe, drawing a shriek. "You're no better than us," he said. "Everybody has their own special enhancements."

"Shut up back there!" the shuttle pilot roared. "I ain't got no time to babysit!"

"Where do you think we're going?" Loco whispered.

"Extraction and evacuation," Nancy replied.

"Funny name for a place."

Loco must have been joking, but Nancy didn't get it. Most of the brainiacs didn't get jokes. "It's not a place, moron, it's a process. We're being evacuated to somewhere safe, so we can grow up to fight the Hok."

Derek nodded, accepting the unacceptable. "That means we're losing."

"No shit," Nancy said, rolling her eyes.

"What about the rest of the people on Oceanus?" Loco asked her, as if hoping her answer would be different from Derek's.

"Sucks to be them. The planet's gonna be hurting for a while. Good thing my parents are dead."

Derek stared at her. "Why is that a good thing?"

"I never liked them anyway."

Loco and Derek exchanged glances. "She always was a loony," Loco whispered.

"My hearing is excellent, and I'm not a loony," Nancy said. "I'm a high-functioning sociopath. That means I can kill you and not feel any remorse."

The dragon of anger inside Derek reared up, and his eyes bored into Nancy's. "If you do, you better get us both, or you'll die too. Or the Enforcers will get you. I'm a physical, remember? I can snap your neck before you even see it coming. I'm going to be a mechsuiter."

"Yeah, me too," Loco echoed.

Nancy looked away and shut up.

That's good, Derek realized. If she's afraid—if *everyone* was afraid—then I'm safer.

He felt slightly ashamed for bullying the rude girl until he remembered her threats. Was it bullying if you got bullied first, and you bullied back?

Everything seemed to be changing around him, the ground shifting under his feet. One minute he wanted to hug his classmates, the next, he wanted to strangle them.

Nancy might be right, though. He digested her assessment of the military situation while they were transferred aboard a fast transport, where the crew treated them like special guests.

A day later, the transport popped out of sidespace and shuttled the seven boys and girls to a hollow asteroid-moon. The gas giant of Darania glowed above like a minor sun, while the system's real star hung in the sky nearby, fainter than on Oceanus. Even with the two, the converted asteroid's surface temperature remained below the freezing point of water, according to Nancy, who rattled off facts and statistics like a robot.

"Welcome to Academy," said a stocky, unsmiling man as he met them on the other side of the airlock. "I'm Colonel Oglala. This will be your new home for a while."

"How long exactly?" Nancy asked. "We weren't supposed to come here until we graduated from Secondary."

"That's 'how long exactly, *sir.*'"

"How long exactly, *sir?*"

"Until you're trained."

"For what, sir?" Nancy asked.

"For whatever you were designed to do."

Nancy raised her chin and sniffed. "I was designed for intelligence work."

"Then no doubt you will be put to good use. This is wartime, Cadet Sinden. You'll graduate as soon as you're ready."

Loco spoke up. "Me and Derek are going to be a mechsuiters, sir."

Oglala stared flatly at Loco. "Perhaps. If you measure up."

Derek grabbed Loco's elbow and pinched, to keep him from running his mouth. He'd seen enough vids about military training to know the instructors were never nice. At least not at first. They were *not* your friends. They were mean and tough, and they made you mean and tough. Then later, they made you proud. That was the formula for warriors.

"You're unmodified, aren't you, sir?" Nancy said to Oglala with a superior air.

"Not exactly."

"What's your strain, then?"

The man's face turned to stone. "I'm Lakota, from Old Earth."

"Hmph. I'm a blend of seven different strains, modified for mental acuity."

"I think you'll find, Cadet Sinden, that Nature has a way of *modifying* everyone. And that raw intelligence and experience are two very different things. I suggest you judge people not on their genetics, but on their demonstrated abilities. You're supposed to work in Intelligence, right?"

"Yes, sir."

"Don't you think it's wise to gather as much information as possible before making a judgment about an opponent?"

"Are you my opponent, sir?" she asked.

"It seems you're making me into one, Sinden. That demonstrates you may be smart, but you lack wisdom. Now, Sergeant Ryan will get you squared away. Dismissed."

"Listen up, recruits," said a marginally more pleasant woman, waving the flextab in her hand. "Mentals follow Specialist Reynolds to the left. Physicals follow Corporal Feldman to the right. Do it now. Quick-march!"

Derek elbowed Loco and quick-marched to the right.

Chapter 4

Planet Corinth, low orbit. Present day (2817 A.D., Old Earth reckoning).

Flight Lieutenant Carla Engels experienced a surge of affection for her boys as she released them to fall toward the embattled city of Helios. Though only in her twenty-ninth year, she felt decades older. The grinding schedule of combat wore everyone down.

The ground fire shifted away from her dropship, focusing on the mechsuiters directly. That gave her a moment to breathe and think. Stretched out below her was a scene that might have been beautiful—all streaks of light, wisps of smoke and sparkling seas—if it hadn't have been so deadly.

The war seemed to be accelerating—more missions, less recovery time. That was the norm lately. The mechsuiters didn't seem to feel it yet. In their physical primes and never defeated, combat fatigue hadn't started to catch up to most of them. But Engels felt tired all the time, deep in her bones. Professionalism and stims and the battlenet wiped exhaustion away when the time came to fight, but the feeling always lurked in the background, to return when the battle ended.

Maybe soon they would get a break longer than a week or two of R&R. Unlike his squadmates, Derek Straker had shed his youth and become a man she could respect, maybe even let herself love… though she'd never say it out loud. Not until they had some kind of chance together.

Not until it was allowed by military protocol—or at least until they knew they'd live past thirty…

The battle shifted again as the Hok fleet took aim at her ship. Shaking herself out of unproductive thoughts, she hauled the Marksman dropship around in a tight turn, throwing herself out of the way of incoming swarms of microshot. Composed of thousands of tiny metal balls, the clusters had been fired from warship shotguns: cheap, numerous cannon that vomited forth sprays of projectiles.

While they moved slowly compared to energy weapons or railgun bullets, these had been launched counter-orbitally, adding brutal force to their velocity. If they struck her Marksman they might knock her out immediately. At the least, she'd lose half her sensors and possibly some weapons emplacements.

Worst of all, it would *hurt*. As with the mechsuiters, she was linked fully with her dropship, which meant feedback manifested itself as pain. They said it kept pilots sharp. Negative reinforcement, the psychs called it.

Rolling so her underbelly pointed back along the incoming tracks, she aimed at one of her tormenters, a Hok frigate twenty times her size, now engaged with friendly warships trying to screen the drop.

Triggering her railgun, she sent a duralloy penetrator slamming into its hull, aiming at the center of mass. Her targeting systems were designed for fire support, and so weren't good enough to aim any more accurately at orbital distances.

She registered a hit, but there was no telling how much damage she'd done. Her weapon could obliterate the largest tank on the ground, but a warship had armor thicker than any ground vehicle, strengthened even more by internal and surface-conformal fields.

Friendly ships engaged the frigate, and the danger faded. She veered off to leave the naval battle to Fleet, who were already counterattacking the enemy from the flank.

Orienting herself, she tried to see through the flak and countermeasures below, estimating the position of the enemy headquarters by the deployment of the division in the lead. Recharging her capacitors seemed to take forever, as always. The railgun required a lot of juice.

Loosing a bolt at the enemy mobile HQ made her feel better, even if she couldn't see through all the mess to get a good target lock. Anything that inconvenienced the Hok would help the Foehammers below.

As she waited for the recharge again, she fired a couple of her defensive lasers at low power, blinding ascending missile seekers, and once, she launched one of her meager store of antimissiles. A Marksman was, after all, an assault support craft, not an independent gunship, despite her one heavy punch.

Though it felt like ten long minutes, recharging only took ninety-three seconds. By this time her boys were over the city, and she decided to save her big stick for when it was most needed. She'd wait for information relayed from the mechsuits to pinpoint her next target. The battlenet was always spotty on a drop, until the suits hit the ground and the uplinks stabilized.

In the meantime, she accessed the strategic overlay to update herself on the Fleet battle.

＊ ＊ ＊

Admiral Lucas Braga picked himself off the deck of the bridge of the Hundred Worlds battlecruiser *Vigilant* and scrambled back into his chair. He fastened the restraints, though he hated them. Most of the time inertial compensators made such primitive things superfluous, and he believed it damaged his command image to be strapped into his chair like a toddler.

That said, falling out of it was worse.

Getting pummeled like this wouldn't be a problem if he could command from a proper dreadnought or super-dreadnought, but neither of the largest classes possessed the speed he needed, not in sidespace or in normal space. Instead, he'd raced ahead on a converted battlecruiser to get here to Corinth in time, leaving his heaviest assets to follow almost a day behind.

"Evasive, course ninety mark thirty," his flag captain, Lydia Verdura, snapped. She commanded the ship itself so Braga could direct the overall battle. "Forty-five degrees port-roll. Beams four through seven, target that Hok bastard's main gun."

"Which Hok bastard?" asked the eight-armed Ruxin weapons officer, but apparently the question was rhetorical, as four pulsed particle beams lashed out, blowing the centerline railgun on one enemy cruiser to scrap. Battlecruisers had no more armor than a heavy cruiser, but they carried double the capital-grade weaponry.

"That one, yes, Lieutenant Zaxby," Verdura replied drily. "Helm, get us back into line of battle. Remaining weapons, fire at will."

"Poor Will, always taking fire," Zaxby muttered. Apparently the octopoid alien had a penchant for providing running comic relief.

Braga restrained himself from issuing a reprimand. He liked a tight, no-nonsense bridge crew, but this wasn't his usual flagship. Still, *Vigilant* had the best record among all his battlecruisers, and a ship's reputation directly reflected her captain: in this case, aggressive, stubborn, highly effective. If Verdura tolerated the chitchat, he could too.

Never repair the unbroken, he told himself.

Examining his screens, Braga noted that the mechsuit regiment had reached the ground with only two put out of action, completing his first objective. Unlike conventional forces, which must be brought by landers to the surface of any planet, mechsuiter organic insertion was relatively easy. He should be thankful.

Phase Two was always harder, though—holding the skies and space above the battlefield. Ensuring a win required orbital supremacy, or at least superiority. Once he cleared the enemy from orbit, his destroyers and frigates could drop low and slam ordnance into the enemy ground forces from above, guaranteeing victory.

If he couldn't gain superiority, parity would have to do, with each space fleet canceling the other. That would allow the ground forces to duke it out. The mechsuiters would still win—he'd never seen them lose a battle outright—but the cost would rise precipitously, and the Hok seemed to have endless divisions to throw at the Hundred Worlds, while the Hundred Worlds operated under a heavy and constant resource strain.

What we couldn't do with a thousand systems worth of production, Braga mused, but that was mere fantasy. We've got what we've got, and not only do we have to win, we have to do it without losing too much materiel.

"First Squadron, tighten up above Helios, standard geocentric formation," he said, touching screens to define his desired area of operations. His command staff sitting around him at their bolt-down consoles, hastily added to convert the battlecruiser into a flagship, relayed his orders in more detail.

His four battlecruisers, including the one in which he sat, adjusted positions and continued to exchange fire with the three Hok battlecruisers and nine heavy cruisers trying to drive him off.

Six heavy cruisers joined the Hundred Worlds battlecruisers, making the fight almost even. His ships had the edge in crew training and technology, while the Hok had the numbers, as usual.

Braga didn't bother to issue specific orders for the dozen destroyers in First Squadron. Two had been lost already, and eight of them had been assigned to shadow his cruisers, covering their vulnerable stern arcs against leaker missiles while adding their lighter railguns and lasers to the firepower mix. The other two destroyers, all Braga could spare right now, rolled inverted and concentrated on supporting the ground battle.

"Second Squadron will advance to envelop the enemy," he ordered.

That section of his fleet was composed of all ten of his light cruisers, units fast enough to turn the corner and powerful enough to smash any corvettes, frigates, or destroyers in their way, with sufficient firepower to damage heavier ships if they could sneak behind to target their more vulnerable sterns.

Like most naval battles close to a planet, this one had a floor defined by the atmosphere and the desire of both fleets to stay close to their ground forces. Otherwise, they would have simply stood off in space and fought in all three dimensions.

Standard tactics would seem to dictate gaining the "high ground" above, but if either side did so, they would be allowing the enemy temporary aerospace superiority above the planetary battle. Therefore, the engagement tended to be fought in two dimensions, as if the combatants sailed the surface of a spherical ocean.

In response to Braga's order, Second Squadron's light cruisers raced ahead on the right flank while First Squadron furiously held the line against the heavier Hok vessels.

In response, the Hok shifted lighter units to screen their bigger ships.

Soon… soon… Braga forced himself not to micromanage. Second Squadron's commander was a good officer, a veteran of many such battles. He was stringing them out, setting them up…

As one, the ten light cruisers turned to port, describing a perfect inward-curving line with all forward weapons pointed at the enemy's flank and rear. This concavity naturally concentrated their firepower. They launched a heavy salvo of shipkiller missiles while opening up with their centerline railguns, much larger cousins of a Marksman's fire-support weapon.

Each railgun projectile streaked past the intervening enemy escort vessels to target one of the three Hok battlecruisers, aiming at its vulnerable stern area. Though still heavily armored, the back end of each ship housed its main fusion engines, the openings of its exhaust ports exposed.

Yes, ships could maneuver on reactionless impellers alone, but only sluggishly, at perhaps one-tenth acceleration. To fight effectively, their fusion engines needed to expel high-speed streams of reaction mass.

Three of the ten projectiles slammed into the battlecruisers. Two gouged impressive but largely meaningless chunks out of the Hok ships' armor, but one caught the inner edge of an engine port and tore into the interior, causing an enormous secondary explosion as at least one fuel tank ruptured.

Braga could imagine the hell inside the enemy ship, contained by blowout panels and damage control systems but undoubtedly killing everyone within the engine and engineering sections. His heart burned with satisfaction as he contemplated the aliens' incineration.

With their main guns waiting on a slow recharge—the inevitable downside of putting such heavy weapons on smaller ships—Second Squadron's light cruisers drifted to their flanks and engaged the Hok destroyers and frigates with their secondaries. Profligate missile use and a superior suite of close-in lasers tore through the enemy escorts. This was classic cruiser work, its cut and thrust so different from ponderous capital-ship battles, and a joy to behold.

As usual when facing superior firepower, the Hok shifted to near-suicidal tactics, closing to point-blank range and aiming to ram their ships into their enemies. Orbital space was wide enough that, in most cases, they didn't actually strike home, but their suicidal runs evened the odds as the smaller vessels gained effectiveness at hull-scraping range, shooting past the Hundred Worlds ships to end up in their rear arcs, trying to rake their sterns.

In response, Braga's light cruisers were compelled to swing and follow their enemies, turning a set engagement into a swirling dogfight of smaller ships. Braga wished he had attack craft to send along with his light cruisers, but carriers were too slow to keep up with the fast task force he'd been forced to assemble.

One of his own battlecruisers and two heavy cruisers took severe damage and were forced to fall back, while the Hok lost two more heavy cruisers of their own.

The effectiveness of the damaged Hok battlecruiser dropped to almost nil. It still fired its weapons at a high rate, but its targeting systems seemed to have been degraded to the point most of its weaponry hit nothing but empty space. This victory alone made his flanking gambit worth the risk.

Agonizing minutes passed before Second Squadron gained the upper hand, finishing off the enemy escort units. Eight of the original ten light cruisers showed combat-effective, while two limped away on curving courses designed to rejoin First Squadron. Hopefully their damage control would restore them enough to allow them to snipe with their main guns.

Now, though, came the decisive moment. Braga leaned against his restraints as if that would help him better see the screens and displays. His eight light cruisers slid into salvo formation, one in the middle and seven in a circle around, and aimed all their now-recharged capital railguns at one of the two undamaged Hok battlecruisers.

Without harassment to spoil their aim, six of eight rounds smashed into the enemy, despite evasive maneuvers. At least one of the projectiles found a vulnerable area, and the Hok battlecruiser staggered, venting gas and plasma. It ceased to return fire.

"All units, concentrate on the third battlecruiser," Braga ordered. "If we knock him out, the rest will have to retreat or die."

He watched as the last of his fleet's shipkiller missiles volleyed in a wave designed to overload the enemy's countermeasures. Such weapons were usually the first to run out, unless specialized missile cruisers or ordnance tenders could be brought along, but he'd held one salvo in reserve for just such an opportunity.

Without further orders, his ship captains timed their railgun and laser strikes to support the missiles, distracting and blinding enemy cruisers that tried to thin out the salvo and relieve pressure on the battlecruiser. Once it became clear that at least half the volley would slam home, the Hok cruisers turned to charge the Hundred Worlds ships, repeating the tactics of their lighter units in hopes of doing as much damage as they could and, Braga inferred, delaying Hundred Worlds space superiority over the battlefield as long as possible.

"Yes!" Braga cried as the Hok battlecruiser crumpled under the impact of at least one nuke. His staff and the battlecruiser's bridge officers cheered. It was rare for a capital missile to actually strike a ship; most of the time their proximity sensors triggered detonation at the closest point of approach, but such had been the concentration of firepower that they'd achieved a contact strike, the holy grail of every launch officer.

However, Braga's exultation was short-lived as his sensors officer barked, "New fleet contacts, bearing one-eight-zero mark neg-nine."

Well versed in astrogation, Braga instinctively recognized that heading meant something approaching from directly astern and low... from behind the planet of Corinth.

Horror blossomed in the pit of his stomach as Braga saw an intact, undamaged Hok flotilla, including at least nine battlecruisers, emerge over the horizon, heading straight for his battered command.

Chapter 5

In close, light infantry can exploit its small arms skills while denying the enemy effective employment of his superior firepower. Light infantry hugs the enemy and forces him to fight at short ranges on its terms.

—The History of Light Infantry; *The 4GW Counterforce* by William S. Lind and LtCol Gregory A. Thiele, USMC.

Planet Corinth, at the edge of Helios city.

Straker aimed the mechsuit's force-cannon with his right forearm and triggered it. Inside, two volatile metals and a surge of energy combined to launch a bolt of superheated plasma. Contained within an invisible tube of magnetic force, the bolt pierced the nearest Hok heavy tank. It impacted precisely where he wanted, at the weak joining between turret and hull, and the turret blew sky-high with the detonation of ordnance within.

Immediately he threw himself sideways and rolled, the fifty-ton mechsuit mimicking his body's movements perfectly via his neural link. In a ballet of death, Straker opened up with the gatling in his left arm, tiny super-dense needles of collapsed duralloy lancing out in a fan as he swept right to left, mowing down battlesuited enemy infantry.

Those soldiers, humanoid but not human, seemed to be moving in slow motion compared to Straker. They died like bugs sprayed by pesticide as he hosed them with deadly projectiles. Their armor didn't save them.

I'm the best mechsuiter ever born, he told himself, and believed it might be true.

He needed all that confidence as four heavy tanks advanced against him and Loco, firing. Their railguns gouged his outer layer of armor with grazing strikes or missed entirely as he dodged. His accelerated time sense and the processors in his suit allowed him to see the turret snouts and predict the exact trajectory of the enemy projectiles. His task was simply to make sure these lines never met.

To the Hok it must seem like magic, but it wasn't. It was superior genetics, training and technology, combined with a desperate need to protect the Hundred Worlds. Humanity, despite its advantages, was losing. They had been losing for quite a while now.

All the more reason to fight hard and kill everything in sight, Straker told himself.

It was time to use his overhead assets. He uploaded a data packet, feeling the battlenet reach out, and then followed it up with the required verbal backup call. "Engels, fire mission! Heavy tanks in the open, azimuth zero-eight-five, danger close."

"Roger, Straker. Shot, over."

"Shot, out."

A column of cyan appeared. The railgun penetrator moved so fast it could only be seen by its glowing trail through the atmosphere. One of the heavies vanished, smashed into the ground like a bug under a fist, transforming into a ball of blazing fuel that swept outward, and then rose to form a tiny mushroom cloud.

The others spread out and fired patterns of obscurant grenades in hopes of hiding from the godsfire above. The ninety-three second recharge time of the Marksman's weapon granted the enemy temporary salvation.

Two hovers swept around Straker's flanks, their autocannon a greater threat than the harder-hitting tank guns. More shells meant more incoming to track. Given enough enemy fire, even an expert mechsuiter could make a mistake, or be boxed in so tight that there was nowhere to go, no way to dodge.

The key to battle was not to get hit, Straker recited to himself like a mantra. If I don't get hit, I don't get damaged. If I don't get damaged, I don't get killed. If I don't get killed, I kill Hok and live to fight another day.

The streams of smaller shells tracked him as he triggered the boosters in his feet and threw himself flat along the ground, the arc of his dive taking him over a slight rise and then into the hollow below. Loco did the same twenty meters over. When the hovers came around the tiny hill, he blew one to smithereens with his force-cannon while Loco shredded the skirts of the other with his gatling.

Its air cushion lost, the vehicle slammed into the churned-up dirt of the battlefield and ground to a halt, still firing. The mobility kill had disrupted its crew's aim, though, allowing Straker time to shift his own gatling and chew through its light armor.

A warning signal told him six guiders were inbound, volleys from the Hok missile tanks farther back. They had his and Loco's general location now, and the seekers on the warheads were discriminating enough to guide on the mechsuits if they got close enough.

"Incoming!" he warned, and Loco grunted in response.

Straker only had to form a thought, and the clear crystal lenses on top of his helm and shoulders blazed with laser light, cued by the active radar system built into the skin of his armor. The coherent beams speared the missiles, not powerful enough to destroy them, but blinding and burning out their seeker heads. The weapons impacted nearby with powerful concussions, but mechsuiters could shrug off anything less than direct hits.

Straker used the cover from the spewing dirt and swirling dust to move to his left. His battlenet showed Orset close by, and he used his comrade's presence to secure his flank while he set up an ambush. Loco turned to engage another enemy platoon, thereby keeping Straker's six clear.

When four heavies churned over the slight hill, assaulting toward Orset, Straker drove a force-cannon bolt into the side of the closest where he knew the armor to be weak.

Plasma vomited from every one of the tank's joints. The crew inside was flash-cooked. He waited for a secondary explosion, but it didn't come. The enemy vehicle's suppression system had done its job, preserving the equipment for salvage, but not the lives.

Three surviving tank guns slewed toward him, and he moved again, hiding behind the gutted heavy. He brought up his battlenet view provided by a combination of a cloud of friendly insect-sized drones blanketing the battlefield and by the regiment's dropships above. With this real-time targeting intel, he launched one of his precious antitank missiles.

It leaped vertically off the recessed slot in his back and arced over the barrier he crouched behind. When it destroyed its target heavy, Straker moved again, circling farther to his left, using the explosion as cover in hopes it had overloaded the enemy sensors.

A railgun dart passed so close it wiped off a line of Straker's sensors. The shockwave within the atmosphere stripping adaptive nano-camo from his skin. A centimeter closer and he might have been put out of action, his arm torn off.

With a surge of cold anger, Straker charged forward to get too close to the enemy for their main guns to follow. Automated secondaries opened up, antipersonnel rounds chattering against his skin, but he shrugged off the high-velocity slugs. His mechsuit weighed as much as a Hok light tank, but kilo for kilo had far better armor, with overlapping duralloy plating reinforced by superconducted conformal fields.

Now he was close enough to grab the relatively delicate barrel of the heavy tank's railgun and, like a man with one horn of a steer, he used his grip as leverage. Placing a foot on the turret, he bent the tube to uselessness, and then released his hold to throw himself backward onto the ground.

Ducking the aim of the final enemy, he set himself, grabbing the lower edge of the vehicle he'd just disarmed. Servos whined and feedback against his body showed he was nearing the physical limits of his mechsuit as he lifted the heavy tank from the side and rolled it. He pushed and shoved, pushed and shoved again, forcing it to continue its motion, top-side, bottom-side, juddering toward the last enemy.

Able to see the final tank's railguns pointed to his left, Straker stepped to his right and, before the gun could traverse, fired a precise bolt of metallic plasma into the nose of the turret. It didn't penetrate the main armor, but the big gun softened and sagged at its base from the intense heat.

The tank reversed and began a frantic withdrawal, escaping before Straker's force-cannon could recharge. He chose to save his missiles and let it go. With no main gun, it was out of the battle.

"First Squad, SITREP!" he called into the brief pause he'd earned. Checking the battlenet was all well and good, but the man in the suit was always his best source of information.

"Gatling's jammed up good, no surprise," Paloco said. "With my luck, I'll probably lose my force-cannon soon and have to withdraw. There's too many of them. I'm trying to back up toward you, but I'm pinned by enemy fire."

Straker located Paloco on his tactical display and surged into a run, staying low. The quickest way to a hero's grave was by bounding too high and presenting his mechsuit as the target for multiple enemy guns and missiles.

"On my way," he said. "Hang in there, Loco."

"I hang, you hang, we're all well hung. Well... I am anyway."

When Straker reached Loco, he saw three full platoons of Hok advancing on his friend. Loco was sheltering behind debris, but that wouldn't last long. Light tanks pounded at the mechsuiter's position while hovers skittered around the flanks, firing bursts from their autocannon.

Squads of battlesuited infantry bounded forward. If they reached Loco, things would get a lot harder. If a mechsuiter had a weakness, it was at the battlesuiters' hand-to-hand range. Like a man beset by monkeys, he would take a few with him, but soon succumb to their molecular cutters.

Straker announced his arrival by hosing a long burst of gatling fire at the largest concentration of battlesuiters. He thinned them out and forced them to go to ground. Simultaneously, he hammered a force-cannon bolt into the rear of a light tank. Its power plant detonated in a burst of superheated fuel, and the vehicle tumbled to rest on its top, severed tracks whipping like legs on a dying cockroach.

The speedy hovers were first to react, swinging around in floating curves while redirecting their stabilized chain guns in shining streams of tracers. To Straker's accelerated senses, the bright lines reached for him like lazy ropes of Christmas lights. He dove between them and rolled up into a run, instinctively causing the enemy to mask each other's fire, reducing the number of weapons that could be aimed at him.

Abruptly, the ground shook and his visor darkened as it struggled to adjust to photonic overload. He threw himself into a hollow for long enough to determine that whatever had caused the effect remained far enough away not to be a direct threat. When he rose, he saw multiple gouts of flame and several mushroom clouds, the signatures of Fleet orbital strikes behind enemy lines. He glanced upward to see the traces of ships skipping off the edge of atmo, getting as close to the battlefield as possible while retaining their speed.

Despite the welcome firepower, he knew the velocity of the vessels meant Fleet had lost space superiority. Otherwise, they would be remaining above the battlefield, hovering on the brute force of their drives, their computers talking to his battlenet.

Without top cover, things would get even more hairy in the open. If the Hok ships could bring their own capital weaponry to bear, they would overwhelm the mechsuiters one by one, sacrificing their own troops if necessary.

"Come on, Loco," Straker said. "We have to retreat to the city so we can hide among the buildings."

"If we give up the close-in battlefield, we'll lose our advantage," Loco protested. "Let's stay here and keep shoving it up their asses. They'll crack soon. I feel it."

"No, there's too many. We have to change tactics. We've done a lot of urban sim under vertical suppression."

"I know—and it always turns out bad. What the hell is wrong with Fleet anyway?"

"I'm sure Admiral Braga did his best. Remember, he doesn't have any dreadnoughts. Now get moving toward the city. I'll cover you." Straker ran across Loco's position toward the flank, drawing enemy fire.

Loco launched his remaining two antitank missiles. They arced upward, causing enemy vehicles to detect them and take countermeasures.

Hok tanks and battlesuiters alike scattered under the threat and retreated rapidly to try to avoid the top-attack weapons.

Loco used this time of distraction to hightail it toward the line of low-rise apartments defining the edge of Helios city.

Straker took the opportunity to reverse course under the lee of a high berm, popping up long enough to smash a bolt into an unwary hover. It tumbled and disintegrated as it bled off velocity.

Caught between the deadly high-tech missiles and the even more deadly mechsuiters, their rear areas under bombardment, the enemy facing Straker retreated—firing all weapons wildly in defensive mode. This allowed Straker to follow Loco without being shot in the back.

Straker used this short breather to check his battlenet for instructions from Regiment. The command WITHDRAW TO NEAREST KILO RALLY POINT flashed in the C3I box.

That confirmed it: the CO's assessment agreed with Straker's. If they didn't get some top cover soon, they'd be slaughtered.

Straker keyed his comlink. "Triple-one, this is Straker. Withdraw toward the city. Rendezvous at rally point four-kilo." He switched to tactical and saw Orset and Chen's icons off to his left to the south, but they weren't moving as fast as they should be. "Loco, I'm diverting to help Orset and Chen. Break open the resupply module and see if you can get your gatling working again."

"Yeah, I call dibs on all the Chicken a la King. Suckers!"

"If your mouth ever gets in the way of your shooting, Loco…"

"Yeah, yeah, heard it all before, boss."

Straker shrugged. Loco would never change, and what he said was true. His never-ending blather didn't seem to keep him from posting above-average battle stats.

At a dead run, Straker reached his men's position within thirty seconds. He saw Chen dragging Orset's mechsuit while trying to keep some low, landscaped hills between himself and the enemy. Straker quick-fired a bolt at the nearest tank, destroying its track on one side and sending up a spray of dirt, and then grabbed one of Orset's arms.

"Run!" he ordered.

The two hauled their downed comrade along the ground. As they ran, Straker accessed Orset's datalink. It showed no life signs. "Dammit, Chen, he's dead!"

"I'm not leaving him," Chen snapped. "Besides, if this gets as bad as it looks, we'll need the spare parts."

"All right. Keep running."

They hit a major road toward Helios and used it to accelerate. Showers of sparks flew from beneath Orset's suit as the two mechsuiters dragged it along the concrete surface.

Scattered fire reached out from the buildings in front of them, but when he automatically computed trajectories, Straker dismissed the attacks as non-threatening. The shells and beams reached beyond the running mechsuiters to strike at the Hok chasing them. It must be the efforts of dug-in militia.

Straker felt a hot spot between his shoulder blades and instantly dodged to the right, losing the speed and ease of the highway but disrupting the enemy laser targeting. Flashing red showed he'd taken some damage, but as long as he didn't get struck from behind again, he'd manage.

Mechsuits had a limited nanotech self-healing mechanism, but it took time and energy for the microscopic robots to patch and rebuild. Even then, they were only good for simple repairs, filling holes and cracks, or thickening thin spots.

He'd had to let go of Orset, and Chen had dragged the mechsuit in the opposite direction, so Straker circled behind an overpass and used it to snipe at the enemy. He tried to access an overhead drone. It took longer than expected, and the view wasn't optimal, coming in from long range and at a difficult slant. The close-in recon network must have been ripped to shreds by a combination of orbital strikes and enemy defensive fire.

Still, he got enough of a lock to fire a missile at the heavy tank constituting the nearest threat. The weapon leaped off his back and arced upward.

The target blazed with countermeasures, but too late. The missile exploded above the tank, firing a self-forging hypervelocity projectile directly through its thinner top armor. Flame shot out of every port, and Straker felt grim satisfaction as he envisaged the crew blown to bits.

Like his mother, his father, and his sister so long ago.

Straker nursed the hot coal of rage that drove him, giving new energy to aching, tiring legs. He dodged across the battlefield under the confusion of the tank's explosion and grabbed Orset's arm again, joining Chen in a section of sunken light rail that allowed them to reach the city in relative safety.

"This way," he said, leading Chen toward RP four-kilo. The mark on the map turned out to be a courtyard set among apartment blocks. Loco waved at them.

Straker looked up. "This won't hide us from above once the Hok have overhead supremacy. We have to burrow into the buildings."

"We take care of Orset first," Chen said with gravel in his voice.

"All right."

A moment later the dead man's capsule extruded from the back of his suit. Chen picked up the thing that was now their comrade's coffin and placed it gently on the ground. With one giant gauntlet he scooped out a trench. In less than thirty seconds, it yawned three meters deep.

Kneeling, Straker carefully set the coffin into the bottom of the grave and said the words the regimental chaplain spoke at every mechsuiter's funeral. "Ashes to ashes, dust to dust. Unknowable Creator, into your hands we commend his body and his spirit. As he was worthy, resurrect him on the Final Day, that he may fight honorably in your Celestial Legion once more. Amen."

"Amen." Chen covered the body with dirt and packed it down. Then he turned to the empty mechsuit. "Loco, you need a new gatling?"

"Yeah." The two men detached Orset's suit forearm from elbow to hand and replaced Paloco's, one for one. It integrated immediately and effortlessly, as designed.

"Where's the resupply pod?" Straker asked.

Loco pointed at an open vehicle door in a nearby block. "I stuck it in there."

"Let's reload and juice up. We don't have much time."

The three quickly opened the drop pod, replenished ammo and power, flushed wastes, and topped off water and medical supplies. All during the process, Straker's shoulder blades had begun to itch, his battle-tested intuition urging him to hurry. "As soon as we're done, split up the rest of the ammo three ways and shove the power module back inside," he said. "One orbital shot could take out all three of us."

"Roger, sir," said Chen.

"Yes, Mom." That was Loco.

Accessing his interior optics, Straker gazed for a moment, as he did so often, at Mara's Glory Girl action figure, mounted securely inside his suit. Other than his memories, it was the only thing he had of hers. The only thing the Hok had left him.

Murderers of children. War criminals. Beasts.

Straker's hatred revived with his suit charge. He unplugged after loading ammo and extra missile packs. Chen and Loco did the same.

"We fight like we trained," he said, "as an urban infantry fire team. We shoot, we scoot, set up and shoot again. Chen, take the north, Loco the south. Burrow in and let me know when you're ready. They'll hit us soon."

Chapter 6

Planet Corinth. Orbit.

Caught between the suicidal remnants of one flotilla ahead and a new, fresh enemy force crawling up astern, Admiral Braga saw only one option. "All units, at my order, advance through the remnants of the Hok ahead of us. They're in bad shape. After we break through, turn to form on my flagship. We won't be able to win this fleet action, so we have to help our ground forces to hold. To do that, we need to keep their ships busy."

Braga paused to let his staff relay his orders and prepare. "Execute!"

His battlecruisers leaped ahead, slashing at the battered enemy as they slid by, gaining distance from the Hok reinforcements behind. *Stalwart* took a glancing strike from a frigate and wobbled, but righted herself.

Braga's flagship, *Vigilant*, pressed her bulk through the enemy line, smashing the beat-up smaller ships in her way with point-blank fire. Covered by a screen of cruisers and destroyers, *Stalwart* soon rejoined *Vigilant* and the rest of Braga's command. This formation turned to begin a slow retreat, sniping at the fresh enemy force as they advanced.

"Orders to all light cruisers and destroyers," Braga personally broadcast on the command channel, "maximum firepower is to be directed at the enemy ground forces for the next... two hundred seconds. Dive down until you brush the upper atmosphere and rain hell on them. When time's up, continue in low orbit to circumnavigate the planet and join us from the other side."

His staff double-checked to make sure every ship had received his instructions. Shortly afterward, his larger ships wheeled to face the new threat from behind. What was left of his command stood at bay, facing the fresh Hok battlecruisers.

In response, the scattered remnants of the Hok flotilla he'd smashed through fled to join their relief group.

As ordered, Braga's light elements dove below the oncoming enemy. They relied on their speed and evasive maneuvers to preserve them as they unleashed all of their weaponry against the divisions of Hok ground forces below in one mass strafing run at the edge of the atmosphere. The bombardment lacked precision, but for three minutes their enemy suffered a blizzard of death from above.

In response, a dozen Hok destroyers peeled off and fired their engines in retrograde to swoop down behind the Hundred Worlds light units. Braga estimated they could harass his fast squadron, but the enemy wouldn't catch them before they made their attack runs on the Hok divisions and fled around the curve of the planet. In this case, momentum was their ally.

As his battlecruisers and heavy cruisers dueled with the oncoming Hok, Captain Verdura turned to face him across the crowded bridge, punching up a private channel in the internal battlenet.

"Sir," she said, "we need our light elements' firepower to help soften up this new flotilla. Without it…"

Braga shook his head. "Even with it, we'll lose. They outnumber us two to one, they're fresh, and we're out of shipkiller missiles. It looks like they anticipated us, expecting us to send in a fast force instead of a full-strength one, as we ended up doing. They're trying to trap us and wipe us out, but I'm not going to let them. Since we can't win, we're fighting for an overall draw. They're going to dominate the battle in space, but if our ground forces are victorious, we can hold the planet until our heavies arrive."

"At which time the Hok may perform a strategic bombardment and run, leaving Helios a smoking ruin. We have to gamble, sir! We should try to win right now!"

Braga worked his mouth to moisten it and cleared his throat. "I feel your pain, Captain Verdura, but I'm not going to sacrifice my fleet-in-being on the faint chance of taking the whole ball game. The smart thing to do is to tie up the enemy for as long as possible. Our dreadnoughts and super-dreadnoughts are on their way. We have to be here to join them when they arrive."

"What about our dropships, sir? We're leaving them behind."

He'd forgotten. "Tell them I'm sorry, but we can't cover them. They're on their own. If they can't rejoin us, they should land or punch out. We'll come back for them when we're able."

* * *

Flight Lieutenant Engels saw her own death approach as the new enemy flotilla loomed from behind Corinth. Braga's fleet was clearly outgunned and would have to fall back, though she had no doubt he'd make a fight of it. Now, she found herself caught in the middle, flying a dropship unsuited for space-to-space combat.

She turned and blasted toward the Hundred Worlds ships, hoping to reach them in time and be taken aboard. She could see the flares of other dropships doing the same. When her gun recharged, she fired its heavy projectile stern-ward, using its reaction mass to give her extra speed. Even as she did this, she felt guilty for not employing her primary weapon to kill another ground target.

Her efforts failed in any case. In front of her, Braga's force accelerated away, driving through the remnants of the first enemy flotilla in order to open the distance between him and the second. A group of Hundred Worlds light units forced themselves downward, their drives flaring brightly.

These dove below her and began strafing the enemy ground units while continuing to accelerate. If they continued, they'd pass under the new enemy flotilla.

Datalinked orders appeared in her battlenet, telling her to evade at will and eject if necessary.

Eject…? She'd never ejected from her Marksman, never even contemplated it. She could see the current rationale, though. In orbit, the enemy would soon pick her off. But she wasn't ready to leave her little ship yet.

Rolling inverted, she pushed her engines and impellers to the redline and forced her craft downward, toward the planet. Without much orbital velocity, she fell with frightening speed toward the battlefield below. Angling westward, she braved the madhouse around her as bolts rained from the Hundred Worlds light ships still making their strafing run. Air defense lasers, guns, and missiles reached up toward her from the enemy divisions below, but without coordination. They had other worries.

Though a pygmy in orbit, she became a relative giant above a ground fight. Her armor shrugged off lasers and gunshells while her defensive beams picked missiles out of the sky. Fortunately, the Hok ground forces had been badly rattled by the strafing destroyers, and the density of fire remained light until after she streaked over the city and out of their targeting arcs.

Engels searched for her boys' transponders and noted them on the east edge of the city, on the battlefront as expected. Slowing, she searched for a place to land among the columns of refugees. She'd just picked out a promising open field when a hot lance of agony drove through her spine. A missile had tracked her after all, and she'd missed it.

She screamed once before automated systems damped the pain feedback, and Engels found her ship in an uncontrolled fall. Minimal airfoils and thrusters got her oriented, but she had no power to fly and only seconds to make a decision.

Aiming for open land to spare the refugees the crash, she waited as long as she could before punching out. After a moment of shock and disorientation, she found herself floating down on nullgrav, tiny thrusters keeping her stabilized. Her gunship, her workhorse and her weapon for years, slammed into a farmer's field a kilometer away and began to burn.

She splashed into the water at a river's edge and stumbled, falling facedown. Hands helped her stand and slog up onto a narrow, sandy beach. She found herself in the company of a squad of militia, clothed in fatigues and carrying battle rifles. Fortunately, her body appeared unharmed, unlike her Marksman.

Popping open her faceplate, she spoke. "Flight Lieutenant Carla Engels. Fleet."

"Sergeant Banden Heiser, Helios Home Guard, ma'am," said the squad leader, a huge, hulking man. "We spotted your ejection. We'll try to get you on a transport."

"Transport where?"

"Evacuating the city. We're spreading out into the countryside for survivability—at least until the city can be secured again."

"Do you need a pilot? Or a driver? I'm rated on ground vehicles too."

"Don't know, ma'am. You can ask the logistics people. We're supposed to keep the traffic flowing."

"Give me a second." Engels shrugged out of her survival suit. It was thirty kilos she didn't need on a fully terraformed planet. She kept her headset, comlink amplifier, sidearm, and the detachable essentials pack. "All right, Sergeant. Lead on."

The four soldiers led her to the nearest bridge where a long line of vehicles sped across. Pedestrians walked along both sides of the road. Bicycles and scooters wove between.

Heiser shrugged apologetically. "I can't stop a vehicle. They have to keep moving. You'll need to walk until there's a slowdown and you get a chance to hop on."

Engels stared with longing back toward the city. Straker was fighting there. She felt like she should be with him. "You sure nobody can use a driver, maybe a gunner?"

Heiser's brow furrowed. "Ma'am, we have plenty of people and lots of light arms. What we don't have are enough heavy weapons: tanks, mobile gun systems, missile launchers. You need to go. There are Home Guard units mobilizing in the larger towns. Join one of them. I'm sure they can use you."

"Dammit... All right." Engels slapped Heiser on a shoulder she could barely reach and said, "Thanks, big man. Stay low." She turned to walk westward, joining the fleeing civilians.

Every time she thought she had a chance to get aboard a vehicle, fate seemed to thwart her. Once, a truck roared away just as she was about to jump aboard. Other times, the occupants waved her off with angry gestures. She could see the fear in their eyes, but she didn't understand their attitude, given her uniform.

Perhaps they blamed the military for failing to protect them.

So, she trudged wearily along on foot, not used to marching. Her feet soon hurt and began to develop hot spots. Flight boots were not made for walking long distances.

Kilometers later, she found herself among a crowd stopped before a bridge. Vehicles crammed the roadway and pedestrians filled in the gaps. As this scene registered on her consciousness, panic swept the mass of people and they began running in all directions—except forward.

Engels found herself trampled in the soft mud of the roadside, bruised and stepped on. When she picked herself up, she saw lines of Hok infantry advancing from all sides. They must have dropped behind friendly lines, seized the bridge ahead, and then deployed to surround this pocket of refugees.

She unholstered her sidearm, staring at it in her hand. What could she do against hardened soldiers in battlesuits? This little popgun probably couldn't even penetrate their armor. It would be a futile gesture. And she was no front-line warrior. She was a pilot, useless without something to fly.

Putting the handgun away, she looked around for somewhere to hide. Spotting a culvert running under the road, she dropped to the ground and crawled through muddy water into the pipe.

Something squealed and she thought of rats, or whatever occupied that ecological niche on Corinth. Ahead, she saw dark shapes and realized that others hid in here with her, also trying to avoid capture. She lay in the cold wet for a long while, smelling dirt, plants, and fear.

In the end, it didn't matter. Hok troops rousted her and the others, threatening to shoot them where they hid. Engels didn't want to die here in a dirty pipe, though she considered it. But where there was life, there was hope. It was her duty to resist and escape.

Survive with honor, said the briefings.

Placing her sidearm and its ammunition on a rock at the faint prospect some resistance fighter might one day find it, she crawled out and let herself be taken.

Chapter 7

The French Chasseurs, the Prussian Jaegers, and the Austrian Grenzer regiments (of the 18th century) followed the ancient Greek concept; in contrast to the rigid maneuvers of their line infantries, the light units were fast, agile, and expected to adapt their tactics to the terrain and the situation.

—The History of Light Infantry; *The 4GW Counterforce* by
William S. Lind and LtCol Gregory A. Thiele, USMC.

Planet Corinth. Helios city.

Almost gently, Straker used his duralloy fingers to rip holes in the back of the apartment building like a man tearing open a child's playhouse. He left as many load-bearing walls and beams as he could, wiggling in among the floors and leaving the roof intact. Overhead cover was most important right now, protection from eagle-eyed enemy destroyers and the drone network that was undoubtedly even now extending into Helios.

Once he was completely ensconced within the blocky four-story apartment building, he peered out the largest window he could find, leaving the glass in place to help mask his signature. He could see the enemy armor and infantry regrouping at three kilometers distance. They wouldn't move in until their aerospace forces softened things up.

The hypervelocity antitank missiles would be ineffective at this distance. Enemy defensive systems would have too much time to react, especially with no threat or other distraction to disrupt them. All Straker and his comrades could do was wait and prepare.

"Soon as you're set, eat and drink," Straker told them.

"Don't forget, I get the Chicken a la King!" said Loco.

"Man, give it a rest," said Chen, and Loco subsided.

While he followed his own orders about eating and drinking, Straker took the time to check the overall tactical situation.

What he saw made his gut ache. Only sixty-five mechsuiters remained, in various states of combat effectiveness. The open battle at heavy odds had taken sixty-three mechsuiters so far, a casualty rate nearing fifty percent, unprecedented in Straker's experience. The Regiment had never been forced to make a last stand; Fleet had always come through to hold up their end.

Maybe they would again, but Straker had to prepare for the worst.

Those who'd made it to Helios had set up much as he had, in ambush positions along the city's edge. Some of the friendly drone network had withdrawn with the mechsuiters, providing decent coverage above the buildings. Straker spotted planetary army and city militia missile teams deployed on rooftops. Artillery batteries could be seen dug within bermed firing pits. Robotic air defense tracks sat in parks and at major road junctions, seeking maximum visibility across the sky.

But there were not nearly enough assets available to cover a city of so many millions. As soon as they got themselves sorted out, the Hok would grind the Hundred Worlds forces to dust. It was a simple numbers game. Despite the losses the mechsuiters had inflicted, the defenders were still outmatched two to one in ground combat power.

If that were all, Straker would feel less pessimistic. The real crux of their bind was the Hok's impending aerospace supremacy.

"Review your bailout procedures," Straker said, startling himself with his own raspy voice.

"That's a little premature, don't you think, sir?" Chen replied.

"I want you guys to be prepared to blend into the captured population. You have a duty to preserve our skills for future use."

"What about you, sir?" asked Chen.

"Don't worry about me." Straker didn't want to say it out loud, but he would never leave his battlesuit voluntarily. He'd fight to the last. Better that than getting hunted like a rat in the sewers.

"How 'bout we don't let it come to that?" Loco said. "On the other hand, I'm sure some of the local babes will be happy to see us."

Straker didn't reply. He looked out of his window, watching the battlefield slowly clear of the smoke and haze thrown up by the friendly orbital strikes. "They'll be coming soon. Everyone's missiles set up for external launch?"

"Yeppers."

"Affirmative."

Straker had placed his own reload racks, which doubled as portable launchers, behind several unbroken windows. When the time came, he would fire one gatling round through each to shatter it, and then ripple-launch the missiles. The three on his back he would save for contingencies.

"Why aren't they coming?" Loco asked.

"If they've beaten our fleet, they're in no hurry. They can develop a coordinated attack plan in order to minimize casualties. It might be twenty minutes, it might be two hours."

"Or it might be now!" Loco called as the sky above them lit with streaks.

Straker lost the drone feeds in seconds, but what little he'd seen indicated the Hok ships were using pinpoint strikes to destroy those Hundred Worlds units visible from above.

The regulars and militia never had a chance. The only ones to survive would huddle in basements and shelters, hoping to spring point-blank ambushes as the enemy occupied the city.

Straker wondered what had happened to Engels and her dropship. He hoped she'd been able to run for recovery and flee with whatever forces Admiral Braga had preserved.

"Stand fast," Straker said, thinking to steady his men. "They can't see us, and they're trying to minimize damage to infrastructure. Otherwise, they'd have commenced a general bombardment. Our job is to make them pay for what they're taking, for as long as possible. We have to hold out until the relief fleet comes."

"What if it doesn't?" said Chen.

"The Hundred Worlds has interior lines and our ships are better. And remember the briefings? The dreadnoughts and super-dreadnoughts are already on their way in a separate fleet. That's why we got here so fast, with the battlecruisers and lighter units."

"They should have stayed together."

"Then instead of defending, we'd be attacking in the open, facing a dug-in enemy, trying to root them out of Helios with restrictive ROE to try to preserve our own infrastructure," Straker replied patiently.

"No point in crying about what-ifs," Chen said. "Here they come."

"BO-fucking-HICA," said Loco in resignation.

They were both right. The Hok armor had shaken itself out and reformed into standard deployments, doing what it did best: frontal assault. They'd long ago learned there was no point in trying to out-finesse mechsuiters. They'd hammer away until they broke the Regiment.

"Remember, as soon as I say so, we bug out to our fallback positions." Straker had already chosen and marked those for his men. "Move fast, because we'll be spotted and engaged from above."

Heavy tanks led the assault, behemoths of over one hundred fifty tons. These were bricks with cannon, deliberately placed out front to absorb attacks and threaten their enemies with the largest weapons, forcing the Hundred Worlders to take them out or be plowed under.

Light tanks followed, with guns almost as large but armor that could only stop smaller weapons. A concentrated gatling burst could drill through one; a force-cannon bolt would destroy one.

Behind and to the flanks flitted the hovers, ground-effects vehicles that relied on speed instead of armor, buzzing about the battlefield like maddened wasps. In conventional battle, these were the infantry-killers. Against mech-suiters, they added firepower and distraction.

At the back of the battle line came the missile tracks, firing heavy guided rockets not so different from the mechsuiters' own antitank weapons. While not as sophisticated as Hundred Worlds tech, the fire-and-forget projectiles had warheads large enough to take out a mechsuiter with a direct hit.

Among them all, battlesuit infantry loped like miniature mechsuiters.

Hok suits massed a ton each, with armor thick enough to fend off small arms. They provided speed and survivability to the troops, along with the strength to carry oversized weaponry. And, of course, the infantry's traditional ability to hold any ground, any terrain. After all, no tank or track could truly occupy a building or root an enemy out of a cave.

"We're fighting their kind of battle," Chen muttered. "This is stupid."

"We're fighting the only battle we can right now," Straker replied, but within himself he agreed with his pessimistic comrade. "It'll get better once they're inside the urban terrain."

"Their aerospace will tear us apart."

"Chen, shut up and do your job," Loco snapped.

"I can do one or the other, dick. Your choice. I don't hear you cracking jokes anymore, huh?"

Straker let them argue. Despite their bickering, they were both professionals, each with years of combat experience. Still, there was a desperate edge to the back-and-forth now, an indication that their morale was sinking.

He waited for commands to come through his datalink and display on his battlenet. The ready prompt appeared, telling him the rest of the regiment was as prepared as he was. "Optimum range. Fire on my mark."

While the missiles technically could reach much farther, optimum range represented a sweet spot at about two kilometers, far enough to allow the hypervelocity weapons to acquire and guide, close enough that the enemy's integrated defense systems had a tough time reacting to take them out.

The prompt flashed red. "Mark!"

Three mechsuiters fired single gatling rounds to shatter windows. Three racks of three missiles each ripple-fired from their positions. All along the edge of the city, more rockets leaped out of windows. Networked and smart, the weapons prioritized targets and deployed their own countermeasures, spinning off decoys and screaming ECM jamming pulses to fuzz enemy sensors.

Immediately after, mechsuiters fired force-cannon bolts and gatling bursts in the direction of the oncoming enemy, not with any great expectation of striking their targets, but simply to add to the confusion. The mass launch was designed to briefly overwhelm the Hok countermeasures—just long enough to wipe out their targets.

In response, enemy armor maneuvered wildly and fired obscurants, instantly wreathing the battlefield in metallized chemical smoke. Shotgun blasts of projectiles reached for the incoming warheads, and active armor plating extended itself temporarily on struts in the hope of intercepting missiles and detonating them before they connected.

Hok infantry leaped high into the air and fired wildly in the general direction of the rockets, trying for lucky hits. Some of them intersected their own armored vehicles' shotgun blasts and died.

They were relentless, Straker had to give them that.

The volley of eight hundred antitank missiles killed over three hundred Hok vehicles. This would have constituted a devastating blow in most battles, but clearly, the aliens had prepared themselves for such casualties. They barely slowed their advance. Fresh troops from behind overran the shattered remnants of their front lines and continued the assault.

Straker began moving before his weapons even struck. "Fall back!" he yelled, tearing himself out of the building that sheathed him and running like a metal godling between the empty apartment blocks. Loco and Chen pounded the ground nearby, taking serpentine routes toward their fallback positions.

From Hok ships above, orbital spikes reached for the mechsuiters at hypervelocity speeds, burning cyan tubes in the atmosphere as friction heated them. They struck the ground with ripping force, though they had no warheads. They contained enough kinetic energy to punch through ten meters of cryscrete.

Or a mechsuiter.

Like ballplayers, mechsuiters dodged left and right until they found cover within large buildings at their fallback positions. Some didn't make it; Straker saw at least a dozen icons on his HUD wink out. The regimental count now stood at fifty-one.

At this rate, we'll be dead in an hour or two, he thought.

Mechsuiters were simply not designed for this kind of battle. The theory went that the urban terrain would provide enough cover, but with full orbital supremacy, the enemy could pick off the mechsuiters any time they exposed themselves.

Unless...

Straker switched to the command channel. "Regimental command, this is one-one-one."

"Command here." The accompanying icon said he was speaking to Major Sanjinar, the XO, which meant Colonel Gormenstahl was likely out of action or dead.

"Sir, we're getting cut to pieces here."

"Tell me something I don't know, Straker."

"We're too big to act like infantry. We have to fight like mechsuiters, which means we must move forward, not back. Let them penetrate the city halfway, then get in among them, use all this cover and rubble. That will neutralize their overhead advantage. They won't be able to fire for fear of hitting their own."

Sanjinar stayed silent for long enough that Straker checked to see the channel was still active. Eventually the major spoke again.

"You're right, Straker," he said. "We have to gamble. I'll put out the word. We'll fall back, then ambush and press forward. We'll turn this city into our playground."

"Sir, any word from Fleet?" Straker asked.

"Seventeen hours."

"Yes, sir." Straker couldn't see any way they would hold that long, and his skepticism must have leaked through in his tone.

"Listen," Sanjinar said, "we have to buy time for the reinforcements to arrive. I know it seems impossible, but it's our only hope. Command out."

A moment later, Straker saw new orders pushed through his datalink and onto his battlenet.

It was time to turn this fight around.

* * *

The Hok battlesuit infantry separated Flight Lieutenant Engels from the civilians, speaking to everyone by employing synthesizers in their faceless helmets. It was enough to control the terrified refugees.

A few militia soldiers tried to resist, firing their small arms, but the Hok battlesuits proved impervious to anything but a lucky hit at a joint. The Hok shot their attackers immediately and left them for dead.

Engels wondered why the militia didn't get issued heavier weapons, something that would penetrate Hok suits. It's not as if the Hok would ship troops all the way from another star system just to drop them into combat with soft gear. No, when you paid that much in energy and logistical resources, you made your units as survivable and self-sufficient as possible.

The Hok separated out military from the civilians—or at least, uniforms from civvie clothing. Engels cursed herself when she realized that was the only discriminator. She should have traded, rations perhaps, to one of the refugees on foot, or even stripped one of the fallen. She yearned for something nondescript to wear.

And now she had nothing to resist them with, not even her puny sidearm. If the briefings were to be believed, there was a fifty-fifty chance they would be herded off a short distance and executed, perhaps after being forced to dig their own graves. She began to mentally prepare herself to run, or to fake being hit and to lie motionless among fallen bodies, if it came to that. She hoped they wouldn't administer killing head shots afterward.

But it didn't come to that. Two dozen or so military personnel were marched to a drop box. All were local militia except her.

By itself, the drop box was a cheap one-way transport for sixteen Hok infantry from orbit down to a planetary surface. It could be dismantled for its materials or abandoned if necessary. It could also be recovered by a lifter and brought back to be used again, needing only new retro modules and parachutes.

A lifter arrived as the prisoners approached the box, squatting atop it like a jealous spider. The Hok herded Engels and the rest inside, and as the door clanged shut she felt the container jerk upward.

She hoped the damn thing was airtight. Maybe the Hok didn't care.

They weren't immediately lifted into orbit. They set down after a few minutes and waited at least an hour. The air grew staler with all the people crammed in. Several militiamen took to banging on the door.

The Hok ignored them.

Eventually, their prison lifted again, this time hauling ass for altitude, she could tell. The air thinned and cooled as it leaked out of the indifferently sealed container.

A few minutes later she felt the shock and sounds of docking, presumably with a Hok warship or military transport. By that time the humans were beginning to suffer from oxygen deprivation, yawning, gasping, some falling unconscious, hypoxic.

Engels herself breathed deeply while remaining still and seated, determined to stay alive and conscious for as long as possible. She was therefore one of the few who saw the door open a crack. The end of a hose was shoved in, spewing gas with a faintly herbal smell.

Since it made no sense that the enemy would take the trouble to sort out the military personnel and spend fuel to lift them into orbit only to poison them, she relaxed and breathed normally, feeling the lethargy of impending unconsciousness steal over her.

Chapter 8

Planet Corinth. Orbit.

Admiral Braga suppressed a sigh of relief as most of his lighter vessels survived their strafing runs and rejoined him on the far side of the planet. For now, he could fall back and face the enemy reinforcements with something like cohesion.

"Harassment mode, all ships," he said, eyeing his three-dimensional holo-plate. Not as useful as his flagship's specialized holotank, it nevertheless showed him what he needed to know.

As his battered fleet assembled, it arrayed itself for long-range sniping, a strategy designed to force the Hok to play his game. They'd either have to withdraw out of range, or fight. If they fought, they had two choices: attack Braga's fleet, reducing their ability to attack the mechsuiters, or stand off and exchange distant shots with him. Either option would take the pressure on the friendlies below.

Braga knew his efforts would probably fail in either case. The simulations showed a greater-than-ninety-percent chance the mechsuiters would be wiped out before Braga's heavies joined him. It would take them seven or eight hours just to get here from their arrival point far out in empty space. Due to the physics of FTL travel, the larger ships had to emerge from sidespace farther away from the strong gravity created by stars and planets.

"Set fleet vector anti-spinward, forty-five degree climb planetary relative," Braga said. His battered squadrons rose and backed away from his adversaries circling Corinth in cautious pursuit. Now that he'd given up on trying to cover the mechsuiters, he had more freedom to maneuver.

His ships did their jobs lobbing railgun shots and beams at the enemy. Braga called up a space-time curvature map, and he waited impatiently as software predicted the arrival point of his heavy reinforcements. He overlaid the diagram on a real-time long-range sensor plot—and he quickly found his worst fears realized.

"They're setting up an ambush," he breathed as he took in two dozen signatures of enemy dreadnoughts and super-dreadnoughts, a force slightly larger than his own incoming task force of twenty-one. They waited at the predicted arrival point. Readings showed the enemy weapons were hot, the ships arranged in omnidirectional battle formation. They parked themselves at the optimum sidespace exit point.

The accuracy of the enemy intel was disturbing. Certainly, they could predict arrivals as well as he could, but this ambush indicated they knew ahead of time there were incoming reinforcements. Or maybe he was just too damn predictable. Had he been the enemy, he would have assumed a capital fleet was coming.

Worse, he couldn't warn the arriving ships. In sidespace, no communication was possible, nor detection of anything except gravity. They might pop out in the middle of the Hok heavy fleet and be shot to pieces before they could even lock their weapons on.

Standard military doctrine called for a fleet to always choose a random, non-optimal point of emergence. By staying away from the very best exit location, an enemy would have to get ungodly lucky to ambush arriving ships, which came through dispersed and disorganized due to fluctuations within sidespace.

But the commander of Braga's heavies, Commodore Downey, was an unimaginative, plodding officer. She had a reputation for conventionality and unwillingness to deviate from any obvious path. Braga wished mightily he could have replaced her with someone else, but she had too many political connections.

Therefore, he'd assigned her to a position that seemed to align with her proclivities, rather than give her command of the advanced task force and taking the heavies himself. He'd expected her to keep her ships together and slug it out with anyone who got in her way. At the start of this operation, that stolid attitude had seemed advantageous, or at least not harmful.

But the Hok had somehow gathered a superior force. They must have pulled units from systems up and down the front in hopes of smashing Braga and his mechsuiters here at Corinth. If they were also able to ambush his dreadnoughts and super-dreadnoughts, the battle would quickly transform from a severe setback into a military disaster for the Hundred Worlds.

It might even be the beginning of the end, if the Hok crushed the best Hundred Worlds ground forces and wiped out a quarter of its fleet units in one battle.

"May I help you with that, Admiral?"

Startled, Braga looked up into the rubbery face of the Ruxin weapons officer, Zaxby. The alien was surrounded by its open, clear suit helmet.

"Why aren't you at your post, Lieutenant?" he asked.

"I've been relieved. Watch change is already overdue. However, my species doesn't need as much rest as yours, so I thought—"

"Zaxby, stop annoying the admiral," Captain Verdura barked across the bridge, very publicly. "Sorry, sir, he's incorrigible. If he weren't the best weapons officer in the fleet, I'd have canned him long ago."

The octopoid turned to the captain. "Canned me? Captain, is that an insulting reference to seafood processing?"

"No, it's a reference to the gaps in your knowledge of Earth idioms."

Braga held up a hand. "It's all right. He might be of some use." He peered at the octopoid. "The pronoun 'he' is correct?"

"Acceptable. My species actually changes genders during our life cycles. I am currently in a non-breeding phase, so it hardly matters."

"Fine, 'he' it is. Now, what did you want?"

"I noticed you creating a predictive space-time curvature plot of our heavy reinforcements' optimum exit location. I also noticed the fact our enemy has a great deal of force arrayed in ambush, assuming our ships arrive near there."

"You noticed?" Braga demanded. "This display is on my personal screen."

"Apologies, admiral, but my eyes are sharp and sensitive even at distances you humans find difficult to resolve. To me, it was obvious what you were doing."

Braga cleared his throat. "Very well. What do you have to say?"

"Not only am I a superb weapons officer, I'm an aficionado of immersive wargaming strategy."

"This is no game, Lieutenant Zaxby."

"It most certainly is, Admiral. A deadly game we must win."

"Not at catastrophic cost to our forces," Braga insisted.

"I submit to you that losing this entire battle would be infinitely more costly than even the most expensive win. In any game, sometimes pieces must be sacrificed. It's regrettable when those pieces involve loss of life, but this fleet must be preserved. One hundred twenty-eight mechsuiters and some thousands of militia must be balanced against a similar number of Fleet personnel. More importantly, your naval task force must not be thrown away. It represents twenty-six percent of Hundred Worlds offensive naval strength. And, if you can win the fleet battle, you can retake Corinth."

"What's left of it..." Braga rubbed his eyes. "I know all this. What I don't know is how to win. If we withdraw and head for the ambush fleet in an attempt to combine with Commodore Downey's flotilla, the Hok ships at the planet will follow us and we'll be no better off than before."

"Sir, with the discovery of the enemy heavies in ambush position, my calculations indicate your present strategy is likely to fail. You must—"

"Zaxby," Verdura interrupted, "leave the admiral alone! You're off-shift, so go to your quarters! Sorry, sir, but he doesn't know his place."

"Belay that, Captain. Keep our ships sniping. I'll listen to the alien. Cosmos knows I could use some inspiration right now." Verdura relayed his orders while Braga rubbed his eyes again. "Go on, Lieutenant Zaxby."

"Well sir, the calculus is elementary. If the Hok catch our reinforcements in an ambush, the battle, and thus the star system, will be lost. If they don't ambush our forces, given Commodore Downey's usual combat methods, it is likely she will fight a battle of attrition that will leave both sides combat-ineffective, a Pyrrhic victory at best. As we are also unlikely to win against our present opponents, it stands to reason that our only chance is to combine our forces and attempt to destroy one enemy group or the other."

"You make it sound easy, but—" Braga began.

"Combining on the ambush fleet is your only option, sir. Then you can take command of all our ships and apply your expertise instead of letting

Commodore Downey use our forces ineptly. However, I believe I have a way to improve our odds, to give the enemy a surprise."

"Like what?" Braga asked, his eyes narrowing.

"I've been working on some unconventional weapons ideas, using materials we have at hand."

"Go on."

"If you'll permit me, Admiral…" Zaxby reached across with two curling arms and ran his fingerlike sub-tentacles across the console. In a moment, new displays showed a weapon schematic.

The admiral peered at it, puzzled. "That looks like a standard fusion mine."

"Correct, a weapon almost undetectable because of its stealth features. When properly placed, a mine is powerful enough to incapacitate or destroy a ship in one strike."

"They're basically useless to us," Braga said flatly. "Mines are very hard to employ. Space is too vast and getting the enemy to run into them, even using proximity fuses, is nearly impossible. Mines haven't significantly influenced a battle since Alabaster Prime, eleven years ago."

Zaxby bobbed his oversized head. "Yes, sir, the problem has always been getting the mine and the enemy to intersect. That's why we have railguns: to cause a projectile and an enemy ship to meet, violently."

"But railguns can't fire mines."

"That's not entirely true, sir."

Braga paused, staring at the alien. A few of Zaxby's limbs churned impatiently as he waited for the admiral's response.

"Are you saying you want to fire *mines* as projectiles?" Braga asked. "Through the railguns?"

"Yes, sir. Properly adjusted, our railguns could launch them into the paths of enemy ships."

"I saw a proposal about that a couple of years back…"

"Yes, sir. I submitted it to Systems Development. It was rejected."

"Why?"

Zaxby shrugged, a gesture he must have learned from humans. "Production and maintenance expense. It would require manufacturing and distributing a completely new kind of mine, as well as modifying the railguns. That's production. As for maintenance… it's very hard on the railguns."

"How hard? How many of our mines could a railgun launch before breaking down?"

"Perhaps one, perhaps as many as five."

Braga sat back and stared in astonishment. "You want me to wreck half my weapons on this scheme? We're out of offensive missiles. You're going to leave us with nothing but beams!"

"But sir, if it works, we could surprise the Hok and do significant damage to their ships, far worse than we do to ourselves. We might even destroy several outright. They won't know what hit them."

Braga exchanged glances with Verdura. She gave him a tight nod, as he expected she would. Always aggressive, she wanted to hurt the enemy no matter the risk.

"All right, Lieutenant Zaxby. Make whatever modifications you need to."

Zaxby input a series of instructions to the admiral's console. "Done."

"Done?"

"Yes, sir. I had the software package all ready to go. It is even now updating across all our ships, under your command codes."

"*My* command codes?"

"From your console, sir…" Zaxby seemed smug.

"Great Cosmos, but you're an arrogant creature," Braga exclaimed. "Hacking my console? That's a punishable offense."

"These things have been said before, sir. Are you going to win this battle or send me to the brig?"

Braga smiled. "I can see why Captain Verdura keeps you around."

"My incredible competence?"

"No, because you make everyone else seem like models of naval propriety."

"I believe I've just been insulted." Zaxby's rubbery mouth imitated a smile.

"You have, but if this trick wins us the battle, I'll sing your praises."

"I had no idea you were a singer, sir. I myself have a complete set of recordings—"

"Stick to the point, Zaxby!" Verdura rolled her eyes.

Admiral Braga glanced at her. He began to wonder only now how much of this entire show had been a setup. Had Verdura encouraged Zaxby to make this entreaty? If so, it meant she was a cunning woman. If the idea had been shot down, she could have pretended it was entirely the crackpot idea of a crazy alien. On the other hand, if the new approach was embraced, she could claim credit.

"Admiral," Lieutenant Zaxby said, "the gunners now need only select Mine Launch Mode, and I will input the preprogrammed target points."

Braga stroked his chin and examined the data. "These specs... the mines won't travel like normal railgun rounds. They'll launch slowly."

"My program takes all that into account, sir. All you have to do is tell me what to hit and let me do the rest. All our railguns will be aimed and fired remotely from the flagship."

"From my console?"

Zaxby squirmed even more than usual for an octopoid. "I have taken the liberty of using your codes to grant my station all necessary permissions."

Braga sighed. "Take your seat again, Mister Zaxby."

"I also have some ideas on tactics. If you—"

"Why don't I simply turn over command to you, Zaxby?"

"Oh, yes, sir, that would be most efficient."

The admiral snorted. "Do you know what sarcasm is?"

"Theoretically, sir. I do have trouble detecting it."

"My last suggestion was an example of sarcasm. Back to your station. You've done enough. I'll take it from here."

Zaxby returned to his seat, displacing the officer there, and his tentacles began dancing over the board.

Braga turned to Verdura, glancing at the main screens. "How are they reacting to our sniping?"

"Sniping back, sir. They've sent light units down to provide overhead firepower for the ground battle, and they're screening with their cruisers and battlecruisers. We need to get in closer to have any effect, sir. Their frigates and destroyers must be raining hell on our mechsuiters."

Braga stared at the readouts and graphics that showed him a synthesized view of the fleet battle. Every fiber of his being cried out to attack the enemy and relieve pressure on the planetary defenders, but he was clearly outgunned. He had to go with Zaxby's advice and abandon them to their fate.

Braga brought up his own displays and began running simulations, mindful of the chrono spinning as time bled away.

He tried and rejected the idea of launching mines at the enemy in their current deployment. Due to the sniping, they were already evading constantly, and the stealthy weapons would only be effective if he could somehow lure his opponents onto a steady, predictable course.

Braga said, "Operations, pass to the fleet to begin retrograde on my order. Plot a course that will take us out to the ambush point, with initial hard acceleration to take us some distance from the planetary fleet. They'll undoubtedly pursue us, so I want to get the jump on them. Keep our external railguns aimed rearward, as if we're merely holding them ready."

"Yes, sir." Verdura and Braga's operations officers began passing orders.

"Zaxby, the enemy will likely follow us. In fact, I *want* them to follow us. As soon as we withdraw out of range, they'll stop evading and their courses should steady in pursuit. When that happens, take your best guess and fire a full spread of mines into their path."

"With exceptional pleasure, sir."

"The fleet is ready, admiral," said the operations officer.

"Execute."

Braga kept his eyes on his displays as his outnumbered task force abruptly stopped sniping and turned away. To the Hok, it would appear exactly like what it was: a sudden attempt to break contact and run. Within moments, the alien commander would deduce his strategy: that Braga was attempting to combine with Downey's incoming fleet.

The Hok should know they'd won, at least in Corinth's orbital region. Braga hoped that would make them complacent, confident of their advantage. But they would still have to pursue him quickly or risk getting beat by a superior force at the ambush point. After all, the Hok couldn't know exactly what would be popping out of sidespace. They'd want to maximize their advantage, so they'd hurry after him.

Braga was counting on it.

"They're pursuing us..." Zaxby said, his odd limbs fidgeting.

"We can see that, Zaxby," Verdura said.

"I'm computing trajectories in four dimensions," Zaxby said. "Did I mention that I have exceptional spatial acuity, a benefit of my primitive ancestors living amphibiously in a three-dimensional semiaquatic environment where they were both predator and prey?"

"No," Verdura replied in a weary voice, "you've never mentioned that. Not in the last hour, anyway."

"Launching mines. My software also reduces the firing signature of the railgun in order not to tip off the enemy to what we are doing."

"Very good, Mister Zaxby," Admiral Braga said. "Can I see the mine cluster as it travels?"

"I will show its projected location on your displays, though obviously there is no positive telemetry from the weapons themselves."

"Obviously. That would rather defeat the stealth factor, hmm?"

"Absolutely, sir. And may I say, sir, you are grasping these principles better than I expected—for a human."

"Oh, Cosmos," Verdura said, palm to her face. "Sorry, sir."

"It's all right, Captain. I'm actually getting used to him. I believe he means well, even if he is one rude son of a bitch."

Chapter 9

The light infantryman is characterized by his mental resourcefulness and physical toughness.... Light infantrymen do not feel defeated when surrounded, isolated or confronted by superior forces. They are able to continue performing their duties and pursue their objectives for long periods of time without any type of comfort or logistical support, usually obtaining what they require from the land or the enemy. They are neither physically nor psychologically tied to the rear by a need to maintain open lines of communication. Their tactics do not depend on supporting arms. This attitude of self-confidence and self-reliance provides light infantry with a psychological advantage over its opponents.

—The History of Light Infantry; *The 4GW Counterforce* by William S. Lind and LtCol Gregory A. Thiele, USMC.

Academy Station. Thirteen years before the Battle of Corinth (2804 A.D., Old Earth reckoning).

"Cadet Engels!"

Carla Engels walked rapidly up and halted at attention, facing Lieutenant Yoshida. "Ma'am!"

"Cadet Straker!" Yoshida pointed at a new boy wearing no hash marks on his collar.

Engels thought he was young even for a Fourthie. This kid couldn't be more than thirteen. She figured he had to be one of the new ones they'd been briefed about.

The cadet raced forward and halted directly in front of the lieutenant. Both Yoshida and Engels were taller than the boy—but no doubt that would change as he grew to his full height.

"Cadet Straker reports as ordered, ma'am!" he said, snapping a surprisingly sharp salute.

Yoshida stared coldly at Straker. "One demerit, Mister Straker: improper reporting procedure. One demerit for double-timing. This is an academic zone, not a training zone. An officer only needs to be told something once, and you were told about these things at least twice during your trip here. Don't make such mistakes again."

"Yes, ma'am."

"One more demerit," Yoshida said coldly. "I gave you an instruction. You will answer 'aye aye' or 'roger wilco' to acknowledge your compliance with instructions. 'Yes' and 'no' are answers to questions. Do you understand?"

"Aye—ah, yes, ma'am."

Yoshida indicated Engels. "This is Cadet Second Class Engels. She is your assigned Upper-Class Sponsor, your UCS. If you need to know something relating to Academy and its procedures, or if you piss yourself in the middle of the night and you're missing your mommy, or even if you're thinking about walking out an airlock because this training is *just too hard*, you will not bother another staff member with your trivial requests. You will see Cadet Second Engels, and she will handle it. Is that clear?"

"Yes, ma'am."

"Dismissed."

"Follow me, Cadet Straker," Engels said. She performed an about-face and strode off, not looking to see if the boy would follow. Footsteps behind her and her superb peripheral vision confirmed he'd positioned himself properly to her left and half a pace back.

She led him to an unused classroom and sat down. Straker remained standing at attention. Engels nodded in approval. "At ease, Mister Straker. Take a seat."

He sat down across the table from her and waited.

"You're a physical?"

"Yes, ma'am."

"Don't call me 'ma'am.' You call me 'Cadet' in formal situations, but this isn't one of them. We're still in the academic zone."

"Okay."

"That's too informal. You're not a civilian anymore."

"Then what do I say?"

"Call me Miss Engels."

"Everything's so confusing…"

Engels offered him a slight smile. "You'll figure it out. It's part of the fun."

"I'll get demerits," he said.

"You're a plebe, a rat, not even a Fourthie yet, Straker. That means demerits will pile so high you'll never have privileges. Not until you make Third, anyway. That's the way it works. The system is rigged. Get used to it. How old are you, anyway?"

"Thirteen last month."

"We've never started cadets so young before."

"I lived on Oceanus. My family was killed. So were a bunch of others at my school. The Hok targeted us Specials. Tried to take us out with spikes."

Engels raised her eyebrows. "I heard about the raid. You *believe* they tried to take you out, or you *know* they did?"

"I—I believe it. Only certain houses got spiked, mostly ones with my friends. More than eighty percent of my class died. I'm supposed to be a mechsuiter. It makes sense they would try to kill us before we get trained."

"Well, Intelligence thinks the same as you do. A mechsuiter, huh? I'm on the pilot track."

Straker raised his eyes to hers. "Oh, you're a physical too?"

He'd been visibly struggling not to stare at her chest. For her part, she wasn't overly bothered, considering her slight breasts to be anything but her greatest asset. Engels was tall and rangy—leggy and athletic.

"Yes," she answered. "Why are you surprised?"

"I guess because *all* the girls in my school were brainiacs, and younger than me. The physicals were all boys."

"Never heard of a school like that before."

Straker shrugged. "That's how they did it."

"Maybe it was an experiment."

"How old are you, anyway, um, Cadet Engels?" the boy asked.

"Sixteen. And you'd better stop drooling over my tits. If the officers see that, you'll be walking tours until midnight."

The boy blushed and lowered his eyes. "Sorry, Miss Engels."

Engels waved his apology away and suppressed a grin. "You'll get it."

Straker raised his eyes to hers. "Why are you being so nice to me?"

"I'm not. It only seems that way in contrast to the staff. Don't make the mistake of thinking I'm a soft touch. Come find me if you need me, but it'd better be important. I've got my own workload. Remember, upperclassmen can give out demerits too, and some of them are worse than the officers." Engels stood. "Dismissed."

* * *

It was all Derek could do to keep from looking back over his shoulder at Miss Engels. She was… she was… he had no words for what she was. Stronger, older, more confident, completely different from the brainiac girls he'd grown up with, who were always younger, and none of them had *curves*. And she was a physical, like him!

His mouth became dry and his heart pounded just thinking about her. More even than the faculty and staff, he wanted to please her, to make her proud of him, to earn her respect. And he wanted to look at her body for hours and hours…

He stopped short in the middle of the passageway. What the hell was wrong with him? The sexuality classes back at the school had talked about attraction and reproduction and how people did it, but it had all been clinical, even kind of disgusting. Now, for the first time in his life, Derek could imagine wanting to be naked with a girl, wanting to do the sex thing.

"Plebe, what the hell's wrong with you! Brace the wall, you stupid rat! Make a hole!"

Derek slammed himself against the nearest wall to let the officer pass. "Sir, yes, sir!"

The young man didn't pass, though, but stopped to lean down and put his nose two inches from Derek's. "Don't make a sir-sandwich out of me, scumbag! One demerit for that, one for failing to respond with 'aye aye' to an instruction, and one more just because you're the scrawniest, ugliest, stupidest rat I've ever seen in my life!"

Derek realized the person yelling at him wasn't even an officer. Rather, he was an upperclassman, a Cadet First, which meant Derek wasn't required to brace the wall, merely to stay as far to the right as practical when passing. The First's name tag read *Skorza*.

"Pardon me, Cadet First," Derek said, slipping out and continuing on his way.

"Get back here, rat!"

Derek stopped and turned around. "Cadet First, I have to keep to my schedule." The schedule was sacred, he'd been told. "Failure to repair," as the military called missing an appointment, was a serious offense.

"You need to drop and give me fifty pushups, that's what you need to do, sub-Fourth. Time to get you into shape!"

Other cadets were gathering around, watching. Some grinned, some looked worried. No officers were in sight.

Straker considered complying, although upperclassmen had no authority to order pushups, or in fact do anything punitive other than issue demerits. But no, that wouldn't be right. He'd always been taught to insist on what was right, even if it was hard. Besides, he felt instinctively this was a bully, and he didn't like bullies. His father had told him to stand up to bullies, though until now that hadn't been difficult.

"No, Cadet First," he said evenly. "You're not authorized to make me do pushups."

Skorza's face whitened, and his tone turned deceptively conversational. "Everybody does pushups for Firsties. It's tradition, no matter what the regs say."

Straker looked around at the watchers.

"Eyes front! Stand at attention, rat!"

Straker did, because that was in the regs. But he still thought he shouldn't be dancing to this guy's every tune. "I have to go, Cadet First. Pardon me."

Skorza leaned into his face again. "You'll do as I say! Now drop and give me a hundred! I know you can do it. You're supposed to be some kind of wonder-boy. Top scores in all physical measures." His tone turned sneering. "Come on, show us what you can do."

"Come on!" cried several cadets gathered around. Others clapped and made encouraging noises.

He almost did it, but realized at the last moment that this would also be a victory for the bully. "No. I'm sorry, Cadet First, but I have to go." Derek turned to dodge around Skorza and double-time away.

"I'm watching you, rat!" The angry, frustrated words floated after him, accompanied by laughter from the cadets nearby.

The amusement ceased as a lieutenant rounded the corner in front of Derek. This time he braced the wall properly. The officer ignored Derek as he walked by.

Derek double-timed onward. He thought he'd handled Skorza as well as he could, though he'd been unprepared. He resolved to focus better, not to get confused by the artificial rules, whether written or unwritten, or by the deliberately imposed abnormality of Academy. He brought the image of his smashed home to mind and felt clarity wash over him.

No matter what the distraction, no matter his body's lusts or fears, he was here for training and education. Academy wasn't interested in chickens, or people trying to hook up. It wasn't as if any sixteen-year-old hottie would even look at a kid like him. And she was a physical, so he couldn't impress her with his speed and coordination.

So, he'd have to impress her some other way...

* * *

Mechsuiter, mechsuiter, can't you see?
This little run ain't nothin' to me
I can run all day, I can run all night
I can run on through to the morning light

The chanting formation of two hundred cadets rounded the course's final hill, running in perfect step to the cadence-caller's voice, bringing their barracks complex into view. Above them arched the practice fields, ranges, forests and rivers of the inside of the giant cylinder that was the heart of the training complex on Academy.

Forty kilometers long and ten across, the converted asteroid station spun on its axis to create the effect of gravity, actually centrifugal force, much cheaper and easier than gravplating such an enormous base. Occupying that axis, a thick tube, the spine of the station, held mechanisms to produce sun, rain, clouds, any weather the controllers wished. The structure also contained observation posts, control machinery, glider launch and suit-drop platforms, and zero-G combat gyms. He'd been here only a month and it had become his world.

"Always nice to get home," muttered Loco beside him between lines of the song.

"Ten kilometers every day," Derek replied.

"I don't mind the exercise. It's just so damn boring—and easy."

"Shut your holes, rats!" an upperclassman roared from nearby. Cadet First Skorza, in charge of the road guards, ran over to talk briefly with the speaker. When he jogged away, he had a grin on his face.

> *Mechsuiter, mechsuiter, where you been?*
> *Down in Shangri-La drinkin' gin*
> *Whatcha gonna do when you get back?*
> *Ten more klicks on a running track*

As the runners approached the edge of the barracks, Skorza signaled a left turn with broad waves of his arm. Instead of heading in to the showers, the cadets proceeded past the buildings and down the road, back out into the countryside for another ten-kilometer lap. "You have sub-Fourthies Straker and Paloco's mouths to thank for this, everyone," Skorza bellowed. "Be sure to give them your regards."

A collective groan, barely suppressed, ran through the training platoons. "Nice job, assholes," a Thirdie said from behind Derek. One cadet kicked him in his thigh. Another punched him in the middle of his back. Loco got similar treatment.

Whatever. Hazing was a part of paying your dues, and if the Firsties wanted to run their rats some more, they didn't need a good reason. The rest often fell in line, passing abuse downhill when they had an excuse. The books and vids on leadership talked about modeling good behavior, but most of his classmates seemed powerless to resist modeling the bad too, despite the regulations printed in black and white.

Derek resolved he'd do it differently. When he moved up, he wouldn't be an asshole to the rats just because the people before him were assholes. He'd model leadership with respect. He probably couldn't change anything in the long run, but at least he wouldn't be a part of the problem.

> *Mechsuiter, mechsuiter, have you heard?*
> *I'm gonna drop from a big-ass bird*
> *If my jets don't save my hide*
> *I'll be splattered on the countryside*

But for now, getting through every day was challenge enough. He settled down, blanked his mind and let the cadence carry him along.

Sometime later in the dark of the night, Straker awoke in his bunk to feel himself held down by his blanket, powerless to get out of bed while large, dim figures pummeled his body with their fists and forearms. He curled up to protect his groin. At the end of a solid minute, they left him bruised from calf to neck.

"Skorza says hello, shitbag," hissed a voice in his ear. "Hope you enjoyed your blanket party."

Then they were gone.

A groan of pain and anger escaped his throat, but he refused to give in to it. He stumbled to the shower while the other sub-Fourthies in their bunks nearby turned away from him, pretending sleep. The water helped, cool, then hot, but it was all he could do to get through the next day, and the next.

He didn't report it, or go to sick call. He could handle his own problems.

* * *

A week later, Derek took a wrong turn coming back from chow. This wasn't as surprising as one might think. Academy was a sprawling space station and the staff seemed to take delight in reconfiguring the corridors every few days to keep the cadets on their toes… or, Derek surmised, to provide them with ready-made mistakes.

As he rounded a corner, he saw two adult-sized shapes in front of him. His hyper-alert mind, trained by excruciating attention to the arcane regulations of Academy, registered the Firstie uniform, and his body reacted by moving as far to the right as possible in order to slip by.

A large hand contacted his chest and shoved him forcefully backward, hard enough to make an ordinary kid tumble. Derek's reflexes saved him, barely, allowing him to retain his feet.

That didn't matter. A blow fell on his back, more of a slap than a punch. Glancing over his shoulder, he saw two more Firsties, and then he focused on the one in front of him.

Skorza.

A shiver of fear and a thrill of confrontation shot through him. He'd never failed in a one-on-one physical challenge, even against non-enhanced adults, so he had no reason to think this time would be different. Besides, whatever might happen, he would survive it like he survived the blanket party, just one more bump in the road toward becoming a mechsuiter. After all, this time he wasn't being pinned down by a blanket held at its four corners.

As Skorza reached for him, he twisted away and dodged forward, intending to dash beneath the outstretched arm and be on his way. However, the hand caught his collar and yanked him backward and into the midst of the four Firsties.

He'd forgotten many of the cadets here were also genetically enhanced physicals, or at the very least they were selected examples of the fastest, sharpest, most competent adolescents from across the population of the Hundred Worlds. Add in that these boys were older, further along in their development, and it didn't seem as if he was going to avoid what was coming.

"Okay, Cadet First, what's this about?" Derek said evenly. "I need to be on my way." He glanced around at the wide spot in the corridor, noting that the cameras within sight, oversized ones visibly set there to show the staff were watching, had socks slipped over them.

If he'd designed Academy, he'd also have micro-sized video pickups scattered around for just such an occasion, but he had no idea if the staff thought in those terms.

"This is about you being out of uniform," Skorza said, lifting Derek by his collar and shaking him, his feet dangling off the ground. His old-style tunic, made of materials grounded in the traditions of the service, wool and cotton and only a smattering of synthetics, began to split at the seams. The four laughed uproariously.

"Also," said one of the others from behind him, "your underpants have become inoperative." A hand reached past his waistband to seize his regulation military briefs and pulled, tearing the material as it friction-burned his man-parts. More laughter followed.

Derek should have taken the abuse, should have played along, but a deep sense of injustice seized him. This wasn't how a future hero of the Hundred Worlds should be treated. He lashed out with his foot, planting it right in Skorza's crotch.

The move caught the Firstie by surprise. He dropped Derek and hunched over, groaning.

As soon as Derek's feet touched the ground, he bent at the waist and mule-kicked backward, aiming again for the groin of the cadet behind him, but instead making heavy contact with his abdomen. A grunt showed some effect, and Derek whirled, hands up in proper defensive combat stance, weight balanced on the balls of his feet.

This turned out to be a rookie mistake, he realized, as his four opponents instinctively did the same. He should have continued to attack wildly and then run when he had a chance. Now...

He gave as good as he got. Even at thirteen, he was faster, sharper, better than any single one of them. But against four bigger, older specimens with more training and excellent reflexes, his advantage evaporated.

They left him curled on the deck, bruised and battered across every bit of flesh he could feel. One eye was closed, the other barely open, and several teeth seemed loose. He suspected ribs had cracked from their heavy kicks after he was knocked to the ground.

"Try that again, you stupid shit, and things will get worse. A lot worse. And don't think that bitch Engels will protect you either. I got her number. And the staff? They won't help you if you can't help yourself." Skorza hawked and spat, the glob landing on Derek's cheek. "Have a nice fucking day, rat," he said as he and the others left. "Mechsuiter, my ass."

Chapter 10

"What happened to you?" Cadet Engels asked when she next saw Straker. She realized as soon as she'd asked the question that his bruises told her everything she needed to know. "You go hand-to-hand with a battle-bot?"

"No, Miss Engels. I fell down some stairs."

"Right... A physical with your scores. Lying violates the honor code, remember?"

Straker stared at her, his eyes angry. "Then I'd really rather not say."

Engels returned the stare, trying to decide what tack to take. This wasn't the first time someone had taken a beating at Academy, but it was the first time for anyone in her charge. "Fine. Somebody kicked your ass and you don't want to admit it."

"I don't want to make it official, if you must know. Tattling to the chain of command will make me look weak. I'll survive, and I won't quit, so it really doesn't matter."

Engels crossed her arms over her crisp, creased tunic. "It matters if it gets worse. What will you do then?"

"I have a plan."

"Tell me about it."

"I respectfully decline to answer, Miss Engels. And please don't tell the faculty or staff. I have to take care of this myself. That's what they expect."

"They expect teamwork," she said. "You're not a lone wolf here, Straker. We succeed by working together. Like whoever gave you that beating did. I bet they trapped you, didn't let you run, right?"

"I respectfully decline to answer, Miss Engels."

Engels sighed in exasperation. Males. Teamwork didn't come naturally to many of them, especially the ones who thought they were destined to be heroes. "Fine. At least keep your buddy Loco or someone else nearby. Don't go places alone. That'll make it hard for anyone hazing you. Academy is a big place and it's not nearly as tight as they'd like you to believe. There are abandoned spaces on this asteroid where you could hide a body that would take months to find, maybe years. Or never."

Straker stared at her, processing this news. "You mean the cadre don't know what's going on at their own station? I was depending on them being smarter than that."

"There's a big war on. Everyone is stretched thinner than they want us to know. A lot of this program is veneer. Think about it. In peacetime, Fleet might have the luxury of sending a full complement of the best and brightest to teach at Academy, but right now, they need those people at the front, on fighting ships and in critical ground force positions. So they're understaffed, using less-than-outstanding officers."

Straker's bruised eyes clouded. "I didn't realize that."

"So you see, you need to tell me what happened. I promise not to refer it up the chain unless you want me to. I'm your UCS. I'm on your side."

Straker lowered his gaze. Engels thought he might be tearing up. Tough kid, but she'd found even the toughest had soft spots, especially those who'd lost sisters and mothers, like his file said. She wondered if she'd been assigned to him for exactly that reason.

"Thanks, Miss Engels," he said, staring at his shoes. "You figured it out. Skorza and three of his buddies jumped me in section 6-X. They covered up the cameras. I fought back, and they did this."

"You shouldn't have fought back. You're a sub-Fourthie. Everyone puts up with some hazing."

"I had to. It was the right thing to do. What would you have done?"

Engels shrugged. "I don't know. Some bullies, you punch them once in the nose and they run away. Some will keep doubling down until someone gets hurt... or killed."

"That's what I'm going to find out."

"What do you mean?" she asked.

Straker lifted shining eyes, a smile on his face that abruptly frightened her. "You'll see. And you'll be there." Then he walked off, without even asking to be dismissed.

Cadet Straker had changed, Engels realized. He'd turned some kind of corner. It must have been the beating, or what it meant to him. Most kids would have pulled in, turtled up.

Not this one. This one would attack a problem until he destroyed it.

Or until it destroyed him.

* * *

Four days later, during self-directed workout time, Derek walked up to Engels in the gym, where she was pumping iron on an overhead press machine. Loco trailed him at a distance, and Derek saw one of Engels' friends exchange glances with her as he approached.

"Miss Engels, Cadet Straker requests permission to speak freely."

"Speak."

"Skorza's in the ring." Derek faced across the hangar-sized sport-hall toward the section containing the hand-to-hand section and pointed with his chin. "He's always here during this period. I hear he takes all comers. Thinks he's the best fighter here."

"He *is* the best fighter here, Cadet Straker," said Engels' classmate, a squat, muscular girl, Cadet Second Melkin. "At least, the best striker. And if you're thinking of going up against him, you're sure not big and strong enough to take him to the ground and win there. In fact, you're crazy to even think about it, no matter that your scores are off the charts, wonder-boy."

Derek raised an eyebrow at Engels. Had she blabbed what he'd told her?

In response, she made a lips-are-sealed gesture and shrugged.

Okay, Melkin had made a lucky guess, Derek realized.

"I *am* going to challenge him. And I'm going to beat him. The trick is to beat him in the best possible way. For that, I need to know how he thinks."

Engels took a deep breath and wiped her hands on a towel. "What do you mean?"

"I mean, should I fight him to a draw? Will that earn his respect? Or should I humiliate him in public?"

"What you ought to do is walk away," said Melkin. "If not, go a couple rounds and then lose gracefully. That will let him feel good about himself. He'll probably leave you alone after that."

"No way, Miss Melkin. I refuse to throw the fight. If I lose, he'll have to beat me."

"He already *beat* you," said Engels heavily. "You're not even fully recovered."

"I heal fast. And it took him and three buddies to do what they did, with no rules. One on one? In the ring? I can take him."

Engels considered. "He's fifty percent heavier and four years older. But if you think you can, I'd say, finish it right away. The longer you go, the more the fight favors him. If you can crush him fast, do it. Knock him out cold as quick as you can. It will be that much more impressive."

"I'm with Engels." Melkin gave him a mock salute. "But I'll believe it when I see it. It's your funeral, kid."

"No," Derek said, squaring his shoulders. "It's his."

He strode across the gymnasium, the other three following, until he stood next to the ring where Skorza sparred with one of his classmates, Cadet First Neekers.

Derek recognized Neekers from the beating. He seemed to be letting Skorza push him around the ring. Straker wondered if this was some kind of submissive behavior, or if Skorza was really all that good.

Best not to underestimate his enemy, though. Derek felt his stomach twist at the memory of the pain inflicted on him. His spirit refused to fear, but his body might be smarter than his mind on this one, the human animal remembering suffering it would rather avoid.

Derek mastered his churning guts to begin taping his hands and pulling on the regulation fight gloves, the smallest, lightest kind that left fingers free for grappling, and incidentally slowed punches the least. He'd already dressed himself in suitable physical training clothes.

"What the hell do you think you're doing, rat-boy?" Skorza said from above him, jumping onto the padded top of the ring's head-high barrier to support himself on his hands and hips. "I'm not done sparring yet. Go find someone your own size to beat your ass."

Raising his voice, Straker said, "I challenge you, Cadet First Skorza. Standard bout rules. Let's see how you do without anyone to help you." He deliberately did not taunt Skorza too openly and risk a charge of disrespect to an upperclassman. With a bully, there was always the chance he would try to claim to be the victim, work the system and appeal to authority. According to his readings on the topic, bullies were insecure. They therefore placed excessive value on their peers' view of their status.

Skorza's eyes narrowed as he glanced around, apparently well aware of how this might make him look. Accepting a challenge from a sub-Fourthie might actually lower his status in others' estimation. Straker hoped to put him in a spot where he couldn't afford to back down.

"Naw, kid. I don't fight rats. It wouldn't be fair."

"You're right about that, Cadet First. But that never stopped you before." Straker moved laterally and entered the ring, Loco holding the gate open for him. "What's wrong? Are *you* afraid of *me*, Cadet First Skorza? Or only of losing?"

"All right, twerp, if you're that crazy. Let's do it. I'll go easy on you, though." Skorza danced around the ring, making eye contact with the gathering crowd, trying to appear the reasonable one.

One of the enlisted physical training staff stepped into the ring. "Do you both agree to this match?"

"Affirmative, Sergeant."

"Yes, Sergeant."

"Standard rules apply. Three rounds of three minutes each. Follow my instructions, protect yourself at all times. Victory will be by knockout, submission, or by my judgment if it goes the distance. Understood?"

"Affirmative, Sergeant."

"Yes, Sergeant."

"Ready?" The noncom held out his hand and arm between them. "Fight!"

Derek advanced, one fist out to touch his opponent's in the standard gesture of a respect.

As he'd hoped, Skorza ignored it, making himself look like a poor sport. Instead, Skorza leaned into a fast, hard right to Straker's body.

Rather than dodging, Derek stepped inside the bigger boy's long reach and slammed the heel of his hand up under Skorza's chin, as hard as he could.

Shock and pain ran down Derek's arm, but he'd executed the strike perfectly, faster than anyone could envision without really understanding what the speed and precision of his genetic enhancement could do.

Skorza went over backward and hit the mat like a sack of meat, out cold.

The referee counted to ten while the stunned crowd began cheering. Derek locked eyes with the three Firsties who formed Skorza's posse, and they all showed fear.

Good, Derek thought. If that's what it takes to keep you out of my way, you *will* be afraid.

Loco and some other sub-Fourthies who'd experienced Skorza's abuse carried Derek off on their shoulders while the training staff gave the fallen Firstie medical attention.

After a shower and change to standard uniform, Cadet Engels found Derek in his squad room. "That was well done, Cadet Straker."

"Thank you, Miss Engels."

"But I doubt that will be the end of it. Skorza will be looking for a chance to get even."

Derek rolled his shoulders, and for the first time, felt almost Engels' equal as he lifted his eyes to hers. "I'm counting on it, Miss Engels."

"What does that mean?"

"Better that you not know, Miss Engels."

"Cadet Straker—"

"Sorry, Miss Engels. I have class now. Thanks for your help. Will that be all?"

Engels sighed. "I guess so. Go."

Derek marched away, head up, shoulders back, aware he'd passed a point of no return.

Chapter 11

An ambush mentality, a preference for unpredictability and a reluctance to follow rigidly specified methods, is the essence of light infantry tactics. The ambush mentality generates other, secondary light infantry characteristics. One is the speed with which light infantry adapts to the terrain. Far from resisting adverse environmental conditions, light infantry exploits them by turning rough terrain to its advantage, using the terrain as a shield, a weapon, and a source of supplies.

—The History of Light Infantry; *The 4GW Counterforce* by William S. Lind and LtCol Gregory A. Thiele, USMC.

Academy Station.

Derek and Loco walked deliberately through the maze of Academy's corridors connecting its many operation and training modules. This one was old, and had not been altered within the short experience of the two sub-Fourthies. It was the ninth time he and Loco had taken this route in the past few days.

Several of the passageway's surveillance cameras were visibly nonfunctional. If Derek hadn't been assured by Engels and others that the staff wasn't trying to fool the gullible cadets, he would have thought the situation constituted a sting, an invitation tailor-made to catch misbehavers and kick them out of the program.

That's the way he'd have done it if he were in charge. But it had become clear over the past few weeks that he thought differently from the adults in command of Academy, and different from the cadets around him.

So, today, he took the chance no one was watching.

No one except other cadets.

As they rounded a likely corner, Derek spotted Skorza and Neekers barring their way. From a side corridor behind them, two other Firsties blocked their retreat.

While Derek stared Skorza up and down, Loco let loose a burst of loud, raucous laughter that echoed down the hard metal passages, and he began making apelike gestures, scratching his underarms, gibbering and hooting.

"You won't be laughing soon, pissant," said Neekers. The two behind chuckled, but Skorza remained silent, apparently puzzled by Loco's antics.

He's not entirely unwary, Derek thought. He's learned caution from me, but not respect. Why was Skorza so stupid, risking his career, even his freedom, to take revenge on a kid that just wanted to be left alone to train?

But Carla—Miss Engels—had said that people like Skorza were so rotten inside, so lacking in self-worth they covered themselves in layers of false bravado. If you peeled back a layer and exposed the corruption there, they couldn't stand it. They had to try to destroy any who revealed their weakness.

So this situation didn't surprise him at all.

Loco kept laughing and posturing for at least fifteen seconds longer than made sense. His odd behavior slowed the Firsties down, made them pause and wonder what the hell was going on, exactly as Derek intended.

"So, you're a coward," said Derek conversationally. "You can't beat me in a fair fight, so you want to gang up on me again. But I'm not alone this time."

Skorza's lip curled. "Your monkey here won't save you. It just means we have two shitheads to finish off."

"Finish off? Why, whatever do you mean, Cadet First Skorza?"

Lips pulled back from the older boy's teeth, though his expression couldn't be called a smile. "I mean, for some reason you two are going to go exploring in the ore tunnels and fall down a long rock shaft. I'm sure your bodies will be found within the next few months. Then we're gonna pull a train on your girlfriend."

"You're going to kill us, and then rape Cadet Engels?" Derek enunciated his words. "Is that what you mean?"

Suspicion crossed Skorza's face for a moment, while Neekers replied, "Yeah, rats, that's what we mean, and nobody will be able to prove a thing."

Derek nodded to Loco. "Got it?"

"Got it." Loco let loose a high-pitched yodeling yell.

Sub-Fourthies swarmed out of the corridors, front and back, at least twenty cadets. They caught the Firsties by surprise and seized them, five or six on each.

Skorza fought, knocking down three before Derek stepped forward and kicked his feet out from under him with a blurring leg sweep. The rest piled on the Firstie and held him immobile.

Derek squatted to look in Skorza's face. He held out his hand to the side and Loco placed a thumbnail recorder into it. Derek keyed the playback to let everyone hear the audio of what had gone on, what Skorza and Neekers had said.

"That's not admissible," Skorza said with a sneer. "You could have faked that."

"Us? Fourthies? We don't have access to equipment to fake audio so perfectly, and this will stand up to any analysis, I'm sure. But, I don't think it will come to a court of law. An Honor Board will believe it, and you'll be out on the street, even if you don't get sent to a penal station."

Skorza strained at his captors, craning his corded neck upward. "Then I'll wait for you as long as it takes, shitbird. You'll never be able to sleep soundly, or any of your friends either. My family's connected."

Derek tipped his head back and closed his eyes in resignation. A saying came to him, something he'd read: *Once I was a child. I thought as a child and I spoke as a child; but when I became a man, I put away childish things.*

"Your family? Skorza, let me tell you about family. Mine and Loco's were slaughtered right in front of us in a Hok attack two weeks before we got here. Now all we have is each other. Us, and these sub-Fourthies, and a few good people at Academy like Carla Engels. Those are my family now. You sure you want to threaten them?"

"We'll crush you, Straker. Command's pussy little wonder-kid and his butt-buddy, and all the rest of you squirming punks, you hear me?" Skorza swiveled his head around and struggled. "You're all dead! Fucking dead, if you don't let me go!"

Derek nodded. "You know what, Skorza? I believe you mean exactly what you say. So here's the deal. You get one more chance to take me. If you can, I'll drop this audio record in the recycler, and you win."

Skorza's face turned crafty. "And if not?"

Deliberately, Derek worked up a gob of spittle and launched it at Skorza's left eye. The older boy jerked, but couldn't avoid it entirely, and the mess ran down his cheek. Derek said nothing, merely allowed his mouth to twitch as if in a smile, though his heart was pounding.

Point of no return.

It passed. Derek saw it in Skorza's eyes.

"Fine, jerkwad. Let's do it."

Derek stepped back, lifted his hands and motioned for the pile of sub-Fourthies to let Skorza go.

The Firstie scrambled to his feet and took a stance, circling warily. "You're not going to get in a lucky strike like last time, rat. You might be fast, but you're not that fast."

"You talk a lot for a coward."

Skorza jabbed and feinted, testing, not to be goaded this time.

Derek leaned back slightly, moving and dodging easily.

Jab, feint, jab. A low kick, no commitment. More jabs and feints.

Derek stayed out of the way. He'd never felt so calm and ready, so at peace with what he had to do, so "in the zone." He'd felt this way in mechsuit VR sometimes, but never in real hand-to-hand.

Until today.

"Come on, chickenshit," Skorza snarled. "Make a move."

"You have to move on *me*, Cadet First. I have the recording. All I have to do is stand here and listen to these sub-Fourthies laugh at you." At this cue the younger cadets broke out in jeers and hoots of delight.

In a sudden explosion of motion, Skorza unleashed a combination, left-right-left, then a whirl of low kicks and body punches, all conservative and undercommitted.

Derek continued to dodge, not striking back. He found Skorza's care interesting. It showed his opponent was cooler and more self-disciplined than he'd expected. But, if he'd really been cool and self-disciplined, he'd have declined the fight entirely.

Or maybe not. Maybe he saw it as his only way out. To convince him of that had been Derek's hope.

Derek's concentration deepened. In his perception, Skorza's motions slowed down, became almost lazy. Whatever made Derek's physiology what it was, the thing that gave him his body's advantage, allowed him to analyze the larger boy's style and ability.

His technique really was good. Skorza should have been proud of his skill. He could have acted as a mentor of younger cadets rather than a terrorizer. But now that he'd declared his evil intentions, in Derek's mind he'd become an enemy of everything good, beyond redemption.

The refrain from Mechsuiter Roundup went through his head. *I defend the Good from the Evil that seeks to destroy it. I place my body, my weapons and my mechsuit between the Dark and the Light. I shall not yield.*

Skorza finally committed to a full-power combination, ending with a reverse elbow strike that would have broken bricks had it landed. Derek stepped in, set his hip beneath his opponent's and caught Skorza's wrists. Then he clenched his core, bending to draw Skorza out of balance and throw him, violently.

A purely defensive maneuver would have released hold of Skorza's arms and let him sprawl heavily against the metal bulkhead. However, with deadly intent and utter lack of emotion, Derek instead snapped the bigger boy's body in an arc, maintaining control of his trajectory so Skorza's head impacted the crysteel with a sickening crunch. When Derek let go, Cadet First Skorza lay on the deck, his skull stove in and his neck bent at an unnatural angle.

Everyone stared for a moment, stunned to silence.

"Loco, run and call for the medics," Derek said, not taking his eyes off his handiwork. He'd killed Skorza, goaded him into this fight and murdered him deliberately, and he refused to look away from what he'd done.

Deep down, a small, unclean part of him rejoiced, and he felt ashamed. But that didn't last long. There'd been no other way. He had to protect the others from Skorza. The older boy had made heinous, unforgivable threats against Carla, and against all his friends.

Against his family.

He'd had to do it. There'd been no other choice.

Hadn't there?

No. Derek refused to feel guilty about anything except his own petty, unworthy glee. But that was a price he could live with. What's done is done, he thought.

Twenty minutes later, before the medics had finished with Skorza, he slipped away and accosted Cadet Engels as she finished a class. He shut the door when only he and she remained.

"It's done," he said. "You'll hear about it soon, but I wanted to tell you myself."

"What's done?"

"Skorza."

"Done… what's done?"

"I killed him."

"You *killed* him?" Engels' jaw dropped. "Intentionally?"

"Yes."

"Are you insane?"

Derek activated the thumbnail recorder in playback mode.

Engels listened, aghast. "He was just running his mouth! He wouldn't have followed through."

"How do you know?"

"I know! He says crap like that all the time!"

"*Said.*" The word fell with a thud. "I was protecting you, and Loco, and the other sub-Fourthies. Protecting the weak against the evil oppressors, just like they teach us."

"So I'm weak now? I can take care of myself!"

Derek stumbled over his words. He'd been sure Engels would approve of what he'd done. "I—I thought you'd be proud of me."

"Straker, I can't be proud of this. He was an asshole, but he was a fellow cadet! We don't turn on our own!"

"He turned on all of us first."

Engels cleared her throat. "He was *not* your teacher, not your role model. Or was he?"

"What do you mean?"

"Straker, my father once told me something I'll never forget. When you fight monsters, don't become a monster."

Derek swayed on his feet, his vision graying. "You think I'm a monster?"

"I—no, Straker, I don't. But what you did was…"

"Monstrous?" Ice crept through Derek's soul. If Miss Engels—if Carla—rejected what he'd done… he didn't even know how he'd face that.

"You can't ever do anything like this again. *Ever.* Murdering people isn't the solution to your problems. And once you start down that road, where does it end?"

Derek tried to explain. "It's what they're training us to be, Miss Engels. Killers."

"For war, against evil aliens. Not this way. Not against your own kind."

"He wasn't my kind." Derek lifted his chin, feeling a cold righteousness sweep through his soul. "Skorza was worse than the Hok. He was a traitor to the Hundred Worlds, hurting other cadets for his own sick pleasure."

"Cadet Straker…*Derek*, give me your word you'll never do anything like this again."

Derek stared at Engels and ice froze his heart. "I can't do that."

Engels turned her back on him. "Then get out. Dismissed."

"Aye aye, Miss Engels." Derek performed a perfect about-face and marched away. When he rounded a corner, his feet became unsteady, and he had to force himself to walk properly.

Thankfully, he made it to a latrine in time to vomit.

The subsequent investigation was thorough, but Skorza's propensities were well known, and Loco's audio had damned the Cadet First by his stated intentions. Nothing could prove Derek had done anything but defend himself, with tragic results.

From then on, everyone stayed way the hell out of his way.

From then on, everyone wanted to be on his good side, but nobody except Loco remained his friend. Not even Miss Engels.

From then on, Cadet Derek Barnes Straker, mechsuiter-to-be, put away childish things.

Chapter 12

Corinth star system, interplanetary space. Present day (2817 A.D., Old Earth reckoning).

Admiral Braga only allowed Zaxby to fire a single salvo of altered fusion mines through the railguns. There were immediate red-light failures, damaging the tubes, but no catastrophes. Repairs would take time, however.

The mines moved steadily, stealthily through interplanetary space. Lieutenant Zaxby had calculated multiple vector influences, including the curvature of space-time due to the planet, its moon, the primary, and every other planet in the star system. Other factors included the launching ships' velocities, the kinetic energy imparted by the railguns, and the probable course of the enemy.

Combined with inevitable sensor errors, achieving strikes on the pursuing fleet of cruisers would be a triumph of multivariate, multidimensional calculus.

But did these humans appreciate him? No! They laughed at him merely because he didn't understand every nuance of their monkey culture, making jokes about canning and eating him, and at every turn telling him to cease his obviously insightful and informative commentary. It was enough to make him swear off aliens and go home to Ruxin.

Unfortunately for him and every other Ruxin native, his planet had been conquered by the Hok eighty standard years ago. So, Zaxby had swallowed his justifiable pride and once again resolved to put up with these annoying and semi-moronic land-dwellers. After all, they had the warships, and Zaxby greatly desired to eventually liberate his homeworld. If that meant enduring abuse, then so be it.

"Impact in four minutes," he announced when he'd finished his calculations.

"If we're lucky," Ensign Stiles mumbled.

Stiles was one of Zaxby's regular detractors. The human was clever enough to keep his insulting commentary below the range of his superiors' detection, but Zaxby heard him.

"It's not a matter of luck, but of extraordinary skill," Zaxby said. "My superior spatial acuity and facility with mathematics has increased the probability of at least three mine strikes to a near certainty."

"Shut up, Zaxby," Stiles singsonged, and others among the hoi polloi echoed him, suppressing obvious laughter.

Zaxby shut up. They were all against him. But he was a superior being, and therefore he must rise above adversity. They would thank him when he won this battle for them.

At least the admiral wasn't a bad sort. Better than Zaxby's fellow officers, anyway. Wise leaders always recognized superior ability in their subordinates, his extensive research of history told him.

"Pass to all ships: plot and target our operating railguns and beams on our pursuers in conventional mode—but do not fire," Admiral Braga said. "As soon as the mines strike, concentrate attacks on the survivors. Our goal is to hit them hard and force them to break off their pursuit. We'll also get some free acceleration from shooting backward."

"A clever tactic, sir," Zaxby said.

"Brown-noser," Stiles whispered.

"I don't have a nose."

"That's because it's so far up the admiral's ass it got lost," Stiles hissed.

"Cease your monkey screechings, Ensign Stiles, or I shall put you on report."

"Go ahead. Nobody cares about what you squids think."

Zaxby went back to ignoring the annoying fellow, regretting that he allowed himself to be drawn into such juvenile banter.

"How many of our railguns survived being misused as launchers?" Admiral Braga asked.

"Twenty-nine of thirty-two," replied Zaxby. "Reports indicate two of the three are severely damaged, but one only needs minor repairs."

"Not too bad…"

The admiral eyeballed their boards along with the rest of the cramped bridge crew. Tension was mounting as the mines traveled backward, and the enemy accelerated in an optimum pursuit curve.

Zaxby watched even more closely because he could read the finer nuances of the intersecting courses. His satisfaction grew as the numbers remained perfectly steady. No unexpected curvature of space-time diverted either vector. No unseen fragment of rock pre-detonated a mine, and the Hok commander remained complacent, choosing the most efficient track rather than varying it as a matter of routine. After all, they were far out of effective range.

Or so they thought. As the countdown reached zero, the crew held its collective breath. Zaxby, as one of the few Ruxins aboard, continued to breathe through his air-gills, his two brachial hearts pumping blood past the membranes, but he experienced a similar thrill of anticipation.

"One… two… three…" Stiles muttered, and then a cheer rose as a dozen explosions blossomed at once.

"Fifteen!" Admiral Braga crowed. "Well done, Lieutenant Zaxby! Well done."

"Sensors," Captain Verdura said, "get me a solid assessment of enemy status. Weapons, keep firing."

"Yes, ma'am," said Zaxby, his tentacles working like a pianist. "Targeting the survivors. Some are evading."

"Fifteen solid hits," said the sensors officer. "Four enemy ships are crippled or destroyed. Eleven are confirmed seriously damaged and out of the fight. Fourteen remain—but we're pounding them now with more beam and railgun strikes."

"Are they returning fire?"

"Not yet, ma'am. They're continuing to pursue, with evasion."

Verdura stood and hung onto the rail in front of the main holoplate in order to get a better view. "Keep hammering them!"

"Naturally, Captain," said Zaxby, expertly coordinating *Vigilant*'s fire on the enemy.

He correctly predicted the position of several undamaged enemy cruisers, based on their likely evasive maneuvers, and was rewarded with evidence of excellent strikes.

At the same time, he passed mandatory corrections to other friendly ships in order to increase the effectiveness of their targeting, using the authority the admiral's command codes granted him. No doubt this minor breach of protocol would be overlooked, given his singular and exceptional performance today.

Admiral Braga leaned to stare pointedly in Zaxby's direction. "Will they catch us?"

Zaxby returned a gaze consisting of two polite eyeballs, keeping the other two on his board. "Not before we reach the Hok heavies in front of us."

"Can you do as well against those Hok heavies?"

"There is no reason to think otherwise, Admiral, as long as I am allowed to fire the entirety of our complement of mines."

"How many do we have left?"

"Sixty-seven, sir. We achieved an approximate hit ratio of fifty percent on the enemy light squadron. If we can match that percentage, we should expect to render approximately one quarter of the enemy combat-ineffective, and another quarter will be significantly degraded."

Braga sat back and took a deep breath. "Leaving about a dozen undamaged Hok heavies... Let's be conservative and say they have eighteen in fighting shape. What does the SAI simulator say in a straight-up fight?"

"Our combined fleet should win comfortably, sir, with you in command," said Zaxby.

"And how long until we can hope to get fifty percent hits on the Hok heavies in front of us?"

"Assuming they remain stationary... We can strike seven hours from now, sir."

"Why *wouldn't* they remain stationary?" Braga asked.

"No reason, sir. Likelihood approaches one hundred percent that they will assume our mine strike was due to a cleverly laid field rather than a railgun launch."

"I hope you're right."

"What would you yourself conclude, Admiral," Zaxby asked, "if you were in their place?"

"I'd be looking for every rational explanation and making sure I wasn't caught napping. Speaking of that, pass orders to maintain routine randomized evasions as we travel." Braga rubbed his neck. "Downey is due to arrive in just under eight hours. Verdura, you have the fleet. I'll take some rack time and relieve you in four hours. Zaxby, you get some rest too."

"But sir—"

"Do as you're told, Lieutenant. I want you fresh for when you launch our next mine strike."

"Aye aye, sir." Zaxby headed for his quarters, looking forward to getting out of his water suit and soaking in his hydro-tank.

Several hours later, Zaxby returned and took his station. He relieved the Second Weapons Officer and pointedly stared at Stiles, who studiously ignored him.

It appeared to Zaxby he'd scored a social victory to match his military triumph. Perhaps that would reduce the crew's obvious ape-bigotry toward octopoids. After all, nothing else explained their clear antipathy toward someone so obviously superior. Now, they could not fail to appreciate him. He felt sure they'd soon be "singing his praises," as the admiral liked to say. Zaxby had looked up the phrase and added it to his repertoire of idioms.

After checking and rechecking all of his calculations and programming, Zaxby used the admiral's codes to access the shipnet chat logs of everyone aboard and found some shocking violations of verbal protocol. He amused himself by composing multiple negative reports on his crewmates.

These, being so honest, sincere and accurate, would undoubtedly endear him to everyone from the lowest rating to the most senior officer. After all, they couldn't help but appreciate anything that improved the efficiency of the fleet, and thus their survival expectation, could they?

"You ready, Zaxby?" asked Admiral Braga.

"Of course, sir."

Captain Verdura punched up a private channel to the admiral, which Zaxby tapped into using the convenient codes he'd acquired. After all, his efficiency could only be improved by remaining well informed.

"Sir," Verdura asked, "why are we timing the mines to hit the enemy almost two hours early? Wouldn't it be better to put them in a state of confusion just as our fleets arrive?"

The admiral replied, "Because they won't sit there until the last moment. They're likely to get ready, begin evasive maneuvers and so on, perhaps an hour prior. Even weapons testing might shift their positions enough to make the mines miss."

"Understood, sir." Verdura closed the private channel. Zaxby found it odd that she'd bothered to make this private contact. Wouldn't the crew have benefited from their commanders' insights? It must be more ape-culture, something to do with embarrassment, he surmised.

"You may fire when ready, Zaxby," said the admiral.

"Naturally, sir." Zaxby rechecked the computer-initiated launch timing for the fifth time, and then waited until the chrono read zero. "First salvo of mines away. Nine railguns failed."

"Why so many?" Braga demanded, frowning.

"Firing the first salvo put great wear on them, you will remember. Each is likely to fail after 2.43 shots."

"2.43, hmm? Not, say, 2.44?"

"No, sir," Zaxby said. "2.43, rounded to two places. Firing second salvo. Fourteen more railguns failed, seven remaining. Third salvo. Four failures, three remain."

"Cease fire."

"Sir—"

Braga growled, "I said cease fire, dammit! We might need a few railgun batteries for something, even launching a last-minute mine. We don't want to have them all down. Verdura, double up on our engineering crews working on repairs."

Zaxby's limbs twitched in irritation. "The salvos are, of course, timed to arrive simultaneously. It took a serious effort utilizing my deep understanding of four-dimensional calculus to—"

"Thank you, Lieutenant."

"And—"

"Shut up," said Verdura. "The admiral can't hear himself think."

Zaxby choked off another reply. He was bound to stay quiet by the direct order, but he wondered to himself how one could hear thinking in the first place.

"Now we wait," said Braga.

Zaxby silently put up the impact countdown, reading nearly an hour.

Propelled by the railguns, the mines flew ahead of the cruising squadron, underway for their secret rendezvous. The tension on the bridge built, broken only by frequent randomized evasive maneuvers in case of something unexpected.

However, as the five-minute mark approached, the sensors officer sang out, "I have sidespace incursions, multiple ships." The man turned toward the admiral. "Sir, it's the heavies, appearing at optimum position."

"Damn it all to hell!" Braga roared. "Downey, the one time I needed you to be your same old slowpoke self, you hurry! Pass to the fleet: all ahead flank, minimum time course. Weapons, engage at extreme range."

As soon as Zaxby had coordinated with the other weapons officers, his sense of self-satisfaction deflated. He watched with horror as the Hok fleet ambushed Downey, accelerating away from their static positions toward the nearby just-arrived dreadnoughts and super-dreadnoughts.

Unfortunately, that meant his carefully launched formation of mines, for which the fleet had paid in broken weapons, would have zero chance of striking the enemy.

The Hok launched a full spread of shipkiller missiles, expensive and deadly, but compared to railguns and beams, slow and easy to counter.

Easy to counter when prepared for battle, anyway. Downey's heavy squadron, arriving by ones and twos and out of formation, could establish no coordination, no teamwork. Flights of missiles overwhelmed individual ships' countermissile abilities; or if they did not, then the hard-driven Hok beams and railgun projectiles slipped by the saturated defensive nets to pound the big ships with impact, energy and radiation.

But these were enormous vessels, thick with energized armor that was reinforced by conformal defensive fields. They didn't die easily.

Zaxby watched as *Niagara* lasted far longer than expected, twisting savagely with brutal, graceless overloading of her fusion engines and impellers, smashing back at her tormenters. But eventually she tumbled, broken, through the void.

Saxon and *Kinshasa* drew together and seemed to stand back to back until finally overrun by eight enormous enemies, ramming one at the last to swallow three in a colossal explosion.

Spirit of Manchester, Downey's flagship and pride of the fleet, managed to hold off the attacks long enough to gather three, four, then five sisters around her and mount a networked defense. For ten full minutes the ether blazed with stupendous energies thrown back and forth with profligate abandon at point-blank range.

The Hok assembled half their force to face Downey's reduced group, while more Hundred Worlds ships arrived over a space of long minutes at random points. This had the effect of allowing the Hok to concentrate at odds of two or three to one against each. Even given the Hundred Worlds edge in individual ship strength, this was a losing proposition.

Zaxby was amazed anything could live through such a point-blank battle of titans. Electromagnetic pulses from fusion warheads overwhelmed *Vigilant*'s sensors for a time, and when it cleared, those on the bridge let out groans and gasps of horror. All of Downey's ships had been reduced to hulks, except for three that had managed to escape back into sidespace.

All eyes turned to Admiral Braga. Bleak-faced, the commander opened his mouth to speak when *Vigilant* shuddered under a heavy impact. Alarms blared and gravity rippled as power fluctuated.

"What the hell was that?" he said into the noise of shouted orders and the sound of breaking metal.

"A missile, sir," said Zaxby, immediately synthesizing this deduction from all available data flowing across his console. "They must have cold-launched them, running them on impellers. As you know, impellers have no discernible emissions, and at flank acceleration as we are, any weapon we detected would have been unavoidable. If we hadn't been making routine evasive maneuvers, we probably would have been destroyed outright."

"How bad off is our remaining flotilla? Operations?"

The ops officer replied, "Eight ships are still effective. Five have working sidespace drives."

"*Vigilant?*"

The officer shook his head. "Only *Keegan, Coriol, Turlock, Grizzly,* and *Mauberge* retain sidespace capability."

Zaxby watched Admiral Braga's face crumple. While the nuances of humans' language sometimes escaped him, he had learned to read their expressions quite well. Zaxby felt himself mimicking it as similar feelings coursed through his expansive brain, a brain that right now stuttered, trying to find some way out of their situation.

Braga said, "Order all ships to escape and evade. Those with sidespace engines head for the nearest friendly worlds, but separately, to ensure somebody survives to report this trap... this debacle."

The operations officer nodded and relayed his orders. "And those without sidespace, sir?"

"Tell them to spread out and try to run in normal space until repairs can be made. How are we?"

The ops officer looked pointedly toward Verdura, and after a moment, so did Braga.

Verdura said, "We're on a ballistic course that will take us near the battlefield. Fusion engines and most of our weapons are down, though we do have impellers. I've ordered maximum lateral acceleration, but I think..."

"Go on."

"If they want to match courses and board to capture," she said, "we're easy meat."

Zaxby watched Braga search the faces of the crew around them. He sensed this was not the time to offer an opinion. The admiral was a sensible human. He would choose the only logical course.

Braga said grimly, "Rig for self-destruct. I won't let them take her, but I'm not going to ask you to sacrifice yourselves. We'll abandon ship in the boats and pods and try to evade them. Several moons in this system are marginally habitable, and Hundred Worlds forces may be able to return and retrieve us eventually."

The crew on the bridge hung their heads, and Zaxby couldn't help imitating them, even if it was not a standard Ruxin physical response. In fact, he felt like wrapping his head in his arms and hiding from the world. His superior intellect had failed him. He should have predicted the impeller missile trick, as he'd pulled something similar on the pursuing enemy with the mines.

In fact, he did indulge in head-wrapping during the long lonely days in the escape pod after *Vigilant* vaporized herself. By the time the Hok picked him up and threw him into a thankfully damp cell, he'd come out of his funk and resolved to face his penance with as much fortitude as he could muster.

Chapter 13

Light infantry tactics are offensive in character, even during defensive operations. Light infantrymen do not hold a line. Light infantry tactics follow the principles of maneuver warfare, attacking by infiltration and defending by ambush. It uses ambushes on the offensive as well, by ambushing withdrawing or reinforcing enemy units, sometimes deep in the enemy's rear. Light infantry applies an ambush mentality to both planning and execution.

—The History of Light Infantry; *The 4GW Counterforce* by William S. Lind and LtCol Gregory A. Thiele, USMC.

Planet Corinth, Helios city.

Straker and his two remaining men dodged back among the buildings, naturally gravitating toward the taller structures at the city's heart. It seemed an immutable law of planetary economics that each colony's starting city would grow to overpopulated extremes. Eventually, the downtown real estate grew expensive enough to build farther and farther upward. Tramways and hovercars increased accessibility, but the most valuable commodity of all was skilled personnel, and those individuals needed the ability to meet and work together, quickly and efficiently. Inevitably, tall buildings sprouted at every capital city.

Virtual reality, despite its promise, had turned out to be a poor substitute for human-to-human contact. Business at the top was always done better face-to-face, where all the players could be confident they weren't being fooled by overlays or false data feeds. Netlinks were left to the drone workers in their warren of cubes, but even they needed to unplug and socialize in the break rooms and cafeterias. Those who could afford it met in restaurants and gallerias.

All that workspace was deserted now as Straker, Paloco and Chen swerved left and right, deliberately avoiding the razor-straight roads and winding footpaths of the city. Instead, they spread out and angled across parks and cut through intersections. They leapt over sheds and outbuildings, using the tall structures to their advantage by hugging them, reducing by half the vertical angle of potential attackers.

Kinetics fell from the sky, slamming into concrete or turf. They spitted geysers of either dirt or shards of concrete and rocks, always leaving behind deep smoking craters. With no explosives, the spikes damaged what they struck, but little else, the better to preserve the city for its eventual conquerors. The Hok were still betting on precision to take down the defending mechsuiters.

Beams also lanced down from the skies to set the ground afire with tuned spectra, flash-heating anything that would burn. Some were pure infrared lasers, cooking the surface of whatever they touched. Others were gamma-ray lasers—grasers—their X-rays reaching deep inside all but the densest materials.

Mechsuits were built to resist both of these, but they weren't impervious. Each strike peeled a little more protection from every man's armor, degrading more of their systems by thermic shock or electromagnetic overload.

What really worried Straker were the capital-class ships with their particle beam cannon. Used mostly in the vacuum of space, they could be employed for brute-force application against ground troops once a besieging fleet achieved total space supremacy. This was wildly inefficient, as much of the beam's punch would be absorbed by any planetary atmosphere, but whatever reached the ground transferred so much energy to its target that it simply exploded on contact, like a tiny nuclear detonation.

Mechsuiters included.

He hoped the Hok remained unwilling to wreck their prize, but as he'd learned early in his career, hope was not a plan.

Two spikes fell nearby, bracketing Chen front and back. A moment later a graser tore a piece out of a building near Loco.

"Chen, keep up your lateral dodging," Straker ordered, "vary your pattern every one to two seconds."

"Aye aye, sir."

"We're almost there."

"Yes, sir!" Chen said as he dodged a fresh fountain of brown earth and smoke.

"BOHICA!" cried Loco suddenly.

"Damn," Chen said, "would you please *shut up*, Loco?"

"Not a chance. If I ever stop talking, I'm dead."

"Seems like a fair trade."

Straker had picked out a building for his ambush point, one built with a partially open first story designed for groundcar parking beneath its structure. As they approached, he saw most of the vehicles had departed, evacuating. That was a break, for sure.

"There, that one," Straker said, designating his goal. "Get under it. It's a financial complex. They won't want to destroy the computers and networking gear."

"Yeah, because they love alien porn on the hard drives," said Loco.

"If they do try, at least we'll have sixty stories of skyscraper above us," Chen said.

"Or sixty thousand tons on top of us," Loco said.

"Exactly. Call it top cover." Straker got there first, diving headfirst into the garage like a goalkeeper trying to block a shot. Immediately he rolled to his feet and crouched. He couldn't quite stand, but the mechsuit cared less than his body, masking any strain on his muscles with biofeedback links. The other two made it into the spacious interior a moment after.

Straker eyed the ramps leading down to the parking sub-levels, but it looked like those had been built to minimum height, less than three meters clearance. A mechsuiter could barely crawl into a space that tight.

"Take cover behind a corner," he said, pointing. The building stood atop five pillars, four at the corners and one larger for access in the center, holding lift systems. "They'll do their best to track us, but as long as they're trying to limit collateral damage, we'll be all right." He said it with more confidence than he felt.

"How's Tactical looking?" Chen asked. Only the squad leader had access to the higher-order battlenet, the better to ensure line troopers concentrated on their own affairs. It was easy to get so lost in the godlike overviews that you didn't pay enough attention to the details.

Straker brought it up on his HUD. "Fifty-seven of us are still kicking. We're stretched out in a ragged band along Phase Line Charlie, approximately the boundary of the downtown. We want them to get everyone inside the most built-up area before we spring our trap."

"Yeah, but who's trapping who?" Loco muttered.

"Getting tired of that defeatism!" Chen snapped.

"Hey, when facing certain death, I make jokes."

Straker broke in. "Can it, you two, and focus. The enemy will be here within the hour."

Speeding through everything was another advantage of mechsuiters over traditional ground-pounders. Their suits could maintain ninety KPH over the roughest terrain, with sprints up to a hundred-fifty. Unlike other heavy vehicles, they didn't have to worry about curbs, barriers and the anti-tank obstacles the militia had deployed for defense.

Thus, the mechsuiters had so far stayed comfortably ahead of the probing enemy armor. After losing several squads to ambush, the Hok infantry kept well back, waiting for their slower vehicles to provide cover and firepower.

Straker considered tearing his way up inside a building to achieve a position of plunging fire, but he would have to break through ten or twelve floors to do it. Once sited, he would have to either retreat to the interior and down, or leap out and into the midst of the enemy.

Maybe that wasn't such a bad idea. He'd never considered it before, but it might be the surprise that would turn the tables.

"Everyone have full jet tanks?" he asked.

"Yeah."

"Ninety-five percent."

"Okay," Straker said. "This is what we're doing."

He explained his plan, and the others were incredulous.

"You're nucking futs, boss," Loco said, but he spoke in an admiring rather than a protesting tone. "I love it."

"It's the best chance we've got to get inside their lines."

"Should you suggest it up the chain?" Chen asked.

Straker grunted. "I'll shoot the XO a message." He didn't feel like talking right now, and the acting commander probably had a lot on his plate anyway. Still, when he got promoted, Straker vowed he'd drill his troopers in unconventional situations like the one they'd found themselves in today.

Careful not to break holes in a skyscraper's crystalline exterior, Straker, Chen, and Loco tunneled their way upward and made nests for themselves in snipers' positions, with views down the major avenues the enemy armor would have to use.

"Make sure you set your feet on the main load-bearing struts," Straker reminded them. "And activate full jet assist and stabilization before you jump."

"Yes, mother," Loco replied.

"If I was your mother I'd give you a spanking," Chen said.

"There you go, man! Gotta get some good humor in you. I must be rubbing off."

"Don't go rubbing anything in my direction."

Loco laughed, and then Chen did too.

On his battlenet, which was now only updating intermittently, Straker saw the red spots of the enemy flow around and beneath them. Passive opticals let him watch platoons of armored vehicles probing through the streets while battlesuited Hok infantry tried to cover the heights, leaping from rooftop to rooftop on jump jets not so different from his own.

Straker froze as a Hok squad flew past. One trooper seemed to look straight at him through the two layers of window crystal, but he moved on.

"We'll wait as long as we can," Straker breathed, as if speaking quietly would matter within their stealth-encrypted comlink. "Maybe we can bag us a mobile command post. That might disrupt their advance."

"Well, we gotta try something big, that's for sure," replied Loco.

"Sounds good to me," said Chen.

"I figured you guys didn't wanna live forever, anyway," Straker said.

"Uh oh," said Loco. "When the boss cracks a joke, I know we're in deep kimchee."

Light tanks gave way to hovers in standard Hok deployment, and then missile tracks. Straker's HUD showed additional lines of combat units approaching after the usual doctrinal separation. A mobile command post might be lurking within the dead space, or it might be staying well back.

"If we don't see an MCP or get the go-ahead, we'll initiate as the last of these missile tracks get here and hit them from the rear." Straker's battlenet updated, and the order to initiate the mass ambush came through. "Three, two,—"

"MCP in sight," interrupted Chen. "Two o'clock to you."

"Right. Two o'clock, Chen, you take point and we'll flank you."

"It has LADAs with it, sir…"

"Dammit!" Straker said.

Laser Air-Defense Array vehicles provided interlocking beam fire using close-in robotic turrets. Without penetration aids, there was no way the mech-suiters could jump from this height and drop on the enemy like they'd planned. The LADAs would treat them as airborne targets and, at point-blank range, could blind and severely damage them long before they reached the ground.

"Missiles?" said Loco.

"I hate to use them as decoys."

"Use me as a decoy, then," Chen said.

"What?"

"Look, if I break cover first, they'll all snap-shot me. We'll use their own reaction times against them. We set our remaining missiles to launch a fraction of a second afterward, in direct-fire mode instead of pop-up, one per LADA. You guys take out any of them that survive, then nail the MCP."

Straker replied, "Chen, that might work, but at *best* your suit will be ruined. You'll probably be cooked by three dozen lasers."

"I'll set my ejection parameters to punch me out if things get too hot."

"There has to be another way!" Straker said.

"There's no time to think about it, sir. We've got about thirty seconds before we lose our best chance."

Straker came to a hard decision. "We'll all hit them at once. That will split their fire."

"If we do that, we'll lose our missiles as they launch. No, you *have* to use me as a decoy."

An idea blossomed full-blown in Straker's mind. "No, we don't. We have to use your *suit* as decoy. Dismount now, Chen, but maintain tele-operation. Hurry! Suicide your suit directly at the MCP."

"Leave my suit?" The horror at the unthinkable in Chen's voice came through clearly.

"Better than being the main course at a laser barbecue. Do it now! That's a direct order!"

"Roger wilco, sir. Dismounting now." Chen initiated the sequence that let him exit his Foehammer, leaving him standing in the carpeted fiftieth-floor corner office of some corporate bigwig, wearing nothing but his survival rig. "Ready."

"Almost too late..." Straker said. "Two, one, *go*."

Chen's suit leaped straight out, bursting through skyscraper windows never designed to hold back fifty tons of duralloy. A tenth of a second later, Straker and Loco followed, their target-locked missiles firing.

As expected, Chen's rockets never made it out of the zone of death. Thirty-six lasers, focused by ultra-quick mirrors, speared his suit and everything attached to it. Blazing with heat, the Foehammer's external fittings melted and some ignited. The missiles' warheads detonated as they left the rails.

The suit itself, though mortally wounded, flew true. It headed directly toward the mobile command post and its flock of escorts. Gatlings, shotguns, and every other defensive weapon targeted the suit in an attempt to bring down the threat identified by the enemy computers.

Those artificial brains outsmarted themselves, as Straker had hoped. Before they could register the fact they'd grossly over-allocated their firepower to the initial target, and before the Hok controllers could override their systems, the squad's last six antitank missiles streaked past the laser phalanx.

Five struck home, turning a maniple of lightly armored LADAs into burning wrecks. The final LADA exploded with the impact of Straker's force-cannon bolt. "Kill the MCP, Loco!" he roared, hosing the big crawler with gatling fire as he waited for his main weapon to recharge.

Chen's wrecked Foehammer crashed next to the MCP. He would have been dead had he not dismounted. Straker had no time to congratulate himself, though, as he flipped end for end and triggered his landing jets to keep from joining Chen's suit in a smoking hole.

As he hit the ground running, he saw one metal end of the MCP crumple under the impact of Loco's primary bolt. The crawler was big, though, over fifty meters long, and compartmented for survivability. It had been hurt, but it would take several more shots before they could count it as destroyed.

Incredibly, a few humanoids dragged themselves out of the damaged section. One ran, burning from head to toe, and threw itself into the mud in hopes of putting out the flames.

Straker fired one precise gatling round into the figure and blew it apart, then another, then another, waiting for his force-cannon to recharge. He felt no remorse about gunning them down. They deserved no mercy, for they gave none to the Hundred Worlds.

Belatedly, obscurant charges triggered off the MCP, adding to the smoke and dust of the battlefield. Straker took this stroke of luck as a sign of fate. It would hide the entire scene from the enemy fleet overhead for several minutes.

Finally, his capacitor telltale turned green and, in the relative calm of this storm's eye, he aimed carefully at the crawler's engine compartment and narrowed the aperture of his force-cannon for maximum armor piercing. The plasma bolt speared into the enemy power plant. As he'd intended, its hydrogen-deuterium fuel supply ignited.

Even then, the MCP remained, but its effectiveness had been eliminated. With no power to move and several compartments breached, it couldn't command a Youth Brigade troop, much less an armored division.

Straker yearned for a satchel charge or limpet mine, but those had been used up long ago. Perhaps...

"Chen, you read?"

"Here, boss. I can't see you for all that crap, but I detect hovers and infantry circling back, and missile tracks reorienting on your position. You got about one minute before they land on you like a ton of bricks."

"Understood. Do you still have a good battlenet datalink with your suit?"

"I do, but it's nothing but a processor and a power plant anymore."

"That's enough." Straker told him what to do, then shifted to Loco. "Help me with Chen's suit."

"It's a total loss, boss. We gotta get out of here."

"Shut up and help me, dammit."

"Right-o." Loco grabbed one side of the mangled Foehammer and Straker the other. "And do what?"

"Shove it under the MCP, between the two side tracks."

"Whatever you say." Loco dragged the thing and, with Straker's help, forced it halfway beneath the command track. "That's it."

"Chen, do it," Straker said.

"Doing it now."

Straker waved a massive arm at Loco. "Follow me to the river!"

They ran.

Behind them, Chen's suit gave its all for the war effort as its fusion plant overloaded, cracking the MCP in half and sending wreckage flying in arcs a kilometer long. The explosion further obscured their section of the battlefield.

Straker led Loco perpendicular to two enemy lines—those turning back and the next wave advancing—which gave them temporary respite from the ground units.

The fleet overhead, however, was a different matter. Spikes fell like thunderbolts as the mechsuiters dodged left and right at full speed. Particle beams blasted gouts of steam from the river next to them.

"There!" Straker pointed at a sports stadium. "It's our only chance."

They'd almost reached the massive complex when Straker felt pain flare in his right foot, and he stumbled. He turned the incipient fall into a roll and managed to scramble under the concrete overhang of the super-sized building.

The bombardment ceased.

Straker looked down to see his suit's right leg end in a stump. A spike had taken it off at the ankle. "Shit," he said.

"Yeah, for sure," Loco agreed.

"I can still fight. I just can't move fast," Straker said. "We'll have to make our stand here."

"Two Foehammers? We won't hold them off for long. Not static, like this."

Straker took a position of cover behind a reinforced wall, where he could see back the way they'd come. In the near distance, hovers spread out to the flanks while a line of infantry advanced deliberately, sacrificial lambs. Behind them, missile tracks sited themselves. They'd fire their suit-killers as soon as they located and targeted the two mechsuiters. That would be the beginning of the end.

"Got a better idea?" he asked.

Loco sucked in a long breath. "Nope. What's the tactical situation?"

Straker almost didn't want to look. He couldn't imagine good news, despite their destruction of the MCP. When he pulled up the display, the results were better than he'd feared, worse than he'd hoped.

He transmitted the details to Loco, and to Chen listening back at the financial center. "Thirty-one suits left," he said. "The two lead Hok divisions are shattered, but their third is at full strength and moving in, and they have reserves after that. We're still inflicting heavy casualties, but it's only a matter of time… time we don't have. If not for the strikes from overhead, we'd have a chance, but every time we move…" He stuck out the stump of his suit's leg in illustration.

"Um, guys?" said Chen. "I think I'm done for. I'm hiding as deep in as I can, but my sensors show Hok battlesuiters searching the building. They must know I'm here. I'm gonna go EMCON. Maybe I'll get lucky."

Straker cleared his throat. "Good luck, Chen."

"See you on the other side, brother," said Loco. "Survive with honor. Oh, and keep some lubrication handy. I hear they go for the pretty ones like you."

Chen didn't respond.

Straker reduced his comlink power to minimum. "Just us now, Loco. You can give up on jerking Chen around."

"But boss, it's so much fun." He sighed. "How long until our fleet arrives?"

Straker cleared his throat. "You can read a chrono as well as I can. Nine hours. No way we're holding out for nine hours."

"Ah… Derek?"

"Yeah?"

"Remember when they spiked our houses back on Oceanus?"

"How can I forget?"

"Yeah, sorry… I meant, remember how we hid in the food warehouse?"

"Yep."

"We could try that here. Set our suits for auto-fight, send them running as far away as possible while we try to evade. Find a basement. Maybe get into the river to hide our IR sigs."

Derek considered his friend's suggestion, rejected it. "No. You can if you want to. That's not me. I always knew I'd die on a battlefield, killing Hok. It's fate. I'll be happy to join the Celestial Legion."

"You really believe in that stuff?"

"I don't know. Maybe. Better than thinking it all ends here."

"Guess so." Loco shifted over to park his suit next to Straker's and sat, back to the same wall, two giants relaxing. He pointed in the direction of the cautiously advancing enemy. "What do you think? Five minutes?"

"I give us ten, maybe fifteen. They know they've won. They'll do it deliberately, by the book. At this point they'll want to minimize casualties and infrastructure damage."

"Infrastructure, infrastructure. It's a bunch of stuff. Is that what we're dying for, Derek? Some bureaucrat's balance sheet? Some war-billionaire's mansion?"

Straker shook his head, his suit mimicking the motion. "No. We're doing it for the people, to keep them safe. We're defending ourselves. Just look at this. They invaded us, invaded the Hundred Worlds, when they could have lived with us in peace. They enslave our civilians and make them work until they die of exhaustion. They take our planets, turn them into production centers and use them against us. We *have* to fight."

"I know. I know. But I'd barely even heard of Corinth until this op. Hard to care when I don't know these people."

"They're human beings. They're citizens, doing their jobs like we are. That's what matters." Straker slapped his friend's armored shoulder with a ton of mechanical gauntlet. "They'll remember us."

"They'll remember you, maybe. You're the best to ever pilot a Foehammer. Most kills, best record." Loco chuckled. "Assault Captain Derek Straker, Champion of the Hundred Worlds. They'll make holovids about you. You'll have a Heroic Action Figure. If I'm lucky they'll make one of your faithful sidekick Loco."

"Ever wonder why they only make showvids about dead heroes?" Straker asked.

"I don't wonder. I *know* why. It's because dead heroes can't refute the bullshit they show."

Straker sighed. "I'm beginning to think you're right."

"You always did buy too much of the party line, Derek."

"You don't believe in defending the Hundred Worlds?"

"I believe in you, Derek. I believe in us, in two brothers-in-arms. That's what I believe in." Loco raised his chin to peer at the enemy forming up out of easy range. "But it ain't gonna matter. We're goners."

"You can still try to escape. Rejoin what's left of the regiment, or hide until Fleet comes back. I'll cover you."

Loco turned to slap Straker's faceplate. "That's why I love you and hate you, man. This straight-arrow routine. We're gonna die because you can't stand to live with defeat. But *I* couldn't stand to live if I left you here."

"Thanks, Loco... and sorry."

"That's enough bromance for me," Loco said, rolling to a crouch. "Time to go out in a blaze of glory."

"One more thing, though."

"Black box burst?"

"Yes. You'll have to do it."

"Upload me, and I'll find an open spot."

Straker told his suit to transfer all his accumulated data to Loco's drive. Once done, his friend wormed his way through to the interior of the stadium. He'd aim at the clear sky and send an encrypted wide beam burst into the ether.

Hundred Worlds warships and scout drones always had automated receivers listening for such transmissions. With a little luck, their last stand would be noted. Maybe Command would learn something from this disaster: the annihilation of First Regiment, the Hundred Worlds' best ground combat unit.

It'd been a masterful trap, Straker thought. The Hok had put the Hundred Worlds into a damned-if-you-do, damned-if-you-don't position by seizing Corinth, a heavy-industry planet located deeper into friendly territory than they'd ever attacked before.

Then they'd conned Command into believing they were trying to capture the planet, to hold out the promise that a fragile but speedy fleet could mount a successful counterattack. The operation was made to seem tough but achievable, and one that couldn't wait.

In retrospect, all of this was done to assure Command would commit First Regiment to the battle, and then lose it to the Hok's unexpectedly superior numbers. They must have kept part of their strength hidden, running silent and lurking behind moons or near asteroids, and brought it in late to close the trap.

Straker's military musings vanished when Loco returned. "Looked good, boss. Didn't see any major jamming. It should get through. I couldn't reach anyone else on the comlink, though."

"Consolation prize." Straker climbed carefully to an upright position on one foot. "Looks like we can use these reinforced concrete box structures to fire through, like windows. Move over three or four and wait. Once the shit hits the fan, change position frequently to break their locks."

"Roger that." Loco shifted laterally. "Derek..."

"What?"

"I scouted below us. There's some basements full of equipment, waiting on the next season, I guess. On the off chance our suits get disabled but we're still alive..."

"Okay, Loco. If we get that lucky, we'll dismount and try to evade."

"Oh, I know *I* will. I wanted to make sure you do too."

"It'll be like old times, hiding in the food warehouse. Now shut up and let's kill some Hok."

"You got it, hero."

Straker turned his view briefly inside his cockpit, disengaging his hand from the suit systems to reach out and touch Mara's Glory Girl action figure with a fingertip. He hummed a tune badly. "*For the glory of the Hundred Worlds...*"

Loco joined him, a smile in his voice, and they recited the mantra of the old Mechsuiter Roundup show once more, together.

Once they'd entered Academy it seemed cheesy.

Today, not so much.

"*For the honor of the Hundred Worlds, I shall not yield. I shall never surrender. I defend the Good from the Evil that seeks to destroy it. I place my body, my weapons and my mechsuit between the Dark and the Light. I shall not yield.*"

"*I shall never surrender*," Straker finished. He set himself, aiming his force-cannon through a corner of the concrete frame. "Come on, you bastards. Come see how a mechsuiter dies."

Part II: Traitor

Chapter 14

Location unknown, aboard a Hok ship.

The battle was brief, and it didn't go as expected. Straker groaned and rolled over on his hands and knees, feeling the cold of poured cryscrete. Against all expectations, he'd survived the battle for Corinth.

The enemy had been heedless of losses, but they'd clearly had a clever goal: to capture two mechsuiters.

Instead of targeting them directly, a barrage of fire from ground and space had collapsed the stadium structure on top of them, pinning them under hundreds of tons of rubble. The Hok had then hit the area with sustained EMP bursts that ate away at their major electronic systems until they went dead.

Straker had tried to dismount as he'd promised Loco he would, but the damage and rubble collapsed above him prevented it. His last act had been an attempt to trigger a power overload, but even that failed. The best he could do was to initiate a core purge, denying the enemy all data and burning out the most delicate of his electronics.

At the end, the Hok infantry had taken his mechsuit apart like they were opening a tin of meat. They hadn't been gentle. He remembered burns, and the pain of links ripped out along with the sockets embedded in his body.

Now his body shook as if with ague and he vomited a thin stream of bile onto the floor. Oddly, this made him feel better. Hunger pangs replaced the feeling of weakness, an improvement.

He stared at his hands, still supporting him above the watery puddle of sick. Harsh white light made his eyes ache, and he squinted against the glare, sitting back against a wall and lifting his right palm close to his face. A damaged thing of bruised fingers and ripped nails, it barely looked like his own flesh—which according to his clear memory was elegant and perfect, suitable for the fine motor control of piloting a mechsuit.

Slowly, painfully, his eyes adjusted to the brightness. They watered profusely, as if he'd been asleep for days before being suddenly shoved outdoors into a blinding field of snow or sand. Painted a dirty white gloss, the concrete surfaces of his prison dazzled him.

He held his injured fingers over his eyes and peeked out between them like a child so he could see the room he occupied. A pallet and a bare toilet-sink fixture were all it contained. Oh, and a roll of crapping paper. Did the Hok normally use the stuff? He didn't know. He'd never thought to ask.

He examined the metal door to his cell. It contained a slot at eye level and another at the bottom, and was painted with the designation 4A. Or at least that's what it looked like. Maybe the symbols were Hok letters that merely resembled 4A. Or perhaps it was marked for his benefit. A mystery.

He listened there, pressing an ear to the door's inner surface. He sensed a faint hum and received the impression of vibrations made by impact, *clunks* and *clangs* more felt than heard.

By this, he intuited he was on a ship. A ship with cells made for holding involuntary guests. The only other possibility was he'd been dumped into a VR environment—in that case, he could be anywhere.

He touched his brainlink sockets. They seemed intact. Usually, when in VR, the sockets disappeared, but if the enemy was really clever…

After perhaps half an hour of recovery, Straker's eyesight improved almost to normal. All the skin he could see that wasn't covered by a thin yellow jumpsuit showed signs of abuse, just like his right hand and arm. Fresh bruises and cuts caused him to ache and left blood spots on his coverall.

If this environment was all a sim, it was a damn good one. Usually, the training virtualities betrayed imperfections, conveying a dream-like feeling and lacking certain details.

After lying on his back on the pallet, thinking, Straker decided to treat what his senses told him as real. If it wasn't, then he was completely at the mercy of the Hok. But if it *was*, perhaps he could do something…

Resist, maybe? Escape even? He'd love nothing more than to return to the Hundred Worlds.

He fantasized about escape until he fell asleep. His overtaxed brain half-remembered and half-dreamed of a happier time.

* * *

"Nothing like a little R&R," Loco said, sipping a rum punch and staring at the parade of bikini-clad women strolling down the beach as if for the troopers' exclusive viewing pleasure.

"Doubtless," said Orset, standing and flexing his buff, cut torso and arms. "They can't resist this prime rib, baby." He ambled toward the strand and the legions of hotties.

Chen rolled his eyes. "I'm going to play some volleyball," he said, and strode off toward a nearby game.

"And... let me guess," Loco said, "Straker's gonna sit here and brood. At least get a beer and relax, man. We've only been on Shangri-La for twelve hours and you already look like you're planning our next mission."

Straker shook his head tightly. "I'm not planning the next, I'm reviewing the last. My kill percentage is slipping. I'm trying to figure out why."

"We ain't getting any younger, Derek," Loco said. "Maybe by the time we retire, the war will be over. I'm saving my pay for a cabana right here."

"Here?"

"Somewhere on this world. Half the planet is covered by tropical islands." Loco waved at the perfect scene—a light breeze, clear blue water, surf and sun. "Maybe I'll buy a bar. Bar owners get plenty of action."

"You're never short of action, Loco. All you have to do is mention you're a mechsuiter, and they jump into your bed." Straker tried to keep the disdain out of his voice. He had no real objection to his comrades taking advantage of willing 'suiter groupies, but he'd moved past shallow one-night stands a long time ago.

Well, mostly. A man had needs, after all. But over the last few years he'd felt like something was missing, and whatever that something was, he wanted it. Filling anonymous holes didn't fill the hole in himself. Only killing Hok did that, and only for a while.

"I have no shame about a shortcut to action," Loco said, laughing. "I take the risks. I might as well get the rewards. You should, too, like you used to. I'm beginning to worry about you, buddy. You need to get your ashes hauled at least once every R&R."

Should Straker tell Loco he strongly suspected Command arranged for the groupie entertainment? That some or most might not even be volunteers but professionals instead? It was all too easy, and it felt worthless.

But even if he could communicate that, why should Loco care?

Why should I care, either? Straker wondered. He was young, fit, and relished his role as the defender of human worlds. Yet, he'd begun to feel old…

He wasn't sure why he felt this way. His comrades seemed to be able to slip easily from combat to carefree celebration, living for the day, shedding their stresses like clothing dropped on a bungalow floor.

"Eat, drink and be merry, for tomorrow we die," he muttered.

"Same old Derek," Loco complained, "reading ancient books on a beach! Come on, man, find a girl and get laid. Hell, find two or three. They'll share."

Straker grunted, pondering. "Loco, you ever had anyone turn you down here on Shangri-La?"

Loco's brow furrowed. "Oh, sure. I think. Maybe once or twice. Until I tell them I'm a mechsuiter. That always brings 'em around."

"And did any of your willing women ever say no to anything you wanted to do? Like, in bed? No matter how freaky?"

"Hmm, not in bed, no. And I *do* get freaky. Sometimes they don't want to go surf-sailing or scuba diving or something like that."

"Don't you think that's odd? That these hotties are catering to your every whim?"

"Not really," Loco said with a shrug. "This is an R&R complex. There are three categories of people here. Military on leave—which to the civpop means *heroes.* Civilians who come here to hook up with us heroes; and last of all, employees. Which is okay by me."

"You sure there aren't only *two* categories of people?" Straker asked.

"Huh?"

"Think about it."

Loco appeared to consider. "You trying to say the civvies are really all employees?"

Straker shrugged. "It crossed my mind."

Loco chuckled. "So what if they are? I can't tell the difference. In fact, I don't want to know. I'm going to go find a couple girls and have me some afternoon delight, eat a few dozen oysters and drink fruity drinks to regain my strength—then maybe I'll find a poker game. You can sit here and wonder about what's behind the curtain, brother. I'm gonna enjoy the show."

Straker watched Loco swagger off in search of fun. His eyes wandered to the firm young women parading by twos and threes down the beach, as if for him alone. When they saw him watching, they waved and giggled, and he felt a surge of interest.

The first few years after he was commissioned, he'd availed himself of their charms with a teenager's gusto, but now, a decade later… where was the challenge? Where was the depth? What did it matter, if everything was free?

Or just possibly… not even real? He scratched at his brainchip port, wondering. How come they seldom let a mechsuiter go home, even to visit his family's graves? Mandatory R&R was the ticket, they said. No time to go for long sidespace trips to Oceanus. Elite status had its privileges, and also its sacrifices.

Yet Shangri-La didn't feel real, or right. He wanted a connection with someone. Something more permanent.

In years past he'd tried to establish a rapport with groupies, fishing for congruence to these civilian girls with their safe little hobbies and their perfect plastic dreams. Some of them professed to want to marry military and have children, but the ones who admitted to that seemed too eager for promises and rings on their fingers before the R&R was over.

Were they looking to escape from their circumstances? The war meant that some parts of the Hundred Worlds lived in proud poverty, on minimum rations and without luxuries. Others were rich by comparison, especially the Central Worlds. Each planet had its peculiarities, and ships couldn't be spared to carry massive quantities of goods to balance the circumstances of each.

This thought brought a sharp guilt to mind. He thought of himself living in the midst of plenty, sitting here on a perfect beach while less fortunate citizens toiled every day in the war industries. He figured that feeling also played into his reluctance to take advantage of people who might have no other way out of misery than volunteering to be a paid concubine.

"Hey, Straker. Mind if I join you?"

He looked up to see a comely female face and body, though she was unlike the others within his sight. Late twenties, well formed… he couldn't quite put his finger on the difference. Maybe she was on the fitter side, without the usual voluptuousness of the groupies.

High, exotic cheekbones, olive skin, short black pixie cut, little makeup. That was also unusual. Most—all?—of the girls around here had long hair and looked like they'd just stepped out of the salon. And her eyes… not young at all. In fact, they seemed aged, radiating a knowing stare.

"We've met before?" he asked.

"Of course we have."

Suddenly, he realized this was Carla Engels. He didn't know how he knew. Just as suddenly, he recognized he was dreaming, though in the manner of dreams it didn't seem to matter that he held two realities in his head simultaneously.

Yet at some level he remained aware that this was *not* how he and Carla had really met: not on a beach, not on R&R. He'd met her at Academy Station and crushed on her right away. She'd been the older, more experienced girl, although he'd never done anything about it. After all, fraternization among cadets was prohibited, and Derek Straker… he always followed the rules.

Later on, as a junior officer aboard ship, such relationships were strongly discouraged if not outright forbidden. Sex, maybe love, was for R&R, not to distract during mission deployment. Straker was determined not to put his effectiveness as a mechsuiter in jeopardy by bending or breaking any rules, written or unwritten.

Until now. They were on R&R, and what happened on Shangri-La, stayed on Shangri-La.

He smiled. Maybe this dream represented how he wished things could have happened.

Straker's heart pounded suddenly in his chest, and he felt lust surge from somewhere south of his abs. Perhaps only in a dream could he have what he desired, with no consequences, and somehow it would all work out.

He was reaching for Carla when the vision shattered, leaving him groaning on the deck, clutching himself with disappointment and frustration.

A plastic emergency ration pack lay on the floor of his cell, near the door's bottom slot. It wasn't exactly like any he'd ever had before, but it was edible. Maybe something the Hok made specifically for humans they captured, or maybe other aliens could eat it too.

Straker ate with his fingers, for the usual plastic spoon was absent. The food had even less flavor than survival rations he'd tasted. Perhaps it was old. To wash it down, he drank metal-flavored faucet water from his hand. Then he slept some more, feeling his aches and pains recede as his bruises and pressure cuts healed.

Nineteen more meals passed. Each "night" the lights dimmed for about a third of the time. If they fed him three times per standard day, and he guessed he'd been in the cell almost a week. Once, a new roll of toilet paper had appeared. Variations in the food itself, in the sounds he could faintly hear, and in his healing body convinced him he didn't occupy a VR sim.

Sadly, his predicament was evidently real.

To pass the time he exercised. He performed every manner of push-up he could: standard, inverted, diamond-hand, handstands against the wall, one-handed, clapping. He stretched too. He punched and kicked the air, recalling the martial forms he'd been taught but had little time to practice between battles lately. He did squats and thrusts, jumps and flips, working himself to exhaustion. Whatever the next stage of captivity turned out to be, he resolved to be ready.

The seventh night things changed.

He awoke to an earsplitting klaxon. Figures in Hok battle armor flung his door open and seized him, dragging him into the brightness of a corridor.

He fought them as they battered him with truncheons. With desperate dexterity and strength he took a billy club from one and struck him down, then another.

But there were too many, and there was nowhere to go, no room to maneuver in the tight passageways. They shocked him with electric prods that doubled him up in helpless agony, and then beat him senseless. They shackled him and dragged him in a daze through cryscrete corridors, leaving skin and blood along the way.

They flung him into a larger room, with perhaps a hundred others. Humans, like him, not Hok. Two women with near-shaved heads huddled near each other in a corner as if to defend themselves from abuse.

Abruptly, he realized one was Carla Engels, He hadn't seen it immediately, what with her shapeless jumpsuit and baldness. "Carla!"

"Derek!" She flung herself at him, clinging to him in a desperate embrace.

He held her tight. "It's good to see you," he whispered in her ear.

She drew back, running a palm over her buzz cut. "I look terrible."

"You look amazing."

They simply stared at each other for a time, ignoring the other people looking on.

"We should see who's in here with us," Engels eventually said.

"Yeah." Straker rose and turned. "Listen up!"

The people in the room fell silent and turned to look.

"I'm Assault Captain Derek Straker, First Mechsuit Regiment. Does anyone here outrank me?"

No one replied. They only stared. One man, who had been hidden on the floor behind others, opened his eyes from sleep, and then raised his hand from where he sat against the wall.

"Derek? It's me, Loco. I guess we survived."

Loco gestured, and Straker realized his friend's legs were hidden by thick, crude casts.

"Damn, Loco. You look like shit."

"You don't look so good yourself, boss," he replied. He rapped on the casts with his knuckles. "At least they treated me."

"Don't worry. I'll get us out of here somehow, and we'll get to a regen center."

"Yeah… Sure we will."

It worried Straker that Loco wasn't cracking jokes. "We have to get out of here."

"Where's here?" Loco asked. "Does anyone know?"

"We're on a ship, and we've left sidespace." Engels said. "We're probably inbound to a planet or habitat. Take it from a pilot."

"I thought so," Straker said, turning to the others. "Is everyone else here military?"

Most of the people nodded, though tentatively.

"Anyone not? Any civilians?"

No one replied.

"Any other mechsuiters? How about pilots? Come on, speak up!"

A man raised his hand. "I'm a Panther gunner, sir."

Another said, "Hover driver."

"Sergeant Banden Heiser," said the biggest man in the room. "Home Guard, sir. Infantry."

Engels nodded at him. "I remember you. You helped me when I landed."

"How about the rest of you?" said Straker.

They identified themselves as local troops from Corinth, captured when the city was cut off.

"So they've separated us from the civilians," Straker said. "I presume that means we're being treated as POWs and they have something special in store for us."

"I think we're about to find out what's so special," Loco muttered as the tramp of booted feet approached the door.

"Should we fight?" Heiser asked, balling his fists.

Straker shook his head. "Not yet. They'll be ready. Let's be smart. Watch and wait for an opportunity. Besides, where would we escape to?"

"We could seize the ship."

Engels spoke up. "Not likely. This feels big—at least a heavy cruiser. We can't fight so many. Not without weapons, or some kind of edge."

Their conversation cut off when the portal swung back and bristled with stun guns held by armored Hok troopers. They appeared to be taking no chances this time as the weapons' ultrasonics pummeled Straker and the others into unconsciousness.

Chapter 15

Enemy-controlled space, unknown location.

When Straker awoke, he found himself alone in a hot, humid cell. No vibrations thrummed underfoot, and there was a solidity to the gravity and the floor that indicated he wasn't on a starship any longer.

A tiny window, too small to fit his head through, let a shaft of sunlight in from up high on one wall. That cinched it—he was on a planet now.

The place smelled different, too. Instead of the disinfectants, lubricants and metal of a warship, the noxious aromas of feces and fear assaulted his nostrils.

He saw little in the cell. No toilet, no sink, no pallet. Nothing but old-fashioned concrete and, in one corner, the filth of bodily wastes. That had presumably been left behind by a former occupant. Straker wondered what had become of him.

Or her.

Or *it*? The Hok attacked aliens and humans indiscriminately, which was probably one reason the Hundred Worlds still stood. A little less xenophobia and a little more politicking would have served the Hok better.

After a time, perhaps an hour, he began to hear noises. Footsteps and voices. The voices *seemed* human, and the rhythms and intonations could almost be understood.

Straker pressed his ear to the metal door and strained to hear.

"Come on out, traitor. Come out! Get up, you crapping piece of shite!"

The guard spoke Earthan! The primary Hundred Worlds language, but with an accent that rang oddly in his ears. What the hell were Hok doing speaking Earthan?

But of course, they had to use a human language to communicate with their prisoners. Still, the few times the Hok had spoken to him had been through synthesizers. This was different, sounding as if it came from a human throat.

"What do you want?" said a female voice.

Straker recognized Engels speaking.

"Come with us, you whore, unless you want a baton shoved up your ass and then our cocks after."

Straker's hands clenched and scrabbled at his door, but found nothing to grasp. He growled with rage and kicked the portal, rattling it. "Leave her alone, you sick Hok bastards!"

He heard cruel laughter. "Hok? Funny! You'll get to know the Hok soon enough, unmutual turncoat lackey," said the voice. "Don't think only the bitches get it. Some of my boys aren't picky."

Turncoat lackey? Unmutual? What the hell did that mean?

The noises diminished as the tormenters led Engels away. Straker kicked at his door until he'd exhausted himself and bruised his bare feet, but it did no good. The cell was built to keep a strong prisoner inside. Without tools, he had no chance. No hinges, no mechanism was accessible, and his hands, mere flesh, were no match for steel and concrete.

Steel and concrete... more proof he was on a planet. Ships were built from expensive high-tech alloys, not steel, plus light, super-strong cryscrete. The gravity here seemed low to him, perhaps one half a standard G, indicating a small planet or large moon. He leaped for the tiny window, eventually catching the bars by his fingertips to lift himself to see out.

He saw a bleak, concrete courtyard, separated from others like it by metal fences topped with barbed wire. Men and women in prison garb shuffled dispiritedly around a small circuit under a hot white sun. Beyond barriers, towers stood, and still farther, the green of a jungle. That was all he could take in before he lost his precarious grip.

Half an hour later more boots returned.

"Carla?" he called. "You okay?"

"Derek?"

"Shut up, bitch!"

Straker heard the sounds of slaps and blows, then a slamming door.

The boots approached. "Your turn, traitor," said the man—the human—who opened Straker's door.

"What's all this about being a traitor?" Straker asked, facing half a dozen big prison guards, humans in simple unpowered body armor.

The leader sneered and glanced at his fellow bulls. "Funny how all criminals say they're innocent. *'I have no idea what happened, officers! I just happened to kill hundreds of my fellow humans while defending rebel outposts.'* Well, nobody believes your lies here, unmutual shitbag."

"You're the traitors for working for the Hok!" Straker yelled.

"Working for the Hok!" All the men laughed. "That's funny."

"No, boy," one said. "The Hok work for us."

"I hear your exploiter leaders brainwash the weak-minded," said another to Straker.

The leader gestured. "Don't matter. He'll confess and self-critique soon enough. After that, he'll join the fodder. Take him."

Straker made ready to fight them. If he could get one of their shock batons, and with his speed…

They didn't give him a chance. One of the men lifted a stunner and shot him. He collapsed.

As they dragged him down the corridor he realized his mistake. He shouldn't have engaged them in conversation. He should have simply jumped them, tried to take the stunner. His genetically enhanced reactions might have made the difference.

They manacled and strapped him securely to a bolted-down crysteel chair in a brightly lit room. Another, more comfortable chair sat in front of him, along with a table that held a plastic pitcher, plastic cups, and plastic plates with real food, bread and cheese and meat. He salivated, unable to stop himself.

A man entered the room, slim and stiff-spined. He had a hatchet face, dark hair and lizard-black eyes. Not old, but not young, he was dressed in a simple outfit that looked vaguely like a uniform, but without accouterments or insignia. The cloth draped his frame like fine silk, and the shoes the man wore were polished like an Academy cadet's display boots.

"Who the hell are you people?" Straker snarled. "Are you working for the Hok?"

The man smiled coldly. "You misunderstand. The Hok work for us—as will you. It's my sincerest hope you will grasp this in time."

"I'll never work for you!"

"That's what you all say," he said with a regretful chuckle, "but once you hear the truth, and your options, you'll change your mind."

With economical motions the man poured liquid from the pitcher into a plastic cup and capped it with a lid and straw. He held it out so Straker could take it in one manacled hand. "You should have enough play in your chains to drink," he said.

Straker threw the cup onto the floor with his fingertips. "I don't want anything you have to offer."

The man looked down sternly at Straker. "There's no need for such dramatics. Grow up and act like a man, not some pampered war-slave."

"Go to hell."

His captor shrugged. "Your loss." He sat and took out a smokestick, lighting it with elegant, long-fingered hands and taking a deep drag. "Smoke?"

Straker shook his head. "Those are unhealthy."

"So is being a mechsuiter, but you did that." With his free hand the man poured himself a cup of whatever it was and sipped, no straw.

Straker didn't answer, merely glared. Whatever this guy's game was, he wasn't going to play it.

But... the longer he had to think, the more the incongruity of the situation nagged at him. He'd been captured by the Hok. Now some urbane human was interrogating him and the Hok were nowhere to be found.

Something was seriously out of whack. He had to get some kind of answers. Grudgingly, he said, "Okay, I'll take that drink."

The man recovered and refilled the fallen cup, setting it in Straker's manacled hand. "A wise choice. It's fruit juice. Nothing harmful, I assure you."

Straker sipped, and after so many days of water and processed rations, the flavor exploded in his mouth. He recalled all the good things, the luxuries he took for granted, and was ashamed at feeling grateful.

This man was trying to manipulate him, he realized. He'd had resistance training, and now he brought to mind the various methods that might be used against him. But one of the things he'd been taught is, when you can get something with no strings attached, take it and use it to survive with honor.

So he drank. He didn't worry about being drugged. After all, if they wanted to drug him, they could simply shoot him with an injection gun.

The man spoke. "I am Inquisitor Lazarus, though I have to say, I've never needed to be resurrected from the dead. Not personally, anyway."

"What? What does that mean?"

"Didn't they even educate you on basic humanities? Literature, mythology? No—I suppose they wouldn't. I'm surprised you even speak Earthan."

"Why wouldn't I speak Earthan? My ancestors were from Old Earth!"

"As were mine." Lazarus sniffed as if he smelled something bad. "You know, we've been trying to capture a mechsuit pilot for a long time. Now we have two, and your unit has been wiped out, praise to the Mutuality. What I want to know is how you justify your actions."

Straker set his empty cup precariously on the arm of his chair. "Justify what?"

"Fighting against your own people."

"I have no idea what you're talking about. I've done nothing but defend the Hundred Worlds my whole life."

"So you admit it?" Lazarus asked excitedly.

"Admit what?"

"That you've fought against us your whole life?"

"Yeah. That's what I've been trying to tell you!"

"Confession recorded! Good. That's your first step toward rehabilitation, admitting you killed so many of your fellow humans."

"You're crazy. I've never killed a human. Not intentionally. Not in the war, I mean." *Unless you counted Skorza*, he thought, but he doubted Lazarus cared about that. He seemed to be talking about Straker's military actions.

Lazarus' lizard-face sighed. Apparently he'd missed Straker's slip. "Going back on your confession already, Mister Straker? So very unmutual. But, not surprising. You're still confused by your transition to reality."

"Reality?"

"Yes. Your Hundred Worlds isn't the paradise you think it is, and your government has been lying to you."

"I never thought it was a paradise, but it's what we've got, and it's my job to defend it against the Hok. And what's the story with the Hok? That's what I really want to know."

The man smiled without humor. "Of course you do." He sat forward, his burning smokestick still pinched between his fingers. "I suppose you think the Hok are aliens?"

"Of course!"

"But they're not. They're as human as you or I. Or at least they were, until we inject them with biotech that turns them into the perfect soldiers. Human Organic Commandos, they were originally called. HOC."

Straker's mind whirled. "But... but..."

"So you see, you've slaughtered hundreds, perhaps thousands of humans in your career."

"But that was war! It doesn't matter if they were humans or aliens, they were attacking my people."

"Sometimes the Mutuality attacks the Hundred Worlds, sometimes the Hundred Worlds attacks the Mutuality. Do you really think your side is filled with pristine virtue and mine is evil?"

"I..."

Lazarus waved a hand as if shooing flies. "But I agree with you."

"With what?"

"That killing in war is justified. It's natural. It doesn't matter if they're humans or aliens, you just said, and I agree."

"It matters if you're the defenders or the aggressors," Straker said. "We have a hundred systems. You—what did you call yourselves, the Mutuality? You have over a thousand. We would live in peace with you if you'd stop attacking us."

Lazarus shook his head sadly. "We've tried that. After a time, the exploiters that run your lives get greedy and try to take what we have again."

It all sounded so reasonable. What if what Lazarus was saying was true?

Could Straker have been hoodwinked his whole life? He'd always felt something was off. As a kid, his parents and teachers hadn't told him the whole truth, especially about the Hok. On Academy, they'd continued the indoctrination, and during his career, they hadn't ever let him go home, sending him and his comrades to Shangri-La between battles instead of letting him have a real life.

No. This man was a liar, trying to use him somehow. Even if there were things about the Hundred Worlds that didn't add up perfectly, even if some of what Lazarus said was accurate, it didn't mean the man was really being honest with him. The best lies were partly true.

"I want to see the Hok, then," Straker said. "Prove to me that they're human."

"Of course. I imagine you never had a chance to really see one up close."

"Close enough to kill me."

"But your underlings cleaned up the battlefield while you pampered mech-suiters relaxed on vacation with the best of everything, I'm told."

Straker shrugged uncomfortably. "That wasn't my job."

"I know. I don't blame you for being a dupe." Lazarus stood and opened the single door to the room, and spoke to someone outside.

A few moments later, a uniformed Hok strode into the room. He halted and saluted.

"At ease," said Lazarus. "Take off your uniform,"

Straker stared as the creature stripped to the buff. He'd never seen one this close, face-to-face.

Though humanoid, it had grayish-green pebbled skin. No hair adorned its head. Instead, its cranium was covered in something that looked like turtle shell, and ridges of bone protected deep eye sockets. Its hands had thick nails, almost claws, and it was heavily muscled. It was also obviously male, though it seemed to have no testicles.

"Trooper, this is Captain Straker," said Lazarus.

The creature immediately saluted Straker, with no change of expression.

"Captain Straker would like to know your function."

The creature's voice was raspy, but intelligible. "I am a Human Organic Commando, rank one, designation BX-1277."

"So you're human?" Straker asked.

"I was human. Now, I am HOC."

"What's your name?"

"I have no name."

"What was your name before?"

"I have no name. I serve the People."

Lazarus ground out his smokestick in a tray. "You won't get much more than that. The Hok were either volunteers or enemies of the State. In either case, the biotech wipes their memories clean and makes them completely obedient and fearless. It also gives them strength and fast healing."

"It's immoral!" Straker said. "You've stolen their humanity."

"You'd rather we lock up our criminals in prison to rot, or execute them?" Lazarus demanded. "This way, they serve the People and the State."

Straker rattled his manacles. "What's to keep your regime from doing this to anyone, not just criminals?"

"We have laws and procedures. Every Hok is properly tried and convicted, never fear."

Straker wondered about that, but didn't see the point in arguing. Trials could be manipulated… and how serious a crime would it take to turn you into a Hok? Shoplifting? Jaywalking? Criticizing the State that Lazarus seemed so fond of?

"So what do you want from me?" asked Straker. "Why not just inject me with the biotech and add me to your slave armies?"

In truth, this idea terrified him in a way mere death never had. To lose his free will, to be forced to kill his own… these Mutuality people were monsters.

"That's the last resort. But Mister Straker, you're special. You and your comrade are the first two mechsuiters we've ever captured, and we'd like you to work with us to establish a mechsuit program of our own."

"Go fuck yourself!"

Lazarus sighed. "I expected you to say that. I told my superiors that your conditioning wouldn't be bypassed by simple persuasion. As you proceed through your inevitable re-education and rehabilitation, remember that I first treated you with respect, and you chose your own path, a path you can always give up. Just say you'll cooperate, and you'll be treated well."

"Never."

Lazarus opened the door and spoke to the guard. "Take him."

They took him to another room with bright lights and a steel table, strapping him to it before the stun wore off. Metal cuffs clamped onto his waist, neck, wrists and upper arms. They were snapped onto his ankles and thighs and kept his feet projecting over the edge of the table into space. Then a white-coated man stabbed him in the thigh with a syringe, sending some kind of drug burning into his muscle tissue.

Lazarus stood by, watching without expression.

"There's no point in torturing me," Straker said. "I won't cooperate."

"What's your name, traitor?" the man with the white coat asked.

"I'm not a traitor."

He dug a thumbnail into Straker's ribs. Pain shot through his body. "Name!"

"Straker. Derek Straker. Assault Captain, mechsuiter. Service number–"

"I don't care about your lackey number, fool. I simply wanted to know what to call you. Maybe if we can cut through the conditioning, you'll learn how to be mutual. But first, you must confess everything."

The man ran a fingertip down Straker's cheek, then his neck. The pain was unexpectedly severe. Straker took it almost without flinching.

Then a different man, a big man with cruel eyes, stepped forward holding a length of heavy plastic hose. He flexed it in his hands, eager.

"You're about to experience pain therapy," said the white-coated man in a voice that was almost bored. "The drug I administered will enhance the sensations. Eventually, you'll beg to confess. Once you admit your crimes in full, you can be welcomed into the community of the Mutuality. Nothing will be held against you, if only you'll confess."

"I have nothing to confess! I haven't committed any crimes!"

"Of course you have. The fact you were a mental weakling and tricked into slaughtering your fellows changes nothing. You must accept responsibility for your atrocities, embrace reeducation, and set your feet on the path to Mutualist rehabilitation." The man paced, hands behind his back and addressed the air. "But fools *never* confess right away. Resistance must be demolished first. We shall begin now. Corporal?"

He gestured, and the larger man approached—his lips spreading into a grin.

Straker fought down fear. Whatever they did to him, he could take it. That's what he told himself.

He wasn't entirely wrong, but he wasn't entirely right, either.

The corporal took the length of hose and whipped it across the soles of Straker's extended feet, and his world exploded in utter agony. He'd never felt such pain. It crawled up his leg and occupied every nerve in his body, advancing to the base of his brain in a wave that he could feel, could track with precision, as if the anguish were composed of red ants traveling his veins, chewing as they went.

As bad as the first blow was, the second was worse... and the third even more so. Impossibly, each strike to the bottom of his feet brought a new level of anguish, until his consciousness filled with nothing but animal torment. He heard screaming and realized the sound came from his own throat, but found himself powerless to stop it.

Lazarus stepped forward. "Confess, Mister Straker! Admit your crimes against the Mutuality and the therapy will stop."

"Therapy? This isn't therapy, it's torture!"

"Take care when making false accusations!" the Inquisitor boomed, suddenly angry. "We do not use torture here. Torture is immoral. Pain therapy, on the other hand, is designed to cut through your denial and allow you to come to the saving knowledge of the Mutuality. Come now. Give up your foolish individualistic resistance. Admit your crimes against the Mutuality."

Straker choked out, "I only fought to defend humanity!"

"Ignorance of your crimes is no excuse. Confess! Purge yourself of resistance to the collective will of the People and the State! Only then can you rejoin the community of the Mutuality!"

Straker refused to confess to crimes he didn't commit. Fighting in a war wasn't a crime. And shouldn't he have passed out by now? It must be the drug, something that wouldn't allow him the surcease of unconsciousness.

Lazarus droned on, speaking similar phrases, over and over, as if trying to hypnotize Straker into surrendering his will. He lost focus, drifting. He couldn't have confessed even if he wanted to.

The place where his self resided, the tiny kernel of his identity, floated on a lake of fire, a sea of hell that threatened to drown him. In that moment, he might have told them anything just to make it stop. He'd thought himself superior, a warrior, but this was a battle like nothing he'd ever envisioned.

Battle… warrior… *warrior…*

Slowly Straker separated his mind from the horror surrounding it. The pain had finally reached some kind of limit and, faced with a plateau, he found he could fend it off.

His mental processes limped, barely capable of holding one thought at a time and moving on to another, like a man hanging from bars above his head that were spaced barely close enough to grasp. It took everything he could muster to create a bubble around his core and push the agony away.

He wanted to quit, but refused. He wanted to give up, but something within him would not.

I shall not yield, he thought. *I shall never surrender.*

"This all can end, if only you confess," Lazarus whispered close to his ear. "You've already admitted you fought for the enemy and murdered our soldiers. Confess the rest! Tell us how you enjoyed the slaughter. How you bragged about it. Unburden yourself! You will feel so much better! Only then can you rehabilitate."

Two paths lay open to Straker. The smart path, or the hard path.

Nobody'd ever called him a brainiac. Not that he was stupid, but he didn't think he had the raw intellect to duel wits with Lazarus, not from the position of being strapped to a table.

Something within him crystallized instead. The hard path it would be.

He'd give them nothing.

Deep within himself, he resolved to fight back, escape, and eventually stick it to all of these devils.

Somehow…

"Do your worst," he rasped out. "I've done nothing wrong."

Lazarus's face grew long, and he shook his head as if at a child. "How unfortunate. You are only making it hard on yourself. Don't make the mistake of thinking I enjoy this, but it is necessary. Corporal, you may proceed with the second phase."

The "pain therapy" began again. This time, they burned him in random places on his body. He never knew where the agony would manifest next. They continued to insist he surrender his will, but their window of opportunity had closed.

Perhaps the drug wore off, or perhaps the pain overcame its effects, but eventually Straker lost consciousness. When he came to, he found himself in his cell again.

When he tried to rise, he failed. Even if he could withstand the pain, he didn't think he could make his ankles and knees work. His feet swelled like slabs of meat and his skin had split and oozed with hundreds of tiny burns.

Instead, he crawled to the door and pressed his mouth and nose to the crack beneath, inhaling. The air he sucked in seemed slightly fresher, though he smelled disinfectant and death.

"Carla, can you hear me?" he said in a low tone. Receiving no answer, he said, slightly louder, "Loco? Anyone?"

Chapter 16

Facility Alpha Six, day two.

A surge of relief shot through Carla Engels when she heard Derek Straker's voice from down the corridor. The sentiment may be nonsensical, but she felt much better knowing he lay in the next cell. That she was not alone. "I'm here, Derek."

"Did they try to get you to cooperate?"

"Yes. Some asshole called Lazarus did—but I refused."

Straker spoke again. "Did they...?"

Engels' mind shied away from the session on the table. "They tortured me. Beat me, burned me."

"Nothing more?"

"They didn't violate me, if that's what you're asking. Not yet anyway. That Lazarus creepo touched me, though. I'm probably supposed to be afraid they'll rape me."

"Or *I'm* supposed to fear that for you. I remember our resistance training. This is all a mind game. Lazarus is smart, but not as smart as he thinks he is."

"What do you mean?"

"Did they beat the soles of your feet?"

"Yes. It was the worst thing I've ever felt in my life, worse than the burns, even. I still can't walk."

"Did they ask you any questions?"

"Not really. Just kept ordering me to confess."

"Me too. So this isn't about information. It's about breaking us."

Engels thought for a moment. "Get prisoners to confess, and they'll have betrayed their integrity. After that, they'll do anything."

Straker remained silent for a moment. "He said something about conditioning. Do you think we were brainwashed?"

"No," Engels said. "Sure, there was always that simple rah-rah patriotic stuff they fed us as cadets, but we were kids. Nothing really changed when we went to war. We had to fight. The Hok kept attacking us."

"Yeah, about the Hok... did he tell you?"

"Tell me what?"

Straker explained to her about the Hok, or HOC, he'd seen. Then he told her how they were made.

"A nightmare..." she said quietly. "Are you sure?"

"I'm sure."

Engels sighed. "We're going to have to talk to these people. Give them something to get something. It doesn't do us any good to keep getting tortured. We're not denying them information, because they're not even asking."

"Carla, no!"

"Derek, I didn't say I was going to crack, and I'm not going to give them anything that matters. But we need to know more about what's really going on."

"Who cares?" he demanded. "What can we do with information as prisoners?"

"I don't know," she said, "but at some point they'll give up on getting us to turn traitor and simply inject us with the biotech. Then we'll be mindless Hok and..."

"No, I think that's an empty threat. They want to use us for our skills."

"You mechsuiters, maybe. You're rare and valuable, but not me. I'm a simple pilot. No doubt they have plenty of those."

"Shit... You're right. We can't let you be turned into a Hok. Okay. You have to cooperate, enough to keep from being injected. But how will you convince them?"

"They *want* to believe. They want me to confess. Besides, I'm a woman. They'll sooner believe a woman cracked than a man."

Derek's voice conveyed puzzlement. "Why?"

"Because women are more sensible, which means less stubborn. Actually we bend instead of breaking, but the guards won't tell the difference. Did you notice nearly all of them are men? I'm going to bet they still have unconscious biases, and I can use that against them. I can play weak—enough to make them believe it, anyway."

"I can't do that."

"Play weak?" she asked.

"I can't," he growled.

"You're not strong enough to play weak?" she asked.

"Don't twist my words. It's not who I am."

"Fair enough. You be the tough guy. It'll make the contrast look even better."

Straker fell silent for some minutes, and Engels relaxed, letting him think. The man was a pure ace in a battlesuit, but he was too much of a thoroughbred racehorse, a one-trick pony. Pilots had to have a wider view, multitasking and shifting their attention among ground and orbit and space.

But it wasn't Straker's fault he was so stubborn. Right now she figured he was hoping to find a problem to attack using his fantastic combat skills. The problem was, as the saying went, when all you have is a hammer, everything looks like a nail. At some level Straker was trying to force their current predicament into the shape of a battle he could fight and win, head-to-head.

Maybe if she put things into his terminology…

"Derek…?"

"What?" he asked.

"You've studied a lot of military history, strategy, that sort of thing, right?"

"Sure."

"When you fight, do you just shoot what's in front of you? Especially when there are too many of them?"

"Of course not," he said. "I look for the enemy's weak spots, move around his flanks."

"What else do you do to win?" she asked.

"Umm… I get ahead of their decision curve. Predict what they'll do and frustrate them. I try to get them tangled up. Make them cross their lines of fire. Use one to shield me from another. Come at them from an unexpected angle. Use the distraction from one weapon to give me the chance to use a different one. Pick my battles."

"And you access recon nets for more information, right?" she asked.

"Sure," he agreed.

"And you call for fire when you get into trouble," she said, "or have to take out a concentration you can't handle yourself."

"Yeah, of course."

"And if you're outnumbered and outgunned," she said, "you hide and wait."

"Not often," Straker said with pride.

"In principle at least?"

"Yeah…"

"So," she pressed him, "you need to start looking at our problems like a whole battle, not just a fight between you and a couple of enemy tanks. Think strategically. Use all your resources. Coordinate with everyone on our side. Only take a shot when it will count. Don't let the enemy know where you're lurking or what you intend to do."

"Yeah, that's smart. But how?" he asked.

"We'll all have to develop new skill sets, Derek. I read something once about every struggle being a part of the same spectrum. Espionage, ground combat, space combat, politics, resistance in captivity—it's not even about killing. It's all about two sides struggling to impose their wills on each other."

"Like me and Skorza—but I had to kill him."

"Maybe. Because he was stubborn, exactly like you, and wouldn't bend his will. But I'm not starting that old argument, Derek. I'm just saying brute defiance isn't the only way to fight these people."

"Okay," Straker said. "I can see that, but I still think it's a bad idea to give them anything. It feels wrong."

"I'll do my best to make sure my cooperation is worthless. Just… Derek, you have to promise me something."

"What?" he asked.

"No matter what you see or hear, no matter what they tell you, I'll never truly collaborate. It will always be me trying to play them. But they might point at me and say, 'Hey look, she's cooperating, why don't you?' Or, 'She turned against you, so why not turn against her?'"

"Yeah, okay," he said. "I promise I won't believe them– Carla?"

"What?"

"You're still…"

Engels waited long seconds. "What?"

"Nothing."

She smiled. "Thanks, Derek. I get it." Engels knew he'd been in love with her ever since his earliest days on Academy Station, but he couldn't find a way to admit it to himself. He treated her like a sister. Some kind of honor thing, as if she were a goddess on a pedestal instead of a living, breathing woman.

For the rest of their time at Academy, she'd been angry with him for what he'd done to Skorza. After graduation, she'd been afraid to break through his reserve. What if the distraction got him killed? What if he was thinking about coming back to her instead of having his mind on the battlefield? That was one of the rationales for strongly discouraging fraternization.

But all that hardly mattered now. Maybe if they escaped together, she could finally make him see her as a woman, not just a comrade.

She enjoyed these fantasies for some time, but all too soon, their captors came for her again.

* * *

Straker shifted within his tiny metal cage, trying to find relief for his half-folded limbs. The closely spaced bars kept him from straightening his legs, and the dimensions of the box wouldn't let them fold up completely either. Agony shot through knee joints that couldn't fully extend, a slow, wearing torture of a sort different from the burns, the foot-beating, the wires shoved under his fingernails, the electrodes attached to his genitals, the thumbscrews…

His prison sat with others in the middle of a separate fenced yard. All were built atop struts that held the cages a meter off the ground and two meters from each other. No shade gave the prisoners relief from the direct sun, no blankets in the chill of night. Insects swarmed on their sores and in the daily bowls of what could only loosely be termed food.

At least once every day, Lazarus would come around and lecture him about Liberty, Equality, and Mutuality, this regime's guiding principles, and ask if he was ready to confess. Every day Straker refused, as did Loco. All the others had succumbed to the threat of being turned into a Hok.

The cleverest torment of all came at unpredictable intervals, when they were taken from their boxes and treated with sudden dignity. Trusted prisoners from other sections would carry or lead them to showers to wash, would feed them decent meals, and would earnestly urge them to confess.

"Just tell them what they want to hear," one pretty young thing told Straker over and over. "They don't really care what you say or what you've done. It's a way to break you down and get you to comply. If they think they're winning, they'll go easy on you." She stroked his hoary cheek. "If you don't, they'll turn you into a Hok."

"If they were going to do that they would have done it by now."

The woman shrugged and whispered in his ear. "I'm just saying what they tell me to say. But if they ever do give up on you, the biotech will burrow into your brain and you won't be you anymore."

"How long does it take after injection? To start losing your mind?"

"About a week, I hear."

"Thanks. But I won't let them win," he rasped. "I don't care what they do. Now go back and tell them you tried."

Later, he was shackled to chairs in classrooms where uniformed drones lectured them endlessly about Service to the Mutuality. They talked about their Responsibility to Rehabilitate, and above all about the importance of confessing their crimes—even crimes they didn't know they'd committed.

They called it "self-criticism." It seemed to be a central tenet of these people's ideology, to tear down the individual and make each person complicit in his or her own slavery. To shame themselves, to become "mutual."

Underlying it all was the threat of being turned into a monster. But that was a last resort. What they really wanted was self-chosen conformity. In a way, using the Hok serum meant they'd lost the battle of wills.

After long hours of indoctrination, interrupted only by a meager but welcome meal, they were allowed to sleep in warm, comfortable cots. If the Celestial Legion and the afterlife existed, he was sure it would be filled with clean sheets and soft beds.

The worst part was the awakening from these happy respites, inevitably roused from a deep sleep. At that point, they'd roughly return him to misery.

Every step he took as the guards led him back to his cage, he had to think about the grinding frustration of another week spent lying naked, half-folded and bruised on rusting steel bars in full view of the others in the next section. In full view of those who'd already "confessed."

Loco helped Straker endure, keeping up his usual patter of dark humor from a cage nearby. Engels supported him and Loco too, even in their degradation. She would come at least once a day to stand at the wire fence and salute them silently, eyes full of concern, as he ached in his cage.

Straker was grateful she didn't plead with him or look on him with pity. His respect for her, already immense, only grew. She might not be a mechsuiter, but she was a warrior, fighting battles in her own way. He didn't begrudge her strategy.

Every day he wished he could be like her—strong enough to do something weak, as she'd put it. But he couldn't. If he gave in, he feared that it wouldn't stop. If he cracked now, he might fall apart completely. He might lose his core, his self.

It was this single fear that drove him on. Was that weakness or strength? He wasn't sure.

He'd read martial treatises that argued differing views on the point. Some claimed an iron will would win the day. Others advised bending like a reed so as not to break. Still more said it was best to flow like water, giving in and vanishing into the earth, but without truly being altered in form.

He longed for the simplicity of combat, to live or to die, not to merely survive like an animal.

Survive with honor. That's what Chen had said. He wondered what had become of Chen. Maybe he'd gotten away. Straker hoped so. Lazarus had said they'd only captured two mechsuiters. If he and Loco didn't crack, their enemies would get nothing.

Chapter 17

Facility Alpha Six, day 37.

Engels sat in the daily self-critique session, reviewing her patter. She'd assembled a speech from snippets of what she'd heard in others, and she could now recite it verbatim. Her main challenge was to come across as spontaneous.

The Mutuals didn't really seem to care about the content, anyway. It was the form that mattered to them, and the sincerity with which it was expressed, not the truthfulness of it. They had their own special jargon as well, and ordinary words didn't always mean what you thought they did.

Her turn came to speak. She stood and faced the rest of the prisoners, adopting her practiced, slightly vacuous tone.

"I was unknowingly recruited to fight against the Mutuality," she said, "when I entered an institution of lies known as Academy Station. There, they implanted chips in my head and brainwashed me into becoming a selfish, unmutual lackey, ready and willing to slaughter anyone I was ordered to assault."

The Dialectic Controller in charge was a fat man called Jeremy. He nodded, encouraging.

Trying not to feel sickened by her own truth-twisting, she continued. "I know now I was being used, and I accept responsibility for participating in this unmutuality against my fellow humans and allied beings. I now understand that only through the principles of Liberty, Equality and Mutuality can I be redeemed and rehabilitated. Mutualism is the ultimate expression of the human collective social system. I hope someday my crimes will be expunged, allowing me to become a productive citizen."

She sat down at last, relieved it was over.

"Very good, Carla. Why don't you tell us something more personal, though? Have you strayed from Mutualist principles recently? Since you arrived at this reeducation facility, for example?" Jeremy leaned forward as if to hear better, eager to take in any indiscretion.

Standing again, Engels racked her brain for something that would satisfy him. "In the Mutual Eating Hall, I saw that another woman's bread portion was larger than mine, and I coveted it."

"And why is that wrong?"

"Because it violates the principle of Equality. Everyone should share equally. No one should have more than another. But I have a question, Controller Jeremy."

"Yes, Carla?"

"I've seen the staff and guards eating food that is better than ours, and more of it. Some of them even get fat. That doesn't seem like equality."

Jeremy smiled as if she were a child, but at the same time he subtly sucked in his ample gut. "That is only because you're not completely rehabilitated yet. Once you become one with the Mutuality, you will share equally in all its rewards. As well, remember some people have slow metabolisms. That's the only reason they're fat."

"But Controller... I also noticed that Inquisitor Lazarus wears fine clothing, and he is picked up daily by a luxury groundcar with a driver. And he's not fat. Do *you* have fine clothing and a driver?"

Jeremy's expression leaked a discomfort he tried to hide. "He doesn't own those clothes or the groundcar, just like a pilot does not own her warship. They are provided by our benevolent Mutuality to enhance the effectiveness of his role."

"I understand the groundcar, but how does fine clothing relate to his effectiveness? Besides, I thought all positions were mutually and equally important, right?"

Jeremy began to raise his voice. "As humans, we're all mutually and equally important. However, genetics and chance have granted us varying talents and skills. Some talents and skills are temporarily more critical, especially during the war we are fighting. The enemy forces compromise upon us, but once we have achieved a victorious peace, the utopia we are all working toward will arrive, as long as we dedicate ourselves to the Mutuality."

Engels noticed Jeremy had avoided addressing how having fine clothing related to the importance of a position. Mutuality officials were supposed to set the example for all citizens, after all.

"But–" she began again.

"Carla," he interrupted loudly, "doubts are a natural part of the dialectic process, but too much doubt can also derail your comrades' rehabilitation. You wouldn't want to seem unmutual, would you? I'd hate to have to report you for reversion. You'd be sent for extra pain therapy, and we wouldn't want that, hmm?"

Engels lowered her head. "No, Controller Jeremy. In speaking freely, I only wanted to comply with the principle of Liberty. I apologize for straying from its strict confines."

She sat back down as if cowed, but surreptitiously glanced at her fellow prisoners. Some met her gaze and nodded or winked. Obviously, they recognized hypocrisy when they saw it. Or maybe they simply liked to see Jeremy sweat.

Some days, even the smallest of victories were enough to keep her going. She continued to listen and learn, to read between the lines, and to gather data. Eventually she'd be able to talk to Straker and Loco, and maybe start figuring out some kind of plan for escape.

Before she did, hope came in a whisper. More than a rumor, but less than a promise. The word was passed: "The Unmutuals are coming."

* * *

The next will-sapping relief-and-indoctrination period brought a change of tactics on the part of Straker's captors. When he and Loco shuffled wearily from the showers—Loco's legs had finally healed—Carla Engels met them instead of an anonymous collaborator.

They'd let her grow her hair out. She'd never looked better to him. He stumbled into her arms.

"No touching!" a nearby female trustee yelled, smashing him across the kidney with her baton.

"Turncoat," he snarled at the trustee as he shoved his tormenter away. "Why are you doing their dirty work?"

"Derek!" Engels hissed. Insistently, she repeated his name until he turned his attention to her. "Come with me. You too, Loco." She led them to an empty room with tables and chairs. "Sit down, both of you."

The two men took seats across from her. When the other woman made as if to sit nearby, Engels pointed at the door. "Stand there and tell me if anyone comes."

The trustee sulked, but nodded and complied.

"You've got her well-trained," Loco said. "You ladies bunkies?"

"Shut the hell up, Loco," Engels said. "That mouth will get you killed someday."

"I—"

"Loco, quiet," Straker said, and his friend shut up. He turned back to Engels, sensing something important was happening. "Tell us what's going on."

"I have an hour, so there's no need to rush it," she replied. "They're watching us, but not listening, I don't think. Even if they are, it won't matter. They want me to tell you as much as I know. They want me to convince you guys to give up and join their collective."

"Collective?"

Engels chuckled. "That's what some of us call it. Just a nickname. Its proper name is the Mutuality, as I'm sure you've heard."

Straker snorted. "Yeah, they've lectured us on the topic a few times."

"Technically there's no difference between the State and the citizenry here. They're all part of the State and the State is everything. Everyone has an assigned role. Liberty, Equality, Mutuality."

Loco snorted. "Not much liberty around here."

"Or equality," Engels agreed. "Some people are more equal than others." She gave them a weak smile. "But there's a lot of mutuality, you have to admit that."

All the frustration of the last weeks bubbled up. "Dammit Carla," Straker said, "tell me something that matters. Tell me how we can get out of here! We don't have clean beds and good food like you sellouts do."

He saw hot tears of anger rise to Engels eyes. "After all I've gone through, the fake collaboration and endless indoctrination and false self-critique and the compromises I've made just to be able to sit here, and now you're calling me a sellout?"

"Sorry..." he said. "It's this place. It's..."

"It's killing us. I know." She covered his hand with hers. This faintest contact felt like heaven.

"No touching!" yelled the trustee from the doorway.

Engels withdrew her hand. "You have to start cooperating. It's all fake anyway. The whole society is based on fear and bullshitting the true believers, acting righteous according to their ideology while actually doing whatever they can get away with. If you don't give in... Derek, the biotech will destroy your mind. Although for you, Loco, that might be a blessing."

"Gee, thanks," said Loco. He turned to Straker. "Boss, it seems like the right play. Survive with honor."

Straker hunched his shoulders. "I can't. I won't confess to fake beliefs just to get out of being tortured. That's dishonor."

Engels' voice grew strained. "But these people don't believe in it either! Everything's built on lies and everyone knows they're lies, so they're not really lies and it doesn't really matter!"

"It matters to me. I can't do it."

She made a sound of exasperation. "Loco, talk some sense into him!"

Loco shrugged. "When did he ever listen to me?"

"Loco, you confess," Straker said. "That way you can help Carla figure out how to escape."

"Dammit," Loco said, "if we all confess, we can all work on escaping together."

"There's another reason to do it," said Engels. She leaned in and spoke in a bare whisper. "I heard something. Something is going to happen. Maybe a rescue attempt. We need to be together when it happens."

Dropping his eyes, Straker said again, "No."

"Damn you," Loco said, his temper fraying. "I suppose I have to keep being abused? You stubborn bastard."

"I'm not stubborn. I'm loyal."

"What you are is a selfish fool, Straker," said a booming voice from the doorway.

They turned to see Inquisitor Lazarus standing there. The trustee lookout hadn't warned them. In fact, she was gone.

"Take him," Lazarus said.

Guards swarmed into the room, pulling the three in separate directions.

A dozen men hauled Straker down a corridor he'd never seen. He kicked and punched them, knocking several down, but they pummeled him mercilessly and dragged him away. They threw him into a different cell.

Inquisitor Lazarus addressed him from beyond the bars, backed by the guards. "Straker, I'm at the point of cutting my losses with you. You would have been a feather in my cap had you rehabilitated yourself and joined the fight against your corrupt former masters. I gave you so much, and you played me for a fool. I let you see your girlfriend. I even bent Mutualist principles to help you understand *why* you should confess and take responsibility for all the men and women you killed as a war-slave."

Straker stood. "That's bullshit. But even if it's true, there's no way I was wrong to fight you people."

"Who cares about right and wrong? This isn't about finding fault, Straker. In that tight military society you were a part of, what was most important, fault or responsibility? We're talking about taking ownership of your crimes, asking forgiveness from society, and rejoining the Mutuality."

"*Re*-joining?" Straker put his face to the hole in the door, so that he was eye to eye with Lazarus. "I was never part of your anthill."

"Every human in the galaxy is part of the Mutuality, Straker. They're just temporarily ruled by someone else right now. What's important is that you can rejoin the Mutuality. We need your help to free the rest, so they can rejoin us too."

"As a mechsuiter."

"As I've said many times. You can spearhead the development program. Until now, mechsuits and pilots have been far too expensive and specialized to develop, build and maintain. The Mutuality is a poor society, not rich like your pampered citizens."

"Whose fault is that? Maybe if you treated people like human beings instead of interchangeable machines, they'd work harder for you and make everyone richer and happier!"

"Once again, you focus on fault over responsibility. The delusional thoughts you cling to are saturated by propaganda. Your citizens' happiness is a pleasant illusion. Consumer goods do not bring fulfillment. Only service to something greater can feed the soul."

Straker stood. "Maybe you ought to let people choose for themselves."

Lazarus snorted in disdain. "Your kind of freedom is an illusion. Our methods might be harsh, but they're honest. We tell you what you have to do, and you get to decide. Even if one choice is a stupid, painful one—it's your choice. We don't breed people from birth to be genetically enhanced warriors, like the Hundred Worlds. You never had any choice, Straker. You were told every day that you were going to be a mechsuiter and that's what you became."

"Choice?" Straker laughed. "If people don't bend to your will, you change them into monsters. That's not freedom."

"As I told you, only incorrigible criminals are forced to become Hok. And, now that it's clear you'll never cooperate, you've fallen into that category." Lazarus waved the guards in.

They seized Straker. He fought them, breaking the jaw of one and snapping the arm of another, but a low-power stunner made his muscles turn to rubber.

Once he'd been subdued, Lazarus entered the cell with an injection gun in one slim fist. Straker struggled again, but he was held immobile while the Inquisitor pressed the device against his neck.

The sharp stink of Lazarus' breath rolled over his face. Hot stinging fluids burned his neck.

"For a few days," Lazarus said in a voice that was strangely gentle, "the effects of the injection can be reversed. After that, it will eat into your brain and the alterations will be permanent. Change your mind soon... or it will be changed for you." He stepped back. "Release him and go," he told the guards.

The guards shoved Straker roughly across the room. By the time he staggered to his feet, Lazarus had retreated out the portal and closed the steel door.

The Inquisitor opened the small portal at eye level. "And Straker... lest you think this is only about you, your two friends have been injected as well.

Just say the word and they will be saved. If not…" The metal door to the hole slammed shut.

Straker heard Lazarus' footsteps fade down the concrete corridor. He sat on the platform and rubbed his bruises. Would he feel it as the biotech invaded his tissues? It chilled him to think he'd be turned into a mindless battle-slave.

Maybe he should pretend to cooperate, like Engels said. That was the sensible thing. But he couldn't bring himself to do it. Not yet, anyway.

Eventually he fell asleep, exhausted.

Chapter 18

Facility Alpha Six, day 39.

Inquisitor Lazarus-176 stared at himself in the mirror, satisfied that his appearance was correct, perfectly Mutual.

His graying hair was combed but not stylish as some of the Committee's pampered, youthful clones wore theirs. His clothing was made from the finest silk blend, but that was only for durability and to appropriately impress those around him, not for his own comfort.

His shoes were polished to a high shine, the product of fifteen minutes of maintenance every night before bedtime. It was important to him that he personally rub the leather with the wax, the cotton cloth and the chilled water, to remind himself of the labor the People had to endure.

He checked his nails. They needed a manicure. Fortunately, there were those with such skills among the prisoners.

"You look superbly Mutual," said his concubine, Tachina-23. She wrapped her hands around him from behind to place her palms flat on his lean chest. Her fingers played with his skin and her long, silky hair tickled his ear as she set her chin on his shoulder.

A discarded pleasure clone, Tachina-23 had been a marvelous find—a diamond among the broken stone that poured through the reeducation facility. She was tall, and he liked them tall. Her other attributes were equally pleasing.

He wondered what she had done to upset her former master. Most such specially bred clones were assigned to high-ranking Party members.

There was no way to be certain of her provenance, and one seldom-bent rule of rehabilitation was that all who came to the camps had their records expunged. Each got a fresh start.

This was a good policy, for the Mutuality recovered humans from wherever it could, whether it be by force or convenience. All had to be processed. All were needed to feed the machine of war. All had an equal chance to rejoin the social order.

He'd spotted her right away in the holding pens. Her long legs, slender waist, natural poise and animal magnetism had clearly stood out, even when disguised by bad clothing and indifferent hygiene. Before taking possession, he'd made sure she was given extra pain therapy and severe terrorization in order to excise any lingering resistance to Mutuality precepts.

When he finally gave her the chance to rehabilitate by sharing his life here at the facility, she'd immediately agreed. After all, the Mutuality was based on freedom and equality, and she'd made the correct—the required—choice to become freer and closer to equal. Now their feelings for one another were mutual, the benefits of their relationship were mutual, and the pleasure she gave him enhanced the effectiveness of his profession—for the betterment of all.

Lazarus' life might almost be declared perfect, if it were not for Derek Straker and those who followed his example of resistance. The man was stubborn, unlikely to change his mind. Yet Lazarus was forbidden to use Level Three techniques on him, or those who'd served as his companion, despite the demonstrated effectiveness of those procedures.

The camp's Guiding Committee had insisted that the mechsuiters must not be broken, for a broken tool was of no use. But they had said nothing about the woman, Engels... and he really only needed one mechsuiter, not two. That meant Paloco was also expendable.

Inquisitors had wide latitude. He could count on being forgiven a deviation from orders if his irregularity yielded the required effect.

Of course, if he failed, the need for resurrection might become all too real. He wondered what another Inquisitor, another Lazarus, might think of Tachina, and vice versa. No doubt the man would bless his good fortune.

For his concubine, of course, little would change.

Tachina shifted her hands downward, sliding them under his belt. "You seem tense, my love."

"That is so," he replied, tempted.

"Let me give you relief." Her hands slid lower.

Lazarus felt his body respond. He almost pushed her away, realizing that this interlude represented a form of procrastination, putting off the dangerous step he was contemplating.

Abruptly, he yielded—deciding he could afford a few minutes.

"We must be quick, my pet," he said as he turned to face her.

Tachina's lips pouted. "I want all of you," she said. "Promise you will make love to me tonight. Perhaps we can share wine?"

She favored wine, and it was difficult to procure in the camps, even for an Inquisitor. "Perhaps," he said, "if you please me now."

As her response, she began her work, and he stifled a gasp.

She was right, Lazarus thought when he departed at last. He did feel better. More relaxed. He was ready to take his gamble, to give Straker one last try.

＊ ＊ ＊

When the mob of guards entered his room, Straker was again hauled down the concrete corridors. He didn't fight them immediately, conserving his strength. He felt strong today, much better than he had lately. Maybe the injection was beginning to work.

They took him to a new room, one he'd never seen before. Wide and shallow, it had three thick, crystal windows opening on three well-lit rooms, empty except for one occupant each.

In the rightmost chamber, Loco stood naked and turned away from the window. His skin looked blue-green. Perhaps it was the lighting.

In the left, Engels was also nude, but stood proudly facing the window. He found himself getting aroused, and then angry. Some kind of stress response, he figured—sex and danger. Her skin also had that odd hue...

In the center room, some kind of alien paced back and forth on all fours. Twice the mass of a human, it seemed reptilian, but moved like a cat, its barbed tail lashing. Doors in its chamber led to the rooms with Loco and Engels. It sniffed at one door, and then crossed the room to nose at the other.

"Magnificent animal, don't you think?" said Lazarus from behind Straker.

"What is it?"

"You don't recognize Miss Engels?"

"You're a funny man, Lazarus, but much too hopeful. After all you've put me through, you think murdering my friends will impress me?"

In the face of losing two prizes for certain, Lazarus was perfectly willing to sacrifice the lesser for a last hope to redeem the greater—for the good of the Mutuality. It was time to get creative. He wasn't exactly going to use Level Three methods, and he now considered his options all but exhausted.

His voice turned pensive as he stepped up beside Straker. Two big guards, armored and helmeted, stayed close behind, their activated shock-prods crackling threats. "I think we're beyond that phase, Captain Straker. I told you I was about to cut my losses. This is my final gambit."

"You're going to threaten my friends unless I cooperate."

Lazarus spread his hands. "At least I'm honest about our system. It's harsh, but necessary. We have no room for sentimentality. If you want friendship, Straker, if you want a chance at the love you won't even admit you hold for Miss Engels, you'll have to act. Be the bigger man. Join us and save your friends! Sacrifice your ego for them, even if you won't do it for yourself."

"You're mistaking my principles for ego, you piece of shit."

"And you're mistaking your ego for principles, Mister Straker. Politeness costs nothing, and I address you with respect, but you keep insulting me. Who's the piece of shit really, hmm?"

Straker almost apologized, until he realized that even this approach was a tactic, a manipulation. Lazarus was trying to reclaim a moral high ground he'd long since abdicated, as if merely being polite made up for all the abuse.

"Get on with it then," Straker said. He calmed himself, taking deep breaths. Whatever the Inquisitor had in store, it wouldn't be pleasant.

"My gambit is simple. There are two buttons in front of you. Each opens its corresponding portal to the left or the right of the Kort, that predator that paces between them. When the door opens… well, the Kort is hungry. It will feed."

A chill settled across Straker. "So simple?"

"The best techniques always are."

"I won't push a button. I won't play your sick game."

Lazarus flipped a switch on the console in front of them, and the two buttons began flashing alternately, one off, one on, switching quickly. After a moment, Straker could see the rhythm slowing slightly.

"Eventually," Lazarus said, "the randomizing mechanism will settle on one of these two buttons. When it does, that door will open, linking the Kort with one room or the other. Then, less than a minute later, the other door will also open. So you see, if you don't make a choice both will die." Lazarus paused. "Remember, Captain Straker, this situation is of your own making. It may not be your fault, but now it's your responsibility. You can end it at any moment. There's no other way out."

"I think you've finally done it," Straker said, turning to face the beaming Inquisitor. He took a step forward, shaking his lowered head in defeat.

At his second step, the guards frowned and lifted their hands—but it was too late.

Straker exploded in a burst of phenomenal speed, slamming an elbow into Lazarus' confident chest to incapacitate him. He continued his turning motion to disarm the nearest guard, who was already striking with his shock-prod. Straker deftly took the weapon and rotated it until he could jam its blazing tip into the second guard's eye socket—his face the only vulnerable area.

The second guard folded in agony. Straker ripped the prod from his eye-socket and hammered the first man across the jaw with the butt of the weapon, hearing bone crack as he fell.

When it was over, Straker picked up the gasping Lazarus and held the prod's crackling tip near the Inquisitor's eye.

"The injections," Lazarus coughed. "We underestimated the effects... such a fine specimen. It's a pity that you now must be put down."

"Stop the mechanism," Straker demanded.

"I can't."

Straker slapped at the switch Lazarus had thrown, but nothing happened. The alternating pulse of the lights continued unabated, slowing toward the inevitable end.

"I'll kill you if you don't."

Lazarus showed no fear. "It's deliberately designed to be unbeatable. Once it starts, it can't be stopped."

"No chance?"

"None, Captain Straker."

"Then I guess I don't need you anymore." Straker punched Lazarus in the gut. As the Inquisitor bent over, Straker wrapped his right arm around the man's neck, locked it with his left, and heaved upward with all his strength.

Breaking a man's neck with strength alone is a difficult feat, but it can be done. Straker did it.

Lazarus' vertebrae came apart with snapping crunches. His feet twitched and jerked against the floor. A feeling of deep, righteous satisfaction coursed through Straker's veins.

He dropped the body, and then seized a baton and slammed it into one of the crystal windows. The material didn't dent, crack, or flex.

Growling, Straker leapt for a door to the left and threw it open. On the other side, a surprised pair of guards hesitated too long. Straker hammered his prod through their open faceplates, leaving them broken on the deck. Then he hit the electronic opener for the door in front of him, one that should lead to Engels's room.

Nothing happened. There was a code pad, and he'd knocked out the guards... and Lazarus wasn't alive anymore. Straker cursed himself for a fool and grabbed another shock-prod.

Running back through the control room, he noticed the seesaw of lights was almost at a stop. In seconds, one of his friends would die, and quickly after, the other.

Roaring with frustration and rage, he opened the other door, the one that led to Loco's antechamber, in hopes it was also guarded.

It was, and they were waiting for him.

It didn't matter. Straker went through them like a hot wire through wax. He'd been bred with speed and reflexes. Now, with the biotech Lazarus had given, him he had even greater physical powers.

For a while at least, he reminded himself. Until he became a Hok zombie.

Straker refused to worry about that now.

Only the fact he had to avoid knocking one guard out caused him to take an electric strike to his thigh. "What's the code!" he yelled at the man he held immobilized, spittle flying from his mouth. "Tell me or die!"

The man told him.

Holding the guard in a headlock, Straker tapped in the code. The door opened, revealing a surprised Loco.

"Get out of the room and shut the door!" Straker barked at Loco, launching his captive past Loco to bounce off the portal to the Kort's room.

Loco scrambled to escape, but they were too late to thwart the selecting mechanism. The alternating light had come to rest—on Loco's side.

Straker gasped with relief. A coin flip had saved Engels's life—for now.

The door flew wide, providing the predator access to the chamber they were in, and the Kort leaped into the room. There, it found a meal waiting on the floor. Its claws were barely slowed by the guard's armor.

A spray of gore washed the room and they closed the door quickly.

"Thanks," Loco said from beside him, staring through the thick window. Then he noticed the woman in the other room. "Is that Carly? She's looking tasty."

Straker slapped his friend on the back of the head. "Stop thinking with your dick and help me get her out of there."

"I meant for the cat thing—not me."

Straker wasn't amused, and he had no patience to continue the exchange. He breathed in deep puffs as he strode back into the first guardroom and punched in the code he'd used on the other door. He let out a relieved sigh when it opened. They hadn't bothered to create two codes.

Engels turned to the two men in surprise and, after a moment, tried to cover her nudity with her hands. "Derek...?"

"No time." He seized her, dragging her out of the room.

"Dammit, Derek, don't–"

The door behind her opened, and all three turned to look through it into the far chamber. The Kort raised its bloody face from its meal to stare at them. In a determined fashion, it began to move in their direction, never taking its odd eyes from them.

"Oh shit," said Loco. "Shut that door!"

Straker slapped the button to close the portal even as the Kort leapt. It slammed into the closed door from the other side.

Klaxons sounded then. The prison was finally being alerted that something was amiss, no doubt because of the violence here in these rooms.

"Now what?" Engels asked.

"Get shock prods and use them," Straker ordered "We have to fight our way out."

They picked up two prods each. "We need to put on the guards' uniforms," Engels said.

Loco grinned. "I'm okay with Carla being naked."

Straker slapped the back of Loco's head again.

"Be a pig in your birthday suit if you want. I need something to wear," Engels said, running into the control room. "Um... Derek?"

"Yeah?" Straker followed her into the room.

She was staring at Lazarus' twisted body, her nudity forgotten. "This is not good."

All the feelings surrounding Skorza's death at Academy came back to the surface. She was scolding him again. How could she not understand?

"He was evil," he said. "He deserved it."

"But now who's going to tell us where the antidote to the Hok biotech is?"

"Somebody will."

Engels began stripping Lazarus' body of its fine silk suit, putting on the trousers and shirt. "Fits all right, with the belt," she said, her back to the two men. "We need to hole up here and wait."

"We can't hole up here! We have to escape," Straker said urgently. Sirens continued to sound. "The longer we sit here, the more likely they'll come with overwhelming force and stunners."

Straker set the door leading into the interrogation area to stay locked, though the staff could probably override it. "Strip these guards, and everybody put on as much armor as you can." He cracked one man on the skull as he began to stir.

"We really should kill these guys," Loco said. "What if we're holding here and they wake up and take us out?"

"No more murders!" Engels said. "Why are you so bloodthirsty?"

"How can you be so *not*?" retorted Loco. "Did you forget the torture?"

"Of course not," she admitted. "But they followed their own code, more or less. They had their reasons for doing what they did. There's a war on. We don't need to be as bad as them. They're not our teachers."

"You're starting to sympathize with them, just like Lazarus said you would," Straker said, pulling on armor and trying to find a helmet that fit. "There's no excuse for torturing us. The ends don't justify the means."

"Oh, really?" Engels asked, staring at him. "That's not what you said when you killed Skorza, and you just said Lazarus deserved it, too. You could have knocked him out or wounded him instead."

Straker ground his teeth, not knowing how to answer her infuriating words. She didn't understand. She'd never been faced with a ticking chrono and a Kort ready to eat her friends.

Things seemed so clear to him when he was in combat. Thinking about them later got tangled—or when Engels started talking. Everything was so much simpler without her... but the thought of a future without Carla just felt despairing.

"Forget it," Engels said. "Let's go."

They grabbed the stunners and Straker led the charge into the corridors.

Chapter 19

Facility Alpha Six, final day.

What was usually an obsessively ordered prison had swallowed a dose of chaos, like an anthill stirred with a stick. Guards scurried through the passageways, many half-asleep and half-dressed.

The real surprise came when Straker found many of them slumped in the hallways unconscious. He couldn't figure that out. Had they accidentally released some kind of riot-suppression gas that had hit their own people?

In any case, it made things easier. There were guards still emerging from every corner of the compound, but alarm couldn't overcome their confusion and grogginess. As it was the middle of the night, the guards not on shift were still half asleep. It all worked in the escaping prisoners' favor.

Straker knocked out the first guard he found who carried a lethal weapon, a slugthrower handgun that wouldn't have been out of place on Old Earth, though the date stamped upon it was from no more than twenty years ago. After that, he concentrated on opening doors and arming more inmates.

Many of the prisoners resisted being freed, cowering in their cells. "They'll come back for me!" some said. "I'm almost rehabilitated!" said others. A few even cursed him for not being Mutual—ruining their chances to gain new futures.

Straker pitied them. No one deserved freedom if they didn't have the balls to seize it. "Leave them with their cell doors open," he ordered. Maybe they would find their courage.

Gathering a force of those willing to fight, mostly from POWs of the Hundred Worlds, Straker ordered the complex cleaned out entirely. Guards who resisted were shot down mercilessly. Those who surrendered, he dressed up in prison garb.

"What do we do now, sir?" asked Heiser, the big militia sergeant from Corinth. He peered out one of the barred windows and aimed his laser carbine, looking through its scope. Bright floodlights shone back at them. A slug pinged off the concrete wall. "Hok troops are holding the perimeter. They have us trapped."

"Only if we're afraid to take a few casualties," replied Straker. "It's been less than an hour since we took over this place. I haven't seen reinforcements, but they're coming. There are over a hundred of us with weapons, and maybe twenty Hok and guards. All we have to do is rush them and get into the jungle. But we have to do it soon, before others arrive."

"And go where, boss?" said Loco. "I mean, I'm all for breaking out, but what then?"

"There's a big spaceport fifteen kilometers north," said Borda, a local truck driver. She was older, with rough skin and bad teeth. The kitchen knife she carried had blood on it. "They have sidespace-capable ships."

"They'll expect us to go there," Heiser said.

"He's right," said Lancaster. He was a Mutualist historian being held for re-education. His crime had been to write a textbook that was true to his research instead of slanted the way the Committee wanted. "They'll be waiting with more Hok. We should scatter into the jungle and try to hide in the population."

"That's all very well for you locals," Engels said, "but for us foreigners, our accents will give us away, and we have no contacts, nobody to get us fake Equality cards."

"She's right," said Straker. "Our only chance is the spaceport, but fifteen kilometers on foot is suicide. Heiser, pick twenty people. Make sure you get drivers like Borda here, who know the area. When we rush the gate, you split off and take the motor pool."

"Roger wilco, sir," said Heiser.

"Derek, we got one more problem," said Loco.

"What?"

"We need the antidote... Unless you want to be a Hok."

"Shit, I forgot. Any medics here?"

A man and a woman raised their hands.

"We have to find the antidote to the Hok injections," he told them. "We've been treated, and we're already transforming."

They slowly backed away from him in alarm, but he ignored that insult.

"Find the antidote and we'll bring it along. Heiser, detail off two infantrymen to escort them. The rest of you, come with me. Bring the unwounded guards. We'll attack in one minute."

At the front entrance to the prison building, Straker spoke to the guards dressed in prison fatigues. "You're going first, straight toward the main gate. If you make it into the jungle, you live."

"Yes, but... the autocannons..."

"You have to get past them. Otherwise," he held his handgun to one man's head, "your dead anyway. Understand?"

The guard nodded vigorously. A stain at his crotch spread as he shook with fear. Straker spared him no sympathy and gave him a hard shove instead.

"Heiser," Straker said. "Get some shooters to the windows. When we go, give us cover fire, and then follow us up and get those vehicles."

He found a powered shield in the riot-gear lockers, picked it up and turned it on. The glow was bright blue around the edges, and a gleaming nimbus covered his hand where he held it. Taking a breath, he readied his slugthrower pistol in his other hand and lifted it overhead.

"For the Hundred Worlds!" he roared, and drove the guards stumbling out of the doorway.

The first surge of captive guards was slaughtered as they exited the building, absorbing the fire of their unwitting brethren and the autocannons that defended the gate. The rest scattered in all directions, some for the exit, others trying to get out of the line of fire around the back of the headquarters. It really didn't matter. His trick had done its job.

Slugs slammed into Straker's shield as he sprinted toward the main gate. He fired in the direction of the floodlights, hitting one and knocking it out. He heard the yelling of his fellows behind him as they followed. The whine of lasers and the bark of slugthrowers were punctuated by the cries and screams of the wounded.

His shield hadn't been built for military action, but it held up well. The autocannons slammed their bullets into it, but they were repelled all the same. Dented and flickering, the reinforced slab of armor kept him alive.

Had most of the guards and Hok not been knocked out inside the cell blocks, this would never have worked, but there weren't many left to try to hold back the inmates, escaping in the chaos. Only a handful of prisoners had lethal weapons, but as soon as the mob got close enough, their many stunners came into play and they pummeled the remaining enemy forces into unconsciousness, and then finished them off.

One Hok with a heavy slugthrower held out in a tower, sniping prisoners with grim efficiency. Straker threw down his shield and climbed the ladder. He leaped over the railing only to find the soldier ready for him.

The Hok's weapon boomed, and Straker twisted desperately aside with shocking speed. But it wasn't enough to save him completely. The bullet tore through his arm.

Before he could feel the pain, Straker's pistol spoke three times, blowing his enemy back over the railing to fall dead on the ground. He grabbed the Hok's dropped slugthrower for himself, holstering the pistol and hurrying down the tower. There, he relieved the Hok of his reloads.

When it was over, more than twenty escapees lay dead, and as many guards.

"Patch up our people as best you can," Straker ordered. "Including me. Where's my transport?"

Loco pointed as a motley assortment of low-tech trucks and groundcars roared out of the motor pool and pulled up at the gate. Borda smiled a gap-toothed grin from the open window of the biggest vehicle, a five-ton cargo rig. "Load up, load up!" she cried.

"You heard the lady, load up!" Straker bellowed. Loco, Engels and Heiser chivvied after the rest until they were on the transports.

The medics ran out of the main prison building, cases clutched in their hands. "We found the antidote," the man said.

"Sir, take five—let me clean you up," a medic called out to him.

Straker looked at his arm and tried to move it, but it had no strength. Now that the adrenaline of combat was wearing off, the pain hit him. His wound sent a sudden wash of agony through him, and he swayed on his feet. "Patch me up on the way," he said.

"Do you humans mind if I tag along?" Straker heard in an oddly formal accent.

He turned to face the voice, the muzzle of his weapon tracking to point at a… He froze, which was the only way to keep himself from firing in reflex. "You're a Ruxin."

"Self-evidently," the creature said.

He? She? It?—Straker decided to use *he* until he found out otherwise. The creature stood on eight boneless limbs, tentacles really, rising to about the height of a short man, looking like nothing so much as a human-sized walking octopus. A *walktopus*, he'd heard aliens like it nicknamed.

"The Mutuality is wonderfully indiscriminate in its attempts at rehabilitation," the alien said. "They allow those of all races and species to enjoy their hospitality. I do thank you for helping me free everyone."

"I didn't even know you were in the prison with us."

"I was with Admiral Braga at Corinth, but we had to abandon ship and they captured me. They kept me in solitary confinement. It was most disturbing."

The alien had rips in its water-suit, and Straker could see the marks of abuse on the alien's mottled skin—scars, possibly bruises. Visible burns emitted a bizarre smell, unmistakably indicating foreign biology. One tentacle seemed to have been severed midway. Another two held a heavy stunner, evidently recovered from a guard.

"An ally is an ally," Straker said.

"I enabled this breakout, did you know that?"

Straker blinked at the alien. Was it actually bragging to him?

"That's right," the creature continued. "It was very clever, given the circumstances. Did you notice that some of the guards were incapacitated?"

"You did that? How…?"

"A difficult task. When I first gained hacking access to their networks, it was due to the fact they had a breakdown in their air conditioning systems. This facility is quite old, you know, and–"

"Could you get to the point?" Straker demanded, losing patience.

Numerous eyes looked him up and down. "Of course... To summarize, they ordered me to help them with technical issues, and I gained some influence over the riot-control systems. I simply reprogrammed the areas of the prison slated to be gassed when the emergency triggers were tripped."

"Ah..." Straker said, pointing a comprehending finger. "You gassed the barracks instead of the prison cells."

"Precisely. It *was* quite clever, you must admit."

Straker hesitated only for a second. Some personalities required a lot of praise. This creature seemed to have that need and yet provided his own adulation.

"Yeah, it was critical," he said. "In fact, it was brilliant."

The creature seemed very pleased. He led Straker onto the armored transport while one fist-sized eye migrated around to its rear, along with the rubbery mouth. "I'm Zaxby."

"Zaxby sounds like a human name."

"Oh, it is. More like an adopted nickname. My name in the Ruxin tongue extends to over one hundred syllables. Most humans simply can't comprehend its majesty, much less reproduce it. What is your name?"

"I'm Straker. Do you always talk this much?" Straker asked as he moved aside to let others load and hurry to the back of the transport.

"Only when I'm nervous, or excited, or interested in something. Or when I'm bored, or tired, or angry, or happy, or–"

"Shut up."

"Why?" Zaxby asked in sudden alarm. His eyes crawled over the landscape. "Are we being observed or overheard? Being quiet seems pointless at this juncture. The gunfire alone makes it moot."

Straker grunted unhappily. "I wish I had a *mute*-button for you. Now shut up and sit down over there! You did a good job in the prison, but I need to think."

Zaxby swarmed over the seat backs toward the rear, not bothering to use the aisle. "Perhaps you should sit down as well," he said. "You look terrible."

Straker growled. "I've been tortured for weeks, I haven't been fed very well, and now I've been shot, so no, I'm not feeling my best. Now for the sake of the holy Cosmos, *leave me the hell alone!*" The lieutenant's large eyes had all swiveled around to stare at the barking soldier.

"Yes, sir."

He was lashing out at Zaxby, and he knew it. His adrenaline was coursing and he was having a hard time controlling his temper. Could it be the transformation Lazarus had initiated? Everything seemed to itch—especially his wounds.

He sat still while the medics treated his injuries as the convoy raced through the night down the jungle road toward the spaceport. The sky was just lightening toward the east, almost dawn.

"The bullet went through cleanly, so I don't think I need to do much," a medic told him as she finished wrapping his arm. "The Hok biotech will prevent infection, and it's already healing you at ten times the normal rate." She opened a medical case and showed him an injector and ampules. "Do you want the antidote now?"

Straker considered it. He'd been injected only yesterday with the bad stuff. He should still have a day or two at least before the mental effects really began to take hold. Until then, the physical benefits might save his life—other lives. "No. Not yet. Give it to anyone else that wants it. I'll let it heal me up some more."

"I'll take it now," said Engels. She eyed Straker as the medic injected her. "Our skin is starting to look like a Hok's. Loco's too."

"It's a small price to pay," he said, "if it gets us to freedom."

"You're taking a big risk," she insisted. "What if we lose the antidote in the next fight? You might get away but turn into one of those *things*."

Straker gave her his 'sincere' face. "Then you'll have a loyal bodyguard."

"I don't want a loyal bodyguard, Derek…"

There was no need for her to finish her thought.

The medic moved down to Loco a couple of seats back.

Straker offered her a rare smile. "So, you want me? About time you said so."

Engels put her head back and stared at the ceiling of the transport. She might've had tears in her eyes or just been pissed off that he was an idiot. "That's not really the response I was looking for."

"Sorry. It's just that we're not safe yet—I still need any edge… Maybe we should talk about this later."

"There might not be a later, Derek."

"All right. Okay. I… I want you too. Yes, I always have. But not like this, in the middle of a fight and with biotech inside us. I can't think about you that way right now. If I do, I might get distracted and let these people down. I have to lead."

She brought her dark eyes down and leveled an emotion-filled stare at him. Even with her hair in ruins, she was suddenly achingly beautiful to him. "I know you do. But you can't put me off forever."

Straker looked away from her piercing gaze. He didn't need the torrent of hormones and confusion that was struggling to surface right now and forced it to stay at bay. Why did women start acting like this, usually at the worst time—in the middle of something urgent. Maybe when they'd fully escaped…

"Roadblock!" called the driver.

Straker leaped forward, trying to see out the front windshield, but the transport wasn't first in line. "Drive around! Try to ram through! Don't slow down for anything!"

The driver cursed and wrenched the wheel to the left onto the narrow shoulder between the road and the jungle greenery, flooring the accelerator. The electric gears shrieked as the armored transport raced past another vehicle, and another.

At the front of the halted convoy, a firefight was in progress. Borda's five-ton had tried to ram. It had halfway broken through a set of concrete barriers, but was now wedged into the gap. Her body hung from the open window. A squad of Hok fired at the convoy from behind cover.

"Ram the back of the five-ton!" Straker yelled. "Push it through! The rest of you open fire!" He opened the transport hatch to let loose a burst of slugs at a Hok, and the trooper fell backward.

When the transport slammed into the cargo rig, the whole mess slid forward and through the gap. Slugs popped and the transport's armored windows starred, but didn't break. Laser bolts sizzled into the vehicle, and Straker heard yells of pain mingled with the cries of battle.

He charged through the open door and climbed awkwardly onto the dead five-ton. Behind the enemy now, he quickly gunned down several Hok troopers that had tried to hold the roadblock. Others overwhelmed the rest of the defending force.

In the near distance he could see the jungle open out, and rising behind it, the shapes of spacecraft. "Come on!" he called. "Load up and follow, now! If that's all they had, we have a chance!" The night had helped them so far, but they had to move fast.

Straker got everyone off the transport except for the driver, who sat behind his crumpled controls, pinned in the wreckage by ramming the five-ton. "Leave me, sir," the man said. "You have to get away and get back home."

"Hell with that," said Straker. He holstered his slugthrower, set himself, and tore free one section of the dashboard, and then another.

"How did you do that?" the injured man asked.

"Biotech." Straker lifted the man into a fireman's carry and loaded him onto a working vehicle in the convoy. This kind of strength reminded him of his affinity to the battlefield—but without the massive hardware. He could get used to this. He wondered if all of it would go away when he was cured.

Straker leaped onto the lead cargo hauler and the reduced convoy roared ahead. A hundred meters later, the road forked as it broke out of the jungle. "Left! Left!" he said. "Head for that freighter!"

"Not that one. It's too slow," said Engels from beside him. She pointed. "That one."

"Do as she says," said Straker.

"Too bad we couldn't have waited for the rescue," she said.

"Rescue?"

"I tried to tell you. I got word there was going to be a prison break from the outside. A resistance group called the Unmutuals is supposed to be on its way."

Anger rose in Straker. "I thought that was all bullshit from Lazarus. So you're saying I should have cooperated?"

Engels shrugged, looking away.

Maybe he should have. Was Lazarus right? Had Straker's ego gotten the best of him? If he'd have cooperated for a few days, maybe these Unmutuals would have broken them out and they'd even now be in sidespace, escaping to some hidden rebel base.

"Maybe you're right," he said, "but it doesn't matter now. Unless you have a way to get in touch with them?"

Engels shook her head. "I have no idea, but somebody might. Get me on the bridge of that ship and we'll see. Worst case, we jump away and find our way back to Hundred Worlds space."

"Agreed."

The convoy pulled up next to the ship Engels had indicated and the prisoners bailed out onto the concrete surface. In the distance they could see flashing lights and scurrying activity.

"This thing's locked!" Loco said from the ship's main hatch.

"Auxiliary hatch, by the canard here," Engels said, running to duck under the ship's belly. "This is a captured Gorman-12C, a fast naval auxiliary. If they don't know about the default code..." She popped the panel cover and tapped the buttons.

The hatch dropped open. Straker pushed her aside and lifted his weapon. "I'll go first."

"Right and up," Engels said. "Get the main door open and the rest inside."

The ship appeared deserted, and within moments Engels had buckled herself behind the helm and powered the ship up.

Something rattled against the hull. "They're shooting at us," Loco said from the operations station. "Small arms so far, but it's only a matter of time before they find a tank."

"That's why I chose a military vessel," replied Engels. "I've got the armor reinforcement fields on, and I've activated the point-defense lasers. Not even a tank should hurt us." She plugged in her brainlink and grabbed the manual controls. "Strap in or lie on the floor, people. This might get bumpy."

Straker buckled himself into the command seat and lay back. A moment later, his eyes tried to roll out of their sockets as heavy acceleration crushed him. He heard Engels grunting in her seat and he rolled his head to look at her. Her face was drawn into a snarl and the tendons stood out on her neck as she screamed defiance at the universe.

She'd never looked lovelier.

The ship shuddered and atmosphere roared against its surface. Straker could see the fusion throttles shoved beyond their safety stops and the impeller gauges redlined.

"Do we really need to push it this hard?" Straker yelled over the noise.

In reply, Engels pointed at the forward sensor display. The green icon in the center must be the Gorman they rode. Four red arrows pointed toward it, two from the right and two from the left.

"Attack ships," she said. "We can't outrun them or outfight them. Our only hope is they don't have shipkillers aboard. If we can outlast them until we reach flatspace, we can jump away."

The noise tapered off to a dull roar as they left atmosphere, but the press of acceleration didn't wane.

"We'll make it past them, but they're going to catch up pretty quick," Engels said. "The problem is, firing straight up our stern the way they are, our engines are vulnerable. I'm running full out, and once they line up I'll jink and evade, but our chances look pretty poor."

"What about those Unmutual rebels?" asked Straker. "Maybe they've transited in already."

"Loco, broadcast in the clear. Try to raise them, or anyone." Engels waggled her controls, and Straker's inner ear wobbled with it.

Loco slipped on a comlink. "Any ship, any ship, this is... shit, what are we?"

"Tell them we're escaping Unmutuals. That should get their attention if they're out there."

"Any ship, any ship, this is Lieutenant Loco of the Escaping Unmutuals. We're in a fast lifter and have four attack craft on our asses. We need help. Please respond."

"Set that to repeat," said Engels.

"Can I do anything?" Straker asked her.

"No. Lie there and rest, and let me do my job, Derek. Our point-defense lasers are on autofire. Those are our only weapons, but I doubt the attack ships will get close enough to bring them into play."

Straker watched as the red icons fell back slower and slower, and then the range stabilized... and began to close.

"They've broken atmo." Engels tapped the display. "They haven't fired shipkillers, which is a clear sign they don't have them. They're single-pilot models, so they can't board us. They'll either have railguns or heavy beams as their primary centerline weapons. I'm guessing railguns, as they haven't begun firing."

"That's good, right?" asked Loco. "Railguns have shorter range."

"Against maneuvering targets yes, but they hit harder. Against fixed targets, their range is as far as a penetrator will travel. They'll have small lasers as secondary weapons."

"How long until we're in railgun range?" asked Straker.

Engels looked over at Loco. "Ops officer?"

"Hey, I barely know how to work this board and you want me to calculate tactical in three dimensions?"

"You'd better figure it out," she replied.

"Perhaps I may be of assistance?"

Straker turned to see the Ruxin, Zaxby, flow across the deck. The heavy acceleration kept the boneless octopoid from standing upright.

"If you could reduce thrust for just long enough to exchange seats," he said, "I believe I can perform operations officer duties with superb efficiency."

"You have six seconds, starting... now." Engels cut the engines, continuing acceleration on impellers alone, and exaggerated her evasive maneuvers.

Loco rolled out of his seat and lay on the deck while Zaxby replaced him and plugged in his brainlink. His tentacles danced over the controls. "You may apply thrust again."

Engels shoved the throttles forward to maximum.

"In answer to your question," Zaxby said, "their hit probability against this ship will rise above ten percent per shot in approximately nineteen minutes. Soon after that, they will close to optimum range and achieve above thirty percent per shot. I calculate it will take an average of seven strikes before at least one of our two engines is damaged."

"Oh, shit. You're a brainiac, aren't you?" asked Loco.

"The proper term is Enhanced Special Mental, I believe—but technically, no. I have no genetic enhancements, but many of my people lean naturally toward intellectual pursuits. In fact–"

"He's a brainiac all right," Loco said. "They always talk too much and have to prove how smart they are."

"You talk too much too, Loco," said Engels.

"Yeah, but I'm hilarious."

"All of you, stick to your business," snapped Straker. "Zaxby, we're glad to have your skills, but we're not brainiacs, so simplify and summarize for us. How long until we lose our engines?"

"Simply put," Zaxby said heavily, "I can only give you probabilities. A lucky hit will reduce the time, or perhaps we will beat the odds. Then again–"

"*Give me an estimate!*"

"Approximately twenty-seven minutes, plus or minus three."

"Finally, a straight answer," Loco laughed.

"Is that transmission still going out?" Straker asked.

"Affirmative," replied Zaxby. "I am activating all sensors and widening the transmission to extend into more electromagnetic bands."

Long minutes passed as the range closed.

"They're firing," said Zaxby in a remarkably calm voice.

Engels immediately increased her evasive maneuvers. "This will slow us down, but it's better than being hit."

"How long until flatspace?" asked Straker.

Zaxby answered the question. "Two hours, four minutes and twelve seconds."

"You sure?" Loco asked.

"Very sure," Zaxby said.

"Because, you know, I wouldn't want it to be two hours, four minutes and *thirteen* seconds."

Zaxby's swiveled two of his four eyes to Loco. "You are an annoying being."

"Yeah well, if anyone was qualified to say so, it would be you, squidly."

"I am a full lieutenant in the Fleet Arm of the Hundred Worlds, and I resent being compared to a squid. Shall I liken you to a simple primate?"

"Would you two shut the hell up?" cried Engels as she worked her controls.

"They're firing again," Zaxby said. The ship shuddered with an impact. "Hull strike, negligible damage."

"I thought you said it would be almost a half hour until they hit us!" snarled Straker.

"I gave you the probabilities. Even my vast analytical capacity cannot exactly calculate future outcomes with so many variables involved."

Over the next ten minutes, four more shots hit their ship.

The fifth changed the game.

The acceleration dropped by almost half. "Crap! We've lost an engine." Engels turned to Straker. "We're not going to make it."

Chapter 20

Enemy space, over Yorinda.

The four attack ships moved in closer as the struggling transport continued to evade wildly. Engels expertly plied her controls and Zaxby fired point-defense lasers at extreme range in order to complicate their enemies' targeting, but eventually the inevitable happened.

The ship rocked, and the rumble of acceleration died. "Last engine down. We're on impellers alone now," said Engels. "They can pick us apart if they want to."

"I am receiving an audio transmission," said Zaxby.

"Put it on," said Straker.

"*Stolen lifter, this is Echo lead. Reverse your course to land on Yorinda or we will continue firing.*"

"That must be the name of that planet we were on," said Engels.

"Don't answer," said Straker. "Keep going. Do we still have hull reinforcement?"

Engels nodded. "Yes, our armor should hold for a while. This is a naval ship, not a civilian model, thank Cosmos."

"Will it hold long enough?"

"No," Zaxby said.

"What, no precise probabilities?" said Loco.

The Ruxin's many eyes narrowed to slits. "The probability of crippling us sufficiently to take us in tow prior to our earliest transit point exceeds the ninety-ninth percentile. I thought you'd like the situation to be summarized."

The ship shook with another strike, then another. "Five more minutes of this and we're going to start losing systems," said Engels. "Ten minutes and we'll be in bad trouble."

"I have something new on sensors…" Zaxby said, swinging all four eyes to examine displays. "An inbound contact ahead of us. It appears to be a frigate."

"Shit. We're done," Loco groaned.

"The frigate is moving toward us at flank acceleration."

Straker sat up in his chair to stare at the tactical screen. "How long until it's in range?"

Zaxby replied, "As I've repeatedly tried to explain, that depends on many factors. There's–"

"Twelve minutes," interrupted Engels, "maybe ten, if its weapons suite is similar to most warships that size. That's not counting shipkiller missiles, of course, which they could fire any time. Why? We can't outrun it."

"I don't want to outrun it. Head straight for it."

Engels complied. "You think it's the Unmutuals?"

"I don't have to think. If it's not, it won't matter. If it is, it's our only chance."

"Transmission incoming, tightbeam, unencrypted," said Zaxby. "Patching in."

"*Escaping Unmutuals, this is the Unmutual frigate Carson. Hang in there. We'll take care of these hornets.*"

A cheer echoed throughout the Gorman, audible via the open door to the bridge. Straker found himself shaking his one good fist in the air.

"Woohoo! Come kick their asses!" Loco cried.

"Missile launches detected," said Zaxby. "Two shipkillers. If this frigate has standard weaponry, that constitutes one salvo. Two more now…" He waved a tentacle at the tactical screen. Two sets of two bright yellow icons separated from the frigate and sped toward the transport and its harassing attack ships.

"The attack ships are running!" said Engels.

What she said was true. The four attack ships accelerated at maximum in a starburst of shallow curves, preserving their momentum while turning away and looping back toward the planet Yorinda.

Straker dropped his head against the seat rest in relief, feeling a sudden exhaustion come over him as his adrenaline levels fell. Though bolstered by the Hok biotech, his body had been through hell. Underfed and tortured, deprived of rest and of hope, and now wounded, he felt as if he could sleep for a week.

Straker awoke from dozing when the hull clanged.

"What's happening?" he said, forcing himself to sit up.

"We're docked," Engels said. She shut down her controls and unplugged. "They've got us now, and they're hauling us back toward flatspace. I sure hope these Unmutuals are better than the assholes we just escaped from."

"They could hardly be worse," Straker said.

"On the contrary, there is no reason they should be less immoral," Zaxby said. "For example, they might be cannibals."

"Cannibals?" Loco demanded. "Where the hell do you get this stuff?"

"I am merely envisioning the worst possibility I can think of. Hopefully, we shall be less disappointed."

"Let's find out," Straker said, standing and heading toward the docking hatch.

"I shall remain on the bridge," Zaxby said. "One never knows how new humans will react when seeing one of my species."

"I know how I'd react," Loco said. "Hot oil and tartar sauce."

"Shut up, Loco," Engels said. "He's a damn good bridge officer and kinda cute."

"Kinda cute? Hmm..." Loco raised his eyebrows.

"Why do I always get the feeling you're thinking something sexual?" she asked as she followed Straker.

"Because I am?"

Straker reached the airlock, where Heiser and several other armed troops waited. "Lower your weapons, but stand ready," he said. "These people drove off the attack ships, but you never know."

When the hatches opened and the pressure between the two ships stabilized, a big woman in combat gear stepped though, blaster carbine in one hand. Her brown hair was short under her helmet. Shaded by the visor, her face was pockmarked, and her expression was unpleasantly suspicious.

"Who's in charge here?" she barked.

"I am," Straker responded. "Derek Straker, Assault Captain, Hundred Worlds armed forces."

The woman grunted. "Hundred Worlds, eh? I'm Major Ramirez, Unmutuals. I'm in charge now, got that? You have no rank unless my boss gives you one. You're just a bunch of rookies as far as I'm concerned."

Straker engaged the safety on his slugthrower and dropped it. Before it hit the deck, he snatched the woman's carbine from her hand and pointed it at her. She stared in shock.

"We're more than novices, Major. Most of us are military. We're thankful for the rescue, but I for one am tired of being treated like shit, and so are my people. I won't tolerate it."

The woman quickly got over her surprise. "You'll do what you're told or we'll blow you off our hull and leave you floating in space."

Straker smirked. "I don't think you will. You got word to the prison that you were coming to our rescue, and you traveled all the way from somewhere in this fine warship just to liberate us. I have to wonder why, out of all the many facilities in the thousand worlds of the Mutuality, you came to this rock."

The major put her hands on her ample hips. "Because I was ordered to, that's why. And if you know what's good for you, you'll follow orders too."

"I'm happy to follow sensible orders from an officer I respect, Major, but I don't know you and I don't know your organization." He glanced at Engels. "We still have sidespace capability, right?"

"Affirmative," said Engels. "Now that we're not under attack, we can use impellers to maneuver to a transit point and jump away."

Straker nodded. "Get back to the bridge and prepare to jump."

Ramirez stared at Straker. "You can't jump while docked!"

"We'll blow ourselves clear if we have to."

"You'll kill yourselves."

"And you too, if you stay aboard," Straker promised. "Feel free to leave."

"You're crazy, you know that?"

"It's been said."

The two stared each other down. Finally, Ramirez sighed. "Fine. I'll respect your ranks until General DeChang decides what to do with you. But I'm still senior."

"It's your ship, it's your rescue. You're in charge, and we'll follow your orders as long as they make sense. But listen to this: we didn't escape from one prison just to be put into another."

"Fair enough."

"And," he added, "we'll keep our weapons."

Ramirez shook her head. "No. We can't have a bunch of unknown people possibly damaging vital systems."

"I'll direct my troops to unload their guns, but we're not giving them up." Straker shrugged. "Call the captain if you need to."

"Why do you think I'm not the captain?"

"Because you're obviously a ground-pounder, like me. This ship has a captain, and it's not you."

Ramirez sighed. "You're a pain in the ass, you know that?"

"That's also been said before. Make the call."

"I don't need to. You can keep your weapons. But you're vouching for your people. If anyone gets out of line, I'm holding you responsible."

"Agreed." He held out his hand.

Ramirez looked at it as if it were a snake. "Save your charm, Straker. Get your people moving." She held out her hand for her carbine. When Straker passed it back, she turned on her heel and stalked onto the frigate.

Straker called for his people to file through the docking port after unloading their weapons. After Loco, Zaxby and Engels entered, he followed in last place, alert for treachery, but it didn't materialize.

* * *

The Unmutuals were wary, but not as unfriendly as Ramirez had been. Some even laughed and joked. The line of the rescued debouched into a bay full of bunks stacked four high, barely roomy enough to cram their bodies into.

"Where are we going?" Heiser asked one open-faced young man called Karst.

"A base of ours. Everything will be explained there. Don't worry. You're all valuable military personnel and will be treated well. We won't discard any of you. Now, strap in."

The Unmutuals rustled the former prisoners into bunks and helped them pull sleep webbing in place. "Sorry, this is the best we can do right now," said Karst as he assisted Engels. "With you people aboard, we're carrying at triple capacity for this run, so it's going to get cozy. The webbing is because we'll be saving grav power where we can."

"How long is the trip?"

"Three days in sidespace. A couple hours maneuvering after transit. Don't worry."

"I'm not *worried*. I'm a pilot, a damn good one, and I like to know where I'm going. What's the captain's name?"

"Captain Gray."

Engels nodded, wishing she were in the cockpit rather than strapped down as cargo. "Thanks. I'd like to talk to him sometime."

"Her. Captain Ellen Gray. She's ironclad." The kid moved on to help the next person.

Where did she get off calling a guy maybe twenty years old a kid? But he did seem young. He didn't have the war-weary aspect of a veteran.

Engels closed her eyes as they flew toward the transit point, trying to process all that had happened up until now. Suddenly relieved of the oppression of prison, she felt as if her mind had become unmoored, like a ship's boat not properly cinched down. Maybe she was just coming down from the Hok poison in her bloodstream.

All her life she'd known what to do, but with this latest disruption, everything had become loose, unpredictable. Was the venom interfering with her in a new way, or was this just the aftermath of extreme duress?

Either way, this new reality had its benefits. The comfortable boundaries had been stripped away. Without any rules or conventions to prevent it, and finally out of prison, Derek could be hers.

Why was her mind going *there* when they hadn't even arrived at their destination, whatever it was? Probably because she felt a measure of safety for the first time since the battle for Corinth.

Freed of constraints, her mind and heart seemed to be running wild. She racked her brain for a reason and remembered a class long ago at Academy Station. The subject had been combat effectiveness and how to maintain it, long-term.

She'd asked why people actually needed R&R—*needed*, not wanted. In her teen years, after all, her energy had seemed limitless, and she'd had no concept of combat fatigue or the frictions of war and their effect on personnel.

The tidbit relevant to her thoughts now had been the ideas of biological release, reproduction, and life-affirmation. Even if combatants didn't actually intend to have children together, their bodies didn't know that. Post-battle, their sex drives would flare up.

That was why they were sent for R&R after every major operation. Otherwise, military personnel would tend to turn to each other for comfort. The rulebook said that might result in unsanctioned bondings, even fraternization, which might undermine discipline.

It had all made perfect sense at the time, and she realized it made sense now. After this horrible experience, her libido was driving her toward him in accordance with her previous tendencies, and his was doing the same.

That meant it was a chemical urge, meaningless animal lust. It wouldn't last, not without more than release from shared misery as a foundation… and she found she wanted more.

That's what she told herself anyway, to rationalize her current state of mind, because if she didn't, she might lose control and do something she would regret. It was so much easier to get into a relationship than out of one. And she didn't want to let that part of her life blossom without some prospect of stability and security.

When the Unmutual soldiers had finished with their passengers and had withdrawn from the crowded berthing spaces, a klaxon sounded, accompanied by an automated voice: *"Sidespace warning. All personnel prepare. Sidespace warning…"*

She felt a twisting, and the ship seemed to stretch. Sidespace engines required a flat space-time curve, which in practical terms mean getting well away from anything that created significant gravity—planets, moons, and stellar bodies.

Then all became smooth. The liberated humans—and one Ruxin— cheered.

They'd made their escape.

Once transitioned, sidespace travel felt no different from normal-space travel. With little else to pass the time, those who did not sleep began to talk.

"Carla," she heard Straker say from the bunk above her. His words barely carried over the faint thrumming of the drive.

"Yeah."

"What exactly did you know about the Unmutual rescue before it happened?"

"I had intel there would be a raid. Nothing detailed. Just that there would be an attempt, and approximately when."

"That's why you tried so hard to get me to confess, right? So we could be together, ready to break out?"

"Of course. I kept trying to tell you, but you weren't hearing me. What did you think? That I *wanted* you to betray your bullheaded principles for no reason?"

Straker remained silent. "Not exactly. Only that maybe…"

"Maybe I'd gone soft? That I was joining them?"

"Never mind. Forget I asked."

"You know what's wrong with you, Derek? You believe anyone that doesn't think exactly like you is wrong. That they're… *unrighteous*."

"If I didn't believe I was right and righteous, why would I believe anything?"

"This isn't about what you believe. It's about trusting your friends, your comrades."

"I trust you!"

"Doesn't feel like it."

Straker released an audible sigh. "I didn't think you were turning against us, Carla, just that maybe you were worn down beyond your ability to stand it. That wouldn't be your fault. You can't be blamed for that."

"You set the bar too high for yourself, Derek. What makes you think you're so much better than we are?"

"I *am* better than most people, in the talents and skills I've been given. I have to use them for something good."

"Okay, how? We may not find our way back to the Hundred Worlds, and even if we do…"

Straker rolled to look over the edge of the bunk at her. "We probably shouldn't even try to look at things the same way again. Lazarus lied a lot, but some of the things he said made me think. Such as, why didn't our own leaders tell us the Hok were bioteched humans, and that there were more humans on the other side?"

Engels grimaced. "I feel like they didn't trust us. They sure didn't trust us to have a relationship outside of work. You may not want to hear this, but I'm not so sure I want to go back, even if we can."

"How can we not go back?" Straker said, but quietly.

She believed that she saw uncertainty in his eyes, and it heartened her. She'd been worried that he would never be swayed from the idea of returning to his life of glory as a mechsuiter.

"You're all about duty and honor, Derek. You'll have to decide where your duty lies, to a government that didn't really respect us—that deceived us about the truth. Or…"

"My duty is to the people of the Hundred Worlds, not to its government."

"I agree. So the question is, how can we best serve them? Maybe we can do more good out here, with these Unmutuals, as a thorn in the side of the enemies of the Hundred Worlds. That way we do our duty and keep our freedom too."

Silence met her words at first. But then he spoke again thoughtfully. "I think I can accept that. I need everyone with me, though. Otherwise, I get the feeling these Unmutuals will simply plug us into their organization and use us for their own purposes."

"We're with you, Derek. Me and Loco, and I'm sure most of the others from the prison will stick with you, too. What's your plan?"

Straker snorted. "Can't call my thoughts a plan exactly. More like an intention to figure out everything that's been going on and not let others dictate our actions. Everyone's got an agenda, and everyone wants to use us. Well, I'm tired of being used."

Engels smiled. "Okay. You're the assault captain."

Straker paused and stared. "I've been meaning to talk to you about that. You've been doing what I say. Yet, you outrank me. In fact, you're actually the highest-ranking officer in our group. You should take charge now."

"No," she said firmly. "You're the natural commander among us, and you're far more stubborn anyway. We're caught in the middle of a war, and someone has to lead. Doesn't mean you get to be a dictator, though, or that I won't tell you when I think you're wrong. Besides, our ranks are meaningless if we're not going to remain part of the Hundred Worlds military."

"We aren't deserting, Carla. We're on independent duty, that's all. We should respect the chain of command."

"Then I hereby put you in acting command. That's an order. I'll keep a veto if I don't like your decisions. Happy?"

"Hmm. Yeah, that could work. Just don't call me *boss*. That's what Loco always says, and I'm glad you're not like him. It may not always seem like it, but I'm glad you push back when you believe you're right."

Engels felt a weight come off her shoulders, though swapped for a measure of guilt at putting it on Straker. She was trained as an officer and leader, but she really preferred the clearly defined responsibility of commanding a ship over men on the ground. "I sure hope I'm not like Loco. He's...." She ran out of banter. "Well, he's not me."

"Yeah, you're a hell of a lot better looking, too." Straker smiled.

Engels became suddenly aware of her compromised appearance before offering, "Thanks." Then she berated herself again for worrying about such trivialities. She was one of the best pilots ever, and far from stupid. What did appearances matter?

But they mattered to men, so they must matter to Derek... so therefore they mattered to her, because Derek mattered to her. *Damn*, she thought to herself, *I think I just need some sleep.*

Maybe things would be all right. Too bad they had no privacy.

Something occurred to her. "Derek, don't forget to get your antidote soon. Your skin is looking more and more scaly." She rubbed her face. "I'm hoping mine gets back to normal soon."

"Yours isn't bad. In fact, the blue-green thing is kind of exotic."

He was watching her like he meant it.

"You silver-tongued devil."

Straker rolled out of his bunk. "I'll go find that medic."

Chapter 21

Unmutual territory, Bayzos system.

Three days later their sidespace journey was over with, and Straker was beginning to feel more normal. His skin mottled was distinctively more yellowy-pink instead of blue-green, but it remained slightly scaly.

They stood in a sealed hangar on the moon where the *Carson*'s pinnace had touched down after the frigate's journey. Engels, Loco, and the others arrayed themselves behind Straker, who had his hand on the butt of his slugthrower.

Confronting them were a dozen Unmutuals, all with weapons ready and almost pointed at those they'd rescued.

"Give me your gun," Major Ramirez demanded. The tough-looking woman had yet to learn good manners.

"I thought we'd settled this already," Straker replied, controlling himself with difficulty. "Why don't you put your own weapons in the armory?"

"We keep our weapons with us at all times," Ramirez snapped. "We're not some Mutuality conscript army that can't be trusted."

"Exactly. I've been a volunteer at war my whole life. You got us out of there so we could fight the Mutuality, right? So what's the problem?"

"The problem is, some of these prisoners are probably spies, and until we're sure who's who, you don't get to be armed. We accepted the situation aboard ship, but now, give it up or we'll discard you."

"Discard? Is that some kind of jargon?"

"It means shove you out an airlock, you ungrateful trash."

Straker's gaze bore into hers, unblinking. "Then I guess we both die right here and now." His hands tightened on his weapon, readying for a fast draw.

These people had no idea how quickly he could move. He could feel his friends tense beside him.

Major Ramirez's eyes widened in astonishment. "We risked our lives to get you out of there. That means we call the shots, and you owe us. Don't be a fool!"

Engels stepped forward to stand between the two, and lowered her voice as if speaking confidentially. "He won't back down, you know. Cosmos knows I've tried to get him to see reason often enough. So if you want us to join up, maybe you'd better play along."

"I think Lieutenant Engels has a point," said an urbane voice from off to the side. "Stand down, Ramirez."

Straker didn't turn, in case it was a distraction, but kept his eyes on Ramirez.

Ramirez's expression blanked, and she let her blaster fall to its slung position. "Of course, General."

At that, Straker did turn to face the man who approached.

He wore a simple, elegant green uniform with starburst clusters on the collar, though no medals or fancy accouterments. High-quality spacer's boots peeked from under his trouser cuffs, and his face showed impeccable grooming, trimmed black beard framing high cheekbones and a generous, smiling mouth.

Straker came to attention and saluted. "General, I'm Assault Captain Derek Straker, Hundred Worlds mechsuiter."

"You *were* all those things, Straker... and perhaps you will be again." The man saluted casually, and then held out his hand to shake. "General Emilio DeChang. Welcome to the moon Aynor and the Unmutual rebellion. I can see you're a man of distinction. The first mechsuiter I've ever known to be captured, and certainly the first one we've ever run across."

Straker clenched his teeth. Was the man impugning him, implying he'd failed? "We didn't go down easy. They set a trap for us."

"No offense meant."

"And then you just *happened* to set up our rescue?"

"Yet you rescued yourself... to a point." DeChang smiled. "Of course it wasn't mere coincidence. Our spies told us about you and your comrades. High-value military, all concentrated in one place. Once the Mutuality brainwashed you into becoming one of their sheep, they intended to use you to improve their effectiveness, perhaps even create some form of mechsuit pro-gram of their own. We decided we'd rather not let them keep you. We want you on our side. Come—and let's *do* call you *Captain* Straker. Walk with me."

Straker glanced at Engels and Loco. Engels nodded and Loco shrugged.

"Now, now, Captain Straker. If I wished you ill, you'd all be in shackles right now. Don't make the mistake of thinking we're like the Mutuality. Quite the opposite. We value the individual and hope you will choose to join us."

"And if we don't?"

"Then you're free to go. Please, let us walk and talk. I'd like to show you our operation."

"My friends will come along." Straker gestured at Loco and Engels.

"Of course. Ramirez, get the others settled." DeChang turned and strolled, hands behind his back, toward a door.

Straker walked beside the general, and Engels and Loco followed, listening.

"So you're the man in charge here?" Straker asked.

"We have a council of elders that sets policy, but I'm the operational com-mander." DeChang led them through an adjoining hangar, this one holding three slim single-pilot attack ships like the ones that had almost killed them.

"Sweet birds," said Engels, running her hand over the skin of the nearest.

DeChang nodded. "And you may fly one if you join us. Most of what's here is built for speed, either to raid or to escape. In the long term we hope to force the Mutuality to change. Perhaps we'll even overthrow it, but for now, we're acquiring, developing, and building."

"How big is your operation?" Straker asked.

"This moon holds about half our assets. The rest are scattered elsewhere, on asteroids or moonlets of several systems."

"That's a vague answer."

"Operational security, Captain Straker. If you join us, you'll be briefed in detail."

"What ships do you have?" Engels asked.

"A few small, fast full-up warships like the frigate you arrived on. Some corvettes, a fair number of these attack ships. Lots of lifters, grabships and utility craft. Several fast freighters, heavily modified."

Straker was beginning to feel a sense of disappointment. He couldn't hold it in.

"A long way from being able to beat an empire of a thousand worlds."

DeChang's nostrils flared. "We're an armed rebellion, not an independent nation. We have to acquire more resources, engineer small victories, bide our time… and most importantly, look for opportunities to grow."

"Ground forces?" asked Straker.

"Nothing heavy. Some hovers, a few battlesuiters, a few hundred infantry, all well trained and motivated, although as I said we're equipped for raiding, not pitched battles. As Ramirez implied, this is a movement of believers, haters of the Mutuality. That multiplies our power."

DeChang continued to stroll, leading them out a door and into a clear plastic dome perhaps a kilometer across. In the sky hung a glowing gas giant, swirling with reds and yellows, and a distant sun added light. "The atmosphere of this moon, called Aynor, is thin and cold, so we have the dome. That's Bayzos above us."

"Quite a sight."

Other than the dome above them, they could have been outdoors. Low buildings squatted among plants and trees, similar to the bases Straker was used to, but more plain. Troops drilled on a nearby parade field next to a hand-to-hand pit filled with soft material like sawdust. He could hear the pops and whines of weapons fire on a range somewhere.

DeChang continued speaking. "Our movement grew out of a group of dissidents from the Mutuality that stole a patrol craft and began raiding, about twenty years ago. Since then, we've expanded, creating a rebellion that will one day overthrow our former masters and free the human race from tyranny."

"What about the aliens in the Mutuality?" Engels asked.

"We'll free them too as we're able. They can take care of themselves, and we're happy to have them as allies, but my main concern is our own kind."

DeChang led them across open fields toward a nondescript industrial building, notable only in that it seemed to be fenced and guarded. Nothing else here on Aynor seemed to have overt security attached.

Straker said, "Listen General, pardon me for being skeptical, but how is it you have a nice military base tucked away on a moon, with hangars and facilities, and you haven't been smashed flat?"

DeChang paused at the locked gate and held up a finger. "First and most importantly, they've never located us. Space is huge. We often forget that fact as we hop from world to world along established routes. The typical star system has five to fifteen planets and hundreds of moons. There are tens of thousands of stars surrounding the area the Hundred Worlds and the Mutuality are fighting over, and billions in the galaxy. We're careful to strike randomly and far from Aynor."

"Okay, sure. And?"

"And secondly, we try not to kill too many non-Hok humans. The raid we'd planned for you would have been the most lethal in recent memory, which should tell you how important you are to us. Mostly we steal supplies and hijack cargo ships, and we release Mutuality personnel unless they join us. We have no facilities or extra resources to manage prisoners."

"So you're pirates," Straker said. "No wonder your Major Ramirez is so unprofessional."

DeChang grimaced. "She serves me and my organization, whatever her rough ways. But I must protest! Pirates work for their own gain. We take what we need as well, but we're a rebellion, an insurgency. We have a greater cause."

Straker remained skeptical, but nodded. "All right. Go on. Reasons you're still alive?"

"Both the Mutuality and the Hundred Worlds are stretched thin, locked in a death struggle. Diverting ships to hunt us down isn't worth it. We also have a robust spy network within the Mutuality that spreads propaganda in our favor and warns us of our enemies' impending actions. They seldom catch our raiders."

Straker stroked his rough jaw, the stubble there reminding him he must look like crap, especially in comparison to the neat General DeChang. "You make a good case, sir, but it still seems like a lot of trouble and risk to free a hundred prisoners."

"Many of whom are valuable military personnel. Especially you and your friend Loco here, no offense to Miss Engels." DeChang waved a guard over to open the gate.

Engels nodded. "You have pilots, but Straker and Loco were the first mechsuiters the Mutuality ever captured, I understand." She crossed her arms and cocked her head at DeChang, a shrewd look on her face. "I'm guessing you already have–"

DeChang held up a palm. "Please don't step on my moment, Lieutenant Engels."

Engels subsided, shrugging. "Lead on."

"MacDuff?" DeChang said.

"What?"

"Shakespeare? Lead on, MacDuff? It's actually a misquote."

"I have no idea what you're talking about."

DeChang sighed and lifted his chin, his eyes filling. "I had hoped… Sadly, the Hundred Worlds and the Mutuality both provide only enough culture to support their crass goals. Humanity has a rich history and body of literature waiting to be remembered. That's one thing we're fighting for: not just human lives, but human culture. Things that have been forgotten."

"You sound just like Inquisitor Lazarus," said Loco. "Like he used to, anyway," he snickered.

DeChang stiffened, and then relaxed. "I suppose it's a natural observation."

Engels, arms still crossed and eyes narrowed, said, "You knew him. Were you in a camp too?"

DeChang gazed into the distance, pain on his face. "Oh, yes, Lieutenant Engels. I was indeed. I'm intimately familiar with Lazarus and his ilk."

Straker spoke up with a hint of impatience. "Well, lead on, General Mac-Duff, please?"

DeChang shook his head ruefully. "Philistines."

"More Shakespeare?" said Loco.

The guard held the gate open and saluted DeChang as he led the three toward the structure.

"No, ancient history," DeChang replied, opening the door to the building. He waved them in without turning on the lights. "Remind me to tell you of the story of David and Goliath. It's appropriate to our situation."

Straker could see huge shapes hulking in the gloom of the hollow interior. "I think I remember that one," he said. "My grandmother had a children's book. Something about a kid beating a giant with a rock."

A smile crept into DeChang's voice as he paused under one dim emergency light. "Yes, but that leaves out an important detail that you should appreciate, Straker. David, who was probably about sixteen at the time, volunteered to face the Philistines' champion warrior, a huge man, heavily armored."

"Like a mechsuiter," Loco said.

"Precisely. And what can bring down a mechsuiter?"

Loco snickered again. "Well, in our case it was a few thousand tons of concrete and steel falling on our heads."

DeChang waved in the air. "An unusual situation. More probably, a lucky or precise shot will do it, correct?"

"Sure," said Straker. "That's why we rely on speed and skill more than armor. Not getting hit is the best way not to get killed."

"So, David used a sling and spun a smooth rock straight to Goliath's forehead."

"Sling?" asked Loco.

"A device for applying centrifugal force to a bullet. With its speed, a stone or ball of lead could burst through skin and break bone."

"I'd rather have a force-cannon," Loco said.

"You're missing the point. Even your force-cannon at point blank range can't penetrate the front glacis of a heavy tank. So how did you defeat one?"

"Hit it in weak spots," said Straker. "But that takes one hell of a lot of skill to do consistently."

"Yes, the skill of David who, as a shepherd, used the sling to defend his sheep against predators from the day he could walk."

"The skill of a mechsuiter..." Straker said thoughtfully.

"Exactly. Even computers can't hit targets as well as a mechsuiter. Not in the chaos of combat, on the move and facing multiple enemies, when the fight becomes more art and intuition than science. And when that one optimized trooper is equipped with brainchips and a fully integrated battlenet, he's death on two legs. Not because of the weapons, you see. It's because of skill and experience. That's one reason why the Hundred Worlds hasn't yet lost against the greater numbers of the Mutuality. Because it's created a synthesis of human and machine that is ten times, a hundred times as effective as anything else on the battlefield. The *mechsuiter.*"

With a dramatic flair, DeChang shoved a lever upward. A heavy *clunk* sounded, and power flowed to the overhead lights.

Straker stared at the thing looming over him, a thing he thought he might never see again.

It was a mechsuit.

Only this one didn't have the clean, perfect lines of a Foehammer, with its teardrop force-cannon in one arm and its slim, lethal gatling in the other. This one sported a heavy, awkward particle beam projector in place of one arm and hand, and a nasty railgun for the other. Instead of an integrated rack of three vertical-fire antitank missiles on its back, an unwieldy four-by-four box launcher sat on each shoulder, loaded with smaller rockets.

"I'm surprised," Straker said. "I didn't think you had the tech."

"We've borrowed much of it, of course."

Straker walked around the thing, as did Loco, inspecting it. They exchanged glances as they ran into various unpleasant surprises. The design of the vehicle wasn't what they'd hoped at first.

"It's a loser," Loco announced suddenly. "You expect me to pilot this thing?"

General DeChang's expression collapsed. "What's wrong with it?"

"It can't possibly be balanced, for one thing," Loco said. "And I can see it can't drop from orbit, it can't run fast, it can't dive and roll... It can't even move through forests or close-in cityscapes without getting those launchers torn off by branches or wires."

"Well..." DeChang sputtered. He looked at Straker for help.

Straker couldn't give him any. Loco was right. The suit was no Foehammer.

Loco, in the meantime, continued his tirade as if unaware he was stepping on anyone's toes.

"It doesn't even have gauntlets to manipulate anything!" he complained, smacking the dangling forearms. "The whole point of a mechsuit is agility. You've turned this one into a weapons platform. You might as well have put your effort into tanks. At least they're low to the ground and heavily armored. And far cheaper."

DeChang again turned to Straker with evident irritation. "My people have worked hard on this prototype, based on salvaged Foehammer parts. We call it a *Sledgehammer*." He gestured at piles of arms, legs, and torsos scattered around the mechsuit, obviously recovered from many battlefields. "It's not what you're used to, but our simulations show it'll be over twice as effective as a Foehammer, when properly supported."

"It's gonna need that support, or it'll die," Loco said. "No antipersonnel weapons at all? It can't handle enemy infantry, especially battlesuits."

"That's because it's designed as the anchor of a combined arms team, not as a jack-of-all-trades. It may not be able to do your usual fancy gymnastics, but it retains the Foehammer's rough terrain mobility. It can crouch for cover, and it has not one but *two* weapons that can punch through anything on the battlefield, even the front of a heavy tank. With your help, we'll get the neural brainlink and battlenet working too."

"My neural link is designed for a Foehammer, and without those 'gymnastics' as you call them, this thing won't last five minutes in a straight-up battle." Loco touched the sockets on the back of his head and neck. "I also don't know what effect the Hok biotech has had. You got any intelligence on that?"

"You should be fine, from the looks of you." DeChang waved his hands. "And I already told you we don't fight straight-up battles. Try to think past what you lost, and see this as an opportunity to wear a mechsuit again. One designed to allow us to make heavier raids on specific targets, not one to fight every kind of combat anywhere as an elite soldier like you used to be."

Loco started to complain again, but Straker waved for him to be quiet. He did so with difficulty.

Straker stared long and hard at the inelegant monstrosity, trying hard to look past its top-heaviness, its patchwork welds and its ugly markings so unlike the Foehammer he once rode. Maybe he could get used to it. He'd felt like a Hundred Worlds Olympics athlete in the Foehammer, and this would turn that sensation into something akin to a pack mule, but at least it would hit hard.

He could use it to strike at his enemies, be a respected part of a military unit again. He'd probably be put in tactical command, as DeChang had said this Sledgehammer would be the centerpiece of a task force.

DeChang took Straker by the shoulders, turning him to lock eyes. "This is what we have, Captain Straker. If you want to drive a mechsuit again, this is your chance. You'll be able to try it and give your expert advice on modifications, and once we work out the kinks, we'll build another for Lieutenant Paloco. It represents the next stage in our ability to hurt our enemies."

"And after that?"

DeChang let his arms drop, lacing his fingers behind his back again. "We have enough materials for two suits. We're optimistic that more can be constructed. I have a plan to obtain more and better parts. We'll also need to run a lot of tests on you two to map and replicate your neural implants, so we can spearhead a program to create more pilots."

Straker found himself aching to put on a mechsuit again, even if it fell short of the smooth perfection he'd enjoyed all his adult life. He rubbed his jaw.

"Okay. Me and Loco will at least try this thing out. No promises, though. And we need free access to information."

"Information?"

"Yeah. Computers, newsnets, sensor readings, databases, stuff like that. I want to know what's really going on out there."

"You want to check up on my claims?" DeChang seemed amused.

"Let's just say I want to see things for myself. Like any good citizen and officer."

"Of course. Major Ramirez can set you up."

"What's her position here?" Loco asked, studiedly casual. Straker shot him a sharp look, and Loco winked back.

"Major Ramirez is my best operational commander."

"What's your regs on fraternization?" Loco said, still deadpan.

DeChang raised an eyebrow. "We don't have any stupid rules like that, Lieutenant Paloco. We're a fighting organization, and we're short on women. Unless you like men…"

"No, I'm a straight ladies' man."

DeChang shook his head. "It's none of my business."

"So when do we start?" Straker asked. "How do we do this?"

DeChang waved airily. "Don't worry. I'll introduce you to Murdock, my brainiac systems engineer and resident mad scientist. Work with him and we'll begin assembling a task force."

"For what?"

"Your first mission, of course."

"Which is what?"

"You called us pirates," DeChang grinned, "and you weren't so far from wrong. We're going to hijack an asteroid."

Chapter 22

Former Hundred Worlds system. Asteroid habitat designated WG604.

Six weeks after Straker joined the Unmutual rebels, he found himself approaching a hollowed-out asteroid habitat.

WG604 was far from hospitable. The target hab closely orbited a nameless, planetless star off the flank of the main stellar battlefront between the Hundred Worlds and the Mutuality. The system had been owned by the Hundred Worlds for generations, but it had been recently surrounded and isolated by the Mutuality offensive.

According to the Unmutual spy network, the system had barely been scouted. In fact, the people here were likely only scarcely aware they would soon be absorbed into the Mutuality. Their asteroid habitats would be taken and used to fuel more conquest by their collectivist enemies, but for now, they continued as before.

Most importantly, the asteroid itself contained factories and machine shops that would double the rebels' manufacturing and engineering capability. DeChang believed that at least one of those facilities built mechsuit parts.

On the negative side, the Hundred Worlds typically fortified all of its facilities, so the raid had been planned with the expectation of opposition.

Though she was fast, the frigate *Carson* had needed eight days to reach the system.

Lieutenant Engels detached her heavy lifter from the frigate. Such warships didn't have launch bays big enough to fit it, so the assault craft had to strap on for the sidespace trip their target. The rest of the Unmutual task force was also attached to the ship's hull, or contained within.

"Beginning Phase One attack run," Engels heard Captain Ellen Gray call from the sleek frigate. She watched *Carson* pull ahead, leading the way toward WG604.

Engels' lifter, and the other, piloted by Zaxby the Ruxin, hung back, waiting for *Carson* to do her work. This pair of lifters held the assault troops. Their inherent velocity carried them slowly toward the asteroid. Two outsized autonomous cargo modules floated behind, their maneuvering computers programmed to bring them to rest next to WG604.

Ahead, *Carson* opened fire with her centerline railgun, a perfect weapon to bombard an unsuspecting base from ultra-long range. The first heavy metal slug slammed into one end of the two-kilometer rock, destroying a propulsion engine. The second struck moments later, wrecking the motor on the other end.

Now, with the asteroid nearly immobilized, it had no chance to move out of the way of the railgun projectiles, always a problem at ultra-long range when the slugs had to travel several minutes before impact.

The Unmutuals had no choice but to begin the bombardment this far away. WG604 might be small for a base, but it functioned like a slow-moving spaceship—which meant it was huge in comparison to the frigate. As close to the star as it was, it collected plenty of solar power to channel through the heavy lasers that were undoubtedly already reaching for the small attacking ship.

But at this distance, *Carson*'s uneven spiral course made hitting her with beams a matter of sheer luck. Decoys and sandcasters filled space between the two combatants with screening debris, detritus that attenuated and revealed the shots of coherent light while inhibiting the attacking railgun slugs not at all.

Over the next twelve minutes, the frigate's bombardment systematically demolished the heavy weapons emplacements on the asteroid, allowing her to approach to close range and use precision firepower to eliminate further resistance.

"Lifters, move in for Phase Two," Captain Gray ordered.

"Already on our way," Engels replied. As soon as the heavy weapons had been silenced, she'd kicked in her impellers to get a jump on Phase Two, and Zaxby had followed.

Switching channels, she asked, "You doing all right, Derek?"

"Five by five, Lieutenant Engels," came the terse reply.

Okay fine, she thought. Straker was still in high-stress military mode, like he'd been for the past weeks while getting ready for this op, with no chance of downtime. Opening the channel to include the battlesuiters and straight-leg infantry inside her boat, she made an announcement.

"Ladies and gentlemen, this is your pilot speaking. Phase One went perfectly. Phase Two is underway. We'll begin the assault on schedule, in approximately one hour and twenty minutes."

* * *

Straker ran a systems check on his Sledgehammer for the tenth time. The railgun in his right arm still had a tendency to jam its reload sequence, and the missiles on his shoulders never locked on as well as Murdock claimed they should. Also, he didn't trust his left hip joint not to seize up when too hot or too cold. Loco's new rig had even less going for it.

What was worse, neither he nor Loco had been able to achieve a working brainlink. The manual backups, though sophisticated, simply didn't compare. The neural battlenets were too finicky, though, needing special equipment to recalibrate and synch.

He couldn't be sure that the Hok biotech hadn't interfered with the brain-link either. His skin still hadn't gone back to completely normal. Maybe it never would. His extra strength hadn't faded, either.

All in all, he was wearing a piece of crap cobbled together by people who desperately wanted it to work, fueled more by hope than by sound engineering. That couldn't be helped, though; the Unmutual rebellion made do with what it had. His suit and Loco's represented a quantum leap forward, so he had to give it his best. Otherwise, he'd end up as nothing special.

After all, without a mechsuit he was just another officer.

This hunk of junk didn't even have the capability to tap into the lifter's systems and see what was going on. He was no better off than the grunts who surrounded him. Worse, really; they joked and played cards, read or watched vids with their squadmates. Now that he'd mounted his war machine, he was stuck inside, cut off except for the comlink.

And Straker didn't have squadmates. He had subordinates and superiors. The general had confirmed his rank of Captain and put him in command of Alpha Company for this mission, once he'd agreed to pilot the mechsuit. Lieutenant Paloco led Bravo Company on Lifter Two.

He'd never been in charge of this many people before. A mechsuit squad boasted plenty of firepower, but had a completely different dynamic compared to a hundred-man company. Maybe he shouldn't have insisted on command, but it had made sense at the time. His Sledgehammer was the anchor of the unit, so everyone would key off him.

But these rebels weren't highly disciplined troops. They were motivated, but they were also quick to deviate from orders and express their opinions when they didn't like something—and they didn't like a newly recruited officer being put in charge.

Major Ramirez was in overall command of the raid, and that took the edge off their objections. Exercising with his new company had helped some more. Seeing what the Sledgehammers could do had also turned them into cautious believers.

They'd become believers in the mechsuits, anyway... Straker wasn't sure they believed in *him*. A few of the troops, especially the handful of battlesuiters, seemed to be coming around faster.

"Ten minutes," Ramirez spoke into everyone's ear. "Drop those cocks and grab your socks, boys and girls."

Straker waited while the troops cleaned up their games and food, beginning final weapons and equipment checks. His half-dozen battlesuiters sealed up their powered armor like pint-sized mechsuiters, readying their blasters. They would cover him against the unexpected, such as enemy infantry getting in close. This was supposed to be a walkover, but he was taking no chances.

"One minute," Ramirez said, still broadcasting to the assault troops. "*Carson* has punched holes through the asteroid's hull as planned. Lifters will fly through the openings and set down inside the habitat. We don't expect heavy ground resistance, but you will treat the landing zone as hot until you secure it. Destroy any threat, but minimize collateral damage. Remember, people, we're capturing this base for ourselves, and we want those occupants to join us. No plundering!"

They'd heard it all before, but it never hurt to tell them again. Straker spoke on his company channel. "This is Straker. Insert by the numbers, people. First platoon with me to capture Sector One Base Control Center. Second and third platoon, Administration and Power. Fourth platoon, secure the lifter and deploy the LADA."

Lifter Two would have similar objectives. Loco would lead Bravo Company's first platoon to capture the auxiliary base control center at the other end. His other platoons would capture Manufacturing and Engineering. Murdock himself was employed on the raid to oversee the technical side of things. With all these key objectives in friendly hands, the civilians should surrender.

The lifter shuddered as G-forces shoved the troops against their restraining straps. Straker kept his suit's elbows and feet clamped into their hardpoints, holding sixty tons of weapons systems in place. Gravplating whined with the strain, and then they set down and the ramps and hatches flew open.

"Go, go, go!" Straker heard noncoms yelling at their troops. Each platoon exited one side of the boxy lifter. He led First Platoon out the large rear door, crouch-walking like a man exiting a cave, his movement rocking the craft until he stepped onto the soil. He sank to his mechsuit's ankles.

Outside, he found himself in an open field of melon plants. A hundred meters to the direction they'd chosen as "south"—opposite the Base Control Center—he could see the other lifter set down beside the hole the *Carson* had blasted through the asteroid's skin, now the ground on which he walked. The atmosphere would be spilling out, but it would take hours to lose enough to become a problem. By that time, it would be patched.

Hundreds of meters above him arched the inside of the hollow asteroid, much closer than the vault of Academy he remembered, though similar in design, as most of these habitats were. Stretched from end to end in its center, a filament of brightness provided sunlight piped in through fiber optics. The rough cylinder maintained only about a fifth of a G, supplied by rotation around its long axis.

"First platoon deploy, inverted V, heading zero-zero-zero," Straker said, turning toward the northern end of the cylinder. He began a slow march in that direction, limited by the speed of his straight-leg infantry rather than his suit. His objective, the Base Control Center, lay only nine hundred meters away. That was short range for his weapons and optics.

Mechsuiters normally did their best work at knife-fighting distance, so close and so agile that armored vehicles couldn't cope. Today he was driving a highly mobile walking tank, a flexible weapons platform rather than a true mechsuit. He had to think like a tanker rather than a 'suiter, adjusting his focus farther out and trusting to his infantry screen to handle the close-in threats.

The rounded domes of the BCC seemed to be pasted to the north end of the cylinder, right on the axis, its structures oddly angled to deal with the weak sideways pseudo-gravity there. No doubt they added gravplating to simplify the working arrangement. Straker was scanning the complex for weapons when his HUD fuzzed for a moment, and he jerked as sensors showed an attack across the front of his body.

Laser! By the weakness of the sting, it was fortunately nothing serious. Rebel intelligence had expected no heavy weapons inside the base, which relied on its space defenses. There's been some question as to whether it would have any internal ground forces at all.

In response, Straker angled to his right, running ponderously to throw off the enemy's targeting and simultaneously pinpointing the source of the attack. He identified a heavy mining laser crawler, normally used to cut through asteroidal rock. With hardly a thought, he extended his left arm and sent a particle beam bolt into the vehicle.

It exploded as the near-lightspeed particles superheated its unarmored chassis and ruptured its fuel cells. Its operator must have died instantly, and Straker felt a flash of regret such as he'd never dealt with when he was killing Hok. After all, his mission was to liberate these Hundred Worlds citizens before the Mutuality scooped them up, rather than exterminate them.

Scanning, he found no other heavy weapons. His platoon took small arms fire from buildings they passed, wounding half a dozen.

He'd hoped the people here would lay down their arms, but he couldn't blame them for resisting. Murdock would be broadcasting on all their networks trying to get them to surrender.

The broadcast apparently didn't work fast enough. Straker had to fire particle beams into several buildings to eliminate nests of resistors and keep more of his own people from getting killed. "Dammit," he growled. "Why can't they just give up?"

"We wouldn't give up if we were defending our homes, would we?" replied Loco.

Abruptly, the chatter on his comlink turned frantic. "Action right, heavy gatling!" he heard, and then: "*Mechsuit!*"

What the hell was a mechsuit doing here? It must have come from the assembly facility, perhaps with a test pilot. Would the man inside be young and inexperienced, or an old, retired 'suiter?

Electricity sang in Straker's veins. Now came the acid test of this walking weapons platform.

"Pull back. I'll handle it," he said, turning toward the action on his right. Within seconds he spotted his nemesis. A Foehammer ran obliquely, guns firing in short, deadly bursts, cutting down his people.

"On my way, boss," he heard Loco call. "Be there in less than two minutes."

"We don't have two minutes," Straker replied, snapshotting a particle beam pulse at the dodging figure. Tactically it might be a bad move to telegraph his presence, but he had to stop his enemy from chopping up his infantry with impunity.

The beam struck the ground at the enemy's feet, spraying a blast of old-fashioned concrete from the pavement. Immediately, the mechsuiter dodged and shifted his attention and his force-cannon to Straker's Sledgehammer.

The pilot was good, whoever he was. No beginner. Must be a trooper put out to pasture, or on rotation from the front. Straker had heard of temporary duty positions like this, but they were few and far between. Bad luck to run into one of them now.

Straker dropped, squatting on his heels to lower his profile as he'd practiced rather than trying to run laterally as a real mechsuit would do. The force-cannon bolt he anticipated sizzled the atmo above his head even as he fired his railgun, leading his opponent slightly.

His right arm bucked with recoil and the penetrator glowed in a streak as it shoved air molecules out of the way, flash-heating the atmosphere like a meteor falling toward a planet. The projectile passed under the Foehammer's arm and impacted the ground all the way across the inside of the cylinder. Without a neural link, he simply didn't have the fine, instinctive accuracy he'd always enjoyed.

In response the enemy fired gatling bursts while his force-cannon recharged. Straker felt the big bullets strike him, doing little damage to his armor. One hit a missile in its launcher, though, and that tube went red.

Straker cursed the fragile design and concentrated on getting a missile lock, standing up and sidestepping to degrade his opponent's targeting. The gatling couldn't put him out of action, but if he didn't use his missiles now, he might lose them one by one.

The reticle blinked ready-lock, and Straker triggered a full salvo. The missiles ripple-fired. Some exploded in midair, struck by incoming gatling rounds. The others missed as the Foehammer dove and rolled, taking cover behind a cargo truck.

The missile volley's reprieve allowed Straker to jettison the ungainly box launchers from his shoulders, and he felt his stability improve. Aiming carefully, he fired his recharged particle beam at his enemy's exposed foot.

The metal resisted for a fraction of a second, then slagged, running like wax. Inside the armor, he knew the enemy circuitry was fizzling and popping.

Straker was sure that would slow his enemy down… until a force-cannon bolt came back at him, striking dead in the center of his chest, knocking him backward onto his ass.

Chapter 23

Disputed asteroid habitat WG604.

Damn, but this guy's good, Straker thought as he checked systems. Almost as good as Straker himself in a Foehammer.

But not good enough, or he would have aimed for Straker's arm or head. The Sledgehammer's center torso protected its pilot and thus sported its heaviest armor, high-tech interlaced composites and superconductors charged with reinforcing energy fields, made to shrug off at least one direct hit from even the heaviest ground weapons. It had held, with only twenty percent degradation.

Straker rolled over and stood to face his enemy, unconcerned about another force-cannon bolt. He knew exactly how long the weapon took to recharge. He lifted both of his own heavy weapons and sighted on the covered position of his foe, who had rolled to crouch behind a pumphouse.

On a whim, Straker tried out his comlink, setting it to standard mechsuiter frequencies. "Mechsuit pilot, surrender and you will be treated in accordance with the laws of war. You are alone and have no chance against our forces."

"Since when did the Hok respect the laws of war?" came the unexpected answer. The voice sounded rough, old.

"We're not Hok. You ever see a Hok in a mechsuit?"

"I got him, Derek," Loco said.

Straker could see Loco's Sledgehammer beyond the enemy, aiming. Between the two of them, and with his mobility cut, the enemy had nowhere to hide.

"Hold up, Loco," Straker said. "You, in the Foehammer. What's your name?"

"I'm Colonel Mitchell Jackson," the pilot said. He sounded surprised and spoke with a provincial accent. "Well, I was a colonel... before they put me out to pasture. Now, I'm just Mitch."

"Assault Captain Derek Straker here. Sir, I read about you in the 'suiter journals."

"Straker? I heard you died at Corinth."

"Captured by the enemy. I escaped and now I'm with an independent movement, fighting against... against the Hok." It would take too long to explain that the Hok were only troops controlled by the Mutuality. "Colonel, it won't be long before this system and this habitat is captured by the enemy. Surrender now, and you can join us in the fight. You can always go back to the Hundred Worlds later if you want, but right now, we have to get this rock into sidespace."

"Get this rock into sidespace? That's impossible."

"We have a way. Now please, Colonel, don't make us kill you."

The Foehammer stood slowly on one good leg, its force-cannon targeted on Straker's mechsuit's head. A hit there wouldn't kill him, but it would wipe out most of his sensors, and with them his combat effectiveness.

"I don't believe you," the colonel said. "This is some new Hok trick. You're not a real human. That's not even a real mechsuit, just some cheap imitation."

"Derek, I got him!" Loco said. "One shot and he's toast."

"Not before I take down your buddy, son," said Jackson. "I've been testing these suits for a long time. I know where to hit one for a single-shot kill, even a custom job like yours."

"Bullshit," said Loco. "You would've done it already."

"I tried, but it ain't easy on the move. Now, though, I got it locked."

"Boss—"

"Stand down, Loco," Straker said. "Colonel, would a Hok even be talking to you?"

"If he wanted to capture me and my suit, he might."

"Would a Hok have called off his partner from shooting you in the back?"

"Same deal."

Straker thought furiously, looking for a way of getting through to this guy. "Colonel, what can I tell you to prove what I say is true?"

"Nothing, probably. Besides, I'm too old to change my ways. You got me dead to rights, and you might be telling the truth, but I can't risk getting captured. Think I'll just punch out for good. I can't win this fight, and ain't no point in more people dying." He lowered his force-cannon and the mechsuit became immobile.

"Power surge, Derek," Loco said. "He's set his systems to overload!"

"Dammit! Everyone back!" Straker aimed his railgun carefully and fired at Jackson's leg, blowing it off and knocking the mechsuit to the ground.

"Still building charge," said Loco.

"I can see that." Straker walked his Sledgehammer forward and aimed at an arm with his particle beam. The discharge not only melted the limb, but sent energy arcing all along the suit. Once the surge cleared, he could see the overload had been disrupted.

He broke briefly into an awkward run, and then slowed to stand above his fallen opponent. Frustrated, he held up his arms. The powerful weapons there had replaced the mechanized gauntlets he now needed to rip open the Foehammer, one more thing the Sledgehammer gave up for its specialized firepower.

Cracking his mechsuit open, Straker dismounted. "I need tools!"

People rushed to him—some his, some local civilians—but none had the equipment it took to cut into mechsuit armor, at least not without killing the man inside.

Straker mounted his Sledgehammer again and plugged into his comlink. "Colonel Jackson, can you hear me? Are you there?"

A crackle and a groan answered him. "Still breathing, son. Not for much longer, I think. Why didn't ya let me blow it?"

"There's no reason to die, sir! You're a mechsuiter! Work with us, for humanity's sake."

Jackson's voice grew fainter, and dreamy. "I overrode my medcomp. Gave myself enough painkiller to finish me off. Let me go, boy. Face your brave new world without me." He breathed twice more, and then came a long, heavy sigh that seemed never to end, until it did.

"Jackson! Sir! Colonel!"

"He's gone, Derek," said Loco, stepping up beside him.

"I hate the Mutualists and their Hok," said Straker, standing above his fallen ex-comrade. "I hate what they're doing to good people."

Loco nudged Straker with his suit's elbow. "Come on. We've got work to do."

Straker stuffed down his anger and nodded, but his mechsuit didn't mimic that motion, so he spoke. "Right. Let's do it. Alpha Company, all platoons, continue your missions. First Platoon, we head for the BCC." He turned to march northward, fighting an unexpected weariness of the soul, leaving the fallen mechsuit for others to deal with.

Within minutes, his platoon reached the Base Control Center, climbing the slope up to the circular complex of buildings, gravity lessening all the way. When he stepped onto the landscaped grounds, he felt gravplating augmenting the spin of the base, and his sense of orientation shifted. Suddenly, his inner ear told him he stood at the bottom of a long cylinder set on its end, gazing upward.

"Secure the facility," he told his infantry. "Battlesuiters, take positions atop the buildings and watch for pop-ups."

Other than Colonel Jackson's surprise appearance, the mission had been easy, a milk run to test out the new Sledgehammers. But it had left him feeling deeply unsatisfied. His whole life he'd spent battling a known, evil enemy. None of this felt like that. Even though they were hijacking the Mutuality's prize, somehow he was still being forced to kill good people.

Straker told himself there would be opportunities ahead to strike directly at the Mutualists themselves. That's what he wanted. But, like DeChang had said, the Unmutual rebellion had to build up forces before making bigger attacks.

"The facility is secure," his platoon sergeant reported after a few minutes. "No further casualties, no problems. Got about twenty prisoners."

"*Liberated* people, Sergeant," Straker replied. "Hopefully they'll all join us. Put them in vehicles and get them to the collection point."

"On it." The noncom got busy commandeering trams and loading up the locals. They'd be assembled near the lifters and given their first briefing on what was really happening.

"Control team, SITREP," Straker called.

"Control team, Murdock here. We're good, no damage to the facility except for a few laser holes. Can't say the same about the fusion engines."

"You know the deal, Murdock. Those had to be destroyed in order to be sure of taking the base."

"I know, but this thing is a pig on impellers only. Do you know how much mass we're talking about here?"

"I don't care. Get it moving in the right direction. We have to get into flatspace before Hok forces—I mean, Mutuality forces—arrive."

"We're already moving, hotshot. You do your job, I'll do mine."

"No problem." Straker found a position in a courtyard from which he could see over the roofs and methodically scan the entire interior of the base. His infantry and battlesuiters settled into covered positions, facing outward.

This end seemed completely pacified. From here, he could see the two lifters with their LADAs set up. The Laser Air-Defense Array weapons spun slowly on their mounts, mirrors ready to aim with machine-precision at anything flying or falling their direction.

Nearby, repair teams had set up super-high-strength synthetic material to cover the holes in the ground, staking it down with meter-long spikes. This would stop most of the atmo leakage, while still allowing egress if necessary.

Thousands of inhabitants gathered in a field between the lifters, their designated assembly area. Some had been trucked in, but many had simply been marched there, as no point inside the cylinder was more than two kilometers from any other.

Phase Two had been completed.

* * *

Engels, sitting bored in her lifter's cockpit, tapped into the *Carson's* sensor feed and watched what was happening outside. After all, with the interior secure, that's what really mattered.

The two cargo modules had come to relative rest adjacent to the base, one at either end. Four one-man grabships from the hovering *Carson* maneuvered them into place. Exo-suited teams removed protective coverings and affixed connections, testing systems and struts to ensure function and controllability.

When they'd finished, two enormous add-on sidespace engines bookended the base.

She still found it hard to believe the things would work. Entry into sidespace was limited by the energy available and its ability to be processed through the machinery. More to the point, the power requirements grew as an exponential function of the mass of the thing to be moved.

Therefore, it got progressively harder and harder to shift bigger masses all at once. This was one reason why ships, whether for war or cargo, hit a practical limit at around super-dreadnought size.

Super-dreadnoughts pushed the upper limits of military mobility. To get bigger, they needed more power from larger sidespace engines, which meant more mass, which took away from additional weaponry. This vicious cycle kept anyone from simply building bigger and bigger, if they wanted to be able to go anywhere.

So, no fortified monster planetoids could be transited from star system to star system via sidespace, crushing all opposition. However, local fortresses with enormous weapons could be built on planets, moons and asteroids, favoring the defense until they could be bombarded into submission. That was one reason territory was so hard to take.

This two-kilometer-long asteroid, though hollow, easily massed double the practical limit.

When Engels had first asked how it could be done, Murdock had given her a bunch of math that was beyond her even though she was a pilot. Multidimensional transport wasn't her specialty, as her dropship had always piggybacked on an assault carrier.

It had taken Zaxby the Ruxin to explain it to her in terms she could understand. They'd been sitting in an Unmutual food facility, sharing a meal, eating versions of the same thing: nutritious algae, textured and flavored, supposedly tailored to each species. Engels wondered if Zaxby's tasted as bad as hers.

"See here, young human female," he'd said, going into his typical lecture mode and ignoring his food. "It's quite simple. First, the curvature of space-time must be extremely small."

"I get that. Space has to be flat. Stay away from gravity sources."

Zaxby sighed. "Gravity has no source. It is a natural effect of the presence of mass, which distorts space-time as a four-dimensional slope. But, I will attempt to stupidize my explanation to suit your simplistic metaphors."

"Stupidize? You mean dumb down?"

"Yes, that was the idiom I was looking for. Thank you. Now–"

"Are all Ruxins so insulting?"

Zaxby brushed at the pocket-vest he wore over his water suit, adapted to carry small objects. "Oh, no. I am quite tactful for my species. I once considered a career as a diplomat."

"Great Cosmos. No wonder Lazarus tortured you."

"I fail to see the connection."

"Did he try to get you to talk, or to shut up?"

"Now that you mention it, I believe he began with the former and proceeded to the latter. Eventually he placed me in solitary confinement."

Engels waved her fork in Zaxby's direction. "Get on with it. Stupidize your explanation for me."

"Please retract your limb. You may inadvertently pluck out one of my eyes with that implement."

"It might taste better than this algae. Plus, you could regenerate another. Now continue with your explanation of exactly how we can shove this huge base through sidespace."

"Very well," Zaxby said, scooting his seat backward and out of range of the fork. "It's simply a matter of getting the math to work."

"Keep it at my level. Layman's terms."

"I will struggle to do so. All right. First, the oversized mass must be moved far out into flat space-time, and its destination must be similar. That is the most important consideration."

"Just like big ships have to enter and exit sidespace far from gravity wells."

"Correct."

Engels put her fork down. "How far out?"

"Oh, well beyond the most distant large planets in a star system. Perhaps four light-hours from the primary. That's a highly approximate figure, though."

"Good enough. You said *first*. What else?"

"Obviously, large engines must be fitted, and enormous power must be supplied."

"Depending on the size of the thing."

Zaxby waved tentacles. "It's about mass, not size. All variables feed into the equation. However, the most important are location, mass, engine capacity and power available."

"So first we move it to a suitable location. We then stick big sidespace engines on it. Maybe we can store up enough power to shove it through. We can't control its mass, though."

"Ah, but if we're ruthless and desperate enough, perhaps we can."

* * *

Engels watched as the next, most unconventional phase of the operation began. She shuddered at the extreme risk of it all, but that very unthinkability was what might allow it to succeed.

The *Carson* began methodically carving at the asteroid's larger projections, using her lasers to carefully blast and cut off nonessential mass. Of course, the base itself had never done so; every bit of rock and ore would have eventually been processed for local use.

But for now, it would all have to go.

Detached chunks streamed outward as the asteroid rotated. *Carson* maneuvered and continued to cut.

In the control center, Murdock and his team would be monitoring stresses on the asteroid and communicating with the frigate, telling her captain where to carve. He was also slowing the asteroid's rotation to a minimum. But the tiny planetoid had never been designed to take such abuse, so every blast and beam carried with it the chance of cracks developing, cracks that would widen and eventually cause the whole thing to fall apart. If that happened, all their work would be for nothing.

Every piece the *Carson* removed would bring the variables closer to lining up in their equation, bring the math that much closer to balancing, allowing the asteroid base to do what its Hundred Worlds builders thought impossible:

to slide into sidespace and be unfolded again in another place, a place of the Unmutuals' choosing, hidden and far from their enemies.

* * *

It took five sweating, nail-biting days of waiting for the possibility of a Mutuality squadron, or even a ship that could outmatch *Carson*, to arrive and wreck all they had done. The asteroid, newly christened *Freiheit*, sailed ponderously outward in a spiral course, the frigate adding momentum by docking and pushing with her own fusion engines and impellers once she had carved off as much as she dared.

But even if a message drone had been sent, Unmutual intelligence had assured the task force it would take at least six days for a response. By that time, they'd know whether their gambit paid off.

The raiders hadn't been merely sitting around. The populace of the habitat needed the time to make mental adjustment, receiving briefings and classes. They sat glued to their screens and vidsets, trying to understand this unexpected new world into which they'd been unwillingly catapulted.

Most of the residents joined the rebellion once they understood what had been done. For some, the conversion was enthusiastic and genuine. For others, it was a way to hang onto stability, keeping their homes, their jobs, and their families in place and hoping the new boss was as generous as the old boss.

Some were too frightened, and they couldn't handle the change. Faced with the disorientation and hardship of life under a new regime, they asked to leave. When told the Unmutuals didn't have a way to send them across space into Hundred Worlds territory, they asked to be left for the Mutuality rather than join a fighting rebellion. Explaining to them how they would likely be treated under Mutuality rule didn't dissuade them all. They seemed in denial even when told plain facts.

"Of course they can leave," Major Ramirez said when the Unmutual officers gathered in conference to discuss the situation. "That was our plan all along. We should be thankful only about twenty percent are such weaklings. We don't want their kind anyway."

"How will we turn them over to the Mutuality?" Engels asked.

"This base has plenty of small craft. They'll be supplied with enough food, water, and air to last for a month. Everyone who wants to stay behind can load up and leave before we fold into sidespace. They can even dock their ships together to make a connected community. They'll survive... probably."

"What if they don't get picked up?"

Ramirez shrugged. "Not our problem. It's their choice. They've been told the risks time and again. We're not in the business of rescuing dead weight. Everyone needs to get with the program, or we cut them loose."

Engels suppressed the urge to argue. She could see the Unmutual point of view—our point of view, she told herself—but it still felt wrong to let people volunteer to enslave themselves. Yet, some would choose secure oppression rather than risky freedom.

If it were simply a question of letting people self-destruct, she wouldn't quibble, but they were being sent to the Mutuality, where they would assist an aggressive system that conquered all in its path.

Engels raised her hand again. "Couldn't we keep them with us and educate them? Give them classes or something? Then they wouldn't be working for our enemies."

"We're not a welfare organization, and we're not Mutualists, with their forced re-education," Ramirez snapped with a glare. "We stand on our own feet and we let people choose for themselves. We don't have a bunch of social-shrinks to hold their hands and tweak their psyches. You want to volunteer to figure out how to re-educate four hundred people against their will while we're running this rebellion? We have no Inquisitors, and we don't want any."

"Sorry, ma'am. It just doesn't seem right."

Some murmured in agreement. Others added their glares to Ramirez's. Straker smiled at Engels and nodded in support of her, as did Loco, Heiser, and a few others.

Zaxby spoke up. "Perhaps we should eliminate them."

"What?" Engels rounded on him.

"It could be done without unpleasantness. Drugs could be administered. They would never be in any pain. This would end any concerns about them helping our enemies or being a burden on us."

"I can't believe what I'm hearing," Engels said. "That's inhuman!"

"I'm not human, as should be quite obvious."

"*Eat shit, squid!*" and worse insults were hurled in the octopoid's direction. Engels was glad this was a meeting for officers only. If the rank and file had been here, there might have been violence.

"You wouldn't make that suggestion if it were *your* people," said Loco.

Zaxby folded several limbs together. "Actually, I would. But then again, I doubt any of my people would choose to submit to enslavement instead of joining a rebellion. Mine is a race of scholars and warriors, without such a high ratio of cowards. Of course, that's not your fault. You can't help it, being primates descended from tree-dwelling apes whose most effective survival trait was to retreat and fling feces."

Many officers jumped to their feet, some yelling angrily at Zaxby, others defending him or trying to calm down the others.

"Shut up!" Ramirez's voice came piercing through the uproar. She hefted her ever-present blaster. "Nobody's discarding anybody without my say-so. Now stick to the plan, and we'll all make it through this. Get back to work. Dismissed!"

As the meeting broke up, Engels grabbed Zaxby. "I thought you were my friend!"

"What has made you doubt that fact? Are some of the humans I suggested eliminating related to you in some way?"

"No, but..."

"Ah. Is it my duty to support you in all public arguments?"

"No, but..."

"Isn't the Unmutual code one of inalienable individual rights and liberties, indicating I should speak my mind? I like that word, 'in-alien-able,' by the way, better than 'inhuman,'" Zaxby said.

"Yes," she said, "you have that right, but rights come with responsibility. Freedom doesn't mean anarchy and chaos, stepping all over anyone else. Those people have rights to their lives too, even if they chose badly."

"So, do the people we kill in battle have rights to their lives?"

"That's different."

"How so?" he asked.

Engels growled with frustration. "It just is! Murdering civilians in cold blood is different from killing enemies in battle."

"Your morality is nonsensical. If they choose to join our enemies, they become our enemies. Eliminating them painlessly would be a kindness for them and for us."

She snorted in exasperation. "Forget it."

"I do not have that capacity. My memory is excellent."

"I mean stop talking to me about it. I don't like you right now."

"I see..." he said thoughtfully. "Human friendship is more subject to emotional whim than I was led to believe. Very well. Please let me know when you like me again and we shall resume our former cordiality." Zaxby moved away, apparently oblivious to the menacing faces on all sides.

"Don't worry about him," said Straker, taking Engels' elbow and seating them both in a corner. "He's an alien. He doesn't think like we do."

"You don't think like I do either, but you wouldn't murder four hundred civilians, some of them children."

"No, but I am having trouble releasing them to help the Mutuality. They have no idea what they're in for."

Engels shrugged. "They won't torture children, and as for the adults... we endured it. They can too. If they're the weaklings they seem to be, they'll cave at the first hint of pain and join the groupthinkers like good little sheep. They'll be enjoying their workers' paradise in no time."

"But they'll still be working for our enemies."

"What if we dropped them on a neutral planet somewhere?" Engels asked.

Straker gave her a thumbs-down. "In all my readings of the Unmutual nets, there's no such thing as neutrality with the Hundred Worlds or the Mutuality. There are only allies, enemies, or planets too distant to be at war. Anything far away wouldn't have many humans, so they'd be refugees among aliens. That's assuming we could even convince the Unmutuals to waste time and effort transporting them there."

Engels massaged her temples. "Dammit. No good choices."

"Nope. We're at war. It will be hard to convince the Unmutuals to expend more than minimum resources on a bunch of cowards."

"I'm glad it's not my decision anyway. Major Ramirez is in charge, acting for DeChang. They'll get left here for Mutuality pickup."

Straker's brows furrowed. "Unless I can convince her otherwise. I'll give it another shot."

Chapter 24

Captured asteroid habitat Freiheit.

Straker failed in his arguments to drop the refugees off at a distant planet. Ramirez stood firm, and Straker eventually accepted her military decision. That's what he reported to Engels.

Engels wished he were as stubborn as he'd been when he refused to knuckle under to the Mutualists, but of course, this was different. They'd all joined the Unmutuals and pledged to follow orders. Otherwise, they could resign their commissions and leave, but Ramirez's decision didn't seem immoral, just problematic: the lesser of two evils.

The time soon came to enter sidespace. Those civilians staying behind loaded all their supplies under the watchful supervision of Unmutual soldiers, and then launched to float in the void far enough from Freiheit to avoid its transit field.

Engels sat in her lifter cockpit again and observed on multiple screens linked to *Carson*. The rest of the Unmutual forces clustered nearby in the open, the artificial sky dark above them in order to channel every erg of power to the engines. They stood ready to load up and flee to the frigate if the attempt failed.

If the attempt succeeded, they would ride Freiheit in comfort and *Carson* would follow at an easy pace. The whole trip back to the Unmutuals' secret star system should take about two weeks.

"Final phase ready," she heard Murdock say over the general comlink. "One minute to transit. Capacitors full. Solar array optimized. Auxiliary generators at one hundred and five percent. Field strength nominal. Sidespace engines, report."

"Engine one nominal. We are go."

"Engine two reading outside nominal parameters. Hold at fifty-five seconds."

"Confirmed, hold at fifty-five seconds."

Soon, the comlink filled with chatter, technical jargon thrown fast and furious back and forth. Engels was able to follow it. Something to do with field balance and the emitters placed around the base interacting with an unexpected ore deposit. They'd have to move them and recalibrate.

She nodded off in her seat. She wasn't on watch, after all. She was on hold, ready to load up and lift if the sidespace gambit failed.

She awoke more than two hours later to the controlled urgency in Murdock's voice.

"Fifty seconds. Forty. Thirty. Twenty. Ten, nine..." She gripped the arms of her seat pointlessly. Whether a jump succeeded or failed, sidespace insertion didn't involve actual three-dimensional motion.

When Murdock's countdown ended, it felt like the end of the world.

"One... We're blurring out."

Engels felt the odd twisting that always came with transit, the impression of being shoved laterally, a sensation that had earned the process its nickname of "sidespace," rather than, say, "hyperspace."

Neither term was very accurate; the alternate set of dimensions they traveled through lay in no particular direction from normal space. No actual sideward motion had ever been detected on even the most sensitive instruments.

Right before the universe disappeared and all the external displays showed the deep gray of sidespace, a flash within a screen caught her eye. The display had been focused on the refugees and their floating village of docked small craft.

Cheering broke out on the broader comnet as it became clear the base had made the transit successfully.

"Congratulations, Mister Murdock," Major Ramirez said. "You've made history. You've doubled our resource processing and manufacturing capacity, not to mention supervised the acquisition of critical Hundred Worlds technology and volunteer labor for us. Well done."

"Thank you, Major, but I couldn't have accomplished it without the efforts of everyone involved in this operation."

The Unmutuals chattered happily on, continuing their back-patting. Engels tuned them out as she pulled up the record of the screen she'd been looking at and shifted it to her large high-resolution holoplate.

After running it repeatedly, it certainly looked as if there had been an explosion among the refugee craft, or at least a large fire. Something that started just as Freiheit went into sidespace. She slowed the recording as much as possible, identifying the very moment when the flash became visible.

A chill settled over her and her heart thudded. She glanced over her shoulder, making sure she was alone in the lifter's cockpit before continuing her analysis. Could the flash have been a laser strike?

She pulled up the external feed from *Carson*, matching it to the chrono readings of the flash, and sighed with relief. The warship's beam waveguides remained stowed in travel position. No railgun had discharged, no missile had been fired.

Missile... she ran the record back far enough to confirm *Carson* hadn't launched a guided weapon, cold or hot, slow or fast, to strike the refugees. She sat back in her padded seat and thought about it.

Maybe it was a meaningless anomaly, an artifact of the optical sensors. Or maybe one of the refugee craft had lit its engines for some reason. A mistake? An attempt to dodge what they feared might be coming? It occurred to her that *Carson*, if she stayed behind, could obliterate them at leisure, with no one the wiser but the crew.

But that seemed unlikely. A horrifying secret like that, shared by so many in the crew, would get out... unless Captain Gray and her crew were far more evil than she believed.

She'd shared drinks with Ellen Gray. She'd eaten with the crew every day. The rank and file were genuinely trying to do good, even if they were wild and undisciplined. One ruthless agent might get away with such a thing, but not the captain and crew of an entire warship.

Then what had she seen? Hmm... The sensor and data store was a full-spectrum electro-optical module, which meant it recorded much farther up and down the scale than mere visible light. Expanding the display, she searched for telltales from various bands—UV, laser, IR, X-rays, particle beam scatter and many more—and located the most energetic one.

Infrared. Heat. She'd been right. It was either an engine on full power, or an explosion. She hunted up and down the bands, looking for the byproducts of a fusion motor, but didn't find them.

Next, she searched for evidence of an uncontrolled hydrogen-oxygen fire, and confirmed it. The fire was real, and from its expansion curve, it had just started when Freiheit transited out of range.

Then, on a hunch, she looked for the spectroscopic emissions from chemical explosives.

Bingo.

Horror settled over her anew. A bomb? Who could have done such a thing?

She downloaded the information onto a data crystal and clipped it inside a pocket of her flight suit, still shaking. Someone else had to see this. Someone she trusted.

Before she found Straker, Engels ran into Loco inside the mechsuit parts factory, working on his partly disassembled Sledgehammer, its guts pulled out for maintenance and repair. She recognized densely packed flexible circuitry, room-temperature superconductors, and electroactive polymer muscles that were, kilo for kilo, a thousand times as powerful as those of humans.

She considered talking to him about the bomb—but changed her mind. His mouth was just too big.

"Hey, Carly-car," Loco said when he noticed her. "How're they hangin'? Still perky?"

"Stop calling me that."

"Okay, *Lieutenant* Carly-car. How does it feel to have Derek get promoted ahead of you?"

She shrugged. "Doesn't really bother me. I already told him he should be in charge, I'm not the commander type anyway."

Loco smiled. "Me neither. What's the latest, then, hotness?"

Engels suppressed a grin. Loco might be incorrigible, but at least he was cheerful. "Where's Straker?"

"Off brooding somewhere. I think that whole thing with the refugees got him thinking."

"Nothing wrong with thinking…" she said.

"Unless it messes with his head. You know Derek, always worried about his honor and integrity."

Engels changed her mind about not telling Loco about her discovery. She had to tell someone. She stepped up to Loco on impulse, putting a hand on his arm. She could see a quip rising in his throat, only to die at her earnest expression.

"What's going on?" he asked.

"Is there a non-networked computer suite around here that you can access privately? Something with holoscreens?"

"I'll ask Manny," he said, giving her a curious look. "He's one of the local mechsuit factory techs helping me. Gonna be really valuable as we ramp up the program." Loco patted her hand and left her standing for a moment.

When he returned, he led her down a hallway. "He said there's a design comp-suite around here somewhere. Here it is."

When they entered the room with its multiple holoscreens, Engels booted up the system and disconnected the network hardlink. "Not even a password... and this is a standard Hundred Worlds setup." She plugged in the data crystal and ran the vid data. "Here we go. What do you make of that?"

Loco leaned into the screen, peering at it from a handspan away. "Looks like a fire or explosion. Meteorite strike?"

Engels colored. "I should have thought of that. For some reason my mind went straight to sabotage or attack. Wait, no! Here, let me show you." She pulled up the multispectral analysis. "This is a chemical explosive signature, so it couldn't have been a meteorite."

"Hmm... Are you sure that signature couldn't be a false positive from something caught in a hydro-ox fire? Batteries, plastics? Explosive bolts? Were any of those boats armed with missiles or mines that might have burned or exploded accidentally?"

"No, nothing that fits this signature," she said. "Not even explosive bolts. All the boats were disarmed and thoroughly prepped. I did some of it myself, along with..." Engels trailed off, staring at nothing. Great Cosmos! She knew the Ruxin's morality wasn't quite like humanity's, but she thought he'd been given clear instructions to leave well enough alone. Dammit!

"What?" Loco asked.

"Who else? Zaxby," she said. "We're two of the most qualified pilots, so we did the prepping."

"But there were other people doing the checks too. Other Unmutual techs. On other boats. You didn't do them all."

"Yes, but it would only take one. Remember how Zaxby suggested we eliminate those people?"

Loco sat back. "Yeah. I'd forgotten. I thought it was funny as shit at the time, but... you think he might have planted something to wipe them out?"

"No... maybe.... I don't want to think so!"

"He's a smart guy, right? An alien brainiac. If it was me, I'd set a bomb to go off at least an hour after we left. Nobody would know."

Engels' voice rose. "But we had that two-hour technical delay... If he planted a bomb, he must have been biting his fingernails."

"That squid ain't got no fingernails, Carly."

"Stop–"

"Okay, okay. You know it's a term of endearment, right?" He leered.

"Never gonna happen, Loco."

Loco spread his hand on his throat. "Oh, dear. Be still, my broken balls."

"Shut up. You wouldn't want me anyway. Not with my skin still scarred from torture and mottled from the Hok biotech."

Loco scooted his seat over until it touched hers and leaned in close. "Can I tell you a secret?"

"Don't go copping a feel."

"If I did, I'd be making my point."

"What point?"

"That you're *not* ugly. Not to me, and not to Derek, because we've known you for a long time. We don't see your skin, or your bad haircut or any of that. We see *you*, no matter what face you got. We both love you."

Engels put fingertips to her cheek. "Thanks, Loco. You're a real friend."

"Ouch, the friend zone. Okay, never mind, I'll stop it. Since I'm such a friend and we're talking like this, I'll tell you something else. You and Derek were made for each other, and I'm not actually trying to get in the way of that. I got a local girl I'm seeing anyway. I just joke around, while I hope you guys will get over your stupid past and....” He mimed an explosion with his fingers. “Boom. It’s gonna be epic.”

“What past?” she demanded.

“You and him were always like binary planets, orbiting each other but never hooking up. Like, you were always afraid that if you did, there would be some kind of disaster. Well, guess what? We’re not in a rigid military structure anymore, and you guys can finally make it happen, but what do you do? You keep dancing around like you’re on eggshells. You’re both afraid.”

“I’m not afraid.”

Loco scratched his head with both hands. “Yeah, that’s what Derek said too, but he is. I think you both got this childish illusion in your heads from when you fell in love at Academy and you’re afraid of losing it. You keep each other at arm’s length because you’re petrified of dealing with reality, just like those people we left on those boats. If someone did blow them up, well, guess what? You’ll be the same as them, hoping so much for emotional safety that the chance for something real passes you up—and then you die. You guys got two weeks in sidespace here on this base. Get busy, girl! Drag that earnest fool into bed!”

“Loco, you make a rotten psych.”

“That’s because psychs don’t tell you what you need to hear. Only friends do that. You know, like you said I am.” He leaned back and pointed a finger at her while winking and nodding with exaggerated drama.

Engels sighed. “Right. Thanks, I think. Back to this explosion... should we report it to Ramirez?”

“No. Better to report to DeChang when we arrive. If Zaxby did it, we don’t want to tip him off. He might kill some more people. If he didn’t, better not to point false suspicion. Lots of people already think he’s a bloodthirsty, alien asshole that doesn’t care about human life.”

“Yeah, we don’t want him hanged by frontier justice.”

“Besides, how’d you hang a guy like that? Where’s his freakin’ neck? And all those ropy arms...”

Engels slapped Loco’s shoulder and laughed. “Stay funny, Loco. We need your sense of humor.”

"Yeah, that's me, the eternal sidekick to the tall, dark, handsome hero. Well, tall and dark, anyway. Okay, maybe just tall." He shrugged. "I don't mind. Not everyone's cut out to be a Glory Girl or a Bravo Boy."

Engels laughed again, and then she felt her face fall. "Those showvids we watched, those action figures we collected… was it all just to program us to be good little patriots? Like Lazarus said?"

"If so, it wasn't our fault. It wasn't the common people's fault, either." He paused. "Do you think that's why Derek isn't pushing to go back to the Hundred Worlds? And why you're not pushing him to push?"

"Maybe," she said. "For my part, I'm wondering where home really is."

"Lazarus got inside your head."

"Lazarus was a lying asshole," replied Engels angrily. "Whatever he said, it was to turn us away from our people and toward the Mutuality."

"Looks like he succeeded with the first part. Nobody wants to go home."

"Because our real home is anywhere we can be with each other."

Loco gazed at her, serious for once. "Got that right."

Engels stood, pulling out the crystal and wiping the system. "All right. This stays under wraps for now. Don't even tell Derek unless he needs to know. And we'll keep our eyes on Zaxby. If he does anything suspicious, try to get the evidence on vid or pics."

* * *

Across the habitat, Frank Murdock in the Base Control Center noticed the mechsuit factory's design comp-suite being taken offline, and then put back online again. He was an obsessive engineer, an Unmutual techno-geek extraordinaire. At Major Ramirez's instructions, he'd already installed monitoring software in all the high-interest facilities, and the mechsuit factory rated just below the BCC itself in importance.

Accessing the system remotely, he reviewed its offline use. Though its first layer of memory had been dumped and erased, his monitoring program kept a backup record of everything.

His jaw clenched and he broke out in a sweat when he saw what had been displayed on the screens. Calling up the factory's closed circuit vid, he watched as two of the new officers, Engels and Paloco, entered and later exited the room, talking earnestly. Unfortunately, he had no audio.

The comp activity and vids spoke plainly. Had these people planted a bomb and killed four hundred civilians, and wanted to confirm it?

After thinking hard for some time, he reached for his comlink.

Chapter 25

Freiheit.

Straker stayed busy tinkering with his mechsuit during Freiheit's sidespace journey, using fresh spares to bring it up to full specs and improve what he could. He also ran live drills with Loco and the rest of the ground task force, forging teamwork and the ability to react instantly to a variety of threats.

Engels tried to get him to eat dinner with her a couple of times, but he was far too busy with important things to waste time on socializing, even with her. He felt bad about it, but this was a matter of survival... and, he realized, Colonel Jackson's suicide had hit him hard. Maybe what he'd done was an echo of Straker's own feelings. The old man had been left with nothing to live for, so he'd simply checked out.

That temptation, that feeling of having the rug pulled from under him, never really went away. He didn't belong in the Hundred Worlds anymore, he hated the Mutuality, and he didn't feel at home here with the Unmutuals either.

He fended off the feeling by working, and by exercising his troops relentlessly.

He got a lot of pushback. Now that they were safe in sidespace, the grunts wanted to slack off and party. Worse, some were taking liberties with the locals, he heard, pressuring or paying them for companionship.

Fortunately, there were few recreational drugs aboard, but there was liquor to be found, or made. Too many Unmutual fighters swaggered around like petty dictators, demanding whatever they wanted and brawling over the few diversions available.

Locals courageous enough to report problems were brought to him for personal interviews. The whiners he dispensed with quickly, those whose lawns had been trampled or who found the communal swimming pools too crowded with off-duty troops. Others he tried to help, those whose homes had been invaded or possessions "requisitioned."

The worst he saw, though, were youngsters who trembled, bruised and battered, telling stories of squads cornering them and degrading them with everything from drunken harassment to serious physical abuse.

The problem was, he could never make a positive identification of the culprits. These civilians had no experience with crime or social unrest. They'd never experienced any major disruption in their peaceful lives. Even after recruiting the intimidating presence of Heiser to work with him and Loco, the incidents only worsened.

Straker faced off with Major Ramirez in the office she'd commandeered and told her what he knew, hoping she would support a cleanup of the situation. She stared flatly at him across her desk. "I understand your concerns, Captain Straker, but boys will be boys and girls will be girls. They're hardened fighters, not programmed Mutuality toy soldiers. They're just blowing off steam. I even hear your buddy Loco has picked up one of these rock-rats for a girlfriend."

"Major, Loco doesn't abuse women, but some of your troops do. This isn't an R&R port of call, accustomed to waves of military. There are no dive bars, no strip clubs, no red light districts, no whores or casinos or VR arcades to absorb their energies and take their money. These people have been isolated for decades. They have close-knit families. They've worked here for generations. There aren't enough single people old enough to accommodate all our troops who are looking for, um, casual encounters. I know for a fact that locals of both sexes have been raped, some underage. I need your help to put a stop to it. It's wrong. Besides, bad discipline brings more bad discipline."

Ramirez waved as if shooing flies. "All right, all right. I'll handle it. Dismissed."

But nothing changed for the next couple of days, and Straker was forced to conclude Ramirez wasn't serious about "handling" things.

"Come on," he told Heiser and Loco that evening. "Let's go to a party."

"A party, sir?" Banden Heiser wrinkled his broad forehead. Part of the core team since the escape from the Mutualist prison, he found it a challenge to relax—his heart always on duty.

"That's what I said. I got some intel."

"You're not really the party type, boss," said Loco, eyeing him. "What's this really about?"

"Some bad shit we need to put a stop to," Straker replied.

Heiser cracked the knuckles of his huge hands. "Sounds fun. We'll watch your back, sir."

When the three men reached the warehouse where the tip told him the get-together would be, they saw forty or fifty Unmutuals, mostly men, but some hard-looking women as well, plus a smattering of unsavory locals. All were armed, as usual.

They were drinking something they scooped out of a barrel. Straker watched Loco grab a cup and help himself, shoving among the others, who greeted him like a comrade, laughing.

"Raw alcohol flavored with fruit and herbs," Loco said when he returned, sipping at the stuff. "Cheap and potent."

"You sure it's ethanol? Might be poisonous methanol or something," said Heiser.

Loco raised his eyebrows, and then tipped the contents of the cup onto the floor. "There's more than one kind of alcohol?"

Heiser rolled his eyes. "Mechsuiters. Hanging out on Shangri-La, getting the best of everything. Some of us had to scrounge for our hooch. The bad stuff will make you go blind."

"I don't think they care," said Straker, looking around the building's Spartan interior. Cheap chairs and tables had been set up, and at one end, a stage had been built, as if for a show.

Suddenly, the lights dimmed everywhere but the stage, and a roar went up from the crowd. Four girls and a boy were shoved onto the stage, all between the ages of about fourteen and twenty. Slow, grinding music started from a player, and one of the girls began to dance and strip.

Obviously she'd done this before, though she displayed no enthusiasm, only resignation. The other four tried to imitate the first one, encouraged by yells and catcalls from the audience.

"Disgusting," said Straker.

"Oh, that one's not so bad, for a beginner," said Loco.

"You think they're volunteers? Take a look at them. They're scared shitless."

"Oh," said Loco. "*Oh.*"

Heiser said, "Yeah, they're being forced to do this. What do you think, Lieutenant? You believe five teenagers from this hick place suddenly decided to become strippers? I've seen that look before."

Loco shrugged uncomfortably. Both men turned to Straker.

"Well, what're we gonna do about it, sir?" said Heiser.

"We break it up."

Loco said, "Uh, boss, I know this isn't the best situation, but it really isn't all that bad. I mean, it's not like they're being sold into prostitution or anything."

Just then, an announcer with a portable microphone spoke up.

"All right, now that the merchandise is naked, let's get on with the auction!" He grabbed the first girl, the one that seemed more experienced. "You all know Rita. Some of you've *had* Rita! And you can have her again tonight! Let's start the bidding at fifty credits! Do I hear sixty?"

"You were saying, Loco?" Straker asked.

"Seventy!"

"Shit," said Loco.

"One hundred, I'm bid!"

"Sir, I'm with you, but we're heavily outnumbered," said Heiser.

"One-twenty, one-thirty, do I hear one-forty? Going once, twice... sold, for one hundred forty credits to Fourth Squad, First Platoon, Alpha Company!" said the announcer.

"Dammit, those are *my* men!" Straker shoved his way to the stage, Loco and Heiser behind him. Rebels gave way when they saw who it was, or perhaps it was the look on his face that backed them off.

"Bring her here," he said to the announcer.

"Hey, we paid for her!" said a man at Straker's elbow. "Oh... hey, sir. Look, guys! It's Captain Straker! You can have the first turn if you want, sir."

Straker ignored the speaker and stepped up onto the stage, taking the girl by the arm and gently pulling her to him. "Your name is Rita?"

"Y-yes sir."

"Do you want to do this?"

"Want to?"

"Are you doing this of your own free will?"

"Me? My free will? They... I... they keep me in a cage all day and sell me every night. They sex me until I bleed. I can't..." Suddenly, hope blossomed in her eyes, and she clung to him. "Please, sir, buy me. Just you. I'll do whatever you want. I'll make you feel good. Just don't make me do it with so many again. They hurt me so bad."

A towering rage flared in Straker. He pointed his slugthrower at the ceiling and fired off a burst, and then waved it out over the crowd. "Listen up!" he roared. "I'm Captain Straker, second in command of this shitty operation. All of you get the hell out of here before I start shooting people!"

Some dispersed, but a hard knot of Unmutuals pushed forward, their weapons dangerously close to being aimed at Straker and his men.

"You can't do this," they said, angry. One, more ominously, yelled from the back, "You ain't got your fancy suit no more, refugee!" Similar comments followed.

Straker handed his slugthrower to Loco and stepped forward, toward the troublemakers, surprising them with his boldness. Quicker than the eye could follow, he smashed two in the face with a Hok-skinned fist, then two more, and then kicked the next two in their bellies. Within seconds a pack of them writhed on the floor. Loco and Heiser covered everyone else with lasers.

"I don't need my mechsuit to deal with scum like you," Straker bellowed, kicking the nearest man in the ass. "Leave your weapons and get out, and I might forget about this. Stay, and you're in the brig! Go on! Go!"

They ran.

Thirty seconds later, the three men found themselves alone in the warehouse, except for the music player and five young locals. The girls started wailing, all but Rita, who picked up a fallen pistol.

"Gimme that, darling. You'll hurt somebody," said Heiser, prying the weapon from her hand. She threw herself at him and refused to let go.

"Looks like you got yourself a girlfriend," Loco said.

Heiser patted her awkwardly. "I ain't... I can't..."

"Loco's right," said Straker. "You take care of her for now. Take her to her family if she wants to go. Otherwise, keep her in your quarters. That way the others will leave her alone."

"What about the rest?" said Loco.

"Take charge of them, Lieutenant Paloco," said Straker. "You're an officer. Act like one. Step up and be responsible for once."

"That's harsh."

"I'm not kidding, Loco. Figure it out and get it done. I'm going to go see Ramirez and put a stop to this once and for all." Straker retrieved his slugthrower, swapped out a full magazine, and then strode out of the warehouse.

* * *

Ramirez only opened her door, pistol in hand, after Straker had banged on it for thirty seconds solid. "What the fuck do you want?"

Straker pushed his way in and shut the door. "I just came from a slave auction. Kids as young as thirteen or fourteen were being sold to be gang-raped. It wasn't the first time, either."

"I take it you handled the situation?"

"Of course."

"Then you did your job. Bravo." Ramirez set her weapon on a table and poured whiskey from a real, labeled bottle, a Hundred Worlds brand. She must have commandeered it from the locals. "Drink?"

"No, I don't want a drink. I want you to give me your word you'll rein your people in. They don't listen to me unless I'm right there. I'm a newcomer. I had to bust heads tonight because they wouldn't recognize my authority, but they'll recognize yours."

Ramirez tossed off her drink. "I'm not their nanny, and neither are you. This is the first operation they've been told not to plunder what they captured and they're doing pretty well. Actually, they're more restrained than usual. I have several of the worst offenders in the brig already. Who cares if they party with a few locals? Stick to your mechsuit, Captain. Leave the discipline to me."

A knot of rage kindled inside Straker. Seized by an impulse he'd never before contemplated, he locked the door and turned to the woman appointed as his commanding officer, one for whom he'd suddenly lost all respect. Slowly, deliberately, he set his slugthrower on the table.

With maximum speed, he took two swift strides and seized Ramirez by the neck, preventing her from speaking and lifting her from her chair to pin her against the wall. She kicked at him, but he held her feet off the ground depriving her of leverage.

Straker growled, barely able to speak. "This is how it feels for a civilian teenager who's never known crime or war or anything but a peaceable society to encounter one of these scumbags you're defending. No one to help you or stop the rape, and if you did report it, half the people you know would blame *you* for letting yourself be polluted."

"Put... me... down..." she choked out as he lessened the pressure slightly.

"No. Not until you feel some of the terror you're making excuses for."

She didn't crack. "I'll throw you in the brig for this. You're DeChang's fair-haired boy right now, but you won't be after he gets my report."

"Then I'll have to kill you and toss your body out into sidespace. 'Discard' you, isn't that what you call it?" His face unchanging, he tightened his hold again.

Ramirez began to panic, squirming and scratching futilely at his iron grip. Straker let her feet touch the floor and shifted his fingers, now grasping her hair behind her head and jabbing his index finger toward her face. "That's what I'm talking about, Major, what you're feeling right now. That's the ugliness I refuse to sweep under the rug. Got it?"

Ramirez nodded, eyes wild.

"You have two choices. You either use your authority to clean up this festering sewer, or I'll do it for you. If I do, that terror you're feeling right now will be the least of your worries. I may not be able to give the locals justice, but I will damn sure put a stop to these crimes. I don't have a brig, but I bet I can find a backhoe to bury you and anyone else that gets in my way. And remember, Loco and I have the only two mechsuits here."

"All right," she growled. "All right! I'll take care of it!"

Straker let her go, and she put her hands on her hips, snarling at him. He grudgingly admired her for that. Nobody'd ever accused her of lacking a spine.

The fear had faded from her eyes. "You just made an enemy, Straker."

"Not my intention," he said, shrugging, "but if that's what it takes to get some military discipline into this outfit, fair enough. Oh, and if you have any thoughts of me having a little 'accident' before we get back, I'll be spreading a few data entries around in the networks, set to send themselves to DeChang if I don't log in from time to time, not to mention a complete report of your troops' crimes."

"They're your troops too, Straker."

"But I can prove I did all I could to correct the situation. Can you?"

Ramirez licked her lips. "I should have discarded you when I had the chance. I knew you'd be a pain in my ass when I met you at the airlock."

He picked up his slugthrower. "When I give my word, Major, I keep it. I'm promising you now: if you do the right thing here, I won't speak to DeChang about it."

"If asked," she said thoughtfully, "you'll say I took care of it as soon as I noticed the problem? And no mention of this little... *incident* between us?"

"I'll be as discreet as you are about it." Straker slung his slugthrower, picked up her sidearm from the table, dropped the magazine, and then cleared and field-stripped it, tossing the pieces into separate corners. "Have a nice day, Major. Tomorrow morning I expect to hear howls of indignation from the troublemakers. By the time we transit in, I want punishment, apologies, and restitution from those convicted of crimes. And there better be quite a few."

"You've made your point. Dismissed, Captain."

Fists clenched, Straker turned his back to her and stomped out.

✳ ✳ ✳

He slept sealed in his mechsuit from then on, all externals locked. During the daytime he remained on guard, keeping Heiser around to watch his back at all times. It wasn't long before he heard reports of Major Ramirez taking steps to remedy the situation.

Karst, the smooth-faced kid who'd first helped them after the rescue, accosted him in the mess hall they'd set up. "Sir, may I speak with you?"

"Of course, Corporal. Sit down." Straker nodded at Heiser, who gave the young man space to take a seat across the table. "What's on your mind? You look worried."

"It's this crackdown, sir. We're suddenly prohibited from social contact with the locals. Official business only. But I've got..."

Straker sipped from his mug of cheap caff. "Go on."

"Sir, there's this girl."

Straker closed his eyes and took a deep breath. "All consensual? No pressure?"

Karst's mouth worked. "No, no sir, no way. She's just... I mean, we're..."

"In love?"

"Yes, sir!"

Straker rubbed his neck. "Look, kid, I don't want to burst your bubble, but think. Is it likely this is real love, or could it be hero-worship and your dashing uniform? These people, they're very parochial. Small-town mentality. It may not last."

"But sir... we're *in love!*"

Straker stared at Karst for a long moment and shook his head. "Yeah, that's the irresistible force. Look, what do you want me to do about it?"

"Talk to Major Ramirez. Get her to let up on us. She's throwing violators in the brig left and right. Some have been *flogged.* You know, like with *whips!* There's a rumor she's even going to execute Master Sergeant Yates. Not that he doesn't deserve it for what he did to that little boy, the bastard, but..."

"But you can't stand not seeing your honey for a few days?"

"I have no idea what'll happen once we transit in. I might get stationed away from her, and never see her again!" Karst seemed as if he might cry.

"Look, kid. Corporal. My standing with Major Ramirez isn't too high right now, and she needed to crack down. Sorry you and your girl got caught in the gears, but that's life. It'll work out. Do what she says for now, and when we get back, I'll try to make sure you get assigned to this base. Either that, or we'll get permission for her to cohab with you. You might have to formalize the arrangement."

"Oh, yes, sir! We want to get married!"

"After knowing each other for what, a week? Maybe you should just do a one-year contract."

"We're in love! We want to be together forever. Haven't you ever been in love, sir?"

Straker massaged his forehead, remembering how he'd felt when he met Engels at Academy... and how their relationship remained unconsummated. Maybe the kid was smarter than he was. At least he was rolling the dice. "Yeah... All right. Just cool it until we arrive. Don't violate orders."

"Yes, sir. I'll try."

"You better do more than try, or I'll flog you myself. Dismissed."

The next morning, Heiser handed him a message. Karst requested to see him in the brig.

"Why am I not surprised?" Straker said. He punched the wall of his temporary office, leaving a visible dent in its surface, and then marched the two blocks to the building Major Ramirez had turned into a brig. He brushed past the guards there as they made abortive motions to stop him. They backed off at the look on his face and the warnings from his bodyguard.

Inside, he spoke to Karst. "What the hell happened, Corporal? Didn't I tell you to stand down for a while?"

"I... I'm sorry, sir. I couldn't stay away. I guess her parents reported me. I got arrested before I even got to see her. They're going to flog me."

"Sounds like you're getting what you deserve for violating orders. Hell, I told you I'd flog you myself, didn't I?"

"Yes, sir. I'm not asking to be pardoned. I just wanted to apologize, sir, and to ask a favor."

"Why should I do you a favor, dumbass?"

"Not for me, sir. Please, go tell my girl what's happened and that it will be all right, that we'll be together soon enough. Her name is Cynthia Lamancha. You can find her house in Section Five. Everybody knows everybody here. Just ask around."

"All right. I'll do what I can. For her, not for you."

"Yes, sir. Thank you, sir." Karst went back and sat down among the dozen other offenders in his cell, grimly awaiting the lash.

The Lamancha family house stood among a score of similar dwellings: small, neat, homey, in the village-like grouping of Section Five. By the time Straker knocked on the door, he had calmed down from cursing under his breath at the idiocy of youth.

A short, plump woman with dark hair answered the door, her face showing tremendous fear. "Yes, sir?"

Straker was surprised and saddened by the intensity of her terror. He didn't think the situation warranted it. Maybe she was afraid he was there to take her daughter Cynthia away on Karst's behalf. Maybe she was afraid he was there to retaliate for wanting to stop the relationship. He sighed under his breath. This was exactly why he'd forced Ramirez's hand. Mix unprofessional fighters in with naïve civilians and trouble always cropped up.

"Sorry to disturb you, Mrs. Lamancha. Everything's all right. I'm not here to… for anything bad. May I come in?" He signaled Heiser to stay outside.

"Of course, sir." The woman backed up into the room.

Her eyes flicked to the left as alarm bells went off in his head. He'd just begun to react when he heard the crackle and felt the discharge of a heavy stunner lock up all his muscles, fry his nerves, and pummel him into unconsciousness.

Chapter 26

Freiheit. Mining entry lock.

Head pounding and nauseated, Straker came suddenly awake to the whining of a half-familiar voice.

"What's going on? What are you doing to me?" he heard a man say in the local accent.

"Shut up," came a reply, and then a heavy thud. "He's out. Goddamn pussy civilians."

A chuckle, and another voice. "Civilian pussy, you mean."

"Yeah, baby. Most of them is virgins, too. Nothing like busting a new cherry."

"What's an old cherry?"

More guffaws and crude jokes followed. Straker slitted his eyes open but remained completely still. Two men moved around the room, setting up equipment. He could see hardwires and electronics.

One was unfamiliar, though he was sure he was an Unmutual fighter. The other he recognized. Master Sergeant Yates, the man accused of raping and murdering at least three locals, one a boy of twelve. He was supposed to be in the brig.

The floor on which Straker lay was crudely finished rock, as was the chamber. It appeared to be a utility airlock, a large one such as led to the airless tunnels that honeycombed the asteroid base's thick outer shell. Mining gear sat here and there, waiting to be used.

Testing, Straker could tell he was bound by fibertape, hands and feet and mouth. The stuff was nearly unbreakable, but it could be cut. Waiting until both of his captors' backs were turned, he edged over to a small ore-crusher and began to try to wear through the tape on a metal corner of the machine. He kept his movements small, and froze every time the others faced him.

"This is gonna make one hell of a bang," said Yates from across the room, patting something as if in affection. "You sure they'll be able to block the hole before we lose all our atmo?"

"Oh, yeah. Remember, the ingress breaches were bigger than this. We let the locals do their jobs. They'll bulldoze a plug and write off this tunnel. Our traitors here'll die trying to sabotage the operation and everything can go back to normal."

"Good. I was getting really tired of play-acting like a good little boy."

"I dunno. I think it was kinda fun. Did you see Straker's do-gooder reaction when we set Karst up? 'Sure, kid, I'll fix everything. I'm your fairy godmother. Let me handle it.' God, these recoverees are such clueless straight-arrows. Act like they're in a kiddie showvid."

"Yeah," said Yates. "It always takes a while for them to toughen up. Wish I could shoot them all, right now."

"Ramirez said no, on the off chance they get dug up later with holes in them. Have to keep up appearances for the local yokels and the general."

"They're gonna have fibertape on them, though. That'll be obvious."

"Yeah, you're right. Stun them again and let's take it off. Then we can set the timer and get the hell out of here."

Straker stepped up his efforts to cut the tape, but the industrial-strength fiber resisted his efforts to wear it through on the corner he could reach. He heard the buzz of the stunner, once, twice, three times, and then it was his turn. He summoned every ounce of power to his arms and tried to break the weakened tape, but he couldn't.

The last thing he saw was the muzzle of the stunner pointed at him.

* * *

Straker awoke again swearing he'd never let himself be stunned again. Repeated nerve overload left him feeling as if he'd been kicked in the groin. His vision wavered and his head pounded. His only consolation was a belief it would have been far worse without the Hok biotech's boost. In fact, it may have saved his life, as they'd obviously intended him to remain unconscious until the blast they'd mentioned went off.

Straker rolled to his feet, free of the fibertape. He found Loco, Engels, Heiser and a citizen unknown to him, all stunned. He grabbed a large, half-empty bottle of water and drank it, then splashed some on the face of each sleeper.

Engels and Loco sputtered awake. The local and Heiser didn't stir. "Come on, you two, get up," Straker yelled, searching the room for the device Yates had left to kill them. When he found it, he groaned in despair.

He'd hoped it would be a simple mining charge, something where he could remove the detonator and that would be that. Instead, he saw the warhead of a Sledgehammer rocket, hardwired to a countdown timer. The numbers on the display read seven minutes and falling. He knew next to nothing about disarming bombs, so he dared not touch it.

As Engels and Loco stumbled to their feet, he tried the room's inner door leading back toward the habitat, but it wouldn't budge. It opened away from him, of course, so loss of pressure on this side would automatically seal it due to the atmo on the other side.

The other door of the mining prep chamber, the one leading out to the tunnels, opened inward for the same reason. With vacuum on the other side, the pressure inside would keep it shut. He couldn't open it. But if there were no pressure...

"Suits! Get into those suits! There's a bomb and we need to get out of here, through the mining tunnels!" Straker yelled, grabbing one of the work suits off the rack. It was a standard heavy-duty model, intended to withstand the rock chips spit out by borers. Fortunately, it had been stored open, ready and fully charged with air and power, all according to Hundred Worlds safety regs.

He dropped the suit, realizing that it would hinder him in getting Heiser and the citizen into theirs. Dragging the unconscious men over to the rack, he selected correct sizes and stuffed them into the things, making sure they were sealed and the air was on.

Engels and Loco reported suited up as well. He got into his own in record time, just like in a loss-of-atmo drill, blessing those who'd trained him to the highest military standard.

Engels found and opened the room's emergency air exhaust valve as Straker sealed his suit. Usually this was used to put out a fire by depleting all the oxygen, but this time it would give them escape.

Their suits inflated as the pressure dropped. "Loco, help me," Straker said, and the two men undogged the outer door and used crowbars to break the seal. The small amount of remaining air rushed out and the door swung inward, wide open.

"Three minutes," Straker said, checking the timer. "We'll take one minute to grab supplies. Carla, can you drive this mini-borer?"

"I can figure it out." She climbed into the vehicle's one-person cab and powered it up.

"Loco, hook up that trailer." Straker grabbed air cylinders and began piling them into the square bed even as Loco manhandled it to attach to the borer. He searched for food and water and added a box of survival rations and a water tank.

"Let's go. Two minutes left. We don't want to be nearby when that thing blows." Engels said.

"Grab these guys," Straker said, and helped Loco set Heiser and the local in the bed of the trailer, both still unconscious. They jumped aboard, and Engels drove the borer out into the tunnel, turning left.

The borer's top speed seemed to be about fifteen kilometers per hour, a trot for a fit person. Several twists and turns ensured that when they felt the shudder of the blast through the rock, nothing but a few wisps of dusty gas reached them.

Engels pulled over in a wide spot and dismounted, turning on all the external lights. "What the hell just happened, Derek? One minute I'm getting into my lifter, the next I'm waking up in a room with a bomb."

"Me too," said Loco. "I was tinkering with my Sledgehammer and…"

"They bushwhacked us and stunned us."

"Who?"

"Ramirez's goons. One was Yates."

"The guy they were going to execute?"

Straker nodded within his clear crystal helmet. "Yeah, I guess that was a ruse to keep us from getting suspicious. I thought I'd gotten her to do the right thing and crack down on these criminals, but it was all a ploy."

"So these guys really *are* pirates," Loco said.

"Pirates with a cause," Engels replied. "Everything can't be an act. They really do want to overthrow the Mutuality, but they're no better than their enemies if they allow their troops to rape and pillage."

"Maybe DeChang doesn't know about what goes on away from his base," said Straker. "Yates said something about keeping him in the dark."

"Oh, Derek, open your eyes," snapped Engels. "I know you wanted to believe the best of him, but he has to have an inkling. As long as the job gets done, he probably doesn't care."

Loco chimed in. "Yeah, these pirates are so used to abusing those they raid, they don't know how to act when they liberate civilians. I think Ramirez really did want minimum trouble, but she wasn't going to piss off her own troops by taking their fun away... until you insisted."

Straker began to pace from rock wall to rock wall. "But that seems pretty extreme. I mean, is she really willing to sacrifice the only two mechsuiters they have, plus a crack pilot, just to let the troops run wild? She could have kept the situation under control without killing us. It's too risky. Unless it's personal. I may have gone a little overboard in making my point."

Engels and Loco exchanged glances.

"Derek," she said, "I don't think this is only about you. If it were, you'd be the only one they bushwhacked. Loco and I found something out."

"What?"

"I recorded an explosion in the refugees' boats just as we were transiting to sidespace. I confirmed chemical explosives. It couldn't have been an accident."

Straker stared at her, trying to reorient his train of thought. "The refugees? Explosion? What does that have to do with anything?"

"Derek, don't you get it? All those refugees are dead! The *Carson* didn't fire on them, and remember, Murdock had a two-hour technical delay in transit. That means someone planted a bomb that was supposed to go off two hours after we left, to kill off the ones who wanted to stay and join the Mutuality. Even Zaxby suggested it."

"I'm just as bad," Straker whispered.

"You didn't want to kill them!" said Engels.

"No, but I viewed them as a problem, not as people."

"Derek, snap out of your stupid guilt mode. It's not always about you and the weight of responsibility on your shoulders. You didn't suggest killing them, Zaxby did. I bet Ramirez gave him the go-ahead and that amoral son-of-a-beach was happy to oblige."

"I say, that was clever aquatic wordplay," came Zaxby's voice over their comlink, "but I assure you I did not plant any bomb or kill any humans. It was clear the consensus was against me, and when there is only one Ruxin and hundreds of humans, it pays to exercise discretion."

"Damned unsecure civilian networks," muttered Engels, looking around as if she could see him. "Zaxby, if what you say is true, then you have to help us."

"Of course, Carla Engels. You're by far my favorite human. What can I do for you?"

"Zaxby, this is Straker. What's going on out there?"

"I believe I was speaking to your female, not you, Derek Straker. Please do not interrupt."

Loco began to choke on laughter within his helmet.

Straker sputtered. "My– oh yeah, my *female*. Okay, Carla, ask this squid what's going on out there."

"Pejoratives will not help your cause, Derek Straker. Squids are a lower form of life."

"You can say that again," Loco commented.

Engels broke in. "Zaxby, answer the question. What's going on out there?"

"The official word is there's been an explosion caused by attempted sabotage, and you, Straker, Heiser and Paloco are among the dead, along with a local miner named Linz."

"And why are you talking to us? Why haven't you reported us?"

"Because I like you, Carla Engels. You treat me with respect, and you give good head rubs."

Loco turned to Engels with a grin. "Head rubs? Ooh, baby, I could use a head rub."

"Shut up."

"This is all starting to make sense to me," Loco continued. "Tentacle-porn!"

"Tentacle porn?" Zaxby asked.

"Look it up yourself, Zaxby," Engels said.

"I just did. Quite graphic. I could do that for you, Carla Engels, if you'd like. It seems a fair recompense for a head rub."

"Zaxby, forget about it and never, *ever* mention it again," Engels growled. "Moving on: how'd you get on this channel?"

"When the excitement started, I began to scan all the comlink bands in order to gain more information. I ran across yours and listened for a while. I am very interested in hearing what sabotage you were planning and how you escaped blowing yourselves up after all."

"We didn't plan any sabotage," said Engels. "Ramirez's goons stunned us and tried to set us up to be killed because we found out about the refugee bomb. Straker got added in because he pissed Ramirez off."

"Because I was standing up for the local citizens," Straker said.

"Yes, that too, and we agree with *what* you tried to do, if not *how* you tried to do it, as usual." Engels raised an eyebrow at Straker. "So what do we do next?"

Straker resumed pacing. "If we could get to our mechsuits, we could crush them."

"Killing cockroaches with sledgehammers—pun intended," Loco said. "I'm in—but we'll still need help. Even with Zaxby and a few other allies, we can't eliminate almost two hundred hardened rebels. Only a few of them would side with us; people from the prison, I mean. The Unmutuals could hold facilities and people hostage, and you know some aren't above murdering civilians to get what they want. We'd end up in a standoff until transit, at which point... who knows?"

"At that point it would depend on General DeChang," Engels said.

"He'd support what I did," Straker insisted, "especially after we show him the evidence of the refugee bomb and Ramirez's attempt to kill us."

"I sincerely doubt that," Zaxby said. "I have learned from my monitoring of all networks that, according to Ramirez, General DeChang authorized anyone not joining the Unmutuals to be 'discarded.' I believe the only reason they weren't simply executed is that you were present. They didn't want to turn their only mechsuiters against them… at least, not until they have more suits built and pilots trained."

"That might be Ramirez's story," Straker said. "She might be going against his wishes."

"Do you really think that's likely?" Engels asked. "Or is it more likely DeChang plays the benevolent father figure and Ramirez is his attack dog?"

"I agree with your female, Derek Straker," Zaxby said. "All indications demonstrate the Unmutual organization is practicing deception in order to influence your behavior to further their own ends in a manner not conforming to your moral structure. DeChang is their leader; ergo, he must know."

"You mean they're lying and using us, and DeChang is a two-faced snake," Straker replied.

"I believe I just said that, in far more precise terms."

"I'm getting sick of everyone thinking they can use me," Straker said.

"And us," chimed in Loco.

"All of us," said Engels. "Zaxby, do you want to stay with these people?"

"Of course not, Carla Engels. They're making far too many calamari jokes for my taste, and my return banter about monkey-meat never goes over well."

"That's the only reason? Because they might eat you?"

"And you are unlikely to. That and your head rubs."

"Tentacles!" crowed Loco.

"I can reach your air hoses, you know," Engels said.

"Shut up, you clowns," Straker growled. "Zaxby, can you access plans of this base without being noticed?"

"I believe so. Murdock has extensive monitoring software installed, but he is no match for my skills."

"Good. Find us a place in these tunnels to live for the next few days until we transit in."

"I've already done so. There's an emergency shelter for miners two hundred meters from your present location. I will guide you, and I will disable all sensors indicating you're occupying it."

"Great. Once we're there, I'll tell you my plan."

Chapter 27

Freiheit's outer hull, the edge of the mining labyrinth.

Two bored rebel fighters sat in a corner of one of Freiheit's small-craft hangars, gambling and sucking on smokesticks. For the last hour the guards had paid no attention to Murdock's voice as it counted down the arrival into normal space. Straker, Engels and Loco had been watching them from behind a row of ground vehicles after sneaking into the hangar through the outer tunnel system. They'd sent Heiser off yesterday to coordinate with other former prisoners, since those people were unlikely to trust Zaxby.

The guards' disinterest was no surprise. Once in sidespace, transiting out was easy. All one had to do was shut off the engines that held the base there, and the vessel in question would slide "down" the gravitic spacetime gradient and pop out once the slope became flat enough. The trick was, of course, making sure you exited in the right place. With Murdock at the helm, the guards no doubt had every confidence of arriving on time, on target.

"I'm surprised they're not drunk or asleep," Straker whispered as they eyed the two guards that stood in their way.

"They're not completely undisciplined," Engels replied.

"It's not gonna matter," Straker growled. "Far as I'm concerned, they're the enemy. No mercy, no prisoners."

"Got it, boss," Loco said.

Engels nodded with compressed lips.

Straker could tell she wasn't entirely pleased with his ruthless order, but they couldn't afford to be merciful. One lucky rebel guard that raised the alarm could wreck all their plans. This had to go perfectly.

When Murdock's countdown reached eleven minutes, Straker said, "Let's roll." He led a stealthy approach from behind parked support vehicles and didn't hesitate before rushing the guards.

He caught them flatfooted, before they even reached for their weapons. Two blinding-quick blows of the crowbar he'd appropriated cracked their skulls, spilling their brains onto the deck.

Loco picked up a stunner and handed Straker a slugthrower. Engels relieved the fallen guard's body of his handgun belt and strapped it around her own waist. Loco held out the other pistol belt to Straker.

"No, you keep it," Straker said. "These are all I need." He hefted the slugthrower in one hand, the crowbar in the other. "Hide the bodies. Cover the mess."

Murdock's voice droned while they dragged the fallen to dump them in an open tank of used lubricant, and then slammed the lid. Engels said, "I'll prep the ship," and headed for the only sidespace-capable vessel in the hangar, a four-seat utility courier with Hundred Worlds markings.

Straker switched on his comlink. "You there?" he said, deliberately not using a name.

"I'm here," came Zaxby's round tones.

"We're securing the objective. Send the rest. Don't forget the databases."

"Affirmative. I am now heading there myself, and will no longer be in control of the network, so maintain operational security protocols."

"Roger." Straker ceased transmitting and made sure he'd found the controls to open the hangar doors, though he waited to do so. Activating them might alert Murdock's monitoring software.

As planned, Loco opened the hatch wide on a twenty-passenger shuttle, and then backed up the mini-borer and its trailer full of supplies right into the craft. He and Straker began to unload food, water and extra oxygen.

The main personnel door opened and more than twenty people rushed in, Heiser in the lead. The big man led the eclectic bunch straight to the shuttle and packed them in, civilians and military alike. It would be very tight. "Glad to hear we're getting the hell off this rock, sir."

"Good to have you with me," replied Straker. He looked more closely at Heiser. "You have something to say?"

"Just that... sir... we thought we were freeing the locals, but they're even worse off now than they were before. Things are getting crazy out there. It's a zoo. They'd almost have been better off under the Mutuality. I wish we could take more of them, not just...."

Straker noticed that Rita, the young woman they'd saved from being sold, was among the ones Heiser had led into the shuttle. "You're right, but we can't fight so many. Maybe someday we can come back and change things for the rest."

Heiser nodded mournfully. "Yes, sir." He began pitching in to transfer supplies. The others did too. Straker recognized most from the battle of Corinth or the prison.

As the countdown approached one minute, a cart drove straight through the personnel door at high speed, scraping both sides as it barely forced itself through. Straker raised his slugthrower, and then lowered it as Zaxby tumbled out and scrambled into the shuttle like a rubbery, stimmed-up spider. He rushed directly to the cockpit. Within seconds, the craft began powering up.

"Everybody aboard?" Straker yelled. "Strap down the cargo and then buckle yourselves in. We'll be lifting as soon as the base dumps transit. Loco, Heiser, get this rig out of the shuttle and board the courier."

"I'd really like to stay on the shuttle, sir," Heiser said. "Rita's there, and with so many aboard..."

"They might need a strong hand to keep order," Straker finished. "All right. Send over someone. We have an extra seat on the courier."

A moment later, a short, smiling man ran to the courier and swarmed aboard. The shuttle door closed, while the courier's remained open.

Straker stood beside the space door controls, his hand hovering over the big emergency button that would override the massive airlock and open the entire hangar to vacuum.

"Four... three... two... one..." Murdock's voice broadcast in even tones. "Transit complete. Egress successful, all systems nominal. Ladies and gentlemen, we have arrived."

Straker hit the button at that moment and sprinted for the open door of the courier. A roar of escaping air began at the edges of the massive steel doors as they swung open. He dove through the portal. "Seal up! I'm in!"

By the time he'd wriggled into one of the vacuum suits, Engels was flying the courier through the access channel, with Zaxby and passengers close behind in the shuttle.

* * *

"Now comes the tricky part," Engels said, her hands white on the joysticks. She hated things being out of her control, and there were too many variables for comfort on this run.

"You can say that again," replied Loco from the copilot seat.

"Now comes the–"

"Hey, you're the straight man and I'm the funny one," Loco protested.

"You're funny all right," Engels said. "If *Carson* is waiting outside and in view, this could be a real short trip with no happy ending."

"Mm, happy ending. Those are fun."

"Loco, don't you ever quit?"

"I ain't no quitter, baby."

"Well, quit yakking now. I have to fly." The courier exited the tunnel and Engels immediately hit the retros, spinning the ship sideways and ducking into a narrow canyon on the asteroid's surface. She activated the gravplates to cling to a rock face. Zaxby followed more slowly, though expertly, in the less maneuverable shuttle.

"I don't see *Carson* or any other warships nearby," Loco said, cycling through the courier's excellent sensor suite. Built for speed and evasion, it was one of the smallest sidespace-capable craft, all engines and power plant.

"That's good, right?" said Straker.

"Yes. It means we won't have to abandon our people on the shuttle," Engels replied. "Not yet, anyway."

Worry lit the extra man's face. He introduced himself as Chief Gurung, an experienced naval noncom, and spoke in a lilting accent. "How are they going to get away? That shuttle has no sidespace engines, and we can't pack all those people in here."

Engels replied, "We're going to attempt something Zaxby claims is possible, but I'd never try if we weren't desperate."

"What is it?"

"This courier can haul a small cargo pod. Even though the shuttle is much larger, we're going to cram it partly into the pod bay, and then grasp it with the courier's waldo arms."

"Can this thing transit with that load?"

Engels gave an elaborate shrug. "We're going to find out the hard way. If we can't, we'll be like two dragonflies stuck together with nowhere to go." She glanced at Straker. "If we're really unlucky, I won't be able to jettison them, and we'll all get captured."

Straker patted her on the back. "Then let's make our own luck. I know you can do it. You were the best pilot in the regiment, and the only thing that's changed is who we work for."

"We don't work for *nobody* no more," said Loco.

"You work for me, Loco," Straker said, "and I'll work for you. I'm giving up on following other people. I'm sick of being used."

"Me too," said Engels, and Loco echoed her. "The only people we can trust are ourselves."

Straker's voice hardened. "And I swear, right here and now, I will bring these bastards down. DeChang and Ramirez, the Mutuality and its types like Lazarus, all of them and anyone else that makes people into slaves. I'll even force the Hundred Worlds to reform, if what Lazarus said was true."

Engels measured Straker with her gaze. "That's a tall order, Derek, but if anyone can do it, you can."

"*We* can," he replied. "I need you. All of you, and a lot more."

"We're with you, boss," said Loco. Chief Gurung echoed him.

Zaxby broke in on the comlink. "We in the shuttle are with you as well, Derek Straker, but at the moment Carla Engels and I must mate."

"What?" yelped Straker.

Loco snickered.

"Our craft," said Zaxby. "We must mate our vessels together for sidespace entry."

"Mate and entry." Loco elbowed Chief Gurung. "I'd like to see that."

"I'm surrounded by teenage boys," Engels said, rolling her eyes. "Zaxby, the slot is open and the waldos are ready to clamp. Line up your belly port with my cargo hatch and insert your docking probe."

Loco couldn't resist a "That's what she said," and gasped with mirth until Straker grabbed him by the back of the neck and squeezed. "Don't distract her," he said.

A moment later, Engels smiled. "Perfect. Zaxby, you're a superb pilot."

"I'm a superb everything, Carla Engels."

"Just 'Carla' will do. Activate your belly gravplating."

"Activating." A *clunk* shook the courier.

"Stand by." Engels manipulated the waldo controls and the ship rattled, squealed and groaned as stresses were placed on the arms and cargo-loading systems, forces for which they were never designed.

"Will it hold?" Straker asked.

"We're about to find out," she replied. "Everyone strapped in over there?"

"Yes, Carla."

"Deactivate all gravplating, structural fields, impellers, and inertial damp-eners. In fact, shut down everything you can. Nothing energetic to interfere with our sidespace engines."

"Confirmed. Carla, we're in your tentacles—ah, limbs."

"Hands, you mean. Here we go."

Engels shut off the gravplating and the courier fell upward, outward from the spinning asteroid base, tumbling slowly. If there were hostile ships any-where, she hoped the simple ballistic trajectory would fool them into thinking the mated ships were merely a metallic boulder that had broken free.

"Using impellers to stabilize… all right, powering up the sidespace en-gines."

Loco said, "I got two corvettes, just transited in. Must be Unmutuals, here to meet the rock. Range, two hundred thousand. I don't think they've identified us yet."

"Good. Only a few more seconds…"

"Uh oh." Loco pointed at a screen. "They're pinging us."

"As long as they don't shoot us." Engels tapped controls.

"They're focusing their sensors on us. One's moving this way."

"I've activated our distress signal. That should keep them wondering for long enough." Engels continued to make adjustments, expanding the sidespace field potential to well above its rated maximum and removing safety interlocks.

Zaxby claimed his calculations showed this would work, but, as with the asteroid, they were near the limits of engine power.

"They're hailing us on the mayday band," Loco said, finger to his earpiece.

"Ignore them," Straker snapped. "Carla, how long?"

"Soon." She shoved two levers forward, letting max power flow to the sidespace engines, building up in their capacitors for the jump.

"They're threatening to fire!" Loco said. "They must detect the sidespace field!"

"Here goes nothing." Engels lifted the protective cover from a large green button and mashed her thumb on it.

Something seemed to shove them sideways and the universe disappeared, replaced on the visiplates by a deep gray. All aboard cheered.

"We're in!" Engels cried. "Zaxby, you're a genius."

"I believe I've told you that quite often. Still, it's nice to hear you say it."

"Good job, Zaxby," said Straker. "How long until we arrive?"

"As I've already briefed you, approximately thirty-six hours, nine minutes, seven seconds."

"Approximately?"

"I cannot be held responsible for quantum dimensional variance."

"Why not?"

"Because there are factors in the multiverse beyond even my enormous intellect."

"Enormous ego, you mean," said Straker.

"I'm not the one vowing to overthrow an empire and more."

"A man's got to have goals in life. Those are mine." Straker reclined his chair. "Wake me up if anything interesting happens."

"In sidespace?" said Zaxby. "Nothing interesting ever happens in sidespace. At least, not as far as we know. Ships have occasionally disappeared in sidespace, which might qualify as interesting, although mainly to those involved, assuming they didn't simply die, or vanish, or dissipate, or disintegrate. Of course, what passengers do in sidespace might become interesting. I still do not have firsthand data on human sexual activities. Perhaps–"

"I'm turning off my comlink now," Straker said loudly, closing his suit's helmet and folding his arms.

"Me too," said Loco.

Gurung nodded and followed suit, leaving Engels to listen to Zaxby's babbling alone.

Eventually Zaxby paused and Engels spoke. "Zaxby dear, we're all going to sleep. I suggest you let your passengers do the same. Emergency contact only for the next nine hours, all right?"

"Of course, Carla. I will amuse myself by continuing my flowchart for our conquest of the Mutuality. Or was Derek Straker planning on reforming the Hundred Worlds first? Because, though that would be easier, it is the one of the few things standing in the way of total Mutuality domination, along with a few allied alien systems. Did you know those of the Trantor system consider the flesh of my people a delicacy? That's—"

"Good night, Zaxby. Switching off now."

"Wait—"

Engels set her comlink to emergency mode and closed her eyes, pitying Zaxby's passengers.

Chapter 28

"Remind me to avoid being cramped in a courier with you guys, like, *ever* again," Engels said as she prepared to transit out of sidespace.

"Beats living in a mechsuit for three days straight," replied Straker. "We get catheterized, and the defecation system never works right–"

"Too much information, Derek," Engels said.

"At least you're not over in the shuttle with Zaxby," Straker said, nodding to Chief Gurung.

"You're right about that, sir," Gurung replied with a shudder. "Does that alien ever stop talking?"

"He talks too much when he's bored," Engels explained. "He's quieter when he's deep into some challenge, or if silence is operationally vital."

"Then I guess I'll have to keep him challenged and operating," Straker said. "He'll be useful to our, um…"

"Insurgency?" suggested Loco.

"No, that's not it. Accurate, but not inspiring."

"Rebellion?"

"Taken."

"Movement?" Engels asked.

"Sounds like we're back to defecation systems."

"Ugh," Engels said. "How about jihad?"

"No, this isn't religious."

"Crusade?"

"Ditto."

"The Cause?"

"Sounds so pretentious…"

"The Struggle?" suggested Loco.

"Lame."

"Uprising, revolt, insurrection, mutiny…" Loco continued.

"When did you turn into a thesaurus?" asked Engels.

Loco pointed to his console. "I pulled up a language database. How about buccaneers? Or freebooters?"

"How about liberators?" Engels asked.

"Better. I'll think about it," Straker said.

"And we'll need a nickname, too," Loco said. "Something catchy and intimidating. Straker's Tigers…"

"Straker's Fakers?" Engels suggested with a wink.

"Ugh," said Straker.

"Bakers, makers, slakers, takers, breakers…" Loco chanted.

"That's the one!" Straker said, pointing at him. "Breakers. We're breaking chains and liberating people."

"Cool," Loco said.

"We're about to emerge into normal space," Engels said, pointing at the chrono. "Zaxby, inform your passengers we're transiting in."

"Why?" he shot back.

"What do you mean, 'why?'"

"Why should they be informed? What can my passengers or I do about transit?"

"Umm… they can prepare themselves mentally?"

"You humans seem to need a lot of emotional support," he observed. "I suppose it's a result of your primate ancestors, living in large social groupings and eating grubs and rotting fruit. Ruxins are, by comparison, much more self-sufficient, even solitary."

"Then why do you love to talk so damn much?" said Straker.

"That is a very astute question, Derek Straker, more intelligent than your average utterance. I shall have to give it some thought. Perhaps I'm anomalous."

"I can tell you why right now," Loco muttered, covering his comlink mike.

"Insecure and compensating?" Engels asked.

"Yup."

Straker's stomach flip-flopped, and the visiplates blazed with the pinpoints of stars, one close enough to seem like a sun. On the long-range passive sensors a large rocky planet loomed, showing four moons chasing each other low around its airless surface.

"There," he said, pointing at the third moon out from the planet. The infrared emissions blazed there.

"Hundred Worlds patrol base 53-G," Engels said. "Four corvettes and a dozen attack ships. The Unmutual database said they're a long way from any action, guarding the rear frontier. Never even had to defend themselves from a raid, so they should be complacent."

"They'll be hailing us in a few minutes, as soon as our emissions reach their detectors," said Loco. "You still want to go in mated like this?"

"At the start, yes," said Straker. "It'll make our story more convincing. Nobody will be expecting a surprise raid from this kludged-up ship."

"We have to detach to land, said Engels.

Straker nodded. "You're the pilot. Loco, you might as well start talking."

"If this weren't a Hundred Worlds courier, this would never work. Hope our IFF codes are still current," said Loco, turning on the transmitter. He spoke in a bored, dull voice. "53-G, 53-G, this is Courier C-421. We are inbound from Base WG604 with dispatches. Got an add-on for you too."

"C-421 this is 53-G, we read. You're not our usual courier. What's going on?"

"Nothing, far as I know. They don't tell me nothing anyway. I just fly these things, you know?"

"I hear you. What's that add-on?"

"I dunno. Extra supplies or something. You order anything special?"

"We've had a hydraulic grav inverter on back-order for months."

"Maybe that's it. They told me you get to keep the shuttle-pod too. I sure don't want to haul it around anymore. Damn thing is hell on my drives and I'm gonna need a new paint job."

"Hey, that'll be useful. Come on in. Hangar Four has plenty of room."

Loco raised his eyebrows at Engels, who nodded. "53-G," he continued, "I'm going to detach the shuttle and bring her in with me on remote. That'll be a lot easier than trying to untangle on the ground. You good with that?"

"Sure, no problem."

"I could use a private room with a shower, too. I'm stinking in this suit."

"I'll have your keycode waiting. The other pilots are already looking forward to swapping lies with you at the bar. See you in a few minutes. 53-G out."

"Nice guy," Engels said, glancing at Straker.

"That changes nothing," said Straker, grim. "We go in according to plan, and we giving warning shots to anyone we see. If they retreat, they live. If not, they die. This is war."

"It was a lot easier when the enemy were faceless evil aliens instead of humans."

"Killing a few isn't as evil as enslaving our entire race," Straker replied.

"Easy to say when you're not being killed," Engels sighed. "You're not wrong, Derek. I just wish we didn't have to kill our own people."

Straker softened. "I know. I'm not happy about it, but we can't let our feelings get in the way of our goal to free all mankind."

"The ends justify the means again?"

"Sometimes." He switched to the general comlink to include those in the shuttle. "Listen up. We've been cleared to land in a hangar and they don't seem to suspect a thing. We have to hit them hard and fast. It's going to be chaos. Remember, we absolutely must secure a corvette. It's the only sidespace-capable ship that's big enough to hold all of us and fast enough to get away. If we're too slow, if they seal up all the corvettes, we'll be captured or killed. This is go-for-broke, people, do or die. Are you ready?"

Growls, cheers and yelps of enthusiasm returned on the comlink. "I think they're ready," Loco said with a grin.

Engels keyed her comlink. "Zaxby, I'm beginning the detachment sequence. Waldos retracting."

"Probe withdrawing from mating receptacle."

Loco snickered again.

Engels waggled the controls in three dimensions. "You're stuck pretty tight."

"I shall release a blast of air inside the cargo bay. That may push us out."

The courier shuddered and there came a crunching sound. "You're free," Engels said. "Damn, I can't close my bay doors."

"We only have to land once," Straker said. "It doesn't matter if this ship is flyable afterward."

"True," Engels admitted. "It just offends my piloting instincts to tear up a ship."

"Forget it and get the job done."

"Don't I always?"

Straker smiled.

The two tiny vessels cruised in to land in Hangar Four, which was empty of all but support equipment. As the craft set down next to each other, Straker stared out the viewports. "No corvette in here. We'll have to move fast, assault the next hangar and hope to find one." He switched to the general channel and told everyone to be ready.

As soon as the hangar closed its doors and pressurized, Straker led the way down the ramp, Chief Gurung and Engels behind him. Loco brought up the rear. Beside them, the other humans and Zaxby spilled from the shuttle, all wearing pressure suits and carrying the small arms they'd brought from their brief service with the Unmutuals.

Two unarmed locals had popped their faceplates open and were on their way to greet their visitors when they were swarmed by Straker's people.

"Remove their helmets," he ordered. "No comlinks, no suit air. If their buddies depressurize the area, they'll be killing their own people. Bring them along."

Dragging their protesting prisoners, the group hustled for the tunnel that connected to the next hangar and burst into it. No alarms had yet sounded. Apparently, they still held the element of surprise.

"Who are you people? What do you want?" one of the prisoners asked.

"We're liberators." Straker didn't explain further as they hurried down the tunnel to the next hangar. "Open the door!"

Inside, they found what they were looking for: a corvette, one of the smallest sidespace-capable warships, and one of the fastest. Its ports lay open, ramps and ladders leading in. Security was lax at this base so far from the front.

Several maintenance personnel stopped and stared as the raiding party burst into the hangar. Preset teams of three attackers each raced, weapons pointed, to capture the locals. Engels sprinted for the corvette while the rest spread out, securing the area.

"Fibertape these people," Straker told Heiser. "Mouths too. Zaxby, Loco, make sure this ship is topped off with fuel. The rest of you, block the personnel doors and be ready to repel a counterattack.

It took six agonizing minutes to detach umbilicals, close hatches, undog lines and power up. Fortunately, the corvette was fully fueled.

As Straker waved his people toward the main hatch, the far personnel door burst open. They must have used breaching explosives. He aimed and loosed a long burst from his slugthrower. Chief Gurung fired blaster bolts from beside him. "Go on, sir! Get in!"

Straker ran to the top of the ramp and stopped to brace his weapon. "Come on, Chief!" He fired bursts of covering fire as armed personnel pushed through the door.

Several opponents fell, wounded. They didn't have battle armor and didn't seem to be combat troops. At best, they were out-of-practice security personnel, or even simply anyone the base commander could scrounge up to hold a gun. They fired wildly, their shots coming nowhere near the two men.

Gurung raced up the ramp and Straker followed him in, saying, "Shut the hatch!"

The portal slammed closed and sealed. Around him the corvette came to life, humming and shuddering as Engels lifted. He made his way to the tiny command center and shoved his way in, displacing two onlookers. "Get off the bridge! Go find someplace to strap in!" he yelled at them.

Engels had the pilot's chair, Zaxby the copilot-gunner's, and Loco sat at the sensors-and-communications board. Straker took the remaining operations station. He strapped in.

"Can they hurt us, Zaxby?" Engels asked.

"No," he replied, "nothing but small arms. A corvette's armor is as thick as a tank's."

Zaxby reached for the weapons controls.

"Don't kill them!" Engels said.

"As you wish, Carla."

"Shoot the hangar doors instead."

"Firing now."

Laser fire blazed from the corvette, and the thin metal that had sealed the hangar vanished, leaving a smoking hole. "What's to keep them from pursuing us in the other corvettes?"

Engels kicked the ship through the opening, rising to hover a few hundred meters above the little base. "Fire on the other two hangars," she said.

"That may kill humans," Zaxby pointed out.

Straker stared hard at Engels, but she ignored him, a determined look on her face. "Do it," she said, hunching her shoulders. "We can't risk them getting a ship into space."

Zaxby played his console like a multi-armed pianist and the corvette slammed two bursts of hot red plasma into the first two hangars, the ones with unknown contents. The buildings exploded, revealing several small craft and two corvettes. Suited figures squirmed like ants in the devastation, the combustion quickly snuffed by vacuum. They should survive. Maybe.

Two more shots, this time carefully targeted, blasted the sterns off the little warships, leaving them helpless to move.

Straker kept his eyes on Engels. Her face was drawn and pained, but resolute. She'll be all right, he told himself. He reached out to place a hand on her shoulder, afraid she would shake it off. "I'm sorry," he said.

She stiffened for a moment, and then leaned into his palm.

He squeezed and let go. "We had to do it," he whispered.

She turned to give him a weak smile. "I know."

"There will be more, Carla. I'll do the best I can to keep from killing innocent people, but…"

"Yeah. Quit talking about it, okay?" She turned the ship away from the base and accelerated toward the nearest flatspace. For a small ship, that location was closer than one a larger ship would need. "Where to now, Derek?"

"Just get us out of here. I need to think and look through the databases." Straker tapped at his console hesitantly. He wasn't a Fleet officer, and these controls were nothing like a mechsuit's.

"Why don't you simply tell me what you're looking for?" Zaxby asked.

"Someplace out of the way, where nobody knows us and nobody's looking for us. Someplace we might be able to rest and figure things out. Where we could make some money, I guess, maybe using this ship as a fast freighter." Straker stared at the bulkhead. "Somewhere I can think. I've been so busy getting us away from things, I have no idea where to go *to*."

"Carla, would you allow me to take the helm, please? Captain Straker, I believe I have just the place."

Straker and Engels glanced at one another and shrugged.

"At this point, I'm willing to try anything," Straker said.

The Ruxin reached eagerly for the controls.

* * *

"Three days of being cooped up in this ship and I'm bored out of my skull," Straker said as he filled a cup with ship's caff. "Only seven more days to go, according to Zaxby." He sat down across from Engels and Loco as he sipped his beverage. "Ugh. This is straight from the waste-tanks. I don't remember Fleet caff being this bad."

She lifted her own mug to her lips and grimaced between bites of protein paste. "This ship wasn't loaded with fresh food, only the standard dietary rations. At least this concentrate gives us nutrition. We won't run out of supplies."

"I wonder what ol' Zax is going to eat?" Loco asked. "Hey, that makes me wonder: Is there any octopus or calamari in there?"

"Oh, that's just wrong," Engels said, but then she began eating energetically.

"Hey Carla, you sure are hungry." Straker raised his eyebrows at her. She was wolfing down food as if it would run away from her plate.

"I've been working hard, so I eat," she replied lightly. "It's not like we have to limit our intakes. Nobody's getting fat off this."

Loco belched loudly. "This stuff sucks," he said, staring at the remains of his meal. "Even in prison, we got a few decent meals. Man, do you remember the buffets on Shangri-La?"

"There were no buffets on Shangri-La," said Straker, "because there probably was no Shangri-La. Just a VR paradise while we healed up in an autodoc on our way to the next battle."

"It hardly matters. I remember the food, and it was tasty."

Straker sampled a brown chunk off Engels' tray. "You're right about one thing, this stuff sucks. And I'm so damn bored."

"How can anyone be bored with so much to do?" asked Heiser as he shoveled food paste into his mouth. "I've never served aboard a ship before, and Chief Gurung is running us ragged. How can someone who smiles so much be so tough?"

"That's a Gurkha for you," said Straker with a grin of his own.

"Gurkha?"

"The ethnic group Chief Gurung is from. Mountain people. They've produced some of Old Earth's finest warriors for a thousand years. Lots of battlesuiters are Gurkha."

"How do you know all this stuff, sir?" Heiser asked.

"Even as a kid, I read a lot of military history. I knew I was going to be a mechsuiter, and I wanted to be the best." Straker pointed his index finger at Heiser. "By the way, from now on, you're not an infantryman. You're a marine. You know what those are, right?"

"Sure, Fleet close combat troops. But they had battlesuits. We ain't got no battlesuits, boss."

"Someday we will, Heiser. Until then, you do what Chief Gurung says and be glad we have an experienced swabbie to help run this boat."

"This is a *ship*, if a small one," said Engels with a hint of irritation. "It's sidespace-capable, it has a shipkiller missile tube, and it has a captain and crew. And, if I may say so, Captain Straker, you need to spend more time with the chief too. If you want to be our leader, you need to get to know your ship."

"I'm a mechsuiter, not a Fleet officer."

"You're a freebooter now, Derek my man. A hijacker," said Loco, putting his feet up on a table. "That's just one step above a plain pirate."

"I'm not sure I like the sound of that," Straker said.

"Too late," Loco said. "That's what everyone is calling the ship: the *Free-booter*, led by the dashing Captain Derek Straker, master and commander. That makes us freebooters. Besides, *I* like it. Makes us sound tough, and we might need that where we're going."

"Where are we going, anyway?" asked Straker.

"Zaxby won't say. Not even to me," said Engels.

"Well, I don't like *Freebooter*. I say we call her *Liberator*, because that's what we do." He looked over at Engels.

She nodded. "That's better."

"Then it's official. Pass the word. This ship is the *Liberator*."

A young woman set a plate of the fried food paste in front of Straker with an apologetic air. "Sorry, sir, this is the best we have."

"I could have gotten it myself," he told her. Then he ran his eyes up and down her. "But that's no problem, ah… it's Campos, right?"

The young woman looked shy. "Yes, sir. Campos. Medic, Second Class. That's who I *was*, anyway."

"You still are. I think you're our only medic. That makes you Medic First Class."

She smiled. "Yes, sir. Thank you, sir. I've inventoried all the supplies and tested the autodoc. It seems to be in perfect working order."

Straker lifted his eyebrows as he ate his food paste. "We have an autodoc?"

"Yes, sir. A good one, too."

"Then that's your baby. Ask around for anyone with tech experience to help you figure out all its software."

"Roger wilco, sir."

Straker's eyes remained unfocused in Campos' direction, as if he were staring through her.

"Sir?"

"Sorry. Just thinking about something. Thanks for the food."

After she left, Engels leaned over to Straker. "They worship you, you know."

"Who?"

"Everyone with us. Especially the former Hundred Worlds people you saved from the Unmutuals."

"They saved themselves. I'm just…"

"Their leader? Their captain?"

"I guess."

"That's a powerful thing. Don't underrate it. Try to remember how you felt as a cadet in Academy, or when you first joined the Regiment, where the officers seemed like gods. That's how they feel now."

Straker sniffed and changed the subject. "What's that smell?"

Engels smirked and set her cup in front of him.

He picked it up and sipped. "Spoiled toilet cleaner?"

"Close. It's hooch. Fermented and distilled from processed fruit juice concentrate."

Straker looked around, realizing most of the dozen people in the mess were drinking the stuff. He was about to issue a reprimand when Engels put a hand on his arm. "They're not on duty, and neither are you. Let them live a little. They've been through hell. We're in sidespace. Nothing can happen here."

"Oh, I bet a lot can happen," he replied, eyeing Loco.

He was now flirting shamelessly with Campos. His girl back on Freiheit seemed already forgotten. Well, that was Loco.

More to the point, everyone seemed to be letting their hair down now that nobody was watching them closely.

Nobody but him. He realized Engels was right. He was the captain. He had a responsibility to set a good example, but at the same time, people needed to decompress.

Engels shifted around the table and held the cup to Straker's lips. "Bottoms up, Derek."

He gave her a sour look, but sipped. "You trying to get me drunk?"

"There are some pleasant stages between sober and drunk, you know." She smiled. "Like, buzzed, tipsy, lubricated, or irrigated."

"Irrigated?" he laughed.

"Why yes," she said. "Now that you mention it. I am, a little." She giggled and slipped her hand into his. "Hey, you said you were bored. I hear the captain lets you use his cabin."

"I *am* the captain."

"Oh, well, in that case…" Engels pulled him to his feet and tried to drag him down the passageway toward the ships' officer staterooms.

Everyone was watching them, Straker realized, and he balked.

"What?" said Engels, still tugging on his hand.

"I–"

Abruptly Straker felt his free arm twisted up behind him and heard Loco's voice hiss in his ear. "Derek, you'd better go with her. If you don't, you'll be rejecting her and she'll never get over it. Take her to bed and prove she's beautiful! Because if you don't, I will, buddy."

Then the pressure was off and Loco shoved him toward the woman who wanted him. *His female*, as Zaxby kept saying.

Afraid of this next step for the first time in his life, he almost turned back, but Carla's pleading eyes pinned him, and his mouth went dry. He smiled a crooked smile and followed her to his cabin.

When the door shut, Carla peeled off her flight suit. She stood naked before him, the dimness hiding the Hok-roughened skin that hadn't yet gone away.

She began unfastening his clothes. He caught her hands.

"What?" she said, worry in her voice. "What's wrong now? Is it my face?"

"No, of course not. Your face is beautiful. Just slow down." Derek kissed her gently, and her lips parted, her hot tongue sending a jolt through his nerves. It seemed as if she would devour him. As they kissed, Carla continued to remove his clothing, somehow never letting her mouth stray.

After an endless moment, the pressure became too much for him. His state of mind progressed from the emotional longing of the thirteen-year-old he used to be, to the culmination of more than a decade of savagely repressed lust.

"Birth control?" he mumbled as they tumbled onto the narrow bunk.

Carla gasped. "My implant should be good for years. Just do it! We've waited long enough!"

"I do love you, Carla Engels," he breathed as she opened to him.

"Damn straight you do, Derek Straker," she said as they joined. "And tonight, you're going to love me until you drop from exhaustion."

Part III: Liberator

Chapter 29

At the edge of nowhere.

"Are we there yet?" Straker asked. As usual, the end of a trip seemed to take the longest.

Zaxby moved his eyes left and right to peer at several of the *Liberator*'s screens, and then focused a pair on one particular display. He tapped it with the tip of a long tentacle. "This is the sidespace engine arrival countdown. It shows approximately three more minutes. When it reaches zero, we shall emerge into normal space at my chosen coordinates."

"Which are?"

"You shall see."

Straker rolled his eyes. "Play your games, then."

Zaxby responded by rolling all four eyes up and completely around in his head and blinking them in sequence.

"Showoff," Straker snorted.

"I am not to blame if my highly evolved physiology gives you an inferiority complex."

Straker snatched the nearest tentacle in a blur of motion and tied it in a knot. "Don't forget who's the boss here."

The tentacle thrashed and flexed, untying itself. "There's no need to escalate a simple discussion to violence. I acknowledge your leadership, Captain Straker, but protest at your evident insecurity."

"I'm not insecure. I'm just getting tired of your smartass ways."

"As opposed to dumbass ways?"

"See? That's what I'm talking about!" Straker snatched another tentacle.

Loco grabbed Straker's elbow and murmured in his ear, "Boss, you're encouraging him. He loves bugging you to get a reaction, especially when you're on edge with nothing to do. He's an intellectual bully, but he can only get to you if you let him. Treat him like any other brainiac. Use his brains and ignore the rest."

"Easy for you to say. He doesn't target you with his bullshit."

"That's because I don't play into it, see? He's a super-brainiac, and we need him, but he knows he needs us, too. You can use that against him."

Straker shrugged off Loco's grip. "Okay." He turned back to the screens and crossed his arms, saying nothing to a couple of Zaxby's further attempts at baiting.

When the countdown ended, the transition alarm sounded and the ship dropped into normal space. Visiplates blazed suddenly with color in greens and yellows and purples. Minor alerts chirped and beeped, and Zaxby manipulated the consoles like a four-armed concert pianist. "Do not be alarmed, humans. We have emerged exactly where I intended, plus or minus a small statistical variance."

"Beautiful," Engels gasped. "We're inside a nebula! We can't even see any external stars."

Zaxby swelled pridefully. "And we are extremely unlikely to be detected from outside. It's far out of the usual travel lanes. The combatants believe there's nothing here to interest anyone during wartime, where every resource must be turned to battle."

Straker eyed the octopoid. "Why are we here, then?"

"Patience, my young captain. You shall see soon enough."

Straker growled and crossed his arms, remembering Loco's advice.

Engels stepped closer to Zaxby and gently scratched at the leathery skin atop his head, where he liked it. "Come on, Zaxy, give us a hint."

"Ah, yes, my dear. Up a bit and to the left. Right there."

Straker ground his teeth, but still said nothing. Engels was obviously trying to butter up the alien. It might be the only way to get answers. Still, he should be the only one she touched like that…

"Please tell us what's going on, Zaxy?" Engels purred.

"Oh, all right." Zaxby manipulated several controls and keyboards simultaneously. The main screen changed to show a false-color representation of the view toward the center of the nebula. Dozens of misshapen lumps stood out in white-rimmed black. "This is a multispectral view which allows us to see through the gas. These are large asteroids. There are many more we cannot see, thousands of them."

"How large are they?" Straker asked.

Zaxby superimposed a scale. "Roughly fifteen kilometers long and larger."

Engels leaned closer to the screen, then squeezed in next to Zaxby and tapped at the controls. "Why can't I find anything smaller? Asteroid fields usually range from large chunks all the way down to dust and sand."

Zaxby waved a couple of tentacles in the air. "Yes, that's an interesting question, isn't it?"

Engels turned on the charm again. "Come on, Zaxy. What's with these asteroids?"

"I believe you will see when we approach one closely."

"You believe?"

"Our presence here is based on many years of research in my spare time, but this is the first opportunity I've had to test my theories directly."

"But where is *here?*" Loco said.

"My people call it the Starfish Nebula, roughly translated. I believe it was the reason we octopoids resisted the Hok—the Mutuality—for so long."

"Riddles," grunted Straker.

"I like riddles," Zaxby said.

"I like answers. Would you please provide some?"

Zaxby's demeanor grew earnest. "I tell you truly, I do not want to get your hopes up in case I am wrong, so indulge an old being's follies."

"Old?" said Engels. "How old are you, really?"

"In human-standard years? I slightly exceed two hundred."

"How long do octopoids live?"

"Perhaps three hundred, if we are fortunate."

Engels smiled. "So you're almost elderly. That explains a lot."

"I beg your pardon?"

"You're getting crotchety, that's all."

"Crotchety: irritable and cantankerous, usually attributed to old age. I suppose that's accurate."

"And we forgive you." Engels hugged Zaxby's rubbery head.

Straker turned away, feeling as if he would explode. He understood that Engels was deliberately manipulating Zaxby, but he still felt... what?

Jealous? But how could he be jealous of an alien that was obviously not going to hook up with a human?

Or could they? Could either of them be genuinely attracted to each other, an octopoid and a woman? Engels treated Zaxby as a cross between an eccentric mad scientist and a pet, while Zaxby soaked up the attention.

That was what really got under his skin, Straker realized: the attention. That kind of attention should be his alone. The touch. He could feel anger building, even while he knew it wasn't rational.

Was it?

He told himself that she was merely being practical. They needed Zaxby's knowledge, so they had to play his games. Eventually, they wouldn't need him so much anymore and he could be moved to some position within Straker's organization—okay, future organization—far away from her.

Straker forced himself to be objective and military. This last week with Carla had been spectacular, but running off alone with her was mere fantasy, what with war and oppression all around them. He was in charge of this tiny crew, and he couldn't afford to indulge in selfish dreams. He had to think of other people and be practical, and that meant love came second for a while. He burned to right all the wrongs they'd suffered.

"So why are we here in this nebula, Zaxby my man?" Loco said in a cartoonishly jolly tone.

"All in good time, Loco my squid."

"Good one. Hey, if you're two hundred, why are you still a lieutenant?"

"I only volunteered for the military ten years ago. Before that, I was a scientist and engineer."

"The usual brainiac stuff. Why'd you give that up? I bet it was cushy."

Zaxby hesitated, as if choosing his words. "I became bored. I was not allowed to research certain things that I wished to know more about."

Loco chuckled. "Bet you're not bored now."

"Not lately."

Zaxby reached for the controls again, but Engels shoved his tentacles aside and displaced him from the pilot's seat. "Let me fly, please. I'm a pilot and I'm tired of just watching. Tell me where to go."

"As you wish, my dear." Zaxby sat at the sensor-comm station and began adjusting it to his obsessive specifications.

For the next half hour Zaxby gave Engels directions as if he were the corvette's captain, while Straker locked his jaw and said nothing. In response, she flew the ship with a deft touch until they approached a designated asteroid. This one measured about thirty kilometers long and half that across, and it spun very gently on its long axis.

Zaxby refined his view on the sensor plates, though Straker didn't notice anything significant. Maybe the octopoid saw into frequencies humans couldn't. "Bring us to the far end."

Engels circumnavigated the rock, and Straker mused on the difference scale made, depending on the objects and the comparison between them. A planet could be called small, but next to it the largest asteroid seemed tiny. Yet now, this medium-sized monolith dwarfed even the largest warship, not to mention their diminutive vessel. And throughout the galaxy there were stars so large they would swallow the inner orbits of a typical system.

Straker wondered whether there was anything even larger than the largest star, and if so, what would it look like? And then he wondered why he was wondering such things. He wasn't a brainiac, but since their escape and the long-awaited consummation of his relationship with Carla, his thoughts had seemed freer to speculate, more likely to wander into areas outside his usual lanes… and that made him wonder if the military of the Hundred Worlds had limited his potential rather than nurtured it.

Maybe thinking too much would have reduced his usefulness as a warrior. If he'd been free to think more, maybe he would have thought more about all the things that didn't fit—about the anomalies, that was the word—in his life as a mechsuiter. He'd wondered about Shangri-La, and what it meant if it turned out to be fake. Now he was starting to wonder about other things.

"There," Zaxby said to Engels, bringing Straker out of his inner thoughts. "Approach that rock formation."

"Okay…" Engels said, easing the corvette in closer. "What's special about that one?"

Zaxby said, "It shows hidden three-dimensional glyphs that only my people are likely to recognize, disguised as random rock formations." He unwrapped his arms to adjust the controls. "I will now send coded laser pulses in an attempt to activate the mechanism."

"What mechanism?" Straker said.

"The mechanism that will open the asteroid. Please be silent. There are many possible combinations to try. I must concentrate." His tentacles grouped around one screen-pad and their tips, with their masses of tiny sub-tentacles, blurred in motion like a nest of worms squirming over an array of symbols, the octopoid written language, no doubt.

"I'm no brainiac," Straker said to Loco, "but I bet trying to crack a code manually could take a long time."

Loco grunted. "Depends on how many slots are in the code. Like, a ten-digit code using normal numbers would have, what, a billion possible combinations?"

"Ten billion," Engels spoke without looking up from Zaxby's tentacle-tips. "But it looks like their language has at least thirty glyphs or letters. That means a whole lot more. It could take days or weeks."

"Correct, my dear," Zaxby said, "but it will take longer if you chatterboxes keep nattering. Or is that natterboxes keep chattering? Your language is endlessly flexible, probably because of its very imprecision. I am amazed such primitive creatures developed it at all."

Engels rolled her eyes, and then made a few emphatic taps on the controls. "Fine. I'm hungry anyway. The autopilot will hold our station relative to the asteroid." She stood. "Well, boys, how about some lunch?"

They made their way to the mess and began unenthusiastically preparing another meal of food paste. Chief Gurung entered a moment later with Heiser in tow. They filled their cups with caff, and the Gurkha gestured for permission to sit across from Straker.

"Have a seat, Chief. How's the ship?"

"The ship is very fine, Captain," he replied in the musical accent of his people. "It is in good repair. The crew is shaping up excellently, even though we have so many aboard some are hot-bunking. They are all wondering what will happen next, though, and they would like to have some shore leave."

"As soon as I figure it out myself, I'll let you know," Straker said, but at Gurung's frown he relented. "Really Chief, I'm not sure yet. Zaxby brought us to a nebula and we're sitting next to a big asteroid hab, trying to access some kind of coded entryway to get inside. That will take hours or days, maybe longer. And no, I have no idea what's in there, except it's something built by his people, but he promises it will be good. As the only things we own right now are the clothes on our backs, our personal weapons and this ship, I'll take any salvage I can get."

"Thank you, sir. I shall pass that on to the crew."

Straker recalled Engels' words, about how the crew—*his* crew—looked up to him. He had to start thinking like a ship's captain and a unit commander, not just a mechsuiter, and part of that was making sure his people knew how much he valued them. "Chief Gurung... thanks. We're damn lucky to have a man like you. Let me and the other officers know how we can help you, but I'm relying on you to keep the ship running and the crew steady."

Gurung smiled broadly. "That's what chiefs do, sir. I won't let you down."

"And Chief... you understand that there's nothing above us out here, right? No chain of command, no regulations, no legal system, just us and the discipline we maintain. In fact, there's no particular reason you should recognize my authority."

Gurung shook his head and pointed a scolding finger. "Oh, yes sir, there is. You are the captain. A crew needs a captain, and vice versa. Otherwise we're as bad as that disgusting mob we left behind. If *you* are not the captain, show me who is."

"Well said. And every captain needs a good chief." Straker looked over at Heiser. "And a good first sergeant."

Heiser snorted. "You're promoting me three ranks? I don't even have any marines! ...sir."

"Chief, how many can you spare?"

The little man's mouth puckered as if he'd sucked on a lemon. "I can give up Nazario and Redwolf, sir. Both of them were dirt soldiers. They're also as dumb as a bucket of rocks. I'm afraid to let them touch anything."

"Perfect," Heiser said, rubbing his hands together theatrically. "I'll whip them into shape."

"Good," Straker said. "You senior noncoms work together and keep the crew too busy to get into trouble. Lieutenant Engels is my second-in-command and Loco—Lieutenant Paloco—is next in line."

"What about Lieutenant Zaxby?" asked Gurung, his face blanking. "The crew is quite unsure about him. There are rumors…"

"Zaxby had nothing to do with any human deaths. He was vital to our escape, in fact. And he's absolutely critical for our survival right now."

"But is he considered a line officer?"

Straker looked up at the overhead, thinking. "Not right now. Listen to what he says and do it if it makes sense. If you have a problem, come to me."

Just then, the intercom chimed. "Captain to the bridge," said Zaxby's voice.

Chapter 30

The Starfish Nebula.

"What's up, Zaxby?" Engels asked as she slipped through the narrow door to the bridge, beating the men there by taking a shortcut through the ship's centerline railgun assembly, a pilot's trick.

"I have opened the way into the asteroid," Zaxby replied.

The octopoid had already taken the pilot's seat, and Engels didn't bother to dispute his right. If this really were a Ruxin facility, it would be better to have him at the controls. She slid into the ops position. "You sure there's no automated defenses ready to blast us?"

"Reasonably sure. I have researched facilities such as this and know all the standard layouts and schemes."

Engels gave him a wide-eyed look. She was learning that sometimes Zaxby's exact phrasing hid lawyer-like pitfalls.

"Facilities *such as* this, but not *this* one?" she asked.

Straker came in then, followed by Loco. Engels held up a hand to silence them, still staring at Zaxby and waiting for an answer.

Zaxby shifted in his seat. "Obviously not," he admitted. "This is an unknown facility. I have been gathering rumors of its existence for decades from any of my people I could speak with, hoping to extrapolate its position by a process of elimination."

"Why didn't you tell anyone before?" Straker asked.

"I did not want to present rumors without proof. In fact, I was just getting ready to take some leave time and rent a sidespace-capable yacht to come here when we were captured."

Straker smiled. "Lucky you didn't, or you'd have led others right to it."

"How the hell could you afford to rent a jump-capable yacht?" asked Loco.

"I'd been saving my pay for decades. In fact, I joined the Fleet specifically so I could learn piloting and ship operations."

"That's some dedication. Good job, Zax," said Engels, trying to get the alien back on track. "Now, what's inside?"

"Why don't we look and find out?" Zaxby accelerated the ship smoothly and lined up on the end of the asteroid, now showing a tunnel barely big enough to fit the corvette.

"Um..." Engels strapped in as the ship entered the shaft and the screens went dark. "Can you see?"

"I can see quite well. Ah, but you cannot, with your limited vision. Adjust the screens, sensors, and illumination, please."

"Right." Engels set the displays to show all sensor returns in human visual wavelengths, while Loco activated landing lights and radar. On the main forward holoplate, the tunnel sprang into view. Zaxby seemed to be piloting the corvette down the exact middle at a leisurely pace.

Minutes later, the tunnel ended in an open space some twenty kilometers long and five wide, the hollow middle of the oblong asteroid. In the very center, illuminated by the corvette's lights and radars, floated one of the oddest, ugliest ships Engels had ever seen.

It rivaled an orbital cargo tug in its ungainly appearance. Most warships were symmetrical, shaped like cylinders with rounded or pointed ends, the better to maneuver and to turn specific aspects to their enemies.

This one, however, looked like a fat groundcar tire with a thick axle running through the middle, one end twice as long as the other. Eight metal tentacles splayed on each end of this spindle, as if for grasping something that wasn't there. The "tire" showed the lumpiness of sensors, drive field emitters, thrusters and weapons ports, arranged with no rhyme or reason Engels could see.

"What the hell is that?" she asked.

"I am certain it's an Archerfish, usually just called an Archer," Zaxby answered.

Straker stared at the monstrosity. "Archerfish?"

"The closest analogy in Earthan. Archerfish attack airborne creatures without leaving the water. Archer warships were some of the most effective my people ever commissioned. I've known of them my entire life, but the only one I ever saw was part of a museum."

"You had time to visit museums?"

"You had your beaches and your rum and your sex, whether in or out of VR. We Ruxins love museums and libraries."

"And sex," said Loco.

"Yes, I admit, and sex. But only during the mating time, after a lovely stroll through a museum with the objects of my affection."

"Objects, plural?" said Loco.

"I told you Ruxins have three genders."

"Nice. Every encounter's a threesome."

"Of course. Much superior to any binary species."

"Would you two knock it off?" Straker said. "Zaxby, tell me about this Archer of yours."

Zaxby focused in closer and extended a tentacle toward the screen as a pointer. "Fusion engines. Thrusters. Missile tube. Laser. Sidespace engine. Underspace engine. Sen–"

Straker interrupted, "Underspace engine? What the hell is an underspace engine?"

"Isn't it obvious? An engine that transfers the ship into underspace."

"And just what the hell is underspace? I've never *heard* of underspace!"

"I have," said Engels, remembering something she'd learned a while back. "Fleet vessels have underspace detectors, but they never detect anything that I know of. I asked a sensor tech once why that was, and she couldn't tell me. Said they trained her to work the machinery and report, but everyone she knew thought it was obsolete tech."

"Perhaps if your female will stop speaking, Captain, I could explain underspace properly."

Engels sputtered, indignant. "I'm not... Well, okay, I guess I am, but you shouldn't talk to me that way, Zaxby."

"I fail to see how I should talk to you otherwise. Didn't you tell me that our friendship should not affect our professional conduct during operations?"

"Doesn't mean you have to be a jerk about it," she said. "Aliens. Just when you think you know them..."

"Jerk: a contemptibly obnoxious person. If I were not a consummate professional, I might be hurt by your characterization. Now do you want the benefits of my copious knowledge, or shall I leave you to your amateurish anecdotes?"

"You ever want a head rub again?"

"I can rub my own head if need be."

"I do that myself every now and then," said Loco.

Engels blanched. "Ew."

Straker held up an emphatic hand. "Everyone shut the hell up. Get on with it, Zaxby. Underspace..."

Zaxby mimicked a very human shrug. "Underspace is a dimensional set, just as sidespace is a dimensional set. However, while sidespace spreads out in all directions, allowing speedy travel by accessing a broad range of locations simultaneously and choosing a different exit point in normal space, underspace spreads only inward, though it is more convenient to think of it as downward."

Loco's brow furrowed. "Huh? Inward? Downward?"

Zaxby nodded happily. "Exactly."

Straker said, "Look, none of us is a brainiac like you, Zaxby, but we understand how to travel through sidespace with a ship. What is underspace used for? What do you do with it, in practical terms?"

Zaxby made a sighing noise, as if putting up with such dense beings pained him. "In *practical terms*, the underspace engine moves the Archer into a different dimensional state, but doesn't facilitate travel. It remains where it is or it can maneuver, congruent to normal space, but shifted downward into underspace, invisible to all but specialized detection."

"Then it's a cloaking device?" Loco asked.

"No, no, no! The ship actually vanishes from normal space and is compressed into underspace."

"Compressed?" said Engels. "I don't like the sound of that."

"Along with the underspace engine, the Archer must use a specialized field to protect itself and its crew from the effects of underspace."

"And if that field fails?"

"Then the ship and everything in it will freeze. Underspace as a whole remains very close to absolute zero temperature. If not protected by the field, all heat will quickly bleed away."

"Why don't they insulate the ship better?" asked Engels.

"Insulation is of no use because the heat is not lost through the skin of the ship. Rather, on an unshielded ship, underspace absorbs the motion, and therefore the heat, from every molecule simultaneously, just as gravity's space-time curvature acts on every atom simultaneously in normal space. You cannot insulate against underspace any more than you can insulate against gravity."

Straker began rubbing his hands as if beginning to see the possibilities. "So this ship can disappear at will into underspace. It can only be detected by specialized sensors, sensors that I bet only warships or scouts have, right?"

"That stands to reason," Zaxby said. "Civilian ships would be unlikely to waste credits, mass, or power on underspace detectors."

"And when in underspace, the Archer is impervious to ordinary weapons?"

"In most cases. Electromagnetics and beam weapons, kinetic energy and conventional explosives have little effect on underspace. Thermonuclear explosions carry over, but weakly, needing multiple direct hits on the Archer's congruent location to do major damage."

"How do warships fight a vessel like this, then?"

"Historically, they carried specialized missiles equipped with their own underspace engines, protective fields, and seeker heads. They would be fired into underspace to attack the undetected ships by homing on them. The combination of field intersection and kinetic collision could severely damage one of these vessels. It would be unlikely to survive more than a few such strikes. Sometimes only one was enough."

"So it's a stealth ship."

"A what?" said Loco.

"You don't read enough military history, Loco. Stealth technology was big on Old Earth in their wet navies—"

"—seawater again?" Loco demanded. "I'm bored already."

"—yeah whatever, but some of our old vessels could submerge for defense and stealth, or even bend light to avoid radar detection and attack targets by surprise."

"These Archers are our proudest military achievement," Zaxby said.

"So why didn't you share the tech with allies?" Engels asked.

"My government determined we couldn't risk it falling into Hok hands. It was our only major advantage. Later, when we were losing anyway, it was too late. The few remaining ships fled to places like this, all but forgotten by those Ruxins like me who managed to reach the Hundred Worlds."

Straker continued to move restlessly in the tiny space, repeatedly slapping his fist into his palm. "But you say they haven't been used in a long time?"

"Over eighty years, I believe, since my homeworld fell. Once shipborne countermeasures became common, my people lost too many Archers, and their use was reduced to only a few reconnaissance craft. Eventually even those were decommissioned in favor of cheaper robotic probes. Unfortunately, these ships were our only combative advantage over the Hok. Without them, our home system was inevitably conquered."

"How does it attack?" Straker asked.

"Our simplest weapons system is the float mine."

"Explain that one…"

"The ship maneuvers to a place close to a target, but not inside it."

"Inside it?" Straker asked in alarm. "How could it be *inside* it?"

"I'm using a crude analogy. There's a point in normal space congruent to the Archer's location. As the ship maneuvers within underspace, the point moves with it. That point can be anywhere, even inside solid matter."

"And what happens when something materializes within solid matter?" Straker asked.

Zaxby rolled all four eyes. "It's not materialization; it's a simple emergence from underspace to normal space. If an object emerges into normal space inside a solid object, then the two sets of molecules tend to interact violently."

"In practical terms?"

"Captain Straker, you seem to be over-focused on the practical. Can you not, even for one moment, appreciate the beauty of my people's scientific and technological prowess without constantly debasing its glory with such venal questions?"

Straker growled, "I'm not totally sure what you said, but it sounded insulting. Don't make me slap you around. Answer the question."

"Your vulgar threats are unnecessary. I hate the Mutuality as much as you do."

"What does that have to do with anything?"

Zaxby shifted to a posture of questioning amusement. "Why, it is obvious to anyone with a brain as large as mine that you wish to employ this amazing vessel to discomfit the Mutuality and their Hok military slaves in some nefarious manner."

"If by all that blather you mean I want to get this ship working again and stick it to our enemies, then yes, you got it. Now keep explaining, and dumb it down to my level."

"That would be an accomplishment indeed," Zaxby replied with an air of longsuffering. "If an object in underspace emerges inside something in normal space, the heat generated is usually enough to melt and mix the two materials, but not enough to cause a spontaneous explosion unless volatile chemicals are involved. Depending on the kindling temperature of the substance, fire is quite likely."

"So, not enough violence to destroy a warship."

"Not by mere emerging, no. Float mines were traditionally equipped with fusion warheads."

"So they would blow up a ship from the inside."

"No, no, no! Nuclear detonation is a delicate process. Emerging inside solid material would cause the warhead to malfunction. Optimally, the float mine was deployed as close to the outside of the target as possible, set to detonate as soon as it achieved normal space. This was a matter requiring great skill and expertise. The best captains and crews became legends for destroying multiple enemies per cruise."

Straker couldn't keep a predator's grin from spreading across his face. "Oh, baby, I can see the possibilities of this ship if we can get it working."

"It is likely we can get it working," Zaxby said. "My people's engineering is impeccable, and this ship appears undamaged. It is also one of the largest, latest models. However, that is not to say it will be easy. There may be no fuel or power after all this time, and any fissionables within warheads will have degraded into uselessness."

"Yeah, but I'm not thinking of going up against military vessels anyway. Not at first, if ever. But with this ship, we can do a lot of sneaky things, especially if they never think to look for us. Our best defense will be the fact that they've forgotten all about these ships."

"It would make one hell of a freebooter," Loco mused.

"Or a liberator," Straker replied. "Zax, you said it has sidespace engines too?"

"Of course."

"And while in underspace, it can maneuver?"

"Yes."

"Does it have any other weapons besides those, um, float mines?"

"Later versions like this one carried missiles in order to stand off farther from their enemies, and mounted beam weapons for use against unarmed targets in order to conserve ammunition or allow for capture of freighters. Of course, as time went on, the Mutuality armed even their freighters and transports."

"Move and countermove," Straker said, nodding. "That's the way war always works. New weapons and tactics bring new defenses, which in turn prompt new weapons and tactics."

"That's actually quite astute for a small-brained bony creature such as yourself."

"Stuff it, Zaxby. There's more than one kind of intelligence."

"Why is it that I speak your language more precisely than you do?"

"Because you're a smug anal-retentive uptight brainiac?"

"That is kind of you to say."

"It wasn't a compliment."

"Too late. You lose."

Tired of the one-upmanship, Engels broke in. "Would you lunatics focus on the task at hand? The Archer?"

Zaxby turned back to manipulating the sensor controls. "Of course, young female. Here, you see? Residual heat. It's still in standby mode. I will try to access it. It will probably take some time. You may all go now."

"Oh, we may go?" snapped Straker, reaching for Zaxby, who recoiled.

"Don't let him get to you," said Loco, grabbing Straker's arm. "Come on, boss. Let him work."

Straker shook off Loco's hand. "Right. I'm sick of being cooped up here anyway. Let's go exo."

"Exo? You mean, like, in work suits?"

"Yeah."

Loco crossed his arms, stubborn. "No way. Those things are unarmored and flimsy. A few layers of fabric between you and hard vacuum. One micrometeorite and you're toast."

Straker shoved Loco toward the bridge exit. "We're inside an asteroid. Pretty sure there's no micrometeorites to worry about. I want to look around."

"How about we do this the smart way," said Engels, following them. "Let's take the gig."

"The what?"

"The ship's small boat. There's only one on a corvette."

"Now you're talking," said Loco. "Travel in style, with the lovely and talented Carly as my chauffeur."

"You can always stay behind and play with Campos," said Engels. "In fact, maybe I should have some girl talk with her about your more vulgar comments toward me."

Loco held up his palms. "Whoa, okay. I surrender."

Ten minutes later the three, plus Chief Gurung, boarded the six-place gig. The chief had invited himself along, saying, "I'd like to take a look at the outside of the *Liberator*, and also this new ship." Somehow, word of the Ruxin ship had already spread among the crew, and Gurung always seemed to know everything going on aboard.

When Engels eased the craft out into the enormous interior space, she could see little except the corvette with its blazing lights, and the ship on which they were focused. The interior walls of the place, kilometers away, showed up on sensors only because of the reflected radar energy, but little detail could be discerned.

"Fly around the Ruxin vessel," ordered Straker, gazing out the wide, wraparound crystal viewports.

Engels flew smoothly over on impellers and approached the bigger ship. "How many people do you think it will hold?" she asked, thinking about Straker's need for troops and crew. If they ever engaged in any kind of… well, not *piracy*, but freebootery, they would need enough personnel to control any situation.

"No way to tell," said Gurung. "But certainly all of us. More importantly, it is a Ruxin ship, yes?"

"Yeah, so?" said Straker.

Gurung said, "Then its internal atmosphere will likely be very wet. I am not well versed in aquatic races, so I do not know the details, but it will likely be rather inhospitable for humans, though we should be able to operate in suits for a time."

"Damn, I hadn't thought of that," said Straker. "Maybe you can modify a part for human use."

"For that, I would need a shipyard and a lot more skilled personnel than I have now," said Gurung.

Engels saw Straker's face grow thoughtful. She knew that look; he was adding to his plans, plans that he'd only dropped hints about, never explained. Maybe now would be a good time to press him. "What are you thinking, Derek?"

"I'm thinking we need more people, like the chief said."

"And how are we going to get them?"

"That's the trick, isn't it?"

Engels let out an exasperated sigh. "Come on, Derek. Let us in on your thoughts. Commander's intent, remember? Like they taught us at Academy?"

"Academy was just somewhere we got indoctrinated."

"Maybe so, but the lessons were real. The Hundred Worlds wanted us to be the best officers we could be. Otherwise, why quote all that military history?"

Straker nodded. "You're right. You're absolutely right. Okay… look, I haven't worked it all out yet, but like the chief said, we need skilled crews to man two ships, we need shipyard facilities, and we need troops."

"To do what, though?" said Engels. "It's all well and good to say we're going to overthrow the Mutuality, but what's the first step? We can hardly even consider taking on an organization the size of the Unmutuals, much less an empire. Right now that's just a fantasy."

Straker showed his teeth. "A fantasy we're going to make reality."

"How? Where do we get troops and crew?"

"I have a couple of ideas. Now let's take a look at this secret weapon."

Great, Engels thought, but it didn't seem worth more arguing to get him to cough up his thoughts. Maybe tonight she could pillow-talk it out of him.

Up close, the Ruxin ship seemed even more inelegant, something cobbled together by the exigencies of war, yet well-built and robust. "It's partially modular," Engels pointed out. "Most of these externals look like they can be swapped around or replaced."

"What are those tentacles?" asked Gurung, pointing at the protrusions at each end of the central spine. "Grabbers?"

"I don't think so. They look more like antennae, if I had to guess."

Gurung snapped his fingers. "I bet they're the underspace field emitters. They resemble old-style sidespace emitters, before the technology was miniaturized and improved."

"Seems pretty vulnerable," said Loco. "Lose a couple and maybe you can't make it back into underspace."

"Stealth tech is generally fragile," Straker said. "Looks like these ships are no different. They're a bit like mechsuits. Not designed to trade heavy hits, but to dodge and weave and shoot from the flanks."

"I'd really like to inspect the *Liberator* from outside," said Gurung.

"Later, Chief, I promise," said Straker. "Right now, I want to see the inside walls of this asteroid."

"Why?" said Loco.

"This is a big place, right?"

"Yeah."

"And there was a lock and a tunnel to get in, right?"

"Right."

"Do you think this ship could have fit through the tunnel?"

Loco's jaw dropped. "Guess not."

"So how'd it get in?"

Engels snapped her fingers. "Underspace."

"Right," said Straker. "The crew knew this place was hollow, and Zaxby said it was of Ruxin construction. Would you build a camouflaged tunnel into it, if the asteroid's only purpose were to serve as a refuge for this ship? Ruxin ships don't need tunnels."

"I see what you're getting at," said Engels.

"I don't," said Loco.

"Watch." Engels turned the nose of the gig toward the nearest wall and accelerated. She switched on the floodlights and directed the navigational radar forward. In a few minutes, they approached the inward-curving interior wall of the asteroid.

"Yes!" whooped Straker. "My guess was right. This place isn't only a hiding place; it's a secret base, and now it's ours!"

Revealed in their floodlights, Engels could see facilities dotting the inner wall of the hollow asteroid. She recognized buildings and structures that, despite their alien origin, shared clear function with shipyards she had seen. In fact, there seemed to be dozens, perhaps hundreds, of small freighters, of a size to easily enter and leave via the tunnel, docked in rows.

"Why the hell would they abandon a place like this?"

"Are we sure they have?" said Loco.

As though he were a prophet, the entire interior of the asteroid came alive with a watery green glow. Beam emplacements, small by warship standards but easily large enough to blow the gig apart, swiveled and aimed directly at them.

Chapter 31

The Ruxin compound.

"Crap," said Loco as he stared at the devices of death pointed at the gig by the newly discovered base facilities.

"I'm getting us out of here," said Engels.

"Wait!" Straker snapped. "If they wanted us dead, they would have opened fire. Maybe it's an automated alert. We don't want to trigger its attack sequence."

"You think it's a machine response?" Engels asked.

"Is anyone trying to contact us?" Straker demanded.

Loco pointed at a flashing icon on one screen. "Comlink laser, unknown protocol."

Engels brought it up. "Running it through the processor."

A moment later, they heard an odd, burbling sound coming from the speakers.

"Dammit, what is that?" said Straker.

"Probably Ruxin, since we're in a Ruxin base." She tapped a screen. "Zaxby, you there?"

"Yes, I...*Great Mother!* I hear Ruxin! Patch it through to me, now!"

"Roger. Patching now."

"Keep us in the comlink, Zaxby," Straker ordered. "Give us a running translation if you can. Is it a machine or a real Ruxin?"

"It is the Ruxin commander... she asks who we are and what our intentions are... I am explaining... she wishes to meet with us immediately."

"Immediately?" Straker's suspicions flared. "Are you certain this isn't a trap?"

"I am in no way certain," Zaxby said, "but her response seems genuine and rational. And, might I point out, if it is a trap, we're all screwed anyway, in your vernacular."

Straker realized Zaxby was right. "Okay. Where and when?"

As if in response, a boat much larger than the gig launched from the surface and flew past, heading toward the center of the base where the two ships floated. "She says to follow. As a gesture of good faith, we will meet aboard the Archer."

"Why is it a gesture of good faith to meet on their ship?" asked Loco.

"Because both sides can have their weapons pointed at it," Straker replied. "In fact, go to battle stations and train the *Liberator*'s guns on the Archer."

"Done, though you will note, all officers but I are away from the *Liberator*," said Zaxby. "Chief Gurung is too. I must come act as your liaison, so who shall command?"

"Okay, lesson learned," said Straker. "Tell Heiser he's in charge and to do the best he can."

"Aye aye, Captain. Lieutenant Engels, please provide me with transport," said Zaxby. "I would very much like to enjoy a Ruxin environment, and translation will be much easier in person."

"Oh?" Engels said. "Now it's Lieutenant Engels instead of 'Straker's female,' huh?"

"You're acting in your official capacity as a pilot, correct?" Zaxby replied.

Loco put his hand on Engels' shoulder. "You can't win with his kind of logic. He'll always have a rationalization."

"I thought he was my friend."

"He is. Think of him as a socially inept brainiac rather than as an equal, and you'll do better."

"Good point." Engels swung the nose of the gig to follow the Ruxin boat toward the Archer and toward *Liberator*, where Zaxby awaited.

* * *

When the humans stepped aboard the secretive Ruxin vessel, they had no idea what they'd find. The answer turned out to be both stranger and more ordinary than they'd imagined.

The air was saturated with moisture, but breathable, like a cool steambath. The deck of the room they stepped onto was awash, knee-deep in water.

The lip of the pressure doors rose to knee height, confining the sloshing liquid, more or less, in the chamber, even if the portal stood open. Of course, everything was outfitted for Ruxin use, with few sharp angles. What passed for chairs looked more like lumpy cupped stools. A greenish glow permeated everything, giving it all the feeling of being in an aquatic environment—which it was.

"Should we seal up?" asked Loco.

Straker sniffed the air. "No, leave our faceplates open. The atmo is good, and I don't think Ruxins and humans can share diseases."

Zaxby pushed past the humans, using his amazing rubbery flexibility to flow between them. He wallowed in the liquid, and then stripped out of his beat-up and heavily patched old water suit. "That's so much better. You're correct, Captain. Our two species generally do not have diseases in common."

"Good." Straker looked around. "I thought your ships would be filled with water, top to bottom."

"You forget we're amphibious, not deep dwellers like our ancestors. We're able to survive in a wide range of environments and utilize the variable advantages of all of them. For example, it's better to flood spaces subject to fire danger, but fill others with air to mitigate shock transmission. Also–"

"Yeah, yeah, all very interesting," Straker said. "Someone's coming."

The Ruxin boat had docked at a different airlock—water-lock?—and Straker wondered what he'd see. Zaxby had called the commander "she." Would a female Ruxin look any different?

The answer wasn't long in coming. A purplish octopoid twice the size of Zaxby swept into the room and plopped itself—herself?—into a chair at the end of what could be interpreted as a table. She waved her tentacles and blatted a noise sounding like a cross between a badly blown trombone and a drunk's beer belch.

Zaxby translated. "This is Freenix, a Ruxin Premier—at least I think that's the closest Earthan word to use. Premier Freenix greets you and asks what the hell is going on. Tell her, now, immediately."

"Immediately, huh?" said Straker, frowning. "I'm not one of her officers. She doesn't give me orders."

"I suppose I need to insert the proper words of etiquette in order to minimize offense," Zaxby sighed. "My people are direct and not given to tact. As I think I mentioned, I am quite diplomatic for one of my race. However, she would like an answer."

"Direct and tactless, eh? I can do that. Tell her we want her Archer, immediately."

"She asks why?"

"To hurt the Mutuality. To eventually overthrow it."

Premier Freenix shook and made even odder sounds, and Straker realized the octopoid was laughing.

"Just because she's chickenshit doesn't mean we are," he said.

"She is amused by the unlikeliness of your goal of overthrowing a thousand-world empire. She also refutes your allegation of cowardice, pointing out that she has many Ruxin lives to consider."

"Many?" Straker leaned forward, placing his hands on the wet tabletop. "How many?"

"More than three million."

Straker's jaw dropped. "How long have you been living here?"

"More than eighty years. The original base personnel have reproduced."

Engels held up a hand. "How long before this base is overpopulated?"

A pause ensued as the two creatures spoke.

"It's overpopulated now," Zaxby said at last, "in terms of resource limits."

Straker nodded thanks at Engels. "So there you are. If you don't do something, you'll just have different problems."

"We *are* doing something. You saw the many small ships we've built. We're preparing to colonize the other asteroids and abandoned bases in this nebula."

"Then you won't need a Archer," Straker pointed out. "We'll also take a shipload of your people off your hands as crew, if you agree."

"This creates a risk of discovery and removes our only defensive warship. What do I get in return?"

"Intel on what's been going on over recent decades. Our goodwill. The morale-building knowledge that you're striking back against the people who conquered your homeworld. We can also try to seize any vital materials you need to expand here in the nebula. We'll hit and run and come back. We will be your eyes and ears. If necessary, Zaxby can captain the Ruxin ship, as long as I'm in overall command."

Zaxby broke off in mid-translation, and Freenix stared at him, waiting.

"What?" Straker asked.

"I do not wish to–"

"Dammit, Zaxby, just translate it like I said," snarled Straker, tired of the Ruxin's slippery ways.

"Very well." Zaxby lowered his head, spoke in his language and then paused.

Freenix began laughing again, and Zaxby looked downcast as he translated in a near-whisper. "Don't be ridiculous. This neuter cannot command a nursery, much less a ship of war. For that, you must have a War Male. We have none."

Straker stared at Zaxby, remembering *he* was technically an *it*. Why did they care so much about what gender Zaxby was? But apparently they did, and they wanted a "War Male," whatever that was, so…

"I am a human War Male, a veteran of many campaigns," Straker said loudly, lifting his hands and spreading them wide, trying to convey a sense of power. "I will command the vessel if you will supply a crew sworn to my service, Premier Freenix."

"Sworn to your service? You want them to swear allegiance to you? Will you then swear allegiance to me, Captain Straker?"

"Absolutely not. I'm in complete charge of my own command. We'll be equals, as allies."

Freenix stared at Straker. "This seems like an inequitable proposition."

"If you mean unfair, then I disagree. You're giving me a ship you don't really care about with a crew of people you have too many of. In return, I'm giving you priceless information, the chance to acquire goods there's no other way to get, and the joy of hitting back at the enemy who did this to you. Oh, and in the long run, the possibility of liberating Ruxin. If anything, it's extremely unfair in your favor."

"Why do you believe I do not care about the *Sweet Pleasure of Inevitable Revenge Against Our Enemies?*"

"That's the name of this ship?"

"As well as I can translate it," Zaxby replied on his own. "I shortened it considerably."

"We'll call her *Revenge*," Straker said. "To answer your purple queen's question, with these shipyards and three million subjects she could have built more ships like this one, or at least more conventional warships, and raided the enemy from time to time. Instead, she's sat on her ass for eighty years and all she's done is make more Ruxins and build colony ships for expansion into the nebula, an expansion she hasn't even started yet. I can't imagine any human society being so cowardly, hiding in a hole and pulling it in after themselves for so long. Zaxby, I thought you said your people were brave warriors."

"Yes they are, when neuters become males, led by a War Male. But males—warriors—must be created by specific hormonal triggers. It appears that, in order to keep peace and order in her inbred society, Freenix has suppressed widespread male production, especially War Males. They're a bit troublesome when there is no war to be fought."

Straker's mind whirled. What kind of insane society disarmed itself of all its warriors when the war wasn't over? Sure, he could see the logic of hiding for a while, but only as a tactical measure, not as a way of life. At best, Freenix was overcautious. At worst, she'd given up her people's long-term survival in order to secure a short-term tranquility. Now, though, the population problem had caught up with her.

"Zaxby," Straker asked, "are you sure a crew of these Ruxin non-males will be competent? Will they fight hard if I lead them?"

"Of course, if they confine themselves to shipboard activities, maneuvering and firing ship weapons and so on, at the direction of an experienced officer like you. However, without War Males, they will make indifferent ground troops."

Straker pounded his fist into his palm. "So we'll still need marines. I have an idea about that." He pointed a dramatic finger at Freenix. "Do you agree? Will you give me my ship and crew?"

"I will think about it."

Seized by an instinct—after all, he'd represented himself as a War Male—Straker strode around the table to loom over the seated Premier Freenix. In his suit, he seemed even larger. He roared, making grand gestures with his hands and arms, "You will give me my answer now, or the trouble you fear begins!"

Freenix shrank back. "You have convinced me. I will give you the *Revenge* and a suitable crew."

Straker remained staring at the Ruxin and said out of the side of his mouth, "Will she keep her word?"

"Of course," said Zaxby. "I believe it's what she wanted anyway. She merely needed an excuse to agree. Your ape-like intimidation worked splendidly."

"And she won't hold a grudge?"

"No. Despite your inexperience, you performed a passing imitation of a War Male. Her instincts are to accept your judgment in all things related to war."

"Good." Straker stepped aside and made a sweeping you-may-go gesture. "Tell the premier it has been wonderful speaking with her and I look forward to the crew's arrival, along with all the food, supplies, energy packs, fissionables and everything else to bring the *Revenge* up to full operating capacity. Make sure she sends skilled shipyard personnel for a thorough overhaul. I'm not going to take such an old ship into battle without a full refit."

Zaxby translated, "It will be convenient to move the *Revenge* to the shipyards. The job will get done much faster that way."

"Agreed. Zaxby, can you pilot this thing?"

"If I do so with due care."

"Do it," Straker said. "Oh, and Zaxby?"

"Yes?"

"You've been bragging about your superior intellect and amazing capabilities for some time. I'm going to test those boasts to the limit. You can begin by vetting all the Ruxins that Freenix sends, and setting up a program to teach them the Earthan language so you aren't the sole translator. After that, coordinate with Chief Gurung to whip the crew into shape."

"Why do you think they'll need whipping into shape, as you put it? All Ruxins rapidly become highly competent at whatever tasks they are assigned."

"Because none of them have done anything like this for eighty years, or maybe ever. Knowledge is good, practice is better, experience is the best." Straker turned to Engels, Loco and Gurung, thoroughly energized. Eagerness sang though his veins and he felt better than any time since waking up as a prisoner, now that his military expertise came into play. "Let's go, people. Life just got interesting."

✳ ✳ ✳

The refit took forty days. The crew of the *Liberator* worked like demons alongside the Ruxin personnel to get both ships as ready as possible.

The first test of the refurbished *Revenge* amazed Straker. He stood on the soaking wet bridge surrounded by Ruxins clad in minimal utility harnesses—they didn't care about clothing in the human sense, unless needed for protection—and after an extended systems check, he gave the order. "Initiate insertion sequence."

Zaxby, now his liaison, spoke Earthan, for all of the Ruxins had been drilled intensively in the language, concentrating on the terminology they would need to run the ship. "Initiate protective field and test."

"Field on," replied the engineer. "Test shows nominal."

"Underspace generators stand by."

"Standing by."

"Full power to generators."

The engineer manipulated heavy manual controls, more reliable than computers during this first test. "Full power. Emitters building the insertion field. Pseudo-singularity is stable. Fifty percent. Eighty. One hundred percent."

"Insert into underspace."

The ship seemed to dim slightly in Straker's eyes, the greenish colors becoming muted. He felt a chill, despite assurances that the protective field would shield against freezing.

Straker stared at the synthetic view on the main visiplate. Since almost nothing leaked across the dimensional barrier between normal space and underspace, the ship's computer system modeled what it knew and saw, and updated the model as they moved.

Of course, the longer the ship stayed in underspace, the more out-of-date the model became. With non-maneuvering objects such as the hollow asteroid shell, this was not a problem. Against enemy ships it became a matter of shrewd guessing, the art of prediction and chance.

"Take us out, Lieutenant Zaxby," said Straker.

"Z-axis turn, ninety degrees."

"Ninety degrees, aye."

"Ahead one-quarter."

"Ahead one-quarter, aye."

The synthetic view rotated on the first order, and then accelerated toward the viewer on the second. *Revenge* leaped at the inner wall of the asteroid, and Straker involuntarily grasped the railing in front of him. Then they passed through and came out the other side as if the solid rock wall were nothing.

"Yes!" he exulted, prying his hands off the railing. For him, that was the acid test. They'd ghosted through a kilometer of rock without the slightest bump. Actually, they'd slipped under it, into another dimension.

"All stop," Zaxby said. "Deactivate underspace engine to emerge."

"Deactivating."

The main visiplate rippled and replaced its synthetic view with a real one, aggregated from its optics and sensors. Nothing but glowing gas could be seen.

"Power down protective field and switch off," said Zaxby.

"Protective field powering down. Protective field is off."

"Rotate Z-axis one-hundred eighty degrees."

The main screen view swung through a long arc, coming to rest pointing at the outside of the Ruxin asteroid.

"That was outstanding," said Straker. "Well done, everyone. They aren't going to know what hit them."

* * *

During the refit, Straker and his officers had pored over the Unmutual databases Zaxby had copied and brought with him. They matched up the information with that stored in the corvette's computer, and they looked for a way to take their first steps toward Straker's goals.

When they slipped into sidespace five days later, Straker had two warships.

He had two untested but well-drilled crews.

And he had two targets.

Chapter 32

Two weeks later.

Inquisitor Lazarus-211 watched with guarded satisfaction as the fast fleet auxiliary *Mutual Lockstep* landed on the snow-covered ground next to Re-education and Training Camp 17. The ship was battered and poorly painted, but appeared to be in good working order. The pilot set her down more skillfully than usual with these vessels, her rounded belly sinking slightly into the frozen landscape.

Although small for a sidespace-capable ship, she was larger than most that could land on a planet. Even a small, cold, miserable one like Prael had an interfering atmosphere and gravity-well. As a rule, ships her size and bigger transloaded cargo and passengers to shuttles in order to reduce the fuel expenditure and wear of landings.

But ships like *Lockstep* had their uses. The Mutuality often employed them as deployment vessels, cheap substitutes for the much more expensive dropships or assault boats. They could jump in with a fleet and, as soon as defenses had been neutralized, they would land and unload troops, combat vehicles and supplies. Once empty, they could stay for extraction or proceed onward to other missions.

In short, they were jacks-of-all-trades, albeit unarmed save for small lasers. They carried cargo comfortably and personnel uncomfortably, using modular bulkheads and removable sanitation pods.

Ships like these were perfect for transporting rehabilitated personnel, mostly those recovered from Hundred Worlds facilities or captured in battle. A few of the transported were recidivist criminals given one final chance to become productive citizens. Those who failed were turned into Hok.

Lazarus's eyes lingered on Camp 17, taking in its barracks, its firing ranges, its parade grounds, its mess halls. An efficiently run re-education program dovetailed neatly with basic military training, creating a useful product. He felt quite satisfied with himself and his management. No doubt the Committee for Public Mutuality would too.

Five hundred men and women marched by platoon out of Camp 17, wearing dull gray-green fatigues and cheap combat harnesses with everything they needed for travel to garrison duty.

Half of them carried mass-produced laser carbines. The other half were unarmed. The weapons would be passed from person to person as needed. These were not front-line Hok, after all. Their tours of duty as militia represented an intermediate status on their journey to returning to a normal worker's life of service to the State.

Or so they were told. In reality, they were often given the Hok biotech and thrown into a desperate fight. What did Mutualist principles matter if battles were lost?

The only thing the product lacked were the power magazines for their rifles. Those would be loaded separately. Naval crews were far too savvy to allow green militia access to devices that could damage their ships.

Lines of personnel boarded the boxy vessel, urged on by armed drill instructors wearing traditional campaign hats that hearkened back to Old Earth.

Lazarus signaled his driver, who maneuvered the groundcar down the unpaved road to stop near the ship. The man leaped out to retrieve two fine travel cases and carried them to the *Lockstep* in Lazarus's wake. Lazarus himself picked his way across the snowy field, thankful for his well-worn, well-maintained spacer's boots.

His cloned Tachina concubine followed with some difficulty. No matter. The exercise would do her good. She was starting to get a little plump, what with all the extra food and wine she wheedled out of him.

He'd made trips like these many times and knew the routine. An Inquisitor's job was, after all, to guide wayward comrades back to full Mutuality, and that meant delivering his product, his work of the last few months, to their new commander.

Sadly, within a year of Lazarus's return to Camp 17, many of those he'd rehabilitated would likely be dead. The cowards or failures would be converted into Hok and thrown into one battle or another, sometimes before the biotech even finished the process. In the struggle against the Hundred Worlds, there was never any want of war.

There was a rumor that a mechsuit program was in the works. Lazarus discounted this possibility, however. He'd heard it all before, how some new technology or trick would bring forth victories for the Mutuality. More often than not, they failed to match the superior Hundred Worlds tech. Even the recent triumph at Corinth had been costly, not to mention the loss of Prison Alpha-Six and the murder of his brother clone, Lazarus-176.

This Lazarus entered the *Lockstep* by the crew door. Spacers saluted him and took his bags from the driver, leading him to Spartan quarters next to the captain's cabin. They'd do the same for his Tachina when she got there.

At least the stateroom was private and clean, with a narrow bed for himself and a pallet on the floor for Tachina. He mused on the sacrifices he made for the People, and felt satisfied.

Once Tachina arrived and began unpacking his things, Lazarus visited the crowded personnel compartments, only one-and-a-half meters high to save space. The inhabitants jammed themselves in with stoic attitudes—at least when he was there. No doubt they joked and entertained themselves when he was out of sight.

He sighed. Jokes were not the lot of an Inquisitor, and his job was his entertainment. That, and Tachina. Unsurprisingly, the pleasure clone had chosen to stay with him rather than be processed into product. That was two years ago. It made for a good relationship, this inequity in power. She knew her place, knew what she would lose by displeasing him, and so became the perfect companion, as she'd been bred to be.

In fact, she pleased him so much he allowed her to come along on these trips, to reduce the ennui of space travel. It was a minor breach of regulations, but if it improved his own efficiency as an Inquisitor, it followed the moral principles of Liberty, Equality, and Mutuality—so he could rationalize it.

After inspecting the soldiers, Lazarus shook hands with the senior drill instructor before he exited the ship. "Enjoy your break," Lazarus said. In five days, hundreds more would arrive at the camp, ready to be re-educated. The schedule wore out even the most mutual.

"Have a good journey, sir," the drill instructor replied, his eagerness to be off peeking from beneath the tiredness.

"Convey my thanks to the staff," Lazarus replied. "You may go."

The man didn't hesitate to hurry back to the camp and his own concubine. Lazarus mused further on the perfection of the Mutuality system: from each according to his ability, to each according to his needs, ensuring all were given functions best suited to them, thus ensuring perfect happiness and harmony.

After all, *he* was certainly happy, as were all around him. He knew, because they told him they were, and nobody lied to an Inquisitor.

Crewmen began slamming and sealing hatches and doors. The soldiers would be locked in until the ship slipped into sidespace. The takeoff warning began to beep and count down in its computer voice. "One minute to lift. Take acceleration positions. Fifty-nine seconds to lift..."

Lazarus strode to his stateroom and strapped himself into his bunk, a familiar ritual. Tachina lay on her pallet. As long as there was no mishap, she would be unharmed by a period of acceleration, two or three Gs for an hour or so.

This was his twelfth delivery in person, an annoyance, but mandated by Committee directive. At some time in the past, an unnamed apparatchik had no doubt determined it would be beneficial for the Inquisitor to hand over his product personally. Perhaps the rule was meant to ensure nothing went wrong with the process, and that his responsibility meshed seamlessly with the militia commanders.

He shrugged, remembering the old joke he'd heard long ago in the crèche, before he donned the garb of Inquisitor: *There's the Right Way, the Wrong Way, and the Mutual Way.* Of course, that was Unmutualist heresy. The Mutual Way *was* the Right Way... but he admitted to himself in the privacy of his own thoughts that, like most heresies, it contained a kernel of truth.

Once through Prael's weak, fetid atmosphere, acceleration was reduced to a comfortable level. The trip became smooth and uneventful out to the transition point. The star system held no other naturally habitable planets, only several heavily fortified asteroid habitats and moon bases for mining various vital minerals.

A pair of aging destroyers served to patrol the area, one generally grounded for leave and maintenance while the other kept watch. Along with a handful of corvettes and a slew of cheap attack craft with mediocre pilots, these served to fend off the occasional pirate raid or Hundred Worlds scout.

There'd been a brief sidespace blip some hours back, but nothing had been found. As the area around the optimum transition point was clear, the *Lockstep* cruised unescorted while the destroyer continued searching on the other side of the system, near the location of the anomalous readings.

Lazarus spent the time on the naval auxiliary's bridge, making the captain and officers vaguely uncomfortable. That too was part of an Inquisitor's job, letting those with responsibility know they were accountable to the Committee and the People.

He sipped fine whiskey from a glass poured from a bottle he did not share, the better to emphasize his superior equality. He looked over shoulders and ran his fingertip above hatches, examining the results with evident distaste even when he found no grime. He gazed at the main and secondary visiplates at the nothingness of space, nodding occasionally to himself as if he really could see something more than the ordinary officer or rating.

Thus it was that he was staring straight at it when an oddity appeared, dead ahead.

Alarms blared, and the ship's anticollision system fired every forward and half of the lateral thrusters, as well as dumping peak power into the impellers, all to slow and deflect the vessel from smashing into the thing that had popped into existence in their path.

"What kind of ship is that?" he asked, forcing calmness into his voice. "And where did it come from?"

"Inquisitor, I've never seen anything like it," replied the captain, a man named Gibson. "It must have some kind of system for hiding itself. Something to deflect sensors. It's on a slow approach vector."

"The ship is broadcasting... in clear Earthan, sir," said the communications rating.

Captain Gibson looked at Lazarus for guidance.

"Can we enter sidespace yet?" Lazarus asked.

"No, Inquisitor, not for over an hour. Not even by overloading our emitters."

Lazarus took a deep breath and laced his fingers behind his back. *Lockstep* had no chance against any sort of warship, no matter how odd or ugly. "Send out a call for assistance."

"Yes, Inquisitor, but it will take at least three hours for help to arrive."

"Then let's see what this intruder has to say. Patch it through, two-way mode with visual."

"...*Mutual Lockstep*, cease maneuvering and prepare to be boarded. I have a shipkiller missile ready for launch, as well as enough beam weapons to cut you to pieces. I say again, Mutuality vessel *Mutual Lockstep*, cease maneuvering and prepare to be boarded..."

"This is Inquisitor Lazarus. You can see me. Show yourself and let's discuss the situation."

There came a pause, and then the main screen changed to show a humanoid in a Hundred Worlds pressure suit, knee-deep in liquid and standing in a command center or bridge. He was lit by a greenish glow and surrounded by octopoids—Ruxins, if Lazarus' copious memory served.

"Lazarus?" the humanoid asked, clearly surprised. It was hard to tell from his green-lit, mottled face. "That's impossible. I killed you!"

"Yet here I stand, I can do no other," Lazarus said, thinking furiously. Obviously, this person had murdered a Lazarus clone at some time in the past. Could this be an escapee from Prison Alpha?

The humanoid recovered quickly. "What, more Old Earth quotes?"

"I see you are not entirely uneducated."

"How can you be alive again?"

Lazarus smiled, enjoying his usual superiority to mongrel humans and aliens. "I would think that was obvious. I'm a clone. The Lazarus cell line has proven itself to be the most efficient ever designed. What could be more Mutual than clones in key positions?"

The humanoid shrugged. "You have a point there, though my friend Loco would say it's probably on top of your head."

Lazarus ignored the nonsense spewing from the creature. "Who are you and what are your intentions? If you intend to steal our cargo, I must tell you, what we are carrying will cause you more trouble than you wish."

"Oh, I highly doubt that. I'm Derek Straker, captain of *Revenge*. She's aptly named, since she's crewed by Ruxins eager to take vengeance on the conquerors of their homeworld."

"The Mutuality treats the Ruxins as well as any other citizens. They have no cause for quarrel."

One of the octopoids sloshed into view and spoke in excellent Earthan. "*This* Ruxin has a quarrel with the Mutuality, as he had the misfortune of experiencing one of your re-education facilities. But I escaped, as you can see, and–"

The humanoid stepped in front of the Ruxin and silenced it with a gesture. "What my officer said is true. These particular Ruxins hate the Mutuality and so do I. You asked what my intentions were, so I'll tell you. I'm taking your ship. If you cooperate, we'll be on our way with a minimum of trouble."

"Cooperate? Cooperate how?" Lazarus asked, buying time. He had no intention of cooperating with these pirates. Even if what this Straker fellow said were true, it was his duty to resist all enemies of the People, even if that meant killing everyone aboard, so promises of leniency didn't matter.

"You and any crew that wish to will board a lifeboat and head back for Prael. Other crewmembers that want to be liberated from your oppressive system can join me. You'll leave the troops locked in their compartments. I'll make a similar pitch to them, and any that want to remain in the Mutuality will also board boats and leave."

"There aren't enough boats to hold all the soldiers."

The humanoid smiled. "Do you really think so many will stay with you after the hell you've put them through?"

"Perhaps a few reversionary criminals will defect, but by and large, yes, I believe they will stay loyal to the Mutuality."

"Then they can triple up in the boats and I'll take the criminals off your hands. If necessary, those who stay can put on exo suits and float in space. Nobody needs to die. Your destroyer is already heading this way at high burn to pick you all up. It will be here in a few hours, but by that time, we'll be gone."

Lazarus pursed his lips and cast his eyes down, miming uncertainty. "I must discuss this with my officers."

"I'm well aware that we're on a ballistic course toward a position where you can enter sidespace. I won't give you the time. You have five minutes to agree, or I'll punch holes in your ship with beams until you surrender or die."

"Then you won't get what you came for."

"I'll settle for as many of the infantry as I can rescue and whatever I can salvage. That's half a win for me, but a total loss for you. If I have to do it, I'll kill everyone left."

"I will call you in five minutes." Lazarus made a chopping motion and the screen blanked.

"What do you plan to do, Inquisitor?" asked Captain Gibson, fear in his eyes.

"We will fight, as is our duty," Lazarus replied. "If necessary, we will overload the power system and self-destruct. Begin the sequence, but do not do anything that will alert the enemy of our plans. Once that is done, open all the troop compartment doors. I will brief the soldiers."

"But sir, the troops will go on a rampage!"

Lazarus stared coldly at the captain. "Don't be ridiculous. They have been re-educated under my personal supervision. A few miscreants like the Ritter brothers will not matter."

Captain Gibson exchanged glances with his first officer, who widened his eyes and slowly shook his head. The others that made up the small crew of the freighter did the same in turn.

The captain opened a compartment in his acceleration chair and removed a compact laser pistol, aiming it at Lazarus. "I'm sorry, Inquisitor. We're not ready to die just yet."

Righteous anger filled Lazarus-211. He pointed his arm, index finger extended, at the treasonous captain. "You will comply with the will of the People, which flows through me! You will carry out my orders, or else–"

"Or else what, Inquisitor? If we do what you say, we die. If we refuse to do what you say, but we don't join these pirates, you'll have us re-educated, or worse. We have families. I can't let them be thrown out of their homes when you brand us 'enemies of the People'."

Lazarus ground his teeth, forcing himself to see things from this traitor's point of view. Now that he'd taken the step of defying an Inquisitor, he had nothing to lose. How could Lazarus salvage this situation? It galled him to bargain with a subordinate, but he was not inflexible. He had an idea.

"Captain, I understand your position. Like this Straker fellow said, I must be happy with half a loaf. If you and your crew will evacuate to the lifeboats, I give you my word as an Inquisitor of the Lazarus cell line that I will not report your momentary weakness. In return for this favor of mine, you will order the soldiers to abandon ship, telling them there has been a catastrophic systems failure, and you will set the self-destruct sequence as we leave. We shall thereby deny the enemy his prize, and we will all survive. In fact, I'll sweeten the pot by putting every member of your crew in for commendations. We can all come out ahead."

The captain motioned his first officer over, never wavering in his pistol's aim. After a brief, whispered discussion, Gibson spoke.

"Sorry, Inquisitor. I have a better plan."

The first laser shot burned into the center of Lazarus' chest, intentionally missing his heart. The wound was cauterized, as designed, to the point at which it imparted enough energy to merely boil blood rather than burn flesh.

Pain such as Lazarus had never known doubled him over. "You... you..."

Lazarus-211 didn't feel that next shot, the one that sliced through the top of his head and cooked his brain.

Chapter 33

Space, near planet Prael.

"It's been five minutes," Straker said, fidgeting and moving from foot to foot. He'd found that pacing in the soggy environment of the *Revenge* was difficult and unsatisfying, so he stayed near his captain's seat. It was only a chair brought in from the *Liberator* and bolted to the deck of the bridge, but at least it was comfortable.

"I will try to contact them again," Zaxby said. "Ah, here they are."

The picture that popped onto the screen showed Lazarus—that *particular* Lazarus, Straker supposed, now that he knew the Lazaruses were clones—lying on the deck, seared brains outside his head. A stocky, grizzled man in a worn, rumpled Mutuality naval uniform with captain's stripes on it stood over the body, laser pistol in hand.

"Captain Straker," the man said, "my crew and I have decided we'll cooperate and join you, as long as you promise to treat us well."

"You'll be treated just as well as all the rest of my people, Captain...?"

"Gibson. We've all volunteered to stay with the *Lockstep*. Hell, we've been aboard her for years. She's home, even more than the places where our families live. But about our families..."

"I can't promise anything, Captain Gibson. I'm on a timeline here and I can't divert to go on a rescue mission to some Mutuality planet."

"I understand, sir. I had to ask."

Straker stroked his jaw. "Are the soldiers all still locked in their holds?"

"Yes. The Inquisitor wanted us to let them loose to fight you, and for us to self-destruct our ship."

"I figured it was something like that." Actually, Straker hadn't figured that at all, and he'd been startled to see Lazarus dead on the deck. However, as Engels had reminded him more than once, it paid to cultivate an all-knowing image. "I'm surprised, though, that you went against your conditioning."

"I wasn't born to this tyranny. I was captured off a Hundred Worlds freighter more than thirty years ago," said Gibson. "I'll never forget the torture the Inquisitors put me through, and I'll never forgive them for it. How they expect anyone not to hate them when they do that to people, I don't know."

"I'm with you, Captain. Now, to business. I believe you, but as a great leader from Old Earth once said, 'trust, but verify.' I'll be joining you on your bridge."

"I'll open the crew docking port for you, sir."

Zaxby skillfully mated the two ships, and soon Straker, Heiser and his two marines Nazario and Redwolf, entered the bridge of the *Lockstep*.

Straker began stripping off his suit after setting a sodden bag on the deck. The other three men did the same, keeping their weapons handy. "Sorry, Captain Gibson, but we've spent two weeks soaking wet. I think I'm beginning to grow mildew between my toes. We'd appreciate a change of clothes while this is being cleaned and dried."

Gibson sent one of his people to find something, and soon Straker and the others had coveralls.

The freighter crewmembers stared as he was changing. Gibson asked, "Captain Straker, why do you look like...?"

"Like a Hok, a little? They gave me the injection but I got the antidote in time."

"I wasn't aware there was an antidote."

"There is, but I still don't know if my skin will go back to normal. Captain, how far are we from earliest transition?" Straker asked.

"Forty-five minutes or so."

"How long until the Mutuality destroyer gets in firing range?"

"They could fire shipkillers at any time. They've been trying to communicate with us, but we haven't answered. So, missiles aside, call it three hours."

Straker nodded. "Good. Now the trick is to get the loyalists off without things going to hell, and here's how we're going to do it."

* * *

After his preparations were complete, Straker spoke over the ship's public address system. The audio clone software the Ruxins had provided made his voice sound like Lazarus.

"Soldiers of the Mutuality, this is Inquisitor Lazarus. A directive has come down from the Committee, and I am proud to pass it on to you. The Mutuality needs your help. Our re-education camps require guards, pain therapists and executioners. Those who volunteer now will be sent back to Prael for training. Once qualified, volunteers will be given privileges commensurate with their new status, including access to luxury goods and concubines. Some of you might even be selected for the Inquisitor program! Troop holds will be opened in turn, beginning with Number One and ending with Number Ten. Volunteers, leave all your equipment with your fellows and report to the crewmen as you exit the holds."

Captain Gibson came on the comlink, speaking quietly. "Opening Hold One now. Looks like... six volunteers. Transferring them to the lifeboat. They seem happy, boisterous. They don't look like bad people. Captain Straker, are you sure...?"

Straker's words were piped into Gibson's headset. "You agreed to cooperate, Gibson, and you agreed this was necessary. Anyone that would volunteer for that kind of duty is scum. They deserve their fate."

"Yes, but... my people and me, we're not killers."

"You are now, Gibson. You already killed Lazarus. You've joined a war, and in war, we kill the enemy. These are the enemy. If you can't accept that, get in a lifeboat and bail out. Are you with me?"

Gibson swallowed. "I'm with you, sir."

"Good man."

Straker watched internal feeds on the screens as the crewmen led the scumbags to the main airlock. The crew dogged the hatch, and Gibson, after hesitating slightly, input commands into the control panel there.

"It's done," Gibson said heavily.

"And it will have to be done again," said Straker. "You don't have to feel good about it, but you have to do it."

"Aye aye, Captain."

Even now, the scumbags who'd entered the airlock were ejected into space. Without helmets, they died quickly in vacuum. Straker watched as Gibson headed to Hold Number Two. There, he repeated the process of collecting the volunteers. Out of the fifty in each numbered hold, he led a handful to the 'lifeboats.'

Straker felt no twinge of conscience, no more than when he'd killed Skorza or Lazarus. Those people had put themselves on the side of evil. They were self-declared enlistees to torture and murder their fellow humans in exchange for a few privileges.

Fortunately, Engels wasn't here to complain about it. He loved her dearly, but he got tired of her objections when it came to getting rid of filth. There was no way such men would serve under him without treachery.

He was glad when it was over. The next step might be a lot trickier.

Straker checked the chrono and the approach of the Mutuality destroyer. Two and a half hours until the warship was in effective weapons range, or less if they decided to fire missiles. The *Revenge*, still mated with the *Lockstep*, was making slow impeller maneuvers to foil any long-range fire. He had to work fast.

"Do you have those Ritter brothers separated out yet?" Straker asked Gibson as he pulled on his own clothes again, a fancy naval captain's uniform he'd had made for this operation. It had been dried out in the ship's laundry. Though it still smelled like Ruxin seawater, it looked impressive. Heiser and the other two donned clean marine-style fatigues and Ruxin-made body armor.

"Yes, Captain Straker. They're in the wardroom."

"Good. I'll be right there."

When Straker and his bodyguards swaggered into the guarded wardroom, he saw three men: one small, one middle-sized, one as large as he, all with the same family look. The smallest was blond, the middle one dark-haired, and the largest sported a flaming red mane, just beginning to grow out. They stared at him in consternation from under sullen brows.

"Who za hell are you?" the smallest said in an odd accent that made all his consonants sound harsh.

Straker smiled. "I'm Captain Derek Straker, your liberator. With the help of the crew of *Lockstep*, I've seized this ship and all aboard her. Are you really brothers? The Ritter brothers?"

"Half-brothers," said the biggest one. "Father had three wives."

Straker chuckled grimly. "Liberty, Equality, and Mutuality?"

"Our family wasn't part of this disgusting system. We're from Sachsen, an independent planet until these Mutuality scum arrived and conquered us with their Hok freaks."

"Well, you're free now."

"Free?" said the middle one. "Free to do what?"

"To join me, if you like. I've looked at the files on this shipment of 'product,' as they call the re-educated. They say you three are troublemakers with disloyal tendencies, not to be allowed to associate. They also say you refused to self-critique and have cycled four times through the camp."

"All true," said the largest. "We also refused to rat on our fellow prisoners or help turn them. The only reason we're here now is they threatened to turn us into Hok, so we decided to play along in hopes of something breaking our way." The man grinned. "I suppose something has."

"If you join me, you'll have a chance to strike back at these tyrants, and liberate as many people as possible. Are you in?"

"Hell, ya!" said the last, the smallest one. The others echoed him. "Eventually we'll want to liberate our homeworld, though."

"I can't promise that, but it's a possibility. Once these near-term operations are over, you can leave or stay as you wish. Until then, you're under my command. Agreed?"

The largest held out his hand to be clasped. "Captain Straker, the Ritter brothers are with you. I'm Aldrik, this is Bernhard, and the little one is Conrad."

"Good. You have any military experience beyond your recent training?"

"We are freeholders, Captain. All of us receive military training from a young age... but our only experience was a losing battle against the Hok."

"Good enough. I'm making you sergeants. You'll report to First Sergeant Heiser here. I have a job for you. Follow me, keep your mouths shut, and do what I tell you."

"*Jawohl, Herr Kapitän.*"

"Yah what?"

"Sorry, Captain. Sometimes we lapse into the old tongue."

"One of the pre-Earthan ones? Like American or Español?"

"Yes, sir. This one is called Deutsch, or German in modern Earthan."

Straker slapped Aldrik on the shoulder. "I've heard of it. Your ancestors were a great people. But stick to Earthan for now. Your accent is funny enough as it is. Follow me." He turned to lead them toward the hold. "And get these men stunners," he told one of the crew.

"I don't have an accent," Aldrik said from behind him. "Everyone else has an accent, *ja?*"

When Straker reached Hold Number One, he met Captain Gibson and four of his crew, nervously clutching laser pistols. "Open both holds, numbers One and Two. We have to speed things up."

"But sir," Gibson said, "there will be twice as many people to control. If things get out of hand…"

Straker loosened his pistol in its holster. "Be ready to stun them and slam the doors shut… but if that happens, I'll have failed. With this group, at least. Now open them up."

The two doors to the cramped Holds One and Two were so close together, Straker could speak into both of them at once. When they opened, he could see about forty men and women in each. They sat or knelt against the wall, for the ceiling was too low to stand. Dim light showed faces, all curious as to what was happening.

"I'm Captain Derek Straker, your liberator," he said, loudly and proudly. "I impersonated Inquisitor Lazarus' voice to separate out the scumbags that wanted to torture people and keep sex slaves. What better way than to let them identify themselves by volunteering?"

He laughed then, as if he'd told a fine joke.

Some of the people in the holds laughed as well, nervously, glancing at each other.

Straker went on, "My goal is to oppose tyranny and free those who've been enslaved. I want to make a place where people can be free. Eventually, I'll overthrow the Mutuality system and liberate all humans and friendly aliens."

"What if we don't want to join you?" said one man in the front.

"I'm going to let anyone return to the Mutuality who wants to. The life I offer you is a hard one. If you join me, some of you may die in battle, but at least you'll die free. Each of you must choose for yourself."

The group hesitated, surprised.

"Don't look at your neighbors!" Straker boomed at them. "They can't choose for you! If you want to go back to your oppressors, leave your gear and come out, hands raised, single file. You'll be put aboard lifeboats to be picked up within hours. But if you want to be a free man or woman under my command, stay where you are."

Some immediately rose to a bent-over positions and dumped their equipment on the floor to come out, hands spread. Others followed more slowly, until there were no more volunteers to return. The rest stayed in place.

Out of more than eighty, some thirty had chosen to return to the Mutuality. Straker noticed with satisfaction that they were almost all male, as he had hoped, though he wasn't surprised. The camps were doubly hard on females. He couldn't imagine many women wanting to risk another bout of "re-education." Those that did… perhaps they had children they wanted to return to. Their choice.

"Captain Gibson, show them to the lifeboats and help them launch."

"Aye aye, sir," Gibson said with satisfaction, gesturing to the loyalists to begin walking. Since these would survive to be recovered by the incoming destroyer, the freighter captain was obviously much more comfortable with this task.

Turning to Aldrik Ritter, the oldest of the brothers and obviously their leader, he said, "You know most of these people? Their strengths, their weaknesses?"

"Among us three, yes, we know many."

"I need you to take a look at everyone. Stun and bring out anyone you wouldn't trust to fight beside you. I don't want criminals, cowards or spies with me."

"Yes, sir."

The Ritter brothers found nobody meeting Straker's criteria in Hold One, but they dragged out one man from Hold Two.

Aldrik said, "This one is Morton. He's a snitch. He sold out a dozen people for minor infractions in order to gain the favor of the guards and Inquisitors." Aldrik lifted his eyes to Straker. "Shall we kill him?"

Straker smiled coldly. "No. Put him with the loyalists and tell them what you told me. They deserve each other."

Aldrik showed his teeth.

* * *

Straker repeated the winnowing process with Holds Three through Ten. At the end of it, he had almost two hundred and ninety potential infantry and had gotten rid of most of his troublemakers. The results were, he had a regiment that was nearly half women.

He didn't care about gender balance when it came to fighting. He'd use whoever he had available for as long as necessary. But after this operation was over—assuming it was successful and Straker survived—he would have to lead not just a regiment, not just a ragtag squadron of freebooter ships, but a free society that would grow, eventually producing children.

For that, there had to be roughly the same number of women as men, a base from which to build, made up of people there by choice. His experience with the Unmutuals and their pillaging had shown him that a force of hardcore fighters with no homes and families to anchor them was asking for trouble.

After passing final instructions to Zaxby, who commanded the *Revenge* in his stead despite Freenix's objections, Straker ordered the two ships separated. He and his three men would stay aboard the *Lockstep* for now. He'd asked Gibson if he wanted to rename the vessel, but he'd declined. There were worse names for a ship than *Lockstep*, he supposed.

"The destroyer has launched a shipkiller missile," the sensor officer said, his voice tightening to a squeak. "I think it's aimed at the *Revenge*, not us."

"Impacting when?" Gibson snapped.

"Nine minutes."

"Plenty of time," said Straker. "Zaxby, you hear me?"

"That is not the proper ship-to-ship protocol, Captain Straker. You should say, '*Lockstep* to *Revenge*, *Lockstep* to *Revenge*, do you read?' and then I say—"

"I'm in charge and I make the protocol, Lieutenant Zaxby! Now move away and transit into sidespace like I told you, unless you want to welcome that shipkiller personally. We'll meet you at the rendezvous."

"Aye aye, Captain Straker—which is the proper response, I might add."

"Wonderful. Get moving."

"Are you certain you don't want us to use an underspace attack profile to destroy that destroyer? Oh, that's a bit of ironic wordplay, isn't it? A destroyer being destroyed. It would do wonders for crew morale."

Straker's voice hardened. "There's no reason to risk our Archer against a warship just for morale purposes. Besides, the Mutuality personnel in the lifeboats would be witnesses. We don't want anyone suspecting that we have an underspace vessel, or what it can do. Just transit into sidespace. Get going, now!"

"There's no need to yell. A little courtesy goes a long way, or so you humans say."

"Zaxby–"

"Transitioning now." *Revenge* winked out.

"Missile still inbound. It appears it has changed targets to acquire us."

Straker put his hands behind his back. "Gibson, you may jump when ready."

A moment later, the screens turned gray with sidespace and Straker silently let out his breath. The first phase of his plan was over with.

Now came the hard part.

Chapter 34

Heading for Freiheit to right some wrongs.

Now that *Lockstep* was cruising safely in sidespace, Straker got back on the public address system to speak with his new troops. "I have good news and bad news, ladies and gentlemen. The good news is the crew will be reconfiguring the holds to give you standing room and more deck space, now that there are far fewer of you. The bad news is, the trip will take longer—about nine days instead of three—and it's going to strain our resources. Rations and hygiene facilities will be short. When we arrive, you'll be going into battle within hours."

Straker could imagine the initial cheering and then the grumbling his words would bring. He hoped the relief of being out of Mutuality hands would keep morale high. Along with the training program Heiser had planned, it would stave off any serious problems.

That, and the oldest human recreational activity of all.

"First Sergeant Heiser and his noncoms will be coming around to get you organized into squads and platoons. They'll appoint sergeants and corporals from among you and schedule training. I'll be briefing you on our mission in detail. Until then, take heart in the knowledge that you'll be freeing more of those in thrall to tyrants, and you'll be seizing a home for yourselves. Remember, this is a military organization, and I expect you all to act with discipline and common decency." He turned off the public address.

"You're getting to be quite the charismatic speaker, sir," said Heiser. "But if I may speak freely…"

"Sure, go ahead."

"You explain too much. It makes you look wishy-washy and insecure. Just tell them what to do."

"I never liked that method when I was a cadet, or a cherry lieutenant."

"Nobody does when they're on the bottom and in the dark, sir. But if you get them thinking, then they'll think. It's not good for the common soldier to think too hard. They might start thinking how they know better than you. Or their First Sergeant."

"Point taken. I'll try to cut down on the verbiage, but despite what I said, this is more than a military unit. It's the foundation of a free society. It's not going to be as clean and simple as an infantry regiment."

Heiser shook his head. "You're the boss."

"Yes, I am." Straker slapped the big man's shoulder. "But you keep telling me what you think. Don't be a yes-man, and I won't be an asshole. Deal?"

"Roger wilco, sir."

Straker winked. "That's 'aye aye,' Heiser. You're a marine now."

"Uh... sir, please don't make me talk like a swabbie."

"Just kidding. Use your best judgment. I trust you."

Heiser took a big breath and let it out. "Thank you, sir. I'll be getting to work now."

"Dismissed."

Shortly after Heiser left, Straker saw a woman, not young but certainly not old, step onto the bridge. She moved like one of the eye-candy on Shangri-La, though she was older, in her late thirties. She was dressed in a provocative red silk sheath, slit from hem to hip, with matching slippers. With long blonde hair, plump lips, and a chest that made everyone in the room stare, she seemed as out-of-place as a rose in a dung heap.

"Who are you?" he asked.

"She's the Inquisitor's concubine," Captain Gibson answered for her. "In all the excitement I forgot about her."

"Concubine? Is that like a slave?"

Gibson frowned. "Pretty much. No different from the rest of the Mutuality. If someone with power wants you to do a job, you do the job or get sent to a camp. That includes... personal services."

"I'm a Tachina." The woman's bold gaze speared Straker.

"A Tachina? Not just Tachina?"

She shrugged. "Tachina-119, if you like. I'm a clone."

Straker nodded with compressed lips. "Miss Tachina, your Lazarus is dead. You're free now."

Tachina mimed sadness. "He wasn't a bad man."

Straker didn't contradict her, though to his mind, all the Lazaruses were bad men.

Gibson spoke. "Ah, Captain Straker, will you be taking the Inquisitor's quarters? It's the best stateroom we have."

"Not very equal or mutual, hmm?" said Straker. "No, just give me a standard stateroom. Let the lady stay there."

"There is no empty stateroom for you. The Inquisitors' is the only one not occupied by my crew. We could put her in with the troops, of course."

Straker gazed thoughtfully at the woman. No doubt she was a pampered thing, used to ease and comfort. Given her looks, she could be an incitement to riot. He *could* order she do something to make her look ordinary—like shave her head and put on a coverall, perhaps—but his natural sympathy stopped him from seriously considering that.

"There are two bunks in the Inquisitor's stateroom?"

"No," said Gibson. "She sleeps on a pallet on the floor."

Straker growled. There went an easy solution: swapping crew around. Then again, the troops were sleeping on the deck, so… "Captain Gibson, my apologies, but please have two of your crew move into the Inquisitor's former stateroom. Miss Tachina and I will take the cabins they move out of. My men will stay with the troops."

"That won't work either, sir. Other than the Inquisitor, I'm the only one with a private cabin. My crew are already doubled up this trip."

"Oh, hell." Straker chewed the inside of his cheek. "Can you reconfigure the holds to create a private area, enough to sleep four?"

"Yes, sir."

"Do it. Miss Tachina here can stay where she is. I'll bunk with my own men. Put four pallets in there too, and make sure the doors can be opened from the inside."

"Aye aye, sir." Gibson passed his orders.

"You could stay with me, Captain... Straker, did he call you?" said Tachina, padding slowly toward him like a cat stalking prey. Her perfume reached his nose, a delicate, musky scent.

"I don't think that would be a good idea," Straker replied. Every nerve had snapped to attention, and the other men on the bridge seemed as intent as he was.

"You have nothing to fear from me, Captain." She reached out to touch his arm. "I'll be quiet as a mouse. No trouble at all."

Her touch ran like electricity up his arm. Why was he reacting like this? He had all he wanted in Carla Engels. The easy women of Shangri-La hadn't turned him on like this, so why was Tachina able to do so? Besides, he was ugly. Why would this sex kitten be interested in him?

Because he was the man in charge, of course. Loco said Straker didn't know women, but he knew some were attracted to power just like the ones of Shangri-La had been attracted to glory... assuming those had been real and not mere software. Involuntarily, he reached up to touch the link sockets at the nape of his neck.

Tachina followed his hand with hers. "Something wrong?"

Straker took her by the wrist and gently pushed her hand away. "No, nothing. Return to your quarters. Stay there."

Tachina's lips pouted. "Very well. But I have to eat, and... shower." Her fingers fluttered, mimicking droplets falling on her body, bringing to mind...

"There won't be many showers this trip. We all have to share the one facility we have among all aboard. You can eat in the wardroom with the crew. This bridge and the holds are off-limits."

"As you wish." She turned, showing her shapely backside, and then looked over her shoulder. "Visit me sometime, Captain. I get lonely." Then she was gone, leaving the bridge looking drab.

"Bitch," muttered one of the female watchstanders.

"Hey, hey!" complained one of the men. More joined in to argue.

"Belay that talk," snapped Captain Gibson. "That woman is trouble. She should be confined to quarters." He looked at Straker.

Straker frowned in thought. "I'll leave that to you, Captain Gibson. It's your ship, after all."

"Thank you, Captain Straker. I think I speak for the entire crew when I say it's an indescribable relief to be…"

"Free?" Straker nodded. "We'll stay free, too, I swear—or we'll die trying."

* * *

Straker threw himself into training and organizing his troops, feeling fully at home in his environment for the first time in a while. No relationship issues, no worries that he'd say the wrong thing, no bickering among his friends, just a straightforward military op.

First Sergeant Heiser seemed to be everywhere, along with the Ritter brothers, who became his three platoon sergeants. Nobody questioned this arrangement. The combination of unthinking discipline instilled by Mutuality basic training, the gratitude at being free of an Inquisitor, fair treatment, and the lack of any other option made the process go better than Straker had expected.

They reconfigured one of the holds into a laser range. With the troops' carbines set to ultra-low power, they were able to improve everyone's proficiency. Heiser also ran assault exercises in the passageways and holds. He wore everyone out with twelve hours of training a day.

"Great Cosmos, I'm so glad we don't have to do those stupid brainwashing sessions anymore," Straker overheard one soldier say.

At Heiser's insistence, the slim, ferret-faced Nazario and the hulking Redwolf alternated in accompanying Straker. Neither would make good noncom material for a while, but they were both deadly in a fight. Nazario liked knives, and Redwolf carried a length of crysteel pipe as a baton everywhere he went. On those occasions where a little intimidation was called for, they only had to growl and display their melee weapons to emphasize a point.

"Sometimes, a heavy club or a sharp blade scares a man more than a gun," Heiser remarked to Straker. "Especially in close quarters. The fact that *you* are actually more dangerous than your bodyguards doesn't even matter. This is about hearts and minds, sir, not reality. The commander needs attack dogs, so he can always be the good guy. Nobody does his best for an attack dog. They do it for someone they respect, even love."

"I'm with you, Spear." *Spear* had been a nickname for First Sergeant since the time of the Romans of Old Earth. Straker had remembered this from his studies, and he'd taken to using it for Heiser. "I'll walk around and smile and slap backs. I'll even kiss babies when they show up. I think I'm turning into a politician."

"Babies *will* show up, sir," Heiser said. "Plenty of activity in the holds going on after lights-out, I hear. A bunch of our female troops gonna be useless in a few months, unless they already have implants."

"Useless as soldiers, maybe, but as people, as anchors for a new society, they'll be essential. Nothing will endear us to a bunch of civilians like mothers with children. And you put the word out to the sperm donors that they'll act like fathers or they'll answer to me."

Heiser grinned. "Roger wilco, sir."

"What do you think, Spear? Will they be ready?"

"More than ready, sir. Eager. I've spread a few stories and let a few hints drop like you said, and everyone's hankering to hear the mission brief."

"I'll brief them the day before we arrive. You can tell them that. That way they'll have time to think about it, sleep on it, and get used to it, but not enough time to worry."

* * *

That day, the day before emergence into normal space, arrived quickly. After a short day of training, Straker had the holds reconfigured yet again to create one big open space in the middle, with three doorless platoon sections around the perimeter. They'd sleep that way tonight, as a regiment.

The new people had embraced being called "Straker's Breakers." It made him smile to hear it: the beginnings of esprit-de-corps, military identity and tradition.

"Good afternoon, Breakers!" Straker roared, and the regiment roared back from their positions seated on the deck. A few leaped to their feet to applaud, but he waved them back down while the Ritter brothers bellowed for silence.

"Tomorrow we'll be going into battle. I'll be leading you, but you're going to be doing the hard work, and I'll be depending on you. Unfortunately I don't have fancy projection screens, or even the ability to print out much hardcopy, so with the help of some hull paint, I've drawn graphics on the bulkhead behind me."

A designated crewman turned on a spotlight that highlighted one section of the drawings. "This blob is an asteroid habitat with two thousand people living on it. It has factories, farms, and plenty of space for homes. With my help, the Unmutual rebels stole it from the Mutuality. With your help, I'm going to steal it back, for us Breakers."

Straker would have expected whispering and quiet talk, but the Breakers kept dead silence. Every face stared in total fascination at the crude picture, as if they could leech more information from it.

Aldrik raised his hand on cue. "How are we going to steal it, sir? How do we get away with it?"

"Good question, Sergeant. We're going to do it the same way the Unmutuals did: with sidespace engines. They moved the habitat to a secret location, but I know that location, and when we take control of it, we'll move it somewhere else."

Straker hoped the habitat was where he'd last seen it. If the Unmutuals had moved it again, they were screwed.

"When we first joined the Unmutuals, they showed me their good side. But I'm sure the Spear told you a few tales about their bad side, and the stories were true. These Unmutual troops became corrupt thugs, lacking in human decency and military discipline. Many are thieves, rapists, and murderers. I promise you, that will never happen under my command. Understood?"

"YES, SIR!" the Breakers barked in unison.

Enjoy this while you can, a small voice said in Straker's head. They'd never be this enthusiastic and naïve again. After this battle, they'd be blooded veterans... or dead. They wouldn't be so eager to rush in the future, but they'd follow, if he led them well.

"The Unmutuals call the habitat Freiheit, which the Ritter brothers tell me is the word for freedom in their old German language. I think we'll keep that name, and make it come true. We're going to liberate the civilians, and they'll be given a chance to join us. Anyone offering armed resistance is an enemy, to be killed or captured. If they surrender, treat them properly, but if they resist, shoot them. I have no sympathy, and neither should you."

At this, a rolling cheer broke out, and this time Straker let it flow and die out naturally.

"You might be wondering how we're going to take this rock against hardened enemy troops. But there won't be as many of them as there will be of us, and as soon as they understand what's going on, I'm confident the civilians will swing over to our side. We'll also have the element of complete and total surprise. I'm not going to explain exactly how we'll achieve that, but I can assure you we have allies."

Straker signaled, and the spotlight shifted to show stick figures of an octopoid and a human, shaking hands. At least, that's what he hoped it looked like. "Along with some of my human troops, and ships you haven't seen yet, we have Ruxin allies. They look a little weird, but they're good people. Any Ruxin you see is on our side."

This revelation brought whispering, quickly quashed.

"Now that you know what I want to do, I'll tell you how I want you to do it." Straker went on to brief them.

After he'd explained his plan in detail—too much detail, Heiser again remarked. Straker spent time with the troops, listening to them talk, trying to gauge their morale for himself. He found them as ready as he could expect. The young were eager to throw themselves against their enemies. The older ones, those who'd been through more misery and abuse in their lives, even a few battles, seemed grim and determined. At least, none of them looked ready to run away. The shifty ones had been weeded out.

When Straker was eating dinner in the wardroom that evening, Tachina came in, escorted by an unsmiling crewwoman. She wore a coverall this time, and her hair was greasy from lack of washing, but she still radiated sensuality. Maybe it was the way she moved, and her perfume… He should order her not to wear it, he supposed, but that seemed like the opposite of the freedom he promised.

He realized his tactical error when she picked up a tray of food, simple but hearty shipboard fare, and took the empty place next to him. Her hip pressed against his, her scent filled his nostrils, and he found himself thinking things he shouldn't. Carla Engels was his woman, always had been from the moment he saw her, not this… creature.

"Ma'am," he said, getting up with his half-finished food.

"Don't go, Captain." She grabbed his arm. "I'm so lonely stuck in that room all day. If you won't come see me, at least let me socialize with the crew."

Straker slipped away from her grasp with difficulty. Her hand seemed to stick like a Ruxin's tentacle.

"We're going into battle tomorrow," he said. "After that, you'll get to choose where you go, what you do. Until then, you're nothing but a problem."

Tachina burst into tears, making him feel horrible. He almost responded with kind words, until Captain Gibson kicked him under the table.

Straker met the man's eyes, and Gibson shook his head. He realized the freighter captain was right. The woman's tears might be real, or just an attempt to gain his sympathy. Either way, his responsibility was to the lives of his regiment, not to the feelings of one person.

He stepped back, taking his tray. "Captain Gibson," he said evenly, "I'll be with the troops. Make sure Miss Tachina stays out of the way."

"Aye aye, sir," Gibson said. "Eat your food, miss, and no more shenanigans, or you'll be dining alone again."

Again? Interesting. Apparently she'd been sent to her cabin before.

Later that night, as Straker lay on his pallet in the separated room he shared with his trusted men, he thought he smelled her perfume again.

His memory must be playing tricks on him, he thought. He sniffed his arm where she had touched, and where he had scrubbed with strong soap, and smelled nothing. Still, the aroma seemed to linger in the air, and when he finally slept, his dreams would have resurrected a dead man.

He woke to Heiser shaking him. "Sir, we're half an hour out."

"I told you to get me up two hours ago, Spear."

Heiser shrugged. "You looked like you could use the sleep. I got everything under control."

Straker bit his tongue. Heiser was his Spear, and he had to allow for the man's best judgment. He rolled to his feet and shrugged on his combat tunic instead of his fancy naval jacket. Inspiring the troops was one thing, getting shot by a sniper was entirely another.

He found himself glad of the sleep and the shortness of time. In reality, he had nothing to do but make a quick pass through the troops and stand on the bridge, watching the transition chrono count down. After all, it wasn't as if the battle would start right away.

Or it shouldn't.

But when the *Lockstep* emerged, the active sensors immediately sounded the alarm.

Chapter 35

Just outside enemy space, seeking Revenge.

"Get me an ID on that contact," Straker snapped.

"Warship, sir," Gibson said. "Corvette class. Transceiver says it's the *Liberator*." The sensors watchstander's voice went up a notch. "They've locked us up with fire control."

"Put me on the comlink."

The communications officer punched up the channel. "You're on, sir. They're transmitting."

"–Mutuality freighter, this is *Liberator*. Identify yourself immediately or be fired upon."

Straker spoke. "Damn, Engels! Don't kill your own captain just yet."

"Derek! I mean, Captain Straker, sir? Good to see you. I take it the mission was successful?"

"So far. No sign yet of *Revenge*?"

"Not yet, sir."

"Hope to hell Zaxby hasn't gone off raiding or something idiotic like that."

Engels' voice quavered. "Or something went wrong in sidespace. Mishaps are rare, but they do happen, and that ship is old."

Straker was quite conscious of the freighter crew watching and listening. He put good cheer into his voice. "Let's not start worrying. How far are we out?"

"So far out the Unmutuals shouldn't have detected our sidespace emergence, but that means it'll be a long trip in."

"And Freiheit is still there?"

"In the same stellar orbit we left it, sir."

Straker let out a silent sigh of relief. "What about *Carson* or any other warships?"

"Nothing I can detect on passive sensors. Can't go active."

Of course they couldn't. Active emanations would give them away.

Just then, the collision alarm screamed at the bridge crew. "Shit!" yelled the woman on sensors. "Too close!"

The helmsman threw the ship into a sharp climbing turn, missing the *Revenge* ahead of them by less than a hundred meters, judging from the display. The motion dragged the crew against their restraints despite inertial compensators. Transports weren't designed for such maneuvers.

"Dammit," Straker complained, gripping the support rungs that were placed around the walls of the bridge. "Get me Zaxby!"

"Lieutenant Zaxby here, Captain."

"That was close, don't you think? And you were supposed to get here first."

"We *were* here first, Captain. We've been here for eleven hours. I was taking the opportunity to exercise the precision underspace capability of the *Revenge*."

"Well, next time appear *behind* the friendly ships."

"There was no danger, sir. Our velocities are matched, so we could not collide. Your helmsman simply panicked."

The helmsman began to protest. Straker held up a hand. "Zaxby, not everybody has your iron nerves and piloting skills. Superior abilities mean you have to take others' capabilities into account. Otherwise, you're more trouble than you're worth. Maybe there's another Ruxin who would like to be Executive Officer on the *Revenge*?"

Zaxby hastened to backtrack. "You're absolutely right, Captain Straker. I'd briefly forgotten that with great capability comes great responsibility for the lesser beings around me. I will endeavor to condescend more in the future."

"Is that possible?" muttered Captain Gibson.

"Let's get on with it," Straker said. "Have you rigged for troop carry?"

"Of course, Captain Straker. You may dock when ready."

Straker nodded at Gibson, who directed the helmsman to match airlocks with *Revenge* again. While First Platoon transferred onto the ship with full combat gear, Straker called *Liberator*. "Engels, what do you see? You have the best sensors."

"Bayzos and Aynor are on the other side of the system, more than a light-hour away, so it will take that long to even see us, and about a day for anything they launch to get here. The hard part will be pushing Freiheit far enough out from the star to make the jump. It could get ugly."

"And you're sure there's no sign of *Carson* or any other vessels?"

"Yes, I'm sure. Likely they'll only have a squadron of attack ships."

"And you can handle those?" Straker asked.

"Between *Liberator* and *Revenge*, yes, but…"

"You hate to kill people that are only doing their jobs, right?"

Her voice strengthened with pride. "I'll do my duty."

"I never doubted it. Begin your run, impellers only."

"On my way, Cap'n. You just make sure Zaxby is there on time, on target."

"Oh, I certainly will," Straker said.

Heiser stepped onto the bridge. "Ready for you, sir," he said. "Your gear is already transferred."

Straker reached out to shake Gibson's hand. "Stick to the plan and everything will be fine. My First Platoon might be enough, but I can't depend on that, so you need to push in as soon as the shit hits the fan."

Gibson let go of Straker's hand and snapped off a jaunty salute. "Aye aye, sir. We'll get into the action. I think the troops still aboard would mutiny if we didn't."

Straker followed Heiser through the open airlock onto *Revenge*. Nazario and Redwolf waited for him, along with Aldrik Ritter.

The passageways remained damp, but at least they'd been drained of water. Breakers now occupied every available cubic meter, packed in like sardines. Straker chuckled to himself at the aquatic wordplay, and then sobered as the joke reminded him of Loco. This was the first battle he'd ever been in where his best friend wasn't at his side.

No matter. Heiser was a good man, as were Nazario and Redwolf. The three could hardly be more different, but now, they were brothers in arms—and more importantly, a deadly team.

"Everyone thoroughly briefed?" Straker said to Heiser.

Heiser gave him a mildly reproachful look. "We've gone over it five or six times. We're as ready as we'll ever be."

"Then pass the word to undock and accelerate."

* * *

The inbound trip was excruciating. Despite the best efforts of the ship's systems, the air became fetid with a hundred extra humans aboard. The air-scrubbers were overloaded on every deck. Built to hold thirty Ruxin crewmen, the ship was being used in a way it had never been designed for.

Zaxby had assured Straker the air recyclers could handle it, but some of the troops reported headaches and nausea. Straker had to order more oxygen released from the emergency tanks. He also had the gravity reduced to ten percent to ease the strain on people who had to stand or squat.

It only got worse when the time came to vanish, safely out of detection range. From there, *Revenge* cruised in underspace, navigating purely on the navcomp's computer memory. If something outside changed, if a ripple in underspace moved them from their chosen path, they'd never know until they emerged.

The temperature dropped slowly but steadily. The troops began to shiver, even though the thermometer on the wall showed they should be comfortable. Straker chalked it up to the underspace effect that slowed every molecule within its field. He clenched his jaw and resisted the urge to visit the bridge. Looking over Zaxby's shoulder wouldn't change anything, and would only make him appear insecure. Instead, he tried to project an air of confidence.

Finally, the PA crackled to life and Zaxby's voice said, "We are in position. Emerging now. Firing beam." A pause. "Main power has been cut. Freiheit is crippled."

Straker imagined the stealthed ship's actions, popping into existence less than a kilometer from the northern, Base Control Center end of the Freiheit asteroid. Murdock must be shitting his pants right now, as would Ramirez, if she was aboard. "Move in, now! And give us some heat in here!"

"I cannot do both, and soon there will be no need. Inserting."

The chill came again, but only briefly, as the Ruxin ship vanished and moved directly toward the asteroid. With a solid update from the first pop-up, the navcomp should be able to place them precisely...

"Emerging."

The temperature rose suddenly, the opposite of the chill Straker had felt before. This must be the effect Zaxby had briefed him on, he realized: untold numbers of air molecules being displaced out of the way by the ship's emergence from underspace. Some of them would not get out of the way fast enough and would interact with solid objects, creating heat.

Of greater concern were dust particles or water droplets. A crackling sound briefly permeated the passageways, accompanied by cries of pain as blisters appeared on—and inside—people. Someone screamed, and several soldiers yelled as a power pack ruptured.

This was the price Straker knew they'd pay to emerge within an atmosphere. Still, with great risk came great reward. Now the *Revenge* should be floating within the spinning interior of the asteroid, an utter shock to any defenders. As long as the Ruxins could keep it in position, it could dominate the entire habitat.

Zaxby's calm voice continued. "Firing. Interior defenses neutralized. We are taking scattered small arms fire. No damage. Reducing identified strong-points. Moving toward the BCC."

Now came the tricky part. *Revenge* would approach the northern end cap where the Base Control Center sat. Only at an end could the troops debark, for the ship wasn't made to land on any surface that had significant downward force. Only at the end would the pull be so small, and the speed of the ground whizzing by so slow, that people could jump out safely.

"All right, Breakers! This is it!" Straker roared, and a cheer came back to him. "Don't hesitate at the airlock. If anyone balks, shove them out! The gravity will be below ten percent, so remember your impact rolls and you'll be fine."

The airlock swung open, overridden from the bridge. "Captain Straker, you're cleared to jump."

"Great job, Zaxby."

"Naturally, sir. Good luck."

Straker hurled himself through the airlock, trusting Zaxby's word that they were in position. The ground was close, and most of his velocity came from his jump, so when he struck the roof of the BCC and rolled, the impact was not severe.

Immediately, he leaped up and ran for the nearest access. Seizing the control center was critical to his plan, and every second was precious. Kicking the door open, he swarmed down a ladder, feeling the force of artificial gravity bite after so many hours without it.

The interior of the complex was lit by dim backup lighting. Rounding a corner, he barely stopped himself from shooting an unarmed woman, obviously a civilian local.

"Where's Murdock?" he barked.

She pointed the other direction, a mixture of fear and hope on her face. "Second left," she said.

"Thanks. Hide somewhere," Straker replied, and ran in the direction she pointed. Nazario and Redwolf jumped off the ladder as he passed, and followed.

He kicked open the indicated door and immediately ran along the wall to his right. A beam speared his left arm, causing excruciating pain, which he powered through due to adrenaline and training. He fired a burst that cut down the rebel with the laser, and then another who was aiming at him with a blaster. His bodyguards followed him in, searching for targets, but it appeared there had only been the two.

"Murdock! This is Derek Straker! Surrender and you won't be harmed!" he called into the room. It was filled with workstations and consoles, and most of the light came from the displays. They must be on battery power. "We're taking this rock no matter what. The only question is, do you want to die for the cause, or live for a new one?"

"Don't come any closer, Straker," Murdock answered, still unseen. "I've got my finger on a burn subroutine that will shut down everything on this asteroid—water, air, heat, everything. We'll all die."

Straker motioned his men to hold. He stood and slung his slugthrower, confident in his speed. The hole in his arm was beginning to make itself felt, but

CHAPTER 35   357

fortunately laser wounds were self-cauterizing and this one felt like a through-and-through, a flesh wound that had missed the bone. "I hear you, Murdock, but I'm hoping you're a good man, not like Ramirez and Yates and the rest of these thugs. Do you really want to work for them after all you've seen? Or are you just as bad?"

"You're just as bad as they are. I'm not going to work for a man that murdered hundreds of civilians in cold blood."

"What the hell are you talking about, Murdock?"

"I saw the records, Straker. That woman and that squid of yours set bombs on board the boats that held the people who wanted join the Mutuality."

"That's bullshit. It's what Ramirez wants you to believe, but she had her people do it, probably someone like that scumbag Yates. It was because my friends discovered the bomb and because I tried to shut down their sex trafficking that she framed us and tried to kill us."

"Why should I believe you, Straker?"

"Because you're not blind, Murdock. You're a smart guy, so *think*. Whose actions have been more consistent? Who tried to stop the abuse? Me. And who made excuses for it? Them. You had to have heard the troops grumbling about how I spoiled their party."

Straker heard the scattered weapons fire die down. It appeared Murdock was thinking, so Straker let him think.

Heiser came into the room, freezing at the sight of Straker's upraised fist. "All secure in the BCC, sir. Two dead, five wounded on our side, three civilian prisoners. All northern facilities have been taken, but there's maybe forty or fifty Unmutuals scattered across the south. Lieutenant Zaxby says he could use ship beams on them, but it would cause a lot of collateral damage and civilian casualties."

Straker said, "Tell him to hold their fire unless he can be sure to kill only the enemy. Advance your squads cautiously but don't take big risks. In two hours, the rest of our troops should be here. Once we have reinforcements, we'll finish them off. Get going."

Heiser left.

"Straker," said Murdock's voice, "don't shoot. I believe you. I'm standing up. I'm unarmed."

"All right. Come on out. Hold fire, men."

Murdock's hands emerged, held high with fingers spread, from behind a console. The rest of him followed, stringy blonde hair surrounding a thin face and crooked nose, a tall man with a slight stoop.

Straker moved toward him. "Nazario, guard this guy with your life. Don't let any harm come to him, but take him down if he makes any funny moves."

"Roger wilco, sir," said Nazario, taking a position behind Murdock.

"All right, Murdock. Give me a comlink to my Archer."

"Your what?"

"The Ruxin ship floating inside here."

"A Ruxin Archer...? Holy shit! I read about those things. Even played around with designing underspace equipment, but it was too tricky. That's a real Ruxin-built vessel? Not some clone?"

"Real as it gets, and full of my squids. It's how we cut your power and assaulted this place from the inside."

Murdock's eyes seemed to glow in the dim reflection of the consoles. "What I wouldn't give to get my hands on that equipment..."

"You can play with toys later, Murdock. Right now I need a comlink."

"Right-o." Murdock handed him a headset. "There you go. It's set to the correct freq, though I don't have your encryption code."

"It's Breaker one-nine."

Murdock put in the code, allowing Straker to tap into the secure comlink. "Straker here. Zaxby, do you read?"

"*Revenge* here, Lieutenant Zaxby speaking. I really would appreciate it if you would use proper protocol, sir."

"Give it a rest. I have Murdock. Stand by for further instructions." Straker's eyes bored into Murdock's. "What can you do to help us win this battle?"

Murdock waggled his eyebrows and grinned. "I think you're going to like my answer," he said. Tapping at screens and controls with slim pianist's fingers, he brought up a visiplate view of the interior of a small hangar. Inside it, three humanoid figures stood.

Straker looked closer and a thrill ran through his bones as he noticed the scale of the manlike things. They loomed over equipment sized for human use, standing seven meters high or more.

"Mechsuits!" he cried. "Our two Sledgehammers and… a standard Foe-hammer?"

Murdock beamed. "I had the factory techs get them in shape. There are guys training on the Sledgehammers using the manual controls, but nobody can get the Foehammer to work properly for them. It's too touchy, too high-powered. Like a racing sloop compared to a utility shuttle."

"I can pilot it," Straker heard himself saying. "I'm *going* to pilot it! With that Foehammer, I can spearhead our assault right away, without waiting for reinforcements. Forty or fifty infantry won't stand a chance against me."

The comlink beeped. "Captain Straker, this is *Revenge*, do you read?"

"Loud and clear, Zaxby."

"We are having increasing difficulty keeping the ship in place. Over half our station-holding thrusters have malfunctioned due to age and overuse. I fear if we do not transition soon, we shall impact the surface and suffer catastrophic damage."

"You want to leave?"

"I believe that is the obvious conclusion."

"Then go. Make repairs and watch for enemy ships."

"Inserting now. *Revenge* out."

"Straker…?" Murdock pointed at the visiplate showing the mechsuits. "I think we have a problem."

Straker watched as two men ran across the hangar floor and mounted the Sledgehammers. "Oh, shit."

Chapter 36

Straker grabbed Murdock's arm and shook the man as he watched the mechsuits powering up. "I need to get to that Foehammer, fast. It's the only thing that can take down those Sledgehammers. How do I do it?"

"*Ow*. Let go, dammit. Without getting killed by rampaging sixty-ton war machines?" Murdock jerked his arm, and Straker let him go. "Use the subway system."

"Subway system? What's that?"

"The first layer of tunnels beneath the surface. Go out the door, to the left, down the stairs to level minus-one. Read the map, take an electric cart. Good luck."

"Good luck? What are you going to do?"

Murdock fixed Straker with a withering glare. "I'm assuming you don't want to sit here and wait for an Unmutual counterattack? If you want this rock to ever enter sidespace, I have to contact my technicians, convince them to defect along with me, restore the power bus your laser-happy Ruxin sliced in half, and make sure everything's working right. It's a damn delicate operation to transit something this big. Not to mention, we're too close to this system's star. We need to get back out to flatspace, and impellers take power too."

"Absolutely right, Mister Murdock. Do what you do best. You're vital to this operation, and I'll reward you as well as I can."

Murdock waved his hands near his ears. "All I want is a chance to do my work in peace, without all this drama."

Straker half-shrugged. "Can't promise that."

"By the way, you'd better secure the south end before somebody thinks to sabotage the sidespace engine down there. We're dead in the water without both of them working together."

"Got it." Straker waved at Redwolf to follow and bolted out the door to the stairs, as the lifts had no power. Three levels down, they emerged into a wide, smooth tunnel with several branches. After checking the map for the way to the mechsuit factory, Straker leaped onto an electric cart and the two men sped down the passageway.

The factory subway station was deserted and dim with the emergency lighting. Straker leaped ahead and ran up the stairs, his bodyguard following close behind. At the top, he stealthily opened a door. The small mechsuit factory seemed equally dark and deserted, and the two men slipped across the robotic assembly floor.

As Straker rounded a giant assembler, something moved. He aimed his slugthrower and took cover. "Come out of there! Show yourself or be shot!"

A small man in a work coverall, tools peeking from a multitude of pockets, raised his hands. "Don't shoot! I'm unarmed!"

Straker recognized the factory tech. "Manny, is that you? It's me, Straker."

"Captain Straker, thank the gods! You have no idea what it's been like these past months."

"I'm here to set things right, Manny. Is that Foehammer fully functional?"

"Yes, but it's only twenty percent charged, and there are no missiles."

"Gatling ammo?" Straker asked.

"Full up."

"It'll have to do."

"The cockpit code is Unmutual123."

"How imaginative." Straker hurried toward the door to the mechsuit hangar.

"They took the two Sledgehammers," Manny called from behind him.

"I know," Straker said. "They're my problem."

He cracked the hangar door and looked in. The big mechsuit portal stood open to the outside, the two Sledgehammers were nowhere to be seen, and the Foehammer stood alone to one side, untouched. His greatest fear had not materialized; the other two pilots hadn't thought to put a shot into the open interior of the 'suit to wreck its naked innards.

Straker handed Redwolf his slugthrower and equipment harness. It would interfere with the sensors in the tight confines of the mechsuit. "Stay here and secure the factory. Manny will help you."

"Roger wilco, sir." The big man turned to the tech and handed him the weapon. Manny took it hesitantly, and that was all Straker saw before he ran for the Foehammer.

He leaped into the cockpit, child's play in the half-G of the spinning asteroid habitat, and buckled in. He tried to plug into his brainlink, to become one with the mechsuit again, it wouldn't synch up. This wasn't surprising; it normally took a day of integration at a specialized facility to blend a pilot's brain with a particular mechsuit's systems.

He'd have to do this the old-fashioned way, using the manual controls. He punched in the cockpit code.

Fortunately, the Foehammer's backup control suite was still quite sophisticated. Cockpit sensors read his body and directed the mechsuit to mimic his every move. A wraparound HUD synched up with audible and tactile cues to give him superb situational awareness. Voice commands would operate his secondary systems, while his primary subroutines allowed point-and-shoot speed and accuracy.

Without his brainlink he'd lost half his combat effectiveness, but he was still the most dangerous thing on this little battlefield.

The mechsuit sealed itself and Straker felt it come alive. Only twenty percent stored power, as Manny had said, but it should serve as long as he was careful. If there was a weakness to a Foehammer, it was its need for power. That was one reason the primary weapon was a force-cannon, using volatile ammo made of exotic materials, instead of a pure beam weapon.

Moving the mechsuit, he became aware of his arm wound and dialed up a painkiller, but nothing happened. Apparently the drugs hadn't been loaded into the system.

As he walked the Foehammer out of the hangar, Straker cursed the absence of *Revenge* overhead. His plan had been to keep the ship floating inside the habitat until they'd secured it. The vessel would have provided both recon and fire support, and could have smashed the two Sledgehammers flat with its ship-to-ship beams.

Looking up, he realized recon would be no problem. The inward curve of the cylinder meant almost every point was visible to every other point. The dimness of the power failure wouldn't hinder him at all. His Foehammer boasted a complete suite of active and passive sensors.

Switching to passive thermal, he easily spotted the line of his Breakers by their body heat and their hot laser carbine signatures. The two Sledgehammers stood out immediately, glowing like bright striding demigods. They were rolling up his infantry's flank, wreaking indiscriminate havoc.

Far from taking care to limit collateral damage, they were firing heavy beams and railguns into every structure, blowing all of them to bits. This showed their inexperience.

Straker suppressed the urge to take a shot from here. He could no doubt nail one, probably taking it out, but that would alert the other. For all its unwieldiness, a Sledgehammer packed not one but two huge punches, either of which could incapacitate his Foehammer with a lucky hit. And, fighting inside this kind of curved interior, the longer the range, the less effective the available cover would be.

No, real mechsuit work took place at close range, where quickness, agility and surprise gave him the advantage.

He loped toward the two enemies, noting their lack of infantry support. The Unmutual troops hadn't figured out that they should be advancing to assist the Sledgehammers' counterattack. The omission would give Straker his chance.

When he reached close range, the inner curvature became moot. Buildings and folds in the ground, built long ago to mimic a planetary landscape, gave him places to hide and dodge.

He approached the enemy from behind and carefully lined up his force-cannon on one, at the most vulnerable point on any mechsuit: the back of the neck. Even though the pilot's cockpit was buried deep in the 'suit's torso, the head of the mechsuit contained most of its sensors, and thus had to swivel and tilt, creating an inevitable weakness. If the sensor head got blown off, a mechsuit would lose most of its effectiveness.

He could have tried for a pilot kill, drilling a bolt directly through the Sledgehammer's back, but that section was just as heavily armored as the chest, being the obvious target. Another choice would have been a hip or knee, settling for a mobility kill, but for his money, the sensor head was the best option.

Straker's bolt lit up the night like lightning, a magnetic shaft guiding a jet of pure superheated plasma little different from that formed by an armor-piercing shaped charge, though even hotter. After cutting through its tough duranium skin, the dense, energetic gaslike stream blasted out of every crack and weakness of the Sledgehammer's cranial dome.

Some pieces fused, some melted, some ignited. The resulting heat burst through the overlapping armor plates and slagged all the delicate parts. The inexperienced pilot would be blinded and, lacking a brainlink, it would take him precious seconds, possibly up to a minute, to access secondary sensors and regain situational awareness.

Eighteen percent of his power remained. Straker shifted his attention to his undamaged opponent, who hadn't noticed him and was still concentrating on advancing against the scattered Breakers. Every second of recharge time meant more of his people dying, blown apart by heavy railgun bolts or particle beams.

"Got to get his attention," Straker muttered to himself, and sent a long burst of gatling fire into the Sledgehammer. He concentrated on a hip, knowing the joints there were underrated for the heavier loads of the modified 'suit. A mobility kill was his best chance until his force-cannon readied itself again.

The Sledgehammer spun with the impact of the cannon stream, and it took a snapshot at him with its particle beam, coming startlingly close before expending its bright blue energy against the soil.

"Won't get me so easy," a voice said on Straker's comlink.

"Karst? Is that you in the Sledgehammer?"

"Straker? Are you behind this?"

Straker crouched in a low spot, extending a telescoping optical from his sensor head to gain line of sight. "Yes, it's me, and you're the only thing stopping me from liberating this base. I already slagged your buddy, and I'm a hundred times better at this game than you are, so *fucking stand down*."

"I can't. They'll kill Cynthia. Sergeant Yates is on another channel right now, talking in my ear, with a knife to her throat. I have to fight."

"Not if he thinks you did your best. I'm going to shoot you now, straight in the chest. It won't penetrate, not on the first impact. As soon as I do it, scream in pain, fire a shot over my head and punch out. Then don't talk to anyone on a comlink. Can you do that?"

"Yeah, all right. I know you tried to help me before, and I owe you."

"Yes, kid, you do. Here we go." Straker stood, moving laterally as naturally as breathing. He trusted Karst, pretty much, but there was no reason to bet his life on it. The kid's Sledgehammer was walking straight toward him, aiming his heavy railgun slightly to the side.

Without conscious thought, Straker put a deliberately widened, attenuated force-cannon bolt straight into his opponent's chest. The armor there should hold. Karst pitched backward as if kicked. To Straker, it looked as fake as a ballplayer's flop, and he hoped any watchers weren't familiar enough with the nuances of mechsuit motion to tell the difference.

Karst's railgun penetrator streaked upward across the cylinder and struck the other side with a flash. A moment later, Karst's mechsuit seemed to explode, though it was only the ejection sequence, blowing him clear within a cocoon of superfast-expanding hardfoam.

Still running laterally, Straker fired a gatling burst at the remaining Sledge-hammer, which was staggering in a circle, still unable to lock up a target. Sixteen percent power remained.

His opponent must have managed to get a view onto his HUD right then, because he raised his arm and triggered a particle beam. Before he fired, Straker had already thrown himself into a diving roll that placed him behind a low building, some kind of storage shed. The beam sizzled through the space where he'd been a moment before and blew a huge divot out of the ground.

Reversing himself, Straker charged out the way he'd come. As intended, he caught the newbie aiming at the other side, expecting him to continue in the same direction.

If he'd had a full power charge, he would have taken the Sledgehammer apart piece by piece, stripping off its legs and weapons until the pilot had nothing to work with. However, he was mindful of Murdock's words about sabotage to the south-end sidespace engine. He had to put an end to this mismatched contest and get on with the liberation.

So, using a low-gravity maneuver a Sledgehammer pilot could never replicate or even expect, Straker leaped over the other mechsuit and fired a bolt of plasma straight down, directly into the mangled head armor. It cut through and blew back out, giving the humanoid machine a crown of fire as capacitors and polymers ignited. Flame, electric charge and plasma leaked from every joint, tearing the mechsuit apart from the inside. The pilot did not eject.

"Dammit," he said. That was one more death he could lay at the door of people like Ramirez and Yates.

In fact, he looked forward to finding Yates the rapist, and recovering Karst's girl. He only hoped she would remain unharmed.

"Engels to Straker, Engels to Straker," he heard on his comlink.

"Straker here."

"I've been trying to get you for a while. There's a shuttle of some kind making ready to launch off the south end. Should I let it go?" Engels' voice sounded hopeful.

"Is it armed?"

"It has a small laser."

"If it's just evacuating, leave it alone, but if it tries to damage the sidespace engines, you have to destroy it. If we can't move Freiheit, all of this is for nothing."

"Aye aye. Engels out."

With no enemy that could stand against him, Straker turned to mopping up the remaining Unmutuals.

* * *

Engels aimed her corvette's short-range comlink at the shuttle and blasted it with several standard contact frequencies. "Small craft, small craft, this is *Liberator*. Respond or be fired upon."

"Hey, don't shoot," came a woman's voice. "We're just trying to get away!"

"Major Ramirez?"

"No, she's over at Aynor Base. My name's Nassimi. You win. I just want to get away. We have civilians on board. You shoot us, you'll kill them."

Engels remained suspicious. The voice sure sounded like Ramirez's. "I have you locked up tight. One shot and you're toast. You can head for your base, but if you try anything…"

"I understand. Nassimi out."

"That was Ramirez," Loco said from the communications station. "I'd bet my next hooch ration on it."

"But what can we do?"

"Chase it down. Try to board."

"Very tricky in open space with a shuttle. Those things are fragile."

"She's probably lying about the civilians."

"Maybe, but I can't take that chance." Engels found herself wishing she had the ruthlessness to fire anyway. Ramirez deserved to be punished for what she'd done, but such a small craft would be hard to disable without killing everyone aboard, and not every Unmutual was equally responsible. Some were only guilty of not being able to restrain their peers. When the chain of command was against you, that was a tough spot to be in. Besides, the part about civilians might be true.

Watching closely, she made sure the shuttle didn't drop anything off or fire its tiny laser to sabotage the sidespace engine bolted to the south end. She was just beginning to relax when the transit detector pinged.

"I have sidespace traffic inbound," said Loco. "From the signature, of frigate size."

Damn the luck. "*Carson?*"

"Getting opticals now. I'd say yes."

"Designate it *Carson*. Give me system tactical." Engels gazed at the main holoscreen, rotating the view this way and that until she got it the way she wanted.

Fortunately *Carson* had transited in at a position optimum for approach to the gas giant Bayzos and the Unmutual base at the Aynor moon. That put it all the way across the system, far from Freiheit.

The frigate would be hearing about the attack on Freiheit and getting instructions from DeChang. The single-pilot attack ships off Aynor would also be launching about now, given the lightspeed delay in learning of the Breakers' attack.

Therefore, Straker's Breakers had at least eighteen hours until a naval counterattack came, probably more like twenty-four unless the Unmutuals decided to go balls-out and make one speedy pass, rather than engage normally. But it would take four days for Freiheit to spiral outward far enough to enter sidespace.

She switched channels. "Engels to Straker."

"Here."

"Bad news. *Carson* or something like her just jumped in. We have about a day before they can get here. What's worse, Freiheit is a sitting duck. In about sixteen hours, assuming a normal approach profile, *Carson* will be able to bombard it from extreme range with railgun slugs or shipkiller nukes. I might be able to intercept a missile, but not a speeding bullet. Not with this little corvette. There's no way to protect the sidespace engines."

Straker replied, "They won't use nuclear shipkillers right away, if at all. They want to recapture Freiheit, not destroy it, and they know they have four days to stop us. We also have to believe they don't know about the Ruxin ship, or at least, what it can do. That's our ace in the hole."

"It had better be, because this corvette can't stand up to a frigate for long."

"Is Zaxby hidden?"

"Yes, he's parked behind the rock. DeChang should be completely in the dark except for whatever reports got sent from the initial attack. Oh, and *Lockstep*'s ETA is two hours."

"Thanks. I have to finish up here. Keep in touch. Straker out."

* * *

Straker cursed under his breath at the report. His primary plan, the one that depended on the Unmutuals' lack of real warships, was now shot to hell. Secondary plans? He had several, depending on the circumstances, but they were all of the more desperate variety.

But right now, he had to finish the task at hand. He switched on his external loudspeaker. "Straker's Breakers," he bellowed, "I have eliminated the mechsuiter threat. Follow me and let's finish off these Unmutuals."

He paused and aimed his loudspeaker forward. "Unmutual combatants, this is Captain Derek Straker in the Foehammer. I don't want to kill you. Lay down your arms and you will be treated in accordance with the laws of war. Keep fighting, and I'll slaughter you like dogs."

Straker repeated these sentences as he strode toward the southern end, aiming for the auxiliary base control center. Unmutual resistance crumbled, and within minutes, all of the enemy had raised their hands and allowed themselves to be captured.

When he reached the control center, he dismounted from his Foehammer. Breakers clustered around him cheering, exuberant after their first battle. Aldrik Ritter found him and saluted proudly. "We've secured the control room, sir."

"Get me a weapon and ammo," Straker said. "Spread out and start telling the populace that it's safe to come out. Brief them to report any Unmutual stragglers hiding out. Collect all the prisoners at the brig the Unmutuals set up, not that they really used the thing right. Where's Heiser?"

"Wounded, sir, but he'll make it."

"You're my Spear for now, then. Carry out my orders. Go." When Aldrik ran off to organize the occupation, Straker took a laser carbine and ammo belt someone handed to him. "I need five men with me."

Inside the auxiliary control room, Straker tapped at keys and tried to get comlinks to work. "Dammit, come on. There has to be..."

"Captain Straker, I see you," Murdock's voice said from one station. "Talk to me. Over here. Touch the flashing icon."

Straker slid into the seat, tapped the screen and spoke into a microphone. "I'm here. SITREP!"

"I should have the power restored in about an hour. Then I'll be able to get this pig moving on impellers. There's bad news, though."

"What?"

"My readouts aren't good. Go check on the sidespace engine at your end. Back door, six flights down, look for a raw tunnel drilled into the wall. Call me when you get there."

"Tell me—" But Murdock had already clicked off the intercom, and Straker had no portable comlink. He waved the five men to come along and headed for the back door. Following Murdock's directions, he soon debouched into the engineering room of the massive sidespace engine.

Straker growled in frustration. All the controls and much of the machinery had been wrecked by weapons fire.

Chapter 37

"Guard this facility from further damage," Straker told his squad of five as he surveyed the damaged sidespace engine controls. "Someone should be here in an hour or two to start repairs." He left the wrecked machinery and returned to the auxiliary control center. "Murdock, this is Straker."

"Kinda busy now, Straker."

"The sidespace engine down here is a mess. Laser burns and bullets, mostly, I'd say. No explosions. You have four days to fix it."

"If it can be fixed."

"You have factories and machine shops on this rock."

"Sidespace engines have highly specialized parts."

"No excuses. Keep working. Requisition techs from the populace if you need to. Tell them if we can't transit this base, the Unmutuals will take over again."

"Public relations is your job, Straker. I can't take time off to go recruiting. Send me everyone who thinks they can help and I'll sort them out."

Straker thought a moment. "Could you use Zaxby?"

"The Ruxin?"

"He hacked your network pretty easy."

Murdock paused. Maybe he was overcoming his irritation with a rival. "Yeah, I can use any Ruxin technicians you can spare."

"I'll send them when I can. Keep up the good work. Straker out."

Straker struggled with the communications console for a few moments. Eventually he gave up on trying to figure out how to make it function for him.

He ran outside to mount his mechsuit and activated the comlink. "Zaxby, this is Straker."

"*Revenge* here, Captain Straker."

"The southern sidespace engine has been damaged. Murdock needs Ruxin help to repair it."

"Of course he does. He is a competent enough tinkerer, but nothing like me."

"So quit talking and start doing. Assemble a team and report to him at the BCC."

"I think he should report to me."

"He's in charge, Zaxby. Take overall direction from him, but you make the repairs happen."

"He's not even a military officer. He has no rank."

"You want me to appoint him a rank exceeding yours? Because I will if that's your main complaint."

"I believe you are favoring him because he is human."

Straker rolled his eyes. "No, I'm favoring him because he knows this rock and its systems inside and out. It's all he's been doing for the past weeks. You might be a better engineer, but he has the local knowledge. Besides, this is temporary for you. You'll have to return to the *Revenge* to fight the *Carson*. It makes no sense to put you in charge of the repairs, then give Murdock back the position when you have to leave."

"You make a strong case, Captain Straker. I will comply."

"I shouldn't have to make a case every time, Lieutenant Zaxby. You're under my command. In fact, I wouldn't take this kind of pushback from a human, so actually, I'm favoring you because you're Ruxin."

"And it makes perfect sense to do so."

"Oh, favors go only one way?"

"They go the way that will get the job done. Will that be all, sir? I need to get started on saving the day yet again."

Straker concentrated on controlling his temper. Command was the art of getting people to willingly do what you wanted, he recalled from Academy. It didn't matter whether Zaxby pissed him off, as long as he did the job. That's what he told himself, anyway. "Yes, go. Do you have a comlink?"

"Integrated into my suit, of course."

"Good. Let me know if you need anything. Straker out."

Next, Straker used his Foehammer sensors to find the largest concentration of people. That ought to be the Unmutual prisoners and his Breakers guarding them. They crowded around the brig, not too far from the mechsuit factory. He quickly strode over to the area, keeping to the paved paths to minimize damage to the fields and crops.

What he didn't expect were the many Freiheit citizens that had begun to gather there. More were arriving all the time, drawn by word of mouth and, no doubt, local comlinks, information passing quickly in the manner of small towns everywhere.

The prisoners had been crowded into the building. Breaker soldiers faced outward, holding back the crowd with the threat of their weaponry, but the locals apparently were in the mood for frontier justice. They yelled curses, and a few began throwing things. The dimness of the artificial night only enhanced the situation's instability.

Well, if darkness emboldened them, then brightness should take some of the starch out of them, Straker thought. He activated his floodlights at maximum power.

Breakers and locals alike raised their hands against the illumination, and Straker stomped forward to take a position in front of the main concentration of citizenry.

"This is Captain Straker," he said using the loudspeaker. "All of you people need to disperse. Go back to your homes. We'll hold trials for these Unmutuals, but it has to be done according to law. I promise you, justice will be done."

Instead of calming the crowd, this seemed to get them more worked up. Rocks bounced off his mechsuit. He tried to sort out what they were saying... something about "give us the Butcher?"

"Who's your leader?" Straker blasted, cranking up his external speakers to maximum. "If you act like a mob, I'll have to treat you as a mob." He swept the muzzles of his weapons across the crowd in naked threat. "I'll consider your grievances, but I need someone to talk to, man-to-man."

"How about man to woman?" he heard as the noise died down. A plain woman in a plain skirt and jacket stepped forward, squinting against the light.

Her lined face was set in an expression of determination. "You gonna shoot me?"

The locals all gave her room, and suddenly became focused on her instead of on the Unmutual prisoners.

"I'm not going to shoot anyone unless I have to," Straker said. He keyed for dismounting. His mechsuit opened, overlapping plates separating like beetle wings to allow him to step out of the cockpit and climb down. He held out his hand. "Derek Straker. And you are?"

The woman stepped resolutely forward and shook his hand. Her grip was firm, dry, and callused. "I'm Bella Weinberg. My husband was the mayor here until the Butcher chopped him up. Now most of the folks seem to think I'm the boss."

"Who is this Butcher?"

"His name is Yates," she said. "He's Ramirez's right-hand man, and the worst of the bunch."

"I know him."

"Then you should also know he doesn't need a trial. He just needs to be dead. And he's inside that building." She pointed.

Straker considered. Insisting on a trial would hold a hard line for due process. It was important that the locals didn't feel they had a license for vendetta, because once that line was crossed, it might never be redrawn. People had to believe in their chain of command and their government. If they lost faith, anarchy would follow.

On the other hand, forcing them to wait might be seen as an attempt to give the evildoers a pass. Straker needed the citizens on his side to help repair the habitat and get it moved through sidespace—or at least, not to interfere. If he was to be their leader, if they were to form the basis for his efforts to liberate humanity, justice would have to begin right here, right now.

Maybe he could split the difference.

"How about if we put him on trial immediately? If he's found guilty of capital crimes, I'll execute him myself."

Weinberg began shivering, her eyes boring into Straker's. "I want to do it."

Slowly, Straker shook his head. "No. This can't be personal, or it's vengeance, not justice. And Mrs. Weinberg... have you ever killed anyone? Especially by your own hand?"

She shook her head.

"I have. Sometimes it has to be done, but any satisfaction you feel will be outweighed by the load of your actions. That's a burden you shouldn't carry alone."

Weinberg straightened. "I'm their leader. Lord knows I didn't ask to be, but that's what they all say. So I'll do it in the name of the citizens of Freiheit Station."

"You still use that name—Freiheit?"

She shrugged. "It's a good name. Means 'freedom' in some old language, I'm told."

"Yes. Yes, it does... Freiheit Station it is." Straker stepped closer so the hushed crowd couldn't hear him. "All right. How should he be executed? What do they want?"

"Nobody can remember a capital crime ever happening, so all these folks know is from history books and vids. On Old Earth, they used to hang people by the neck until dead." Weinberg raised her chin. "That's what they want."

Straker leaned even further in to whisper in Weinberg's ear. "Then that's what they'll get, because he's guilty as hell. But the witnesses have to testify. It has to be done by law."

"What law?" she said, stepping back slightly.

"Breaker law," he replied. "Freiheit law."

"What's that?"

"I don't know. I'm making it up as I go. But if you're the mayor, and I'm the military commander, we both need the people to respect law and order or we'll be no better than our enemies."

Weinberg nodded slowly, and then she turned to raise her hands over her head. "We're going to put the Butcher on trial, right here, right now."

The people gave a wild cheer and crowded around Weinberg. Straker backed up and climbed half into his mechsuit, above the press. He waved at Aldrik Ritter as the noncom came trotting up with a dozen more soldiers.

"Get these people back from my 'suit. Don't hurt anyone, but get them back," he called. "And make damn sure none of those Unmutuals escape."

The Breakers began moving the crowd out of the way, and Straker used the loudspeakers to emphasize his wishes. Soon he had a well-lit area cleared, and tables and two chairs brought from the building.

After giving Aldrik further instructions, he escorted Weinberg to a seat, and then took the other. "Bring out Yates," he said. "Line up the other prisoners and keep a close eye on them, too. I want them to see."

The twenty or so prisoners were lined up against the wall of the building, with a good view of the trial area. Four men dragged a struggling Master Sergeant Yates out to stand in front of the impromptu judicial bench.

"Straker," he said with a sneer. "And the Mayor's bitch…"

The crowd jeered and some surged forward. Breakers held them back. Straker hefted his laser carbine and stood. "Silence!" he roared.

When calm was restored, Straker continued. "Might not want to antagonize these folks. They're out for blood."

"They're a bunch of pussies." Yates spat on the ground. "What do I care? You're gonna kill me anyway."

"Probably. But first, we're going to establish your crimes against the military code."

"You can't establish anything, Straker. You're not in my chain of command."

Straker smiled, a wicked thing. "Actually, as far as I've been able to tell, General DeChang confirmed my rank and never revoked it. So consider this a summary court martial." He turned to Weinberg, who waved up someone in the crowd.

A line of witnesses began to form. The details were grim. Yates claimed they were all lying, willing, or just out to get him. But the testimony was overwhelming.

Straker stood after an hour of it.

"It looks like there are more witnesses lined up, but I think we've heard enough. I'll take the final word. I personally witnessed Yates and another man wrap me and my friends with fibertape and set a bomb to blow us up. That's attempted murder. You've also heard a dozen people who personally witnessed this man raping, torturing, and murdering. That's enough for me. Mayor Weinberg, is it enough for you?"

Weinberg nodded.

Straker banged the butt of his carbine on the table. "Then I pronounce Master Sergeant Yates, also known as the Butcher, guilty of capital crimes. Mrs. Weinberg, as the other presiding judge, sentencing is yours."

Weinberg stood slowly, placing fingertips on the table before her to still their trembling. She stared at Yates with eyes gone stone dead.

"Hang him."

The crowd cheered, and Yates had to be restrained again and clubbed to the ground by his captors. Nearly escaping notice, one prisoner kicked out a window and tried to run, only to be shot by a Breaker and dragged back to the brig.

Sergeant Aldrik Ritter tossed a line over the outstretched arm of the Foehammer, the only structure available that would serve as a gallows. Yates was hauled into place, and then Aldrik tied the rope around his neck in a sliding knot.

A detail of five men seized the other end of the line. Weinberg, with a nod to Straker, walked over to take hold of it as well.

Yates took a breath and yelled, "All you sheep can suck–"

Aldrik signaled his men, and they pulled—choking off Yates's vulgar declaration. The detail held the line taut, facing away from the man dancing in the air. Weinberg, however, backed up and watched, her expression one of deep satisfaction.

Suddenly, like the sun coming out, the fiber optic coil in the center of the habitat brightened. Within thirty seconds the day broke again. With the light, the gruesome scene lost some of its macabre spirit and became merely ugly. Yates's body hung still, and Straker heard someone retch into the dirt.

"That's enough justice for today," said Straker loudly. "We'll put others on trial as we have time, but for now, I need you all to go back to your homes and your jobs and your schools, whatever you'd normally do today. If you think of a way to help your neighbors or your liberators, please do it. More of my people will be here soon. If anyone gets out of line, I want to know about it immediately. Nobody is above the law."

He had to repeat these declarations several times, but eventually the citizenry dispersed. He had Yates's body cut down and wrapped in a tarp. "Toss it out into space," he told Aldrik.

He'd just climbed back into his mechsuit and gotten on the comlink when he heard, "Engels to Straker."

"Straker here."

"Derek, we have a problem."

Chapter 38

Bayzos System, outskirts opposite Aynor.

Engels looked over at the readings on her displays, and then to those at the sensors station nearby.

"What's the problem?" Straker asked over her comlink.

She tweaked the *Liberator*'s heading to give her the best angle for the sensors. "One of two possibilities, both bad. Either a second frigate just jumped in, or the *Carson* performed an in-system transit and knocked ten hours off her travel time. I'm betting on the latter, based on the optimization of her new location. She emerged as close as she can possibly get to us, given the space-time curvature."

"Why can't you tell which?"

Engels rubbed her forehead. "Lightspeed delay, Derek. We're still seeing the *Carson* near Bayzos, but she might have jumped past her own light. We won't know for half an hour."

"I thought you said Bayzos was a light-hour away."

"Dammit, Derek," Engels said. "This is my business. Trust a professional in her own domain."

"I do," he assured her, "but I want to understand. If I'm to command, I need all the info."

"Only if you want to be overwhelmed with detail."

"Just humor me."

Engels let out a long sigh through her nose. "Okay, look. In rough terms, *Carson* jumps from Bayzos, a light-hour from us, to a position half a light-hour from us. We can't see her immediately. When we do finally see her—right now, current time—the half hour has passed. In another thirty minutes, we can look at Bayzos and see if *Carson* transited away from there. We're waiting to see if the original position was vacated. If not, this is a new, second ship."

"Got it."

"In either case, we're in trouble. She can start firing on us in six hours. *Revenge* has to get going now to have any chance of making an interception." Engels hated to accept the situation. She'd hoped they'd somehow be able to avoid destroying the *Carson*.

"Dammit," said Straker. "Murdock needs Zaxby and his tech team to help repair the southern sidespace engine. I'll have to command *Revenge* myself and hope the Ruxin crew's Earthan is good enough. Heiser is injured, and I don't want to leave Aldrik in sole command. He's a good man, but he's still pretty green."

"I'll take over on the ground," said Loco. "Just sitting on my ass here anyway."

"Good idea. Use the Foehammer to get around. Cockpit code is Unmutual123."

"Woohoo! Back in a 'suit, a real one."

"Yes, but I doubt you can get the brainlink working. Have fun. Carla, I'll call you when I get aboard *Revenge*. Straker out."

"I'll get someone to drop me off in the gig," said Loco as he departed.

Engels waved at him distractedly and chewed her lip, staring at the tactical problem as she lounged at the *Liberator*'s helm. Assuming that was *Carson* and not a second ship, Ellen Gray should still be in command. They'd spent some time together on Aynor, back when it had seemed their destiny lay with the Unmutuals. The woman was a by-the-book captain and had seemed to be a decent person. Would that translate into unswerving loyalty to DeChang and his organization, or could she be pried loose by Ramirez's ugly misdeeds?

Derek would want to make the safe play using the ship's most effective attack, which likely meant one or two thermonuclear float mines, properly placed. Given the three-body problem of *Revenge*, frigate, and warhead, she couldn't blame him. One slight variation that caused a miss and their advantage of surprise would be blown.

Did *Carson* have underspace detection gear? Engels was betting that even if they had the tech, they didn't have it active. If they were able to figure out what was attacking them, they might be quickly able to locate *Revenge*. At that point it could become a slugfest—and Ruxin Archers weren't sluggers.

That would mean bringing *Liberator* into play. Doing so would even the odds, but Engels didn't like even odds. No rational commander did. When she recalled the nineteen crewing her corvette, it strengthened her resolve. She hated to think about killing people she knew aboard *Carson*, but she'd be a rotten captain if she didn't do her very best for her own.

Still… was there some way she could make this a win-win? If there was any way to appeal to Captain Gray's decency… Her mind chewed on the problem until Straker called her.

"Straker to Engels. I'm aboard *Revenge* now."

"Enjoying the water?"

"Not one bit. We need to plan our attack, and, as you said, you're the pro. How do I do this?"

"Synchronize our displays on a tight beam. I have tactical up."

"How do I do that?"

Engels hissed in exasperation. "Just tell someone to do it. Stop thinking like a mechsuiter and be the captain. Delegate."

"Right. Somebody synchronize our main display with *Liberator*'s, tight beam." A pause. "There we go. Okay, I see *Carson*, Freiheit Station, *Revenge*, you, and the star."

"Those are the only things that matter to us right now. You see Freiheit's outward spiral course projection?"

"Yes."

"Here's *Carson*'s optimum course inbound, which she's already taking."

"I see it."

"Here's your interception course. It meets *Carson* shortly before she's likely to start firing, assuming she doesn't deviate. The problem is, if you go into underspace for six hours, you won't be able to see anything. One slight alteration in vector and you'll miss by kilometers. Thousands of kilometers, actually."

"So we pop up and adjust."

"You risk being seen."

"What are the odds of that if they have no underspace detection gear?"

"Wait one second…" Engels ran a couple of tests. "Higher than you might think. That's because your best approach is head-on to their course, and they'll be sweeping with active sensors."

"What if we come in from the side?"

"The chances of detection are a lot lower, but she's moving fast. A side intercept will be very tricky."

"Can we slip in behind her and overtake? When do you think she'll decelerate?"

"Not until an hour out. The question isn't whether you can destroy her. It's whether you can do it before she bombards Freiheit's sidespace engines to scrap."

Straker's voice gained a note of irritation. "This would be a lot easier if Freiheit could make any kind of evasive maneuver."

Incredulous, Engels answered, "Do you have any idea how big and underpowered that rock is?"

"I know. I was hoping one of us would come up with some clever trick to improve our odds."

"There's one possibility that has nothing to do with tactics."

"Go on."

"We get *Carson* to defect. I'm acquainted with Captain Gray. She might do it."

Straker stayed silent for a moment. "Carla, are you getting cold feet? Because that's a long shot. Two thousand people aboard Freiheit Station are depending on us for their freedom, maybe their lives. If we can't get out of this star system…"

"Then it's a stalemate, Derek, or maybe we're actually ahead. Think about it."

"Hmm… maybe you're right!"

"Of course, I'm right. Are you foot-dragging because I caught on to something before you?" she demanded.

"Come on, Carla, it's not like that."

"I know you believe that as the commander you should think of everything," she complained, "but you can't do it all. It's easy math—if we lose the sidespace engines but neutralize *Carson*, we still hold the balance of military power in this system. They won't be able to recapture Freiheit, and unless they get reinforcements, we can attack Aynor any time. They'd have to evacuate or capitulate. That will buy us time."

"Time to do what?"

"Find some new sidespace engines, maybe from the Ruxins? I don't know. I'm simply saying it's not an absolute catastrophe if we can't fly this rock out of here on time."

"Good point," he said. "But I have to plan for the worst case. So how do we make the best, highest-probability attack on *Carson*?"

Engels studied her display for a moment. "There's one asteroid near *Carson*'s course. I've designated it M100. It won't be making any maneuvers. If you pop up behind it relative to *Carson*, they're not likely to spot you. You should be able to peek out and update your navcomp readings. The key is not to spook them. You're blind when you're under, so you're operating entirely on predictive analysis at that point."

"I know that. So, once we've updated, I'll go under and move directly into their path, and drop float mines just before they arrive, timed to explode in their face. Afterward, I hightail it."

Engels sighed. "Yes. It's the only way to be sure."

"I'm sorry I might be killing a friend of yours."

"Not a friend, exactly. A fellow ship captain. Someone just doing her job, following orders."

"That's no defense," Straker said. "Not if someone knows their leaders are committing atrocities."

"Easy to say now, Derek, in your black-and-white world. What would you have done back before all this happened, if you knew the Hundred Worlds had massacred civilians? Would you have defected to the Hok? Or would you have made your protests but stayed loyal? How many atrocities would it have taken before you gave up hoping your own chain of command would clean house?"

That brought more silence from Straker. "Okay, I get it," he said at last. "But that doesn't change anything right here, right now. Being a commander means making the hard calls. The chrono's rolling and I have to destroy the biggest threat to our people. Feel free to talk to Captain Gray, but don't do anything to warn her about my attack."

"Understood. Derek...?"

"Yes?" he asked, detecting a different note in her voice.

Engels swallowed. "Good luck and good hunting."

"You too."

As soon as Straker took *Revenge* into underspace to head out to M100, Engels glanced over at Chief Gurung, who stood at the door to the bridge, his usual position. He seemed to consider it the optimal spot on the small ship to watch both the goings-on of his officers on the bridge and the crew in the cramped spaces behind him, inevitably with a cup of caff in his hand.

"Chief, how's everyone feeling?" Engels asked.

The man smiled a compact grin. "Oh, very good, ma'am." His accent made the honorific sound like *mom*. "We're a bit bored, but that is the lot of any navy."

"Are we a navy?" she asked.

"Oh, yes, ma'am. If not a navy, then what?"

"Liberators."

"Then we are a navy of liberators. Even pirates must have discipline."

Engels snorted. "But if they do, are they still pirates?"

"This is not for me to say."

"Chief, I might need that discipline soon."

"Of course, ma'am." He cocked his head. "Is there some particular reason?"

"Maybe," she admitted. "Pass the word to the crew that we'll be getting underway."

"Shall we go to battle stations?" Gurung asked.

"No. It will be hours before we're in even extreme range. In fact, keep all our weapons locked down and unpowered. I want to appear completely nonhostile for now."

"Very good, ma'am." Gurung withdrew to the aft of the ship.

Her sensors operator, a rating named Lorton, raised his eyebrows in question.

"You'll see soon enough," Engels told him as she set a course and began moving the ship out toward *Carson* on impellers. As was often the case, cruising at the helm granted her mind time to wander.

In truth, she didn't want to tip her hand to Gurung or anyone else in case she decided to do the thing she contemplated, a thing that might cross a line in Straker's mind.

Straker was her commander. She could have insisted on the primacy of her commissioned rank in service of the Hundred Worlds, and he would have acceded, but she knew herself. Despite all her training at Academy, all the theory and the knowledge pumped into her, she didn't really want to be the top boss with all these subordinates and civilians depending on her.

Like Loco and Gurung and probably most people, she was happy to be a valued officer, to have autonomy and status, with no one lording it over her, content to be the pilot of a ship–the captain even better.

Perhaps she also thought and felt things deeper than those around her. It made her a particular, empathic type of leader, but maybe it precluded her from being another kind—the ruthless kind that was needed at times like these.

Straker, on the other hand, had all the required drive and stubbornness. He exuded certainty in battle—in any crisis. There was a natural ability in the man that allowed him to do what had to be done and not let it affect him.

Yet in their relationship, in their love and lovemaking, he still had a core of hesitancy, of vulnerability, and that reassured her. Despite his harshness, his willingness to annihilate anything in his path, his darkness hadn't consumed him.

Not yet, anyway. She worried that the more he destroyed on the way to his goals, the easier it would become to see destruction as the first solution instead of the last resort.

The current situation was a case in point. She understood Derek's reasoning, even agreed with it, but she saw another possibility. It was a long shot, but it might pay off big.

The only question was: would she have to attempt it? Or would she get lucky and not need to?

He'd given her the go-ahead to see if Ellen Gray would defect. That was Engels' first gamble, and she might as well give it a try. *Carson* and *Liberator* were as yet far apart, so distant that even lightspeed transmissions would take over ten minutes to reach the other ship, more than twenty to return an answer.

Though every hour of combined travel would knock more than two minutes off that, she might as well get the conversation started.

"Lorton, establish a tightbeam laser comlink with *Carson*. Use a standard automated hailing protocol, then put me on full vid." Engels sat up in her chair and put on her most earnest expression.

"Sending, ma'am… Okay, we synched up. You're on."

"Hello, Ellen," Engels said, addressing a vid pickup. "I'm assuming it's you commanding *Carson*, the ship I'm aiming this transmission at, since naturally you're not squawking any IFF. As you can see, it's Carla Engels here, in command of this stolen Hundred Worlds corvette, which we've christened *Liberator*. By now you know that Captain Straker and I have come back to free the people of Freiheit from Major Ramirez's abusive tyranny."

The tiny jewel-like tip of the camera stared at her, and she took a breath before pressing ahead.

"Your first thought is probably that I'm lying," she said, "because you've been told that we planted the bombs that killed the refugees who wanted to defect back to the Mutuality. Well, it's not true. I'd never be party to such a horror, nor would any of our people. In your heart you must know this is true.

"I figure you know Yates by reputation," she continued. "It was undoubtedly he that did the dirty work at Ramirez's orders. I don't know whether DeChang is in on it, or if he's only guilty of letting his subordinates run amuck. Either way, it was murder, and I found the evidence. That's why Ramirez tried to kill us and make it look like an accident, but we got away."

She leaned back, confident she'd made her case.

"Now," she said, "we're back. Even if you stop us from taking Freiheit into sidespace, we have the habitat, and the Unmutuals will never get it back. The people there are sick of the way they've been treated. We've also brought a regiment of ground troops aboard and enough extra weapons to arm all the locals." They didn't really have that many guns, but Engels didn't mind stretching the truth if it convinced Gray.

"So, you see, you might be able to destroy Freiheit, but you'll never own it. You simply don't have the manpower. At best, this will become an ugly intra-system war that will cripple both sides and kill a lot of people, including yours."

Engels narrowed her brows. "So I'm here to ask you to think about joining us. Or, if you won't do that, at least let us leave in peace. It's either lose-lose, or we win. There's no way for the Unmutuals to come out ahead. The best you can do is cut your losses, because I promise you, we can hurt you badly. Look around your bridge and see which of your friends will die to support a bunch of rapists and murderers." She folded her hands. "Engels out."

Then she waited, cracking her knuckles and staring at the glacially moving tactical plot. Warfare at interplanetary scale was always an exercise in slow motion, punctuated by explosive violence as combatants approached each other. So it would be this time around, unless she could head it off.

"Transmission incoming," Lorton said.

As Engels composed herself again, the main screen dissolved into a picture of a stern older woman with black eyes, full lips and a flat nose, of a type anyone would call handsome rather than beautiful. She had the weary presence of an overworked senior officer, and an anger in her eyes that did not bode well for Engels' efforts.

"Hello, Carla. I'm sorry to see you in these circumstances. I understand your concerns with the situation on Freiheit. It got out of control, but General DeChang assures me Ramirez will be sanctioned and brought to heel, and that individuals who committed crimes will be punished, up to and including execution if warranted. I trust his word. And Carla, no matter what happened, I'm not going to betray my people, any more than you're going to betray yours. I guess we're on opposite sides on this one. Gray out."

Engels sighed. It looked like there would be no easy solutions, but she might as well continue the dialogue. At least it passed the time, and every answer marked twenty or so minutes off the six hours until *Carson* might begin bombarding, and off the dozen hours until *Liberator* might be forced to fight, if the *Revenge* failed.

"Ellen, I hear you. I think I understand your dilemma. I'm sending you a burst with the record of what happened to the refugees. There are two files. One is the raw data, the other, with annotations. I hope you'll examine them and draw your own conclusions. If you survive, you'll have to deal with DeChang, and the evidence of the murder of over four hundred people. Think about that, Ellen. Someone on your side was willing to slaughter a bunch of frightened civilians just to deny the Mutuality their labor—labor that could hardly have affected the course of the war. That's no different from bombarding population centers… no, it's even worse, because at least if you obliterate cities, you can tell yourself that you're doing significant damage to the enemy's economy. This was pure evil, Ellen. There were children. There were mothers and babies on those ships."

Engels couldn't keep her eyes from tearing up. It was so easy to forget those who paid the real price in wars like this. She rubbed her belly, suddenly aware of the possibility of life growing there, someday. Until she and Derek had begun sleeping together, she'd never really thought about motherhood, but now…

"If General DeChang is really a good man as you believe, he'll understand why you let us go. There's no logic to bombarding Freiheit. You'd be killing more civilians than combatants, five innocents for every soldier. If you rupture the habitat, you'll kill *everyone*. You can't destroy Freiheit's impeller; it's too deep inside, so you can't stop the habitat from continuing to accelerate in normal space toward the outer reaches of the system. Best case, it will take you years to mount a takeover. In the meantime, Freiheit will end up as a generation ship, traveling toward some far star. Please, Ellen, think about what you're doing. You believe it's your duty to follow DeChang. What about your higher duty to humanity? What are we for, if not to protect the civilians? Sheepdogs don't attack the sheep. If they do, they have to be put down. Dead children won't care about your abstract principles."

After the interminable delay, Captain Gray's face returned to the screen. "I salute you, Carla. You make a persuasive argument. Understand, this isn't an easy decision for me. I've thought, I've weighed, and I've decided. The evidence you sent didn't change anything; I've already accepted that there's an ugly rot among Ramirez's people. Maybe the whole of our ground forces will have to be purged. But that's only half of the Unmutual movement. Frankly, it's the lesser half. The greater half includes those of our fleet and the civilians living on our bases.

"Also, I think you paint a rosy picture for yourselves. I don't judge your chances to be so favorable. I think once all opposition in space is neutralized, I can use surgical strikes to force Freiheit to surrender. I'll explain the situation to the people there and promise they'll never have to deal with Ramirez again.

At the end of the day, they'll thank us both for bettering their situation. I'll get the other ship captains together and insist DeChang remove Ramirez from any position of authority pending a thorough investigation. If she personally ordered or committed crimes, I'll insist she be punished. So I'll make you the same offer you made me: give up and join us. Join my fleet and work for me. Between us and your Captain Straker, we can go to the Council of Elders and insist on reforms. We can chalk this up to a family spat among Unmutuals and come out the other end stronger than ever. Come on, Carla. You like to talk about babies. Don't throw the baby out with the bathwater. Gray out."

Engels sat back and let out a hissing sigh. Gray was formidable, and she'd made some good points. If Engels really believed Gray was a good enough politician to make that kind of play, to set herself against the smooth, confident and well-liked DeChang, she might even try to get Straker to agree.

However, deep in her gut, deep in her bones, Engels didn't believe it.

First, she didn't believe Captain Gray was the type to openly risk a split with DeChang—a possible civil war within the ranks of the Unmutuals.

Second, she didn't believe DeChang was the man he wanted everyone to think he was. He was a little too urbane and condescending—too clever, smug and calculating for her to trust him. Derek and Loco seemed much taken with him, probably as a father figure replacing those they lost when they were young, but she'd never quite bought it. He reminded her too much of the Lazarus clones.

The only question for Engels now was: how far was she willing to step over this line? Was it worth it for a long-shot effort to save Ellen Gray and most of her crew, even while neutralizing her ship?

That was the optimal outcome, anyway. The worst outcome would be allowing *Carson* to slip by *Revenge*, thereafter to destroy one or both of Freiheit's sidespace engines.

Slowly, Engels sat forward and clenched her knotted fingers together. By doing what she contemplated, she was risking her relationship with Derek. Even if he didn't hate her forever, he would never again see her in the same light.

If it worked, he would forgive her. If it didn't, he might throw her out of his life, or even his command. Where would she go, what would she do then?

The thought of losing Derek and all these people that had become her family over the past months, was excruciating.

Yet, if she was going to stick to her own principles, she had to try.

"Lorton, take a break. Nothing will happen for about four hours. That's when Captain Straker will hit them with *Revenge*, just before they're in extreme bombardment range. When you get back, set up for one more transmission to the *Carson*."

Roll the dice, she thought as she stared at the tactical plot. Go big, or go home. Though in this case, *home* might not even want her anymore.

Chapter 39

Awaiting Carson.

"Plot an underspace run out to M100," Straker said to his Ruxin crew once he was done talking to Engels. The tactical plot drew his eyes, showing *Revenge* still hiding behind Freiheit Station.

"Course plotted."

"Execute."

"Inserting. Moving toward designated emergence point near M100."

The chill manifested, and Straker turned on his suit heater to compensate. The Ruxins apparently did something similar, for the vents on the floor began to swirl with warm water, and the bridge filled with a fog that didn't seem to bother the octopoids.

Six hours was a fair time to be under, though not as long as the trip inward to Freiheit had been, so he had confidence they would make it. Most of the ship's thrusters had been repaired, though he wondered what other mechanisms on this old vessel might fail.

Straker took the time to try to learn his bridge crew's names, but the problem was, they all sounded too similar—Froxen, Lixor, Trunix, Roxov, he couldn't keep them all straight. Eventually he told them he would address them by function, and trust them to carry out his orders. In the future, he planned to mandate that they had their names printed on their suits in Earthan, front and back.

Slowly, too slowly, the tactical plot on the main visiplate display showed *Revenge* crawling toward the M100 asteroid. *Carson's* icon approached at about the same speed. Even though these ships were travelling at high velocity, the vastness of space dwarfed everything.

It made Straker think about what he'd read of Old Earth's early days, launching fragile probes into the void, machines that would take weeks or months to cross planetary distances that now took mere hours.

Finally, shivering despite the heaters, Straker ordered *Revenge* emerged. The main display updated, and he let out his breath when he saw M100 exactly where it should be: between *Revenge* and *Carson*.

"Sensors, do we have confirmation of *Carson*'s course and position?"

"Not yet, sir. M100 shields us."

"Helm, peek out."

"Not understood, sir."

Straker explained. "Move our ship just enough to get a passive sensor reading to locate *Carson*. Minimum exposure. Then return."

"Understood. Moving."

The main screen updated yet again as *Revenge*'s passive sensors collected active pulses from *Carson* as she traveled. Ironically, had *Carson*'s captain not been so concerned about something in her path, had she run silent under emission control procedures, she might have saved herself.

"Compute optimum attack position," Straker said. "Lay in that course."

"Course computed and laid in."

"Execute."

Revenge dove again and accelerated directly into *Carson*'s path, passing through M100. Straker wasn't sure he'd ever get used to that feeling. It seemed like magic rather than science, this ability to move through solid matter. Theoretically, they could slip right into a planet and come out the other side.

"We are in position, sir."

"Weapons," said Straker, edging forward with tension, "prepare float mine."

"Float mine prepared. Warhead activated."

"Set fusing for detonation upon emergence."

"Fusing set."

Straker stared at the chrono counting down. "You will release the float mine at time zero. Do not wait for my verbal order. Helm, when the float mine is released, you will immediately accelerate, all ahead flank, to gain maximum separation."

"Aye aye, sir."

Straker chuckled at the naval jargon. Zaxby had trained the crew well, despite not having War Male status. No doubt he'd flimflammed them with his endless talking. Or maybe Ruxins really were all meticulous brainiacs as Zaxby claimed. In any case, they made good ship handlers, and none were argumentative toward him. Unlike Zaxby, these individuals were all young and eager.

Four... three... two... one... zero.

"Float mine deployed."

"Inserting and accelerating," said the helm, and the ship seemed to tilt with the thrum of the engines.

Time suspended itself for two seconds. Something in Straker's optic nerve sparkled and the temperature inside the ship rose several degrees. For a brief moment, the nuclear blast blurred the lines between normal space and under-space, resonating a broad spectrum of radiation, from hard gamma and free particles to electromagnetics, across the dimensional barrier.

In underspace, such a blast was simply something to be endured, though it was not conducive to the long-term health of the crew.

Outside, though, in normal space, the fusion explosion would scour any ship inside its radius clean of the toughest external fittings and would subject its hull to heat and kinetic stress briefly rivaling the surface of a star. Depending on proximity—in other words, the accuracy of the float mine placement—such a target might merely be damaged or it might be vaporized outright.

"Insert," Straker ordered, his mouth dry.

If he'd succeeded in his sneak attack, *Carson* would be eliminated as a threat, and Freiheit Station would likely be safe for long enough to get it out of this star system—assuming Murdock and Zaxby got the other engine working. However, in killing Ellen Gray and her crew, he might have to deal with the wrath of Carla Engels.

So be it. This was war, and there was only so much he could do to spare the Unmutuals. Maybe he'd emerge to find Gray had decided to defect. Then everyone would be satisfied.

But if his attack didn't succeed, he'd be stuck in a stern-chase. He didn't relish the idea of trying to overtake a faster, more heavily armed warship that was heading straight toward everyone he cared about, in order to kill them.

Despite his doubts, he was damned sure he didn't want to drop the ball at this point.

That was the real reason he had to be ruthless. For *them*. If she couldn't see that… well, he could only be who he was, and do what he had to do.

"Emerging," said the helmsman.

'*Helmsquid*', Straker thought mirthfully to himself. Apparently he subconsciously missed Loco so much he'd begun doing his own jokes.

"Sensors, report," Straker barked.

"There is an excess of radiation in the area, sir. I am collating and filtering the inputs now."

* * *

Engels mentally prepared herself for the transmission. She would have to be earnest and convincing, but give nothing away. She'd made notes for herself, but hadn't wanted to create a script. This must appear extemporaneous, off-the-cuff and urgent, or Gray might not believe her… and she'd lose *Carson*'s only chance at survival.

First, she checked the positions of all the players on her tactical display, making sure nobody had changed course. Naturally she couldn't see Straker's ship, but her system showed his predicted position. *Liberator* continued to fly outward, directly toward *Carson*, though her weapons remained stowed in obviously non-hostile positions.

Carson was still advancing, cruising on inertia in order to save fuel. In a space battle, fuel to accelerate must be matched by fuel to decelerate later, and no captain ever wasted fuel.

The ship's armored nose remained pointed forward at the only conceivable threat, her centerline heavy railgun aimed at *Liberator* and, incidentally, at Freiheit. The crew was clearly preparing for bombardment.

That fact, *Carson*'s travel position, was the only reason her ploy might work.

Finally, Engels was ready. "Record this and hold it in the transmission buffer. Send it only when I say."

"Aye aye, ma'am," said Lorton.

She took a breath and nodded, speaking with urgency. "*Liberator* to *Carson*. Ellen, this is Carla. Do what I tell you and you'll stay alive. If not, you'll die, I swear to the Cosmos. Shunt maximum power to your forward structural fields, armor reinforcement and inertial compensation. Do it quick, do it now. You have to believe me, Ellen. This is not a trick. Do it *now*, please! Engels out."

Then she relaxed, rubbing her neck. "Play it back."

Though fully prepared to do several takes, she decided this one was good, authentic. She checked her calculations for the multivariate problem integrating transmission time, the movements of all the ships, and the precise moment Straker should drop the float mine. She'd insisted he stick to the plan they'd made, down to the computer-counted second, telling him the half-truth that unless he did so, he might miss his window and fail.

What she hadn't told him was the use she might make of his window.

Now all she had to do was transmit the message at the correct time—but by doing so, she might become a traitor.

She remembered an old saying: *Should treason prosper, then none dare call it treason...* In other words, everybody forgives a winner. If she pulled this off, all would be forgotten.

If not... she had no idea what would happen. At the very least, it would destroy Derek's trust in her, and where trust vanished, love was sure to follow.

The chrono counted down. She'd plotted a narrow window to send the message. Too late, and *Carson* would die, because without any known threat, she wouldn't be *wasting* power on armor or structural reinforcement. Too early, and Captain Gray could guess at the threat and take additional measures, such as a violent evasive maneuver. That might mean she would escape completely unscathed.

"Lorton, transmit the message when this chrono hits zero."

"Aye aye, ma'am."

There. It was set in motion.

She stared at the numbers. To play it safe, to avoid risking her love and the lives of her comrades and her... her *family*, all she had to do was cancel the order.

Let them die, said a voice in her head.

Let them die.

Or give them a chance at life and possibly destroy her own.

The chrono crashed into zero like a runaway freighter against an asteroid, and the message flew toward *Carson*, timed to give Captain Gray just enough warning to reinforce her defenses.

Engels drummed her short, bitten fingernails on the console and made minute adjustments to the display. Long minutes passed.

Soon... soon.

There!

Carson vanished as the nuclear float mine detonated just ahead of her—kilometers ahead of her, in reality. At speeds measured in kilometers per second, though, the frigate had no chance to evade. She flew directly into the still-expanding explosion, taking the full brunt of its blast and its storm of hard radiation directly on her nose.

Just as impacting water at a high enough speed would feel like striking concrete, the collision of ship and wave front would sledgehammer *Carson* with enough kinetic force to crack her open—if the reinforcement didn't save her.

Engels leaned forward.

Where was she... where was she...

Carson emerged from the fireball intact.

She breathed a sigh of relief and, taking the helm controls, increased the throttles steadily to maximum. *Liberator* rumbled with the acceleration. Checking over her shoulder, she saw Chief Gurung there in the doorway, leaning against the jamb with a mug of caff in his hand.

"Chief, ready the crew for rescue ops, everyone with sidearms. Bring me one too. We'll be there in under two hours."

"Are they dead, ma'am?" The Gurkha gestured with his cup at the main screen, his face an odd mixture of bloodthirstiness and pity.

"I don't know yet," Engels said. "For sure they're hurt badly, but at least..."

"Yes?"

"Nothing, Chief. Carry on."

"Aye aye, ma'am." He withdrew and dogged the pressure door.

She caught Lorton staring at her. "You have a problem, spacer?"

"No problem, ma'am."

"What do you think of what I did?"

"Not my place to judge, ma'am." His face seemed frozen.

"Speak freely. That's an order." She might as well find out right now how a common crewman felt about her actions.

Lorton took a deep breath. "I honestly don't know, ma'am. As long as they can't attack Freiheit now…"

"Yeah." Engels put her chin on her fist and remained silent. There was no point in trying to justify herself to someone else when she wasn't really sure in her own mind. "Well, we'll find out how big a fool I was soon enough. Aim maximum active and passive sensors at *Carson*. No point in acting non-hostile now."

While Lorton was setting that up, she brought the corvette's weapons to standby positions. Once done, she activated an encrypted broadcast comlink on *Revenge*'s frequency. "Straker, this is Engels. You there? Looks like *Carson* wasn't completely vaporized. If she's knocked out and no threat, check for life signs and try to rescue any survivors. We'll be there as soon as we can and take anyone you pick up off your hands. Engels out."

Of course, she hadn't told Straker about her warning to Captain Gray, a warning that looked like it may have worked. He'd eventually find out, but the later, the better. She waited for his reply, a delay of more than a minute.

"Straker to Engels, I read you. You might hate me for it, but I'm not going to try any rescue missions. We have no medical or berthing facilities for humans and no expertise in treating injured people. Any lives we save have to be balanced against the fact that this stealth technology would be exposed for hours to the scrutiny of both survivors and any other Unmutuals watching on long-range sensors. It's critical to keep this technology secret. It hasn't been used in eighty years, and I don't want anyone alerted to it. You'll have to do the rescuing in *Liberator*. I'm moving to intercept the attack ship squadron. I've tightbeamed updates to your tactical system so you know what I'm doing. Straker out."

Engels sighed with a mixture of relief and frustration. On the one hand, she disagreed with Straker's decision not to help with the rescue, especially as he was on the spot. People might die because of the delay. At the same time, she understood his intention to fight the battle first, and not having him there meant that much longer before he found out how she'd ignored his orders.

She transmitted, "All right, Straker. The key is, you knocked out *Carson*. If she has any fight left in her, we can handle it. Good luck and good hunting. Engels out."

When *Liberator* entered long range, decelerating brutally to match velocities with the apparently drifting *Carson*, Engels had Lorton turn all the ship's sensors on the frigate. It was critical to establish that *Carson* wasn't playing possum, ready to blast anyone approaching.

Chief Gurung reported the crew ready for rescue operations. "Here's your sidearm, ma'am," he said, handing her a pistol belt. He'd already sent up a crewman to take the weapons station, and manned the ops station himself.

"Keep our guns on *Carson*," Engels told the weapons crewman, "but for Cosmos' sake don't fire unless we're fired upon."

"All her antennas and sensor arrays have been stripped away," said Lorton. "All of her weapons I can see are also damaged. The centerline railgun might be operative because most of its parts are internal, and its clamshell outer doors were shut at the time of the blast."

"I'll make sure we stay out of her firing arc," said Engels, adjusting her position to put *Liberator* farther aft of *Carson*. She began a slow spiral in toward the wounded ship.

"It appears," Lorton continued, "that her armor is severely damaged all along the front half of the ship. The rear half, beyond the waist, is much less damaged, but the thermal shockwave has melted most fittings that projected beyond the hull, such as antennas, docking rings, atmospheric control surfaces, and sidespace field emitters."

"How about electronic emissions? Give me a heat map."

He took a few minutes to bring up the correct imagery. Gurung had to lean over and give him some help. "Sorry, I'm not all that good at this yet," Lorton said.

"You're doing fine," Engels replied distractedly, staring at the optical feed on the main visiplate. "I'm seeing something, a light flashing intermittently..."

"Here it comes," said Lorton. The optical display suddenly expanded its magnification, with a false-color overlay showing *Carson*'s electromagnetic emissions spectra from the far infrared up to gamma.

"Looks like main power is still online, but everything forward of the waist is getting cold. The flashing is... can you zoom in?"

"Magnifying."

Engels was able to make out two exo-suits. One appeared to be welding, possibly closing a breach. "Well, that's good news. We didn't kill everyone and they're not maneuvering or shooting at us. They might not even know we're here if they have no operating sensors. Set up a high-power tightbeam, all frequencies, audio only, unencrypted. See if they have a working receiver."

"Aye aye, ma'am. Activated. Go ahead."

"*Carson*, this is *Liberator*. It appears you are crippled. Surrender now and we will render assistance. If you do not, I will be forced to attack until you do."

The comlink crackled, and a faint reply came. It was Captain Gray. "Damn you, Engels. I have a dozen dead and twice that many injured!"

Engels hardened her voice. "I tried to talk you out of continuing, Ellen. I gave you the warning that saved your crew, if not your ship. Without maximum reinforcement, you'd be radioactive scrap. I wasn't about to tell you about the weapon we used, of course. This is war, a war *you* chose to pursue against my advice. Now you have to surrender. I have beams trained on you right now, and I have a shipkiller missile in the tube that I really don't want to use. I also have a working autodoc and a decent medic aboard, and clean, safe bunks my people have prepared. Surrender and we'll do as much as we can for your wounded."

Gray sighed. "I have no choice. We surrender."

"Good. We'll dock at your aft port. I want you to come aboard with the first batch of wounded."

"What, you don't trust me?" Gray demanded.

"I don't want your people to get any ideas. Better that they know you're with me."

"As a hostage?"

Engels shrugged, even though there was no vid. "Call it what you will."

"I have to direct damage control!"

"You and I both know that captains only get in the way when it's time to make repairs. Chief Gurung will bring some technicians aboard to help out. Brief your people that they're prisoners of war now, and to comply with all orders. If there's any trouble, we'll be ruthless. Your remaining crew still outnumbers mine two to one, so I can't afford to take chances." Engels couldn't resist a dig. "I hope you have more control over your people than Ramirez did."

Engels could hear Gray's anguish. "I'd better, or I'm worthless. I'll give the orders. You'll have no trouble. Gray out."

"See you soon." Engels glanced over at Gurung. "Escort Captain Gray to me. Make sure all of their people are disarmed, get the wounded aboard, and then go over there to help make repairs to life support and power. No weapons, no comms, no sensors, though. I don't want anyone getting ideas, or warning DeChang about the Ruxin ship. In fact, I'll make an announcement."

"Aye aye, Captain," Gurung said with a wide grin, and bolted off the bridge.

After using the public address to remind the *Liberator*'s crew not to talk about *Revenge* or the way Straker had taken down *Carson*, she carefully, deftly brought the corvette in to dock with the drifting frigate.

"Captain Engels," said Captain Gray stiffly as she entered *Liberator*'s bridge, giving Engels the title of courtesy aboard her own ship.

Engels stood. "Captain Gray." She held out a hand, which Gray took after a moment's hesitation. Engels held onto it, then placed her other palm atop Gray's. "I'm sorry about your casualties."

"Can't be helped." Gray squeezed Engels' hand, and then extricated hers, grimacing. "You were right. I followed orders, did my duty as I saw it, and so did you. I might have backed down, but you couldn't. I should have seen that, and I should have known you wouldn't make idle threats."

Engels waved Gray to a seat at the empty ops station, taking her own at the helm. "Now I need you to convince DeChang to back off. Straker is on his way to destroy your attack ship squadron, which is the only military space force you have left in the system. He'll be there in…" she glanced at her display, "five hours or so. Given that Aynor base is over a light-hour away, it would be wise to send a transmission soon."

Gray examined the displays on *Liberator*'s bridge. "Straker's on his way in what sort of ship? I never saw it coming. Was that a stealth mine we hit?"

"Sorry, that's classified. Trust me, though. When Straker makes his intercept, it will be no contest. You'll lose a dozen ships and pilots for no purpose."

Engels put more sureness into her voice than she felt, but it was important to appear absolutely confident.

"I really wish we could have cooperated instead of being set against each other, Carla."

"Ramirez and your misplaced support made that impossible. You don't know what it was like on Freiheit. Straker was second in command. Imagine if you were the XO on a ship with a captain that ordered murders of civilians, let the crew run amuck, and then tried to kill you when you tried to stop the madness. You'd mutiny too."

"I suppose I might." Gray idly rubbed her fingertips on the console. "I still think DeChang never intended any of this."

"Doesn't matter. A commander has to take responsibility for the actions of subordinates. Can you truly say DeChang's done his best to keep his house clean? Seems like he's been unwilling to make the hard calls."

"You might be right. So, what do you want me to say in this transmission? I'm not going to be coerced."

Engels nodded at Lorton, who set up a vid recording. "Ready when you are, ma'am. Both of you are in view."

"Just tell him the truth," Engels said to Gray. "Don't speculate aloud about Straker's ship, though, no matter what you've guessed. Your goal—our goal—is to avert unnecessary bloodshed so we can both keep on fighting the Mutuality."

"And the Hundred Worlds? ...I don't see they're much better."

"That's a discussion for later." Engels held up three fingers, then two, then one. "Go."

"Recording."

"General DeChang, this is Lieutenant Carla Engels, commanding the corvette *Liberator*. We've neutralized and captured the *Carson*. As you can see, Captain Gray is my prisoner, as are the survivors. But there won't be any survivors of your attack squadron. Those ships are too small to stand up to our weaponry. The pilots will all die. I'm asking you to order them back. We don't want to kill them, but we will." She nodded at Gray.

"General DeChang," said Gray, "What she says is true. Straker's ship can and will destroy the attack squadron without difficulty. It's pointless for them to continue. We're being treated well, and I've been assured we'll be allowed to return to Aynor. I know it's a blow to the Unmutual movement to lose Freiheit, but we have no way of stopping them. I respectfully but strongly advise cutting our losses at this time." She folded her hands.

Engels continued. "As you see, General, Captain Gray is not under duress. View the attached vid to see I'm telling you the truth. I urge you to think of your people and about not throwing their lives away. Engels out."

"Recording off," said Lorton.

Engels stood. "Let's make a newsvid, shall we? I always wanted to be journalist."

"Really?" he asked.

"No—but this time it's important."

Engels retrieved a suit helmet and put it on, activating its vid and audio recording. She and Gray toured both ships for fifteen minutes, providing commentary on what they saw—repairs being made, wounded being treated, prisoners being held without mistreatment.

"Download this and attach it to our transmission, then send it to Aynor," Engels said to Lorton, passing him the helmet.

The man had no sooner done so than the sensors board lit up with telltales and gave off the muted *meep-meep* of a sidespace detection alert. When Lorton fed the new data to the main tactical overlay, Engels couldn't help herself.

"Holy shit…" Engels said. "We're screwed."

Chapter 40

"Warships," Captain Gray said as she examined the two new contacts on *Liberator*'s main visiplate. "This certainly changes things."

Engels' eyes roved over the display. "Lorton, add a timespace curvature overlay to the map."

"One moment... Added."

Lines resembling a land surface topographical map appeared, with the central star, the planets and moons appearing as hilltops. The areas away from any mass showed as flat, the places where ships could enter and exit sidespace.

Fortunately, the contacts had arrived much nearer Aynor than Freiheit. For now, the rock was safe.

"Are they yours?" Engels asked.

"They're Mutuality ships," Gray said. "One destroyer, one light cruiser. It's a recon in force, or a raid. Somebody found this place—found the Unmutuals, I mean. We've been here for decades, and it had to happen sometime, just by the odds."

Engels shook her head. "That's too much coincidence. If we were able to steal a courier and get away when you made off with Freiheit, maybe someone else did too. Or somebody got off a message drone undetected."

Gray crossed her arms. "Doesn't really matter. They're here now and we're blown. The light we're seeing is more than an hour old. DeChang will already be evacuating on the fast transports." She pointed. "There."

A dozen small contacts rose from the surface of Aynor and curved away from the inbound Mutuality warships, aiming spinward and outward from the planet of Bayzos. "They're heading for flatspace to transit to our preplanned fallback location," said Gray.

"Just in time." Missiles blossomed from the warships and sped toward Aynor. No… Engels realized the missiles were pursuing the freighters. "Shit. They're toast."

"Don't count them out yet," Gray said. "Our ships are fast, and have add-on defensive laser systems for just this kind of thing. Some will get away. Look how slowly the missiles are overtaking. It's going to be a race."

Engels pointed at something else. "Your attack ship squadron has no sidespace capability. They're dead pilots flying if they don't surrender to us. Lorton, set up a transmission. Ellen, tell them to head for docking with Freiheit and keep their weapons powered down. If I see any hostile intent, I'll blow them out of space."

"Understood."

"Ready," Lorton said. "You're both in field of view."

"Attack squadron, this is Captain Gray. I'm here with Captain Engels, as you can see. Dmitri, I know you're lead bird, so listen to me. Two Mutuality warships just jumped in and they're heading for Aynor. DeChang has already evacuated. Your only chance is to surrender to Straker's people."

"The Breakers," said Engels.

"Straker's Breakers…? Catchy." Gray said. "Dmitri, I'm being well treated. These people are our opponents, not our enemies. Everyone's against you and you have nowhere to go unless you join me in surrendering to Straker's Breakers. Give up, unless you want to be killed or captured. It's your choice. I hope you make the right one. If you agree, head for Freiheit, power down all weapons, and wait for further orders. Remember, that rock and its sidespace engines are your only ticket out of here."

Engels chewed her lip. "Straker's gonna be seriously pissed. I wish we could contact him, but he's…" she suddenly realized she was about to reveal secrets. "He's EMCON."

"Why?"

"Part of the secret weapon."

"No, I mean, why will he be angry?"

"Because now we have to take a bunch of Unmutuals with us and you'll know about our secret base and secret technology. I'm not sure Straker will let you leave."

"Better than dying or being captured by the Mutuality," said Gray. "Truth to tell, while I'm not going to betray DeChang, I'm not in love with the guy." She lifted her eyebrow. "Not the way you are with Straker."

Engels blushed. "You can tell?"

"You have that sparkle in your eye when you talk about him. Or sometimes that frustrated frown that means you care too much what he thinks. More than if he were merely your commander, I mean."

Engels smiled. "Guilty as charged. But that's not blinding me to his faults. I've known him for thirteen years."

"And I've known DeChang for more than twenty. I don't think I've misjudged him that badly."

"What about Ramirez?"

"Less than five. She was captured in a raid on a Mutuality re-education camp."

"So she could have been a hardcore criminal, not merely a political prisoner."

Gray shrugged. "I never liked her, but she wasn't my business."

"Maybe she should have been."

"Yeah, rub it in."

Engels shrugged. "Sometimes the truth hurts." She looked at the tactical display again. "Patch me through to Zaxby or Murdock."

A moment later, the comlink activated, audio only. "Lieutenant Zaxby here. Is this important? I'm exceedingly busy at the moment."

"This is Engels," Carla said, fighting to keep a surge of irritation out of her voice. "How're the repairs coming?"

"Better than I expected, Carla," he said. "We should have the sidespace engines functional within a day. Mister Murdock is not completely incompetent, and my team of technicians has doubled the rate of improvement. We are not limited to two hands or two eyes, after all, and so can do the work of multiple humans."

"Even with one brain?" she asked.

"We have *large* brains," he assured her.

"And egos to match," she added.

"Which seems appropriate, doesn't it?" he asked. "How is my ship?"

"*Your* ship?"

"The *Revenge*. Has Captain Straker managed to avoid irreparably damaging it?"

"I thought you could repair anything."

"Some things are beyond even my vast capabilities."

"Such as humility?" she asked.

"Humility is of value to humans, not Ruxins. To return to the question: is *Revenge* undamaged?"

"I believe so. At least, he used it to good effect and took down the *Carson*. Zaxby… Captain Gray is here with me."

"Hello, Captain Gray," Zaxby said. "I do hope your captivity is not too stressful. Perhaps someday soon we may play chess again."

"Maybe so."

"I'm sorry, but I have little time for pleasantries and must return to my technical duties. Zaxby out." Zaxby seemed to be humming before he cut off the comlink.

"You and Zaxby play chess?" asked Engels.

"He's the only one around who can beat me," Gray said. "Perhaps you'd like to play sometime?"

"Yes, in my copious free time."

Gray shrugged. "It's good for sidespace trips." She glanced sidelong at Engels. "So Straker is captaining a Ruxin ship?"

"Nobody said that."

"But it's true, isn't it?"

Engels shrugged.

Gray snapped her fingers. "It's an Archer, isn't it? That's explains everything. I've read about them—but they're obsolete. Old stuff."

Engels glared helplessly at Gray. "Ellen, you can't tell anyone. Not yet, in case people get captured, or are moles for the Mutuality. And it's only obsolete if our enemies are on guard against it. We may not be able to use it against Fleet units, but ships like this one haven't been seen in eighty years." She gestured at the visiplate. "Our only chance of getting Freiheit out of here now is if Straker can destroy or drive off those ships."

Gray rubbed her face with the palms of her hands. "I sure wish they'd shown up a few hours earlier. I'd have an intact ship, and we could be working together."

"Can we work together now?"

Gray eyed Engels. "Yes. I'll place myself under your command or I'll revert to the status of prisoner of war."

"No reservations?"

"No," Gray said.

"What about your crew?" Engels asked.

"They'll follow me."

Engels held out her hand. "Deal. Lorton, get Chief Gurung in here."

A moment later the Gurkha rushed in. "Yes, Captain?"

"How are the repairs coming on *Carson*?"

"Prime power is restored. The engines are undamaged. Life support is adequate. The forward spaces are radioactive, but crew can wear suits until that declines. There are a lot of minor problems, but she came through surprisingly well."

"Captain Gray has given her parole. She and her people are to be treated as allies under my command until I say different or they do something out of line. You may now assist in repairs to all systems, including weapons, just like *Carson* was one of our ships." Engels added bleakly, "Soon, we might need everything we have."

"Oh?" Gurung turned to the main display and grinned. "I see we have company."

"Mutuality fleet units. They'll be on us within twenty hours unless Captain Straker makes them change their minds."

"Excellent." Gurung saluted and left.

"Is he always so happy to be attacked?" asked Gray.

"Good cheer seems to be his response to everything."

Lorton said, "Incoming transmission from the attack ship squadron."

"Put it up."

A round-faced man with stubble on his chin appeared on the screen. The cockpit of a one-pilot attack ship was visible around him. He seemed quite unhappy. "Major Polzin here. Captain Engels, on Captain Gray's advice, and with General DeChang's permission, given the arrival of the Mutuality squadron, I will surrender to you. We have altered course and are on route to match vectors with Freiheit. Our weapons are powered down. See you soon. Polzin out."

Engels nodded. "Transmit this. Thank you, Major Polzin. The situation has changed yet again. Captain Gray?" She gestured.

Gray spoke. "Dmitri, with the Mutuality warships here, the enemy of my enemy is my friend. We're all allies now. Captains Engels and Straker are in charge and I report to them. You report to me. We may have to fight to get out of this system, so be ready. There should be time to catch a shower and some rack time once you arrive at Freiheit, as we estimate nineteen or twenty hours until the enemy comes within range. I'll be waiting for you when you get here. Brief your people clearly: we're now all on the same side, and Straker's Breakers are in charge. Any trouble and heads will roll. Gray out."

Engels nodded. "Thanks, Ellen."

"Nothing like a common enemy to make everyone sing *kumbaya*."

"I don't know what that means."

"It's a song. Like kids around a campfire. Don't worry about it. You were raised in the Hundred Worlds. Apparently they retained only enough Old Earth culture to keep their fools quiet."

Engels stared at Gray in mild astonishment. "I wouldn't have thought you bought into all that negative Mutuality crap about the Hundred Worlds."

"Oh, no doubt your people are better off than those in the Mutuality, but if you think the wage slaves of the Hundred Worlds are truly free, you need to expand your education. Every empire has users at the top, crushing those beneath them." Gray cocked her head at Engels. "Otherwise, why aren't you in sidespace right now, on course for home?"

"Straker thinks he can do more good here, and I don't disagree. As long as we're damaging the Hundred Worlds' enemies, we consider ourselves on detached duty."

"But you're harming us, not the Mutuality, by taking Freiheit."

"That's all about Ramirez and the people of Freiheit. Besides, if we hadn't shown up, you'd have lost Freiheit anyway, now that the Mutuality knows where you are."

Gray sighed. "Everyone's just trying to do the right thing here."

"Yeah, me too," agreed Engels. She chewed her lip and watched the slowly changing tactical situation. "Okay, next order of business: record a transmission for Straker."

"Ready."

"Derek, SITREP," she began. "Two Mutuality warships just transited in near Aynor. DeChang has evacuated. *Carson* survived the float mine with some capability. Captain Gray has surrendered to me and, in light of the situation, has chosen to ally with us under my command. We're repairing *Carson* as fast as we can. The Unmutual attack squadron is also joining us. Zaxby says repairs to Freiheit are proceeding apace and they should have sidespace capability again within a day. I'm including an encrypted databurst update with this transmission. You should be able to load that, and confirm everything using passive sensors. I presume you'll head for the enemy ships. I suggest you go first to Bayzos and use its moons and surrounding debris to hide in and update your sensor readings, then try to take out the light cruiser first. If you can do that, we may be able to beat the destroyer with the forces we have, even if you can't. Engels out."

"Buffered," Lorton said.

"Attach a tactical data log of the last six hours and aim the transmission in a cone toward where he expects to intercept the attack squadron. Set it on endless repeat."

"Aye aye, ma'am." Lorton worked his board.

"What's that?" asked Gray, pointing at a tiny icon.

"Shuttle," said Engels. "I let it escape from Freiheit, as I couldn't really stop it without destroying it. Ramirez might be aboard. The woman I talked with sounded like her, but claimed to be someone named Nassimi and said she has civilians with her, which to me was just a veiled way of saying 'hostages.' So I let them go."

"I don't know any Nassimi. Should we warn them what's going on? A shuttle's sensors won't tell them much."

Engels thought about it for a moment. "No. They're headed for Aynor but it will take them days. None of our ships are nearby and I don't want to divert anyone. Best case, we drive off the Mutuality ships and can decide what to do then. Most likely outcome, we get away and they get captured by the Mutuality. At least they'll be alive."

Gray nodded. "I agree. We can't save everyone. It'll be remarkable if we don't all end up back in labor camps." She stood. "Now that we're allies, I need to get to work."

"Good idea," Engels replied, "You go help get *Carson* shipshape. I'll stand watch here and bite my nails. With Straker out of comlink..."

"It's lonely at the top." Gray saluted with an ironic flip. "Permission to carry on?"

"Carry on, Captain Gray."

* * *

Straker wiped his hands uselessly on his suit. Everything on the *Revenge*'s bridge felt like one big sweat locker and smelled like seaweed rotting on a beach. The warmer water from the vents fought the chill from underspace, resulting in fogs, mists, and ice in the upper corners of the room.

Inside his suit, his heater was losing its own battle, making his skin hot and sweaty while his bones seemed to chill. An intermittent lethargy stole over him, and he wished he had stims. Next time he would bring some.

Fortunately, the trip beneath normal space was finally ending. He watched the ship's predicted location, and her intended point of emergence, overlap.

"Insert," Straker ordered.

"Emerging."

Straker immediately felt warmer, and shut off his suit heater.

The point of emergence was off the attack squadron's axis of travel and ten minutes ahead, a place outside of the little ships' sensor range and arc. Their best detectors were LIDAR, based on a scanning laser focused ahead, for targeting and collision avoidance.

"Where are they?" he asked, not seeing a confirming icon. "Did they deviate?"

"I have readings," said the Ruxin at sensors. "Updating plot."

A new icon flashed, showing the attack squadron had turned and accelerated, and was now out of easy intercept range. "Dammit! We'll have to chase them hard."

"Incoming transmission from *Liberator*," said the communications officer.

"Comlink it," Straker replied.

"This is not realtime, sir. We are more than twenty light-minutes from *Liberator*."

"Of course. Play it."

"There is data attached…"

"Well, process it then!" Straker ordered.

"Aye aye, sir."

Engels' recorded vid played. By the time he'd listened to it, the tactical data came up so he could see clearly what she was talking about. As a ground-pounder, he didn't yet have an instinctive mind for space warfare.

"All right, let the attack squadron go. Sensors, update this data with as much realtime passive data as you can, especially about these two Mutuality warships."

"Sensor data is already integrated."

"Good. Very efficient."

"Thank you, sir."

Straker wiped his eyes and stared at the plots. On an old-fashioned analog clock, with the system's star in the center, the enemy was at the top at twelve, heading downward toward Bayzos and Aynor base at two. DeChang's escaping freighters were at three and outward. Straker on *Revenge* was at four and much farther inward. Freiheit was at six, closer to the star but climbing outward.

Everyone but *Revenge* was moving clockwise.

The Mutuality warships were cautiously approaching Aynor and Bayzos from farther out in flatspace. They wouldn't necessarily know that Aynor Base was now deserted, and would be checking it out.

The destroyer led the light cruiser, both widely separated for maximum sensor coverage and minimum vulnerability to surprise attack, he supposed. Zaxby's trick with the stealth mines at the Battle of Corinth—the Ruxin had bragged about that several times over the past few months—might have made them cautious. They were both banging away with max-power sensor pulses, concentrated forward.

DeChang's fast transports, which must be carrying everyone from Aynor, continued to run like scalded dogs, ahead and outward toward flatspace. Missiles from the enemy ships still pursued, slowly overhauling them. To Straker's eye, it looked like catching them before transit would be a toss-up. He hoped they had good point defenses. There was nothing *Revenge* could do.

Freiheit continued to spiral outward, rising in its stellar orbit, on the opposite side of the unnamed star of this system. *Carson* and *Liberator* hung in space nearby. The star would mask them from a detailed scan. Straker hoped the enemy took their time before personally investigating one asteroid and some ships all the way across the system.

And *Revenge* floated in Bayzos' future orbital path.

Eventually, Straker spoke. "Acknowledging Captain Engels' message and inform her we're heading for Bayzos. Helm, plot a course for Bayzos, to emerge on the opposite side of the planet from the enemy and away from orbital debris."

"Which enemy?"

"The Mutuality ships. They are our only enemy right now."

"Not true, sir. The remnants of the Unmutuals remain–"

"Helm, don't turn into a Zaxby."

"Not understood."

"Don't be too literal. Our only enemy within this tactical situation is those two Mutuality ships. Understand?"

"Understood."

Straker growled, "Great. Now plot the course."

"Course plotted."

"Insert and go."

"Inserting. Accelerating within underspace."

"Call me ten minutes before arrival. I'm going to my cabin."

"Aye aye, sir."

Straker returned when notified, feeling much better after a meal and a few hours of dry napping, though he was chilled again. His wound still ached and itched. His suit, recharged, heated his skin to sweating temperatures.

Upon *Revenge's* emergence, the sensors officer updated the display without asking. The Ruxins were getting better as they gained experience.

It looked like DeChang had gotten away. No wreckage floated near their exit point, and no residual radiation could be seen. Freiheit continued to accelerate slowly, clockwise and outward. However, the Mutuality ships' positions showed unconfirmed.

"Bring us gently around the planet to unmask, using impellers only," he ordered. "Act natural."

"Not understood."

"Keep our flight profile as similar to a natural satellite as possible."

"Understood."

Slowly, slowly, *Revenge* sped up in Bayzos orbit, imitating a chunk of rock, until they could see the moon of Aynor. Nearby, the Mutuality destroyer systematically blasted at the surface, annihilating the base and all its facilities.

Beyond, the light cruiser waited in a stable high orbit, watching over her sister ship, active sensors flooding the area.

Adrenaline surged in Straker's veins as he saw his prey. "Helm, set course to place us directly in the light cruiser's path for float mine deployment, three weapons, extreme proximity."

The alien helmsman turned a pair of eyes toward Straker, as did the weapons officer. "Three weapons? That is wasteful of our limited supply of fusion warheads."

"This isn't a standard war cruise, hunting targets of opportunity. We absolutely *must* get this cruiser."

"It will also be dangerous for us."

"Then make sure we're far from the blasts."

"I'll do my best, Captain."

"Insert when ready," Straker ordered, "and take us there by the shortest vector."

The helm officer brought a third eye around, evidently quite concerned. "That will take us through Bayzos itself."

"Is that a problem?"

"Define 'problem'."

Exasperated, Straker barked, "What's the worst that could happen?"

"This gas giant is large. It approaches the status of a brown dwarf. If we pass near a pocket of proto-fusion, it could leak over into underspace and alter our course, or even damage us."

"How likely is that to happen?"

"Approximately zero point five percent."

"One in two hundred?" he demanded.

"Approximately, sir."

"Dammit, that's nothing! Do it, *do it now*."

"Aye aye, sir." The Ruxin's tentacles flew. "Inserting now."

Straker gripped his hands together behind his back and clenched his jaw to keep from railing at these people for not knowing what was relevant. He told himself that they were technically adept, but young and not blooded at war. They weren't even extensively experienced at space travel. Still, it illustrated why mixing two cultures was fraught with unseen pitfalls.

The predictive plot showed *Revenge* moving down through the planet as it cut across to get ahead of the light cruiser in its orbit. Straker held his breath, waiting for some kind of bump or rumble or other sign, but there was nothing at all.

Until there was.

An alarm screeched. "Damage to the missile and tube," said the operations officer. "Warhead is intact, but repairs must be made in order to fire. Other damage is possible."

Straker sighed with relief. "Get on it. I mean, implement damage control procedures and make repairs. Inspect all critical systems and report to me."

"Aye aye, sir." The Ruxin crew swung into action.

The *Revenge*'s position continued to crawl through Bayzos. If the underspace engine failed, they would die within milliseconds as they emerged inside the crushing pressure of the gas giant. They would be crumpled like an empty drink bulb, never to be seen again, but the risk was worth it. The enemy could alter course at any time.

"Ten minutes to float mine deployment."

Straker said, "Is there any indication the damage threw us off course?"

"Impossible to determine."

"Maintain timeline, then. Deploy on the computed schedule. What I wouldn't give for a periscope."

"A what, sir?" asked the sensors officer.

"A device to look into normal space without leaving underspace."

"Such a device is impossible to construct."

Straker raised his eyebrows in amusement. "So you say. Everything's impossible until someone figures out how to do it."

"That is a nonsensical statement."

"*Gaah!* Are you all turning into Zaxbys?"

The bridge officers permitted an increasing number of eyes to drift and peer toward him. They chittered for a moment in their language. The sensors officer eventually said, "Though we would be happy to become Zaxbys, that is also a nonsensical statement. Have we made the War Male angry by failing in our duties?"

Straker clamped down on his temper. "No, no, it's merely the tension of combat. Carry on, you're all doing well."

"We are pleased. Zaxby is an example to all of us neuters."

"Really? Why's that?"

"He has risen above his gender. We are a downtrodden class. We are not eligible to govern or lay eggs like the females, nor are we allowed to contribute our genes for reproduction or become heroes in battle like the males. We can only work and invent things to serve the others. This is as close as we will come to glory, at least until we liberate our homeworld. Then, perhaps, we will be allowed to improve ourselves."

Straker shook his index finger in the air and paced, sloshing. "Wait a minute. I'm pretty sure Zaxby said something about being a neuter *at the moment*. That it was just a phase. Don't you people change genders throughout your life cycle?"

"You do not understand fully. Only a rare few are selected to become male or female. The rest remain neuter until they expire from old age. They may participate in the reproductive process, which is pleasurable and honorable, but the offspring are only of the male and female involved. At best, the neuter is a caretaker."

"So you're like workers in an anthill."

"I do not understand your reference," said the Ruxin.

"Never mind. But why not make you all male to crew this warship?"

"Premier Freenix fears to alter neuters to become males, beyond a few pampered individuals to provide genetic material. She is convinced too many males cause society to become unstable. They create trouble, she says. Neuters are easier to control."

"What a load of bullshit. Look, I'm no brainiac, but I remember Academy classes where I learned that whenever you oppress one kind of people for a long time, you're asking for a revolution. You neuters are the biggest group, right?"

"That is true."

"Then you could free yourselves and become male or female, whatever you wanted."

"That would lead to chaos in our society."

"Maybe a little chaos is a good thing. Maybe it would make sure there isn't some kind of bigger blowup later. I studied Old Earth's revolutions. They always started with somebody standing on someone else's neck."

"We have no necks."

"It's a metaphor. The little guy always got tired of it, and felt like the only thing he could do was overthrow the system. Maybe you could get more freedom by pointing out how well you performed on this warship. Demand the right to become male if you wanted, so you could fight better."

The sensors officer had all four eyes on Straker by this time. "Your proposal is interesting. We will discuss it among ourselves."

Straker realized he was philosophizing a bit too much. It was an interesting sensation of power, to plant thoughts in the heads of these young Ruxins. It occurred to him he shouldn't give them too many crazy ideas too fast, so he continued. "Just no revolutions until we're done with this operation, okay? I need you to win this battle. That's what it means to be military, regardless of gender. We put our personal desires aside for the good of society, at least for a while."

"Understood. Thank you for your insights, War Male Straker." Most of the eyes turned away again, though all the Ruxins kept at least one turned warily toward their captain.

The chrono ticked toward its appointed time.

"Float mine deployment underway," said the weapons officer. "Mine one away."

"Accelerating," said the Ruxin at the helm.

"Mine two away."

"Altering course."

"Mine three away."

"Inserting and accelerating at flank speed."

The ship shook with the fusion explosions. What leaked less than one percent into underspace would obliterate almost anything nearby in normal space—assuming Straker had placed at least one of the weapons correctly.

He couldn't put them too close to each other or the explosion of the first might destroy the second, and so on, a principle known as fratricide. He couldn't target them actually inside the cruiser, because nuclear detonation mechanisms were delicate things, and emergence damage might turn an atomic blast into a mere dirty bomb, inconvenient but not devastating.

So he had to drop them as close to the enemy ship as possible, but not inside it. Unfortunately, as the cruiser seemed to be on high alert, it probably had allocated at least some of its energy reserves to reinforcing its hull and armor with structural fields.

Thus, the three weapons.

"Back us off. Emerge behind the nearest moon and peek out."

The helm officer said, "Confirm: you want me to gain distance from the deployment site and use the nearest natural satellite of Bayzos in order to hide our emergence, and cautiously survey the situation."

"Pretty sure I just said that."

"I am confirming my understanding of your idiomatic speech, sir."

Straker lifted his eyes to stare pleadingly at the overhead. "And you're doing a damn fine job of it. Carry on."

Come on, come on, Straker thought. I need to know. Did we get them or not?

"Emerging." The visiplate showed a rocky, pockmarked moonlet nearby. "Peeking out." The moonlet seemed to move aside.

The tactical plot updated and showed two large pieces of wreckage and a debris field where once the light cruiser had orbited. "Yes!" Straker yelled, throwing a fist in the air.

All the Ruxins looked askance at the human. "Target neutralized," said the weapons officer.

Straker put his hands behind his back again, resuming what he thought of as a commanding aspect. "Well done, everyone. Uh... where's that damned destroyer?"

Chapter 41

Near Bayzos.

"The destroyer is departing Bayzos orbit," said the Ruxin at the sensors station of *Revenge*'s bridge. The main screen updated to show the vessel fleeing at high speed, directly away from the gas giant.

"Keep an eye on him." Straker waited, though patience was not in his nature. Right now it looked like the destroyer was merely putting distance between herself and the unknown danger. Her captain probably thought the cruiser had hit stealth mines.

Fifteen minutes later, it appeared the destroyer had set course for Freiheit Station. Straker had hoped she would flee outward, running for sidespace, but it appeared her captain had decided to try to stop the prize asteroid from getting away.

This made sense as Freiheit's sidespace engines were vulnerable. Destroying even one of them would ensure the Mutuality could recapture the valuable habitat at leisure.

"Ops," Straker called out, "given the destroyer's course, calculate the point at which they could reasonably attempt a long-range bombardment with railguns."

"Aye aye, sir." The Ruxin's tentacles danced across the controls. "I should remind you that they could fire missiles at any time."

"They have to believe there will be point defenses against missiles," Straker replied. "They can detect the presence of ships in the area. Launching an unsupported missile spread from only one ship would be a waste. The way to get missiles through defenses is to fire a lot of them at once, mix them in with decoys, and be close enough to fire railguns and beams as well. Give the enemy too much to handle."

"I see. That is sensible. The War Male is clever."

"Damn sure hope so," Straker said under his breath.

"Point calculated. Displayed."

"Helm, lay in a course for that point. Can we catch them if we insert?"

"We cannot catch them at all," said the helm officer. "Their ship is much faster than ours."

Straker's eyes roved over the screen. "What if we did an intrasystem sidespace jump?"

"Calculating. No, that would not allow us to reach the designated point any faster. Space is not flat enough."

"Could a transit get us to Freiheit faster than going via normal space? Like the *Carson* did?"

"We would have to travel outward, then transit, then travel inward again, but yes, it would save several hours over a standard course. We would still have to travel from Freiheit to the interception point, though."

Straker sloshed over to the helm. "Do it. If we can't intercept the destroyer, we might as well be back at Freiheit and help defend it."

The helm officer turned two eyes to Straker while continuing to pilot the ship. "How does one defend a non-maneuverable target against long-range bombardment, sir?"

"That, I don't know. But if we're to have any chance, we need to get all our forces together and come up with something."

* * *

"Incoming transmission from *Revenge*," said Lorton to Engels.

She woke from her doze at the helm and stretched. She couldn't help but think that she probably ought to go shower and get a meal before things really heated up. "Put it on."

Straker looked tired and wet, Engels thought as she examined his image displayed on the big screen.

"Engels, this is Straker. We took out the cruiser. The destroyer is heading for you at full speed in normal space. *Revenge* is too slow to intercept, so we're going to perform an intrasystem jump and reach Freiheit as soon as possible. My helm says we'll arrive a couple of hours before the bombardment starts, but I have no idea what to do about it. You need to get your brainiacs working on some kind of solution or tactic. You may have to consider sending all our forces just to tie the enemy up. We have to keep them from bombarding with impunity. Straker out."

Engels examined the tactical plot, noting the new contact that must be the destroyer heading their way. It was traveling anti-spinward in order to get ahead of Freiheit in its rising, accelerating orbit.

Freiheit itself traveled spinward with its southern end forward, rotating on its axis like a slow-motion bullet. Therefore the most accurate position from which to bombard it would be from directly ahead. That also put the south-pole sidespace engine front and center, completely vulnerable.

Could Freiheit be maneuvered? Engels wondered, perhaps to fly sideways to make it harder to hit the sidespace engines? Not within the time allotted. A spinning object of that mass was, in effect, an enormous gyroscope. It would resist any diversion or change of angle. Even if enough force were applied to alter its orientation, the strain would wreck the interior.

What about moving the engine out of the way, or shielding it somehow? Those were vague ideas, but she had no others, and the chrono was ticking. She ran a quick calculation and said to Lorton, "If we have to sortie to meet the destroyer, we'll need to launch within six hours, preferably sooner. Pass the word to Gurung that's all the time they have to get *Carson* in some kind of fighting shape. Tell Captain Gray to meet me back at the gig. Also, hunt down that attack squadron commander. Dmitri somebody–"

"Polzin," supplied Lorton.

"That's the one. And that freighter captain, Gibson. And Loco and Murdock. Tell them all to meet me at the southern docking port. We're holding a council of war."

＊ ＊ ＊

In the docking port's operations room, Engels swept her eyes around the table at those she'd ordered to attend.

"Will this take long?" said Murdock. "I have work to do."

"None of your work will matter if that destroyer wipes out our sidespace capability," Engels said.

Murdock flapped his hands in the air and waggled his head, shaking his stringy blonde hair to fall half over his face. "That's your problem. I need to go."

He began to stand, but Loco put a hand on his shoulder and shoved him back into his seat. "Sit your ass down. You're just worried Zaxby will show you up."

"Or implement one of his crazy ideas without my approval, and I'll have to waste double the time to undo everything," Murdock replied.

Engels rapped on the table with her knuckles. "We *need* crazy ideas right now—crazy ideas that will help and actually work. Maybe I should have asked Zaxby here instead of you, Murdock, if you're not up to it."

He crossed his arms petulantly and stared at Engels. "Fine. What do you want me to do?"

"I need you—or someone—to come up with a way to preserve our sidespace capability against a bombardment. If we can't, then all of our ships will have to sortie out to fight that destroyer, and I don't much like the odds. Without Straker's ship to help, it could to get really bloody. Our enemy is twice the size of *Carson* and is fresh and undamaged. I'll lead us into battle and we'll fight because that's the only way to get Freiheit out, but if I do, some of us will die. I don't feel like dying just yet. Come on, people, let's have some ideas."

"Can we move the southern sidespace engine? Or at least the main components?" asked Loco. "Restore it after we deal with this destroyer?"

"No," said Murdock. "We just got that damn thing repaired and it's jury-rigged to hell and back. If we tried to dismantle it, it might never work again. It might not even work now."

"And I presume we can't reorient Freiheit," said Engels. "Fly sideways?"

Murdock snorted. "Give me a week to ten days and I could, but that means taking the spin off. These civilians couldn't handle being weightless for that long. How would they cook food or use toilets? What would happen to the lake and all the fresh water? This thing is made to rotate. It's a habitat, not a ship."

"How about getting the laser defenses working?" said Loco.

"What laser defenses?" asked Murdock. "*Carson* wiped out the big beams in our original surprise attack when we took Freiheit. We don't have anything to replace them. Nothing heavy enough to shoot down railgun slugs, anyway."

"Could we deflect or block the projectiles?" asked Major Polzin.

Murdock's eyes blanked with thought. "Possible... possible... but with what? Any loose rock on Freiheit gets flung outward by our spin. We don't have time to capture an asteroid big enough to park it in the way as a shield."

"Could we cut something loose?" asked Loco. "Freiheit's two kilometers long. There has to be some chunk we could chop off and shove into the way."

"The outside's pretty smooth right now," Captain Gray said. Her dark eyes were piercing and serious. "All raised peaks and like projections were shaved down before the first trip through space."

"And besides," Murdock said, "anything we cut will weaken the structure itself. We're already at minimum spin for things to work properly—air circulation, liquid flows and so on. I mentioned the lake: that's a million tons of fresh water. If it isn't held in its bed by spin-gravity, it could unbalance us and tear us apart anyway. I'll say this again: *Freiheit isn't a warship.* It's fragile. It's not even designed to fly around this much. It could come apart under any severe strain."

Captain Gibson raised his hand slowly while staring at the table. "What about blocking with a ship?"

"Better," said Murdock. "Ships are designed to take a pummeling. They can be reinforced with structural and defensive fields and they can be maneuvered when an impact knocks them out of position."

"A freighter isn't designed for that," Gibson went on, still not meeting anyone's eyes, until he slowly lifted them toward Captain Gray.

"Oh, wait just a damn minute," said Gray. "*Carson's* already suffered enough. Now you want to turn her into a... a..." She sputtered to a halt.

"A shield. A hulk," said Engels gently. "Ellen, it makes sense. *Carson's* our largest warship. With full reinforcement, her hull and armor can stand multiple railgun strikes. A minimum crew can keep her in place to block any bombardment."

"I'd much rather sortie into battle with a full crew than stand there like some idiotic ring fighter taking a pummeling," Gray snapped.

"And if we do all sortie, and even one missile slips past us?" said Engels.

"Straker's going to be late to the party anyway. He can stay back and intercept it."

"His ship isn't made for missile defense. It has one laser and one missile tube, and no armor."

"Then we can set up a defense in depth! Create a gauntlet to kill any missiles. Come on, Carla, we're just talking tactics now. Don't make me sacrifice my ship."

Engels shook her head slowly. "Any defense in depth against missiles leaking through would reduce our attack. And if even one missile or one heavy railgun shot made it past us, it will all be for nothing."

Polzin stood. "Actually, Captains… With due respect, I believe we must take both paths." He nodded to Gray. "Captain Gray should play goalkeeper in *Carson*. The rest of us must sortie to engage the enemy."

"We can't beat that destroyer," said Engels.

"It's unlikely, but we *can* keep her off balance. We want to force her to deal with us instead of launching high-precision shots at the station. Bombarding Freiheit while under attack herself will be far less effective. At extreme range, she may not even be able to target the sidespace engine. She will have to move in closer, and that means she will have to fight us."

"How long will we have to keep this up, Frank?" asked Gray as she turned to Murdock. "How much time do we have to buy?"

Murdock squirmed. "From extreme engagement range? Two more days, plus. Call it fifty-six hours from now. And we'll only get one chance at transit. This habitat runs mostly on solar power. The farther out we go from the primary, the less we have. I'm keeping the batteries full, but attempting sidespace insertion will drain them, succeed or fail. So I can't push the button early. I have to be sure we're going to make it."

Engels turned to Gray. "Captain Gray, Major Polzin's right. We have to do both, whatever the cost. We'll sortie and keep the enemy busy, maybe so busy you won't even get hit. Straker will follow up and join the battle when he can. Maybe he will be able to sneak up on the destroyer and take it out if we give him the time. Meanwhile, you'll have to prep *Carson* for goalkeeper duty.

Murdock, I need you to pull some people off Freiheit and help Captain Gray turn *Carson* into a defensive monster."

"How am I supposed to do that?" he asked.

"You're the brainiac!" Engels replied. "You figure it out. Put Zaxby and his Ruxins on it. That will get them out of your greasy hair. Maybe one of his crazy ideas will do the trick." She clapped her hands. "Get working, everyone."

"What can I do?" said Gibson.

Engels considered. What was the freighter good for? Carrying things... or people. "How many civilians can you pack in for evacuation?"

"About six hundred, but only for three days. After that, environmental systems will be overwhelmed. Fewer aboard, longer time."

"I'll send the nav data you'll need to reach our hidden base. Figure out how many you can actually take given the time in transit. Work with Mayor Weinberg to prep an evacuation plan for children, nursing mothers and so on. Let her choose who goes. If worse comes to worst... you have to get them away. There are friendly Ruxins at the other end. They should give you asylum." Engels shrugged. "It's better than dying or getting enslaved by the Mutuality."

"I wish my crew and I could do more," said Gibson. "We're not warriors, though."

"We all have to play our parts. Yours is to save lives. I think we'll all feel better knowing our most vulnerable are out of harm's way. Dismissed." Engels grabbed Loco's elbow before he departed. "How's everything going here?"

Loco gave her a bleak look. "Could be better. The locals are scared shitless. There's lots of rumors. They also keep demanding we hang the rest of the Unmutual personnel. I've had to keep all of the Breaker infantry camped around the brig. That kid Karst wants to defect and join us, by the way. Can we trust him?"

Engels shrugged. "I don't know. He said he was being blackmailed to pilot the mechsuit, but he did attack our infantry. Probably killed several of them before Derek took him out."

Loco shrugged. "I'll handle things here. You go out and kill that destroyer. Do some of that fancy pilot shit you always brag about. Wish I could help, but me and my one functioning mechsuit are better on site, keeping order."

"Damn, Loco, you're sounding almost responsible for once in your life."

"Tell you what, Carly. I'll act more responsible if you act more fun. Deal?" He held out his hand.

"Deal." She reached for Loco's hand, and then retargeted to tweak his nose. "Gotcha."

A smile spread over his face. "You're learning. See you later, Carly-car."

"Get your ass out of here, Lieutenant Paloco."

"Aye aye, ma'am."

Engels watched him swagger off and felt her spirits lifted in spite of herself. Maybe there was more to the little clown than met the eye. They used to say at Academy that good leaders rose to the challenges they had to face. Perhaps Loco had simply never been challenged before.

Captain Gray broke that reverie by clearing her throat from somewhere behind. "Let's go, Carla. I have a lot of work to do and you're my ride."

Engels nodded and began to stride toward the docking port hangar. "Too bad nobody ever came up with some kind of personal teleportation, like on the showvids."

"Lots of fictional concepts have turned out to be impossible," said Gray as they walked. "No sensors from sidespace, no faster-than-light communications, no self-aware AI..."

Engels nodded. "And no force fields. At least, none that don't have to be conducted through a material, like armor."

"Maybe not all of it's impossible. The Ruxins came up with underspace ships when nobody else did."

"True. Maybe they'll think of something else, now that..." Engels caught herself again before she spoke more about operational details of the Starfish Nebula base. She had to remind herself that Ellen Gray might not be her ally forever.

"What?"

"Never mind. Classified."

They boarded the gig and soon returned to *Liberator*, *Carson* still attached. Gray immediately resumed work on repairing her ship.

A few minutes later, Zaxby comlinked in to ask that *Carson* dock with Freiheit, the better to work on fortifying her as a shield. Engels decided to detach *Liberator*. The idea of having no warship ready in space made her nervous.

With *Carson* docked and most of *Liberator*'s crew helping to repair her, Engels left the bridge in the care of a watch officer and forced herself to catch a couple hours of rack time.

She'd need to be sharp for the upcoming battle.

Chapter 42

Aboard Liberator, *preparing for battle.*

"Engels to Polzin," Engels comlinked when she returned to *Liberator*'s bridge.

"Polzin here."

"Major, we're less than an hour from sortie launch. I need you and your squadron to mount up."

"Understood. We'll join you shortly."

Next, she ordered Gurung and the absent crew to rejoin *Liberator*. To save time, she brought the ship in to dock and took them directly off. Fifteen minutes later she was back in space, ready to go.

Five minutes after, the dozen ships of the attack squadron rounded Freiheit from their docking at the northern port. The slim vessels resembled four-bladed arrowheads. If they were smaller, they might have been called fighters, but at longer than fifty meters and massing less than a hundred tons, they were actually the smallest ship where a pilot was needed. Any tinier craft were normally unmanned, short-range drones needing a mothership and a combination of remote and semi-AI control.

All twelve of the attack ships put together massed less than her corvette, which was two ship-classes smaller than the enemy destroyer. At best, they had a quarter of their opponent's combat power. Of course, the fact that she had a shipkiller missile launcher made *Liberator* a genuine threat to any ship—even though big missiles seldom reached their targets. Just forcing those targets to run from them, or to shoot the missiles down was plenty of leverage in the thick of battle.

That's what makes the Archer so dangerous, Engels mused. The ability to get a nuclear warhead inside a target's defensive suite was key. The trick, as always, was not in the concept, but in the execution.

Her comlink beeped with an incoming transmission. "Attack One here. Major Polzin, commanding First Attack Squadron, reports as ordered."

Engels set course and eased her throttles forward. "Spread out and follow me."

It would take more than five hours to reach the intercept position, which was only a guess at the destroyer's maximum likely range. In reality, the enemy could lob railgun bullets at any time, but the odds of hitting even a stationary target shrank to near zero beyond a certain distance.

And this guesstimated location was far too imprecise to vector Straker toward it in his ship. If there were to be any chance of *Revenge* making an underspace run, the destroyer would have to remain on course and not maneuver.

Engels had only a vague idea of how to accomplish this feat. The problem was, Straker was three hours' travel time behind her. That meant keeping the destroyer busy for three hours.

But as soon as Engels stopped harassing the enemy and let them cease their according evasive maneuvers, the destroyer would be free to lob shots at Freiheit. She had about four hours to play with the corvette's battle simulation to see if she could come up with a solution.

* * *

Four hours later, Engels brought Polzin and the rest of the attack squadron pilots into her comlink and recorded the discussion for repeat transmission back to Straker for his information. The lag back to him was down to less than ten minutes, but that still precluded true conversation.

"I've run a bunch of battle simulations," she said. "We're going to have to let them fire the first shot. Then we engage."

"Why?" asked Polzin.

"We don't really know how far away they intend to start shooting. We also don't know how accurate they are. It's to our advantage to let them come as close as possible, because every kilometer and every second brings *Revenge* nearer to arriving, and that's what's likely to win this battle."

"So we hang back."

"Yes, we wait until they feel they are close enough to take a shot. *Carson* can absorb at least one round, probably more like seven or eight, before she's wrecked."

"I don't like waiting," said Polzin. "We're *attack* ships, not sitting-on-our-asses ships."

"You'll do as I say. This is a chess match, not a brawl."

"Ah. Very well. We Russians understand chess."

She vaguely remembered the name from history classes. "Russians? What's a Russian? Any similarity to a Ruxin?"

"No. I am Russian. Russians are my ancestors. From Old Earth. Yours were likely Germanic, with a name like Engels. It means angel, something like that."

"Angel. I like that. Warrior angels have wings and swords."

Engels wondered what it might be like to have ancestors, some kind of tribe or ethnic group or family. The only equivalent she'd ever experienced was the camaraderie of Academy, and later the Fleet. She'd left all that behind now.

Now she had only the Breakers. She envied Polzin his Russians.

"So, we let them play the white pieces," continued Polzin.

"White pieces?"

"You said it was a chess match. White makes the first move."

"Ah." Engels smiled. "Yes. You're the pawns, I'm sorry to say, and I'm a bishop at best. Straker is a knight, able only to make short-range but off-center attacks. *Carson* is our rook, protecting our king, which is Freiheit."

"That would make the destroyer a queen, powerful and long-ranged."

"But unlike chess, one attack does not necessarily equal one kill. Except, perhaps, for our knight, or a shipkiller missile."

Polzin laughed. "That is true. The situation is complex. Yet the pawns must play their role."

"As must the bishop." Engels thought for a moment. "I wish I could talk to the enemy. Persuade them to run."

"They are Mutuality Fleet regulars, which means they are crewed by loyalists and by Hok. They will not turn."

Engels' ears pricked up. "Are there ships *not* crewed by Hok and regulars?"

"Yes. Local defense forces are not as fanatical. Generally speaking, the smaller and shorter-ranged the ship, the less they are true believers. The Committee wisely ensures its capital units remain the most loyal. All ships have Hok, but Hok follow orders of the political officers first, the line officers second."

"Interesting." She rubbed her neck. "Back to tactics. We let them take one shot at Freiheit. We then advance to our long range, firing at them while using evasive maneuvers. Remember, our goal is to buy time. Do not press the attack. When Straker gets within coordination range, I'll discuss our timing with him and we'll back off, try to get them to feel safe."

"And then Captain Straker does... what?"

Engels realized that Polzin didn't know much about the technology. Gray had guessed, but had pledged not to tell anyone. "That's classified," she said. "If it works, you'll see for yourself. If not, it won't matter."

Polzin's face turned sour. "Then we are pawns indeed."

"Do you want to defect to the Breakers? If so, I'll brief you."

"I will follow Captain Gray's lead. Keep your secrets. I hope they do not kill us."

"I'll tell you whatever you need to know."

"That's what all tyrants say."

"And military commanders once the operation starts. Fall back now. Let *Liberator* take the lead. Engels out." Damn these argumentative Unmutuals. Can't they see we are on the same side?

At least for now.

"Lorton, send a recording of that conversation back to Straker and Gray, along with updated sensor data." She drummed her fingers on the arm of her padded pilot's chair. "Then sound battle stations. Everyone suit up and prep for damage control. It won't be long now."

"Aye aye, ma'am."

Engels retrieved her suit from the nearby cubbyhole and drew it on, leaving her faceplate open and plugging in the integrated comlink. Wireless was standard, but so was triple redundancy. Then she plugged in her brainlink. It was one advantage the Hundred Worlds had over others, and fortunately this was a captured Hundred Worlds ship. However, as she was piloting a crewed vessel, the link did not immerse her like it did with a single-pilot craft. It merely improved her performance.

Chief Gurung reported the ship ready. Engels watched as the chrono and the integrated tactical plot showed the destroyer reach potential firing position. A close examination of the enemy revealed all her weapons run—out and ready.

"What's she aiming her big railgun at?" asked Engels.

"At Freiheit, ma'am. But her beams are locked on us. We are within extreme range."

"Ops, give me ten percent reinforcement to the forward armor. Raise the percentage as we approach, your judgment."

"Aye aye, ma'am."

"Is she reinforcing her armor?" Engels asked.

"Not yet, ma'am," said Lorton.

"Weapons, can we tickle her with lasers yet?"

"Not at this range."

"How about our railgun?"

"Within range, but hit probability well below point-one percent, assuming they evade."

Engels nodded. "We *want* to make them evade, when the time comes. Keep them locked in our sights."

"Aye aye, ma'am."

Engels wished she could fire, but her simulations had showed it was best to let the enemy fire first. It's a chess match, not a slugfest, she reminded herself. She raised her impeller braking, reducing the rate of closure with the enemy. Soon, she would come to relative rest and actually begin to back up as the destroyer came onward. Polzin would follow her maneuvers.

More than half an hour she waited, aware that every moment brought Straker closer in *Revenge* and reduced the time available for bombardment. But it also meant the enemy would gain in accuracy. Presumably that's what they were waiting for: some threshold of precision to fire.

"Energy surge. Railgun firing," said Lorton. "Target is Freiheit."

"Notify Captain Gray of incoming in case they missed it. Add sensor data and send." Of course, the transmission would beat the railgun bullet by minutes at this range, allowing Gray time to prepare.

"They are recharging for another railgun shot."

"Weapons, you are free to engage."

"Firing our railgun."

Liberator shuddered and the lights dimmed with the power drain from her capital weapon. As with her enemy, the alloy penetrator was accelerated down the centerline of the ship and spat out of her nose with brutal velocity.

In response, the destroyer began rolling in a randomized evasive pattern, impossible to predict. Engels expected that. Nobody took one in the face if they could help it. However, the enemy's combination of movement and extra energy for reinforcement would degrade both her accuracy and her recharge time.

Engels input a random evasion pattern of her own and initiated it at low level, reducing the chance of a lucky hit on *Liberator*.

An alarm's *wheep-wheep* prompted Lorton to report, "They're targeting us with the railgun."

"As expected. Maximum forward reinforcement to coincide with potential impact," Engels snapped, raising the rate of evasive maneuvers instinctively. She was one of two snipers taking pot shots at each other. Unfortunately, though, she had a smaller gun and thinner armor. The enemy could take many hits from her weapon; her own ship, only a couple.

"Incoming." The four on the bridge held their breaths. "No impact."

"Excellent."

Her comlink pinged in her ear. "Polzin to Engels."

"Engels."

"When do you want to advance the pawns?"

"Don't stretch the metaphor. We want to buy time. We'll keep up this dance as long as we can. Chess game, remember?"

"Understood. Polzin out."

Attack pilots. She knew the type, hyper-aggressive and prone to derring-do. She'd unleash them when the time came, but not until.

"Enemy accelerating toward us, flank speed."

"Shit." Engels spun the corvette around and lit her fusion engine, waggling her joysticks slightly to create random jinking. "Wish this baby was equipped with stealth mines. I'd drop a few in our wake."

Polzin came back on the comlink. "Captain Engels, are you sure you don't want some support?"

"No! Stay back. I can handle this. If we get hit bad, you can come in hot and we'll try to slip a shipkiller missile into the mix."

"As you wish, *Kapitana*."

"At least we're faster than they are," she muttered. She examined her board, noting the enemy's speed and rate of acceleration. "I'm going to spin us around again. Weapons, be ready to target and fire."

"Weapons ready, ma'am."

Engels dropped acceleration to zero and whipped the corvette around in place. Now she flew tail-first through space, nose pointed backward. "Fire when you have a lock."

"Firing."

She didn't wait to see the result, spinning the ship again through one hundred eighty degrees and accelerating to stay ahead of the enemy, out of effective laser range.

"No impact."

"No surprise," she said. "Just as long as we keep them busy."

This dance continued for more than an hour. In that time, the destroyer fired at least forty shots, some aimed at *Liberator*, others aimed at Freiheit.

None hit *Liberator*. This was normal for warfare in open space. With nothing to defend, nothing to pin anyone in place, faster ships could remain at extreme range as long as they wished, and *Liberator*, being smaller, was quicker.

Of those shots fired at Freiheit, only four had struck the asteroid, and only one had come close enough to the sidespace engine to need intercepting by *Carson*'s reinforced hull.

But the destroyer was now only five hours from Freiheit. The hab was the anchor of this battle. Fortunately, *Revenge* was only an hour away from engagement.

Engels wondered what the enemy thought of the weird ship approaching, assuming they even spotted *Revenge*. She wasn't sure how much time they were spending in underspace.

Instead of a slim cylinder like most warships, the ship looked more like an orbital station, a donut with a baton thrust through its center, tentacles on each end. Would they have its design in their database? Would they think to turn on their underspace detectors? As a Marksman pilot, she'd never spent a lot of time on Fleet ship operations.

Or would they even notice Straker's ship? *Revenge* had long since ceased using her fusion engines, cruising on impellers only. Impellers were far more efficient, less wasteful of fuel and power, and were impossible to detect at any range. Perhaps the destroyer had lost track of Revenge.

"Lorton, any word from Freiheit or Gray?"

"Last update says they are holding. One shot hit *Carson*, but they blocked any damage to the sidespace engine."

Engels examined her tactical display. "And is *Revenge*'s position confirmed, or only predicted?"

Lorton tapped his board. "Predicted, ma'am. I don't have anything on passives, and I didn't want to aim an active sensor at *Revenge* for fear of highlighting her."

"Good decision. So we actually have no idea where she is?"

"Only a rough estimate. We know they're heading for an intercept in about an hour."

Engels rubbed her eyes. "Then we'll have to keep this up for that long."

* * *

"Insert the ship," Straker ordered again.

This was the sixth time he'd ordered *Revenge* dipped into underspace on the way to the intercept. Every time he did so, he wondered whether he would set off some kind of detector on the destroyer. But he was balancing that unknown and unpredictable possibility with the much stronger probability of being tracked by sensors in normal space.

He wished he could coordinate with Engels, but given the fact that *Revenge*'s course lined her up with both *Liberator* and the destroyer, any transmission, even a laser comlink, might be detected by the enemy, who would no doubt be trying to localize that odd contact if they detected it. They had to still be wondering about the destruction of their sister ship.

The longer he kept them in the dark, the better.

This would be the next-to-last disappearing act before the actual attack. Although the destroyer was evading with random slight heading changes, she remained on a consistent general course for Freiheit. Straker had to pop up from underspace early enough to get a good reading on the enemy and update his data, but late enough to give the enemy minimum warning, and as little time to think as possible.

Straker also had to make one hundred percent sure he emerged ahead of his target, because at the speeds they were approaching each other, he would get only one pass to drop float mines. Reversing course to catch it from behind would be futile.

In fact, the Ruxin ship was a piece of shit as a warship design. She wasn't slim to present the smallest target to the enemy. She wasn't maneuverable for her size. She wasn't armored. She had one laser and one missile tube for a conventional fight, barely enough to intimidate a noncombatant. She couldn't even reinforce her nonexistent armor. All her excess power and mass went for underspace engines and the field to protect herself from the deep freeze.

She was a one-trick pony. Well today, Straker was going to see if her one trick was good enough. He hoped Engels could capitalize on his attack.

Slowly, so slowly, the positions of *Revenge* and the destroyer approached each other. In underspace, *Revenge* flew past *Liberator* and the attack squadron, possibly passing literally through one of the ships, or perhaps "below" was a better term. He'd never know for sure.

Finally, the time came. "Emerge."

"Emerging."

"Update our sensor data." Really, there was no need for Straker to give the order; he'd gone over this sequence a dozen times in the past hour. His officers were following a meticulously timed plan.

"Updating... Completed."

"Insert again! Helm, put us in their path!"

They'd come out off-center, inevitable after almost an hour in underspace with only educated guesses for positioning.

"Inserting."

"Maneuvering," said the octopoid at helm.

As *Revenge* slid again into the safety of underspace, Straker's eyes roamed hungrily over the tactical display. It had updated to a much larger scale, and the destroyer seemed to charge toward him like a mechsuiter at a dead run. He imagined himself a tank commander, dug into a hull-down position, with only one shot at taking down a Foehammer. That's how he felt.

The icon that represented the hidden ship moved directly into the destroyer's path, just in time. Straker hoped Engels had backed off in her harassment in order to lull the enemy into believing evasive maneuvers were unnecessary.

"Deploy float mines."

"Mine one away," said the weapons officer.

"Accelerating," the helm reported. The icon representing *Revenge* leapt toward the enemy, as if ramming.

"Mine two away." A pause. "Mine three away."

Then the two icons merged.

The ship shook with the spillover from the fusion explosions. Water misted up from the sludge in which Straker stood as the vibration came through his feet and rattled his teeth. Lights flickered and went out.

"Damage from spillover. We have lost the underspace engine. Involuntary emergence," said the operations officer.

"Doesn't matter," said Straker, eyes on the displays. "Sensors, as soon as we're up, go active. Get me an update! And get me a comlink to *Liberator*!"

The main visiplate fuzzed and dimmed, then brightened and changed as the computer processed the updated sensor data. Behind him, Straker could see the destroyer, apparently cruising serenely onward.

"Helm, all reverse flank. Chase that destroyer with every erg we have."

"Aye aye, sir." The ship thrummed and water sloshed over to one side as acceleration leaked through overtasked compensators.

"What damage did we do? I need a detailed scan of that ship," Straker snapped.

"Scanning. Details will take several minutes."

"Do the best you can. Give me an optical in the meantime."

"I will make the attempt," said his sensors officer.

A shaky, receding image appeared on the screen. There was no way to tell the state of the enemy.

"Where's my damned comlink?" Straker demanded.

Chapter 43

Battling the Mutuality destroyer.

"Captain Straker on the comlink," Lorton said to Engels.

"Tell him we're busy," she snapped as she shoved the corvette's throttles forward. "Tell him he damaged the destroyer, but she's not out, and we have to hit her while she's trying to recover from the blasts."

"I heard you, Carla," Straker said, his image appearing on a small auxiliary screen. His voice was full of frustration and concern. "Our underspace engine is down. We're reversing course, but it will take a while to get back to the battle."

"Thanks, Derek. You shook them, but none of the mines came close enough to crack their armor. If we're going to finish them off, we have to attack now."

"Keep the comlink open, please," Straker replied. "I can't stand not to…"

"To see me die?" She spread her lips in a wolfish grin. "Not gonna happen today. Don't worry about me, Derek. This isn't like with *Carson*, shooting at people we know. This is war, they're the enemy, and I'm not pulling any punches. Now shut up and let me do my job."

"Aye aye, Captain Carla. Good hunting."

The corvette rumbled and shook with flank acceleration, the fusion engine at the rear pushed to the redline and the impeller gulping power. Her best chance right now was to close in to short range as quickly as possible and kick the Mutuality destroyer while she was down.

Hands white-knuckled on the controls, Engels kept one eye on the tactical plot and the other on her forward view. She curved the course of the corvette slightly outward and then inward to stay off the destroyer's centerline, away from a sudden railgun strike. "Are they maneuvering?"

"No, ma'am. They seem to be on a ballistic course only."

She lined up her own centerline reticle and stabilized for a full second. "Railgun: lock, track and fire."

"Locked," the gunner called back. "Tracking and leading… solution computed, firing."

The corvette bucked with the powerful kick of the projectile launch.

"Laser range?" Engels asked.

"Long, but feasible."

"Begin engagement, distributed fire."

Distributed fire, rather than concentrated fire, would pound a steady barrage of shots against the destroyer. She wanted to keep them off balance and in pain. "Pass this to Major Polzin: attack the queen."

"Passed. Looks like the attack squadron is already on its way." Lorton made the cluster of icons behind the corvette flash. Engels could see they'd begun accelerating as well, and were already overtaking her in their fast craft.

"We are taking beam fire," said Lorton. "One heavy laser in action—now two."

"Reinforce forward armor."

"Already at maximum," ops said. She could hear the nervous twitch in the voice. "We're depleting our reserves. Down to forty percent. At this rate we'll be out of battery power in eight minutes."

Engels considered. Battery power was the only way to keep reinforcement up and weapons firing at the same time. No ship ever had all the energy it needed for every system.

"Reduce rate of laser fire to half for now." She also backed off a bit on the impeller, letting the fusion engine carry the load. "Maintain railgun fire."

The weapons officer spoke up. "Our railgun salvo impact in three… two… one…" The destroyer's image showed a brief flare as the heavy duralloy bullet struck armor near the nose. "Hit on her prow—no discernible effect."

"Dammit… They must still have reinforcement. Continue firing."

The tactical plot showed the attack squadron racing ahead and beginning to fire with their lasers—small by capital ship standards, mere pinpricks.

When the numbers lined up properly, Engels said, "Launch our missile."

"Shipkiller launching."

The big rocket ejected from the corvette's tube and accelerated away at phenomenal speed. With nothing organic inside, it could pull high Gs and its computer would do its machine-minded best to merge with its target and explode. It rapidly began to overtake the attack squadron.

"One attack ship casualty, complete destruction," said Lorton. "It... that must have been a railgun shot meant for us."

Engels shook her head, imagining the hammer blow of the fast-moving projectile tearing apart the attack craft like a rifle bullet through a sparrow. "That's bad news. It means their railgun is still up. If we were sure it was down, we could pull back and pound her. Now we have to make it a knife fight."

"Heavy laser strike on our prow. They're targeting our railgun port."

"Not the shipkiller?"

"Negative. Shipkiller is closing. Passing attack ships now."

"Full laser fire!" Engels gripped her armrests. "Come on, baby..."

On the screen, the destroyer suddenly turned broadside. Spears of light blazed. "Missile destroyed," Lorton confirmed. "Multiple point-defense lasers took it out."

"Yeah, but now you're off centerline, you bitch," Engels snarled. "Pass to attack ships: target their heavy lasers, and then try to rake her nose and tail. Take out her railgun and engines. Weapons, concentrate on her stern until she turns. Ops, reduce forward shielding to twenty percent." With the enemy railgun pointing away from them, the reinforcement wasn't as critical.

"Looks like they've lost at least one fusion engine," Engels remarked. "Otherwise, why aren't they maneuvering faster?"

"Don't know, ma'am," Lorton said.

She hadn't really expected an answer to her rhetorical question. Thirty seconds of relative calm passed, then new contacts appeared.

"Missile launch," Lorton announced. "Correction: I'm seeing multiple missile launches. Four launches."

"Targets?" Engels asked, her heart sinking.

"One on the attack squadron, three on us."

"Shift fire to the ones targeting us," she said without feeling guilty about it. Polzin had eleven lasers to kill only one missile. Engels, on the other hand, had to fend off three missiles with only six lasers.

She considered turning around to extend the range again, but there was no way to outrun the missiles. She was too deep into the destroyer's engagement envelope. She might as well continue to accelerate and evade.

"Vectoring spinward and rolling," she said. That would unmask all of her lasers and force the missiles to turn more and more sharply—to try to predict where *Liberator* would be, and intercept.

Once the predictive software of the three guided weapons had pointed themselves firmly ahead of her, trying to cut her off, she turned the corvette hard into them, then behind them. "Vectoring anti-spinward."

The missiles now had to turn twice as sharply back, in order to try to aim themselves at the new location they expected her to be.

If the opposing missile controllers were on the ball, they could override the semi-AI guidance and use their own analysis to predict her actions better than any machine. However, she was hoping the enemy had their hands full with repairs, and that they had fired the missile barrage in hopes of buying time and keeping their enemies at bay.

Once the missiles had found their new course, she whipsawed them again. This time, they simply could not turn fast enough and she was able to slip past them.

The closest one detonated. "Heat surge in fusion plenum," ops declared.

"Reducing burn," she replied. EMP from the nuclear detonation had sent a thermal pulse up her tailpipe, and with her fusion engine already running at maximum, she couldn't risk overheating.

The other two missiles swept by her and turned for Freiheit.

"Crap," she said. "Message *Carson* that they have two shipkiller leakers inbound."

"Transmission sent."

Engels couldn't worry about those now. She had a much larger fish to fry.

Nine icons still showed from Polzin's original twelve. The destroyer must have taken two more of them out. She lined up *Liberator* again on the enemy, aiming at her nose, which was swinging forward again. "Railgun: lock and fire."

"Firing."

The range had closed now to medium, approaching short, and the alloy penetrator slammed into the destroyer's forward quarter, tearing off a chunk of the hull and creating a spray of debris.

"Yes!" she cried. As she'd guessed, they couldn't reinforce everywhere now that the narrow nose wasn't turned directly toward *Liberator*.

"More missile launches," said Lorton.

Engels acknowledged. "They know they're in a fight to the death, so they're dumping their whole load. Weapons, fire our shipkiller." She had one tube and three missiles total. This was the second launch. "Use it defensively. Intercept theirs. It's still a chess match."

Again, three enemy missiles headed for her, one for the attack squadron. This time, the small ships seemed ready. They shot theirs down right away.

Instead of vectoring away and dragging the missiles this time, Engels remained steady on course directly at the enemy. This caused all the guided rockets to line up. When her weapons officer detonated *Liberator*'s missile, the oncoming warheads flew straight into the fireball, and the remnants of the explosion covered her approach.

"We've silenced one heavy laser," said Polzin. "I'm down to eight effectives."

"Keep hitting them hard, Major. Don't let up!"

As the destroyer loomed larger and larger, Engels braked with her impeller. She had no shot at the railgun, as the enemy nose was now turned away. "Line up our railgun on one of those damned missile tubes. Fire railgun," she said.

"Firing... Impact. Missile tube destroyed."

The destroyer's remaining heavy laser jolted the corvette's nose, and lights flickered.

"Batteries empty," ops called out. "I need prioritization, ma'am."

Engels shut down her impeller. That would leave more power for weapons. "Full lasers, then railgun capacitor. Only reinforce when we have excess. Shut down life support. Our suits will be enough for now."

Air circulation stopped. It wouldn't be long before the temperature dropped, but the battle would be over by the time it became critical—she hoped.

"Shift lasers to concentrated fire. Target their missile tubes, then their lasers, one by one."

In rapid succession, *Liberator*'s six medium lasers obliterated the enemy's missile launchers. They might not have any weapons left to fire anyway, but the shipkillers were the biggest potential threat.

Engels continued to slow her ship as she approached to point-blank range, aiming her railgun but not firing yet. "Give me a wideband transmission in the clear, all standard freqs."

"Transmission open. Comlink not established."

"Well, we'll see if they're listening." Engels cleared her throat. "*Liberator* to Mutuality ship. This is Captain Carla Engels. Surrender now. Continue to fight and we will dismantle you piece by piece."

Nothing but static returned.

"Continue firing. Keep trying to smash her railgun."

"Firing."

Suddenly the destroyer seemed to shake herself like a fish, and her fusion engines flared at full, apparently all back in action. She swung in a tight circle to point directly away from *Liberator*—and incidentally toward Straker's *Revenge*.

"They're running," Engels said.

"It's not over," said Straker. "Keep hammering them. If we let them get distance now, they can come back and start all over again with the same long-range advantages."

"Understood. We'll keep harrying them," said Engels.

The attack ships harassed the fleeing destroyer, buzzing around like angry hornets. It fought back with point-defense lasers, knocking out another of its tormenters. Engels almost called them off, but as Straker had intuited, now was not the time to give the enemy a rest. Two days remained before Freiheit made its jump to sidespace. Letting the destroyer get away to recover would simply reset the battle situation, giving the advantage back to the bigger ship. She couldn't assume they would run clear to flatspace and depart.

Engels pushed the corvette closer and closer, up and to the outward side of the destroyer to get a firing angle past the hard flare of the fusion engine, trying to herd her enemy toward Straker. This battle was balanced on a knife-edge, and she had to use every resource she had, even if it put the man she loved directly in death's path. She knew instinctively that if she tried to protect him at the expense of winning, he might never forgive her.

✳ ✳ ✳

Straker jabbed his fist repeatedly against the nearest handrail, causing himself enough pain to distract from the waiting, waiting, *waiting*. He bit his tongue listening to Engels's open comlink, not interfering with her concentration. He cheered when the destroyer turned to run, knowing the battle was half won. Pride flared in his chest as he watched her throw her corvette at the enemy.

"We have achieved negative extension rate," his helm officer said.

"What? Say that in Earthan."

"I did, sir."

"Then say it more simply. I may be a War Male, but space combat isn't my specialty."

"The destroyer has turned toward us. Combined with our reverse acceleration, we're now closing on the enemy instead of extending away from them."

Straker took another look at the tactical plot and understood. *Revenge* had been clawing to get back to the battle. Now the battle was accelerating toward *Revenge*.

"Any chance of getting underspace back?"

"No, sir," said the ops officer. "The underspace engine will need major repairs."

Straker racked his brain. He had one laser and one missile that had been damaged, and may or may not work. The float mines were worse than useless; without the ability to vanish, deploying them would destroy his own ship.

Unless...

"Can we drop float mines in normal space?"

"Yes, but we would destroy ourselves, sir."

"That might be our final option, but let's not get suicidal just yet. Can we set them for delayed detonation?"

"Yes, sir…" said the weapons officer.

"How about proximity fuses?"

"Yes, they have proximity fuses if you prefer."

Straker ordered, "Helm, keep us directly in the path of the enemy. I want her to run right over the top of us, close as possible."

"Aye aye, sir. I must point out, though, that one railgun strike will wreck us. As will a collision."

"I know. Evade as much as possible while keeping us in their general path. We have to risk it. I'm betting that they're too busy fighting and too low on power to use their railgun."

The destroyer's icon began flashing red. "Unfortunately, sir, your supposition is incorrect. They have fired their railgun," said the sensors officer.

"Evade!"

"I have done so, sir," the helm officer said with the appearance of calm. "In fact, by the time you spoke, the projectile had already missed us. I took the liberty of evading before your order. I hope the War Male is not displeased."

"Hell no, I'm not displeased," Straker said, slapping his helm-squid on the back—or at least on the part of his torso that was facing away from the console. He wasn't sure Ruxins really had fronts or backs, considering they had eyes and arms in all directions.

The helm officer shrank from him. "Why are you striking me, sir?"

"It's… it's a human gesture of comradeship and approval."

"Ah. Very well." The Ruxin slapped Straker's chest with a tentacle.

"No, not… never mind. You'll get it." Straker refocused his attention on the tactical plot, trying to estimate when to make his play. "Ready float mine deployment. How many do we have left in inventory?"

"Seven."

"Use six, keep one in reserve. Set them to proximity fuse, with a timed activation after we have moved out of range. Drop them every ten seconds once we're approximately two minutes from crossing paths with the destroyer. Weapons, choose the exact times to drop based on our relative ship courses. Work with the helm to plant them directly in the enemy's path."

"Aye aye, sir." The Ruxins began chattering in their own tongue.

When the destroyer and the hidden ship were two minutes apart the weapons officer began deploying them as ordered.

Because the *Revenge* was still accelerating directly toward the enemy, the mines fell back to her stern, but continued on a ballistic course in her wake. Ten seconds separation should eliminate the possibility of fratricide and give each a chance to detonate when its proximity fuse detected the destroyer… assuming they didn't see the mines.

Straker had one more trick up his sleeve. "Weapons, aim our laser at them, wide beam, continuous fire."

"That will do no damage, sir."

"I don't care about damage. I want to screw up their sensors."

"You wish to reduce their ability to detect our mines?"

"Of course. Get with the program."

"Not understood."

Straker sighed. "I mean do it *now!*"

"I am already doing it, sir. The fact that I am conversing with you doesn't preclude my carrying out your orders. I am Ruxin, after all."

"You sure are." Straker waited until the intercept chrono hit forty seconds. "Prepare to launch missile."

"Missile ready."

At thirty seconds, he gave the order. "Launch!"

"Missile away. Running true, no malfunction."

"Open secure broadcast comlink to all friendly ships."

"Secure broadcast comlink open."

"Straker to all ships. Break off now! I have laid mines in the enemy's path and have launched a shipkiller missile. Move to the side and get out of the way!"

The comlink channel burbled as their replies stepped on each other. Straker might have given more warning, but he couldn't risk letting up the pressure on the destroyer, or by their actions, giving anything away. The enemy had to remain distracted and miss the threats in their ship's path.

The missile failed to detonate—perhaps because of a malfunction, perhaps because it had been plucked out of space by a point-defense laser—and the intercept chrono dropped to single digits. Straker held his breath as it reached zero. If the unlikely happened and the two ships crashed head-on despite the vastness of space, he'd never know it. The Archer would be obliterated, and the destroyer would probably be crippled.

The two icons merged on the tactical plot, and then separated with no collision. Those of the corvette and the attack ships passed by the *Revenge*, well outside the line of travel. The six pips representing the float mines pulsed ominously, and Straker held another breath, waiting, waiting…

The destroyer's icon met a mine, which disappeared. "Give me a tight optical, maximum magnification!" Straker barked.

"On screen."

The screen cleared to show the destroyer still traveling, her fusion engine flaring without letup.

"Must not have been close enough," he muttered.

"That appears to be the case," said the weapons officer. "The disadvantage of proximity fusing is, detonation is only triggered when the target ceases approaching and begins moving away. This reduces the impact of the blast."

Straker rounded on the weapons officer. "Why didn't you tell me that?"

"You're the War Male. I'm following your orders."

"Dammit! Can you command-detonate the mines?"

"Yes."

Holding a tight leash on his temper, Straker said, "Then do so, as effectively as possible. Don't forget to take transmission lag into account."

"Of course not, sir." The weapons officer skimmed two tentacles over his console. "Mines two and three command-detonated."

The optical view whited out again, and when the destroyer was again visible, it appeared crumpled, bent in the center.

"Is she still on course toward more mines?"

"No, sir. The explosion diverted her path."

"Save the mines, then," said Straker. "Shut them down. We'll recover them later. Comlink to *Liberator*."

"Comlink remains open."

"Carla, you there?"

"I'm here, Derek."

"I think we got them. We're shutting down the mines. You're cleared to approach and see if there are any survivors. Don't..."

The optical view flared yet again with a large fusion explosion.

"I thought I said to shut down all the mines!"

"That was not a mine, sir," said the weapons officer. "That was an internal detonation. It appears the enemy triggered a fusion warhead inside their own ship."

"Damn fanatics. What's wrong with these people?" Straker stared for a moment at the spreading debris, somehow feeling cheated by his prey. He deliberately reminded himself of the larger issues, and the fact that they'd won.

"All right. We did it... Stand down everyone. Let's go home."

"Home?" asked Engels.

Straker took a deep breath, sighing with relief. "Freiheit. That's home now."

Chapter 44

Aboard Freiheit.

As he walked along a paved path from the mechsuit factory toward the Base Control Center, Straker imagined the gray of sidespace surrounding Freiheit and he shivered. For some reason the asteroid, as large as it was, felt more vulnerable to the oddity of the alternate dimension, as if the void were trying to break in and devour everyone. Maybe it was because there was so much space inside Freiheit, without the nearby walls of a ship or the cocoon of a mechsuit cockpit to swaddle him.

Private Redwolf walked behind Straker at a few paces' distance. Heiser had insisted he keep a bodyguard nearby at all times in case of spies or assassins. Anyone could be a sleeper agent. Straker thought it unlikely, but he accepted his spear's judgment for now.

He lifted his hand to greet or salute people—*his* people, he reminded himself—as he passed by them. They walked from place to place or worked the fields or drove ground vehicles stacked with goods and parts, working hard. The repairs were still ongoing, of course, as the community transited toward the refuge of the Starfish Nebula.

Straker was glad his fight, this campaign, was over for the moment, like an R&R break before the next inevitable battle. Freiheit was no Shangri-La, but despite its flaws he found it much more satisfying than the fantasy planet, much more real.

There was no parade of plastic women throwing themselves at the warriors here, but with vibrant society composed of two thousand souls, he thought most of his troops would eventually join the community rather than just partying between battles. He might not have an instinct for people, but he

knew Old Earth history—or as much as the Hundred Worlds had bothered
to preserve—and he knew a free society had to be founded on lasting values:
integrity, stability, hard work, family.

Too bad the Unmutuals that had fought alongside them had left. Straker
had thought of them as the "good ones."   Captain Gray had done her
part—*Carson* had blocked the one shot that would have destroyed a sidespace
engine—and so Straker had honored Engels' promise to let her go back to
DeChang, along with her crew.

Gray had taken Polzin and his surviving attack ship pilots aboard *Carson*,
but the slim craft themselves were now parked inside Freiheit's northern dock
hangar, for they had no sidespace capability.

Straker had thanked the Unmutual Fleet crew for their efforts and their
sacrifices. In other circumstances, Gray and Polzin would make excellent
comrades-in-arms, even friends. He hoped they could force DeChang to purge
the Unmutuals of their sickness and corruption. Nobody expected military
people to be saints, but what Ramirez had allowed was beyond the pale.

Speaking of Ramirez... he still wondered about her fate. It had probably
been her, masquerading as "Nassimi" on that shuttle, but despite sensor sweeps
and open transmissions, the tiny craft hadn't been located. Maybe she'd hidden,
correctly assuming Straker's justice would fall on her like the stadium had fallen
on him and Loco at the battle for Corinth. Maybe she'd try to make it to the
ruins of Aynor Base and survive there until pickup.

"Sir, sir... Captain Straker!" Karst, now wearing a Breakers uniform coverall and corporal's stripes, ran up and saluted. "May I speak with you?"

"Sure, Corp. What's on your mind?" Straker didn't stop walking, and Karst
fell in besides him.

"My girl, sir. Cynthia Lamancha. She's gone."

Straker raised an eyebrow. "Ran off on you? I'm sorry, but sometimes..."

"No, no, sir. I mean, she's vanished. Nobody can find her. Nobody's seen
her since Yates had a knife to her throat. I've spent the last two days trying to
find her, or maybe her..." He gulped.

Straker nodded in sympathy. "Her body?"

"Yes, sir, but there's nothing. I didn't want to bother you until I'd checked
all the tunnels and hiding places."

"And have you?"

"Lieutenant Paloco says the troops have searched everywhere for stragglers. They found a few Unmutuals hiding out, and a pile of bodies of murder victims, but…"

"No Cynthia. I'm sorry, Corporal. Is there something more I can do?"

"Maybe, sir. I heard about that shuttle that Ramirez got away on."

Straker raised an eyebrow and looked at Karst sidelong. "That's not been established."

"I listened to the audio. It sounded like Ramirez. She said she had civilians aboard. I bet she has Cynthia."

Straker stopped and stepped off the path, getting out of the way of the bustling traffic. "That's possible, I guess. But we're already in sidespace. Even if I wanted to, I couldn't send anyone back until we reach our destination. That would be a risky long-shot anyway."

Karst's face became a study in controlled desperation. "I know that, sir, but I ask you: how would you feel if it was Lieutenant Engels? I bet you'd never rest until you found her."

Straker looked away. The kid was right. He'd move mountains to find the woman he loved, but there were two thousand people depending on him. That was the problem with being the boss: suddenly you found yourself with less freedom, not more, despite the power and authority.

"Okay, what do you want to do about it?" Straker said. "Stick to what's possible."

"I don't know, sir. Some kind of search. It would be good for everyone to get her back, and any other civilians with her. Show the people you care."

"You trying to blow smoke up my ass, Corporal?"

Karst straightened to attention. "No, sir! But wouldn't you like to put Ramirez on trial too?"

Straker growled. The kid was right again. There was good reason to give it a try. "I'll consider it once we get to where we're going, but no promises. There are a hundred other things to do first."

"And I want to go along on the search, sir."

"If it happens, you'll go. Happy?"

"Yes, sir!"

"Get back to your duties then. Dismissed."

Karst saluted, grinning, and bolted away double-time.

Straker continued walking. When he reached the Base Control Center, he found Murdock there as he usually was, sixteen hours a day. He might even spend more time there than that... he probably had a bunk somewhere within the complex. The man was the ultimate techie, never happier than when playing with his machines.

"How's the sidespace system?"

Murdock ran his hand through his stringy hair. "Lucky that once we're underway, it's easy to stay in and travel. I've got a lot of fluctuations and had to make so many repairs I'm amazed we made it into sidespace at all. When we transit out, we won't be going anywhere for a while. Not without a complete rebuild."

Straker slapped Murdock's back, rocking the skinny man. "I hope we won't be going anywhere at all in Freiheit. How's the power problem coming?"

"I've rigged up all available sources," Murdock said, "such as our parked ships' reactors, but we really need something a lot bigger. Preferably two or three somethings, in case one has to be taken off line."

"When we arrive, I'll get the Ruxins to provide reactors. Their population numbers in the millions, and their habitat is a hundred times this size. They're expanding to other asteroids, building habs. I think you're going to have a lot of fun."

"With Ruxins?" Murdock asked in dismay. "They're all a pain in the ass."

"They're brainiacs like you," Straker insisted. "Find a way to get along with them, because you'll be seeing a lot of them."

Murdock looked bleak. "Hoo, boy... I'll try."

Abruptly, an aroma drifted to Straker's nose. Perfume? Not something he often smelled since leaving the Hundred Worlds.

"Frankie, aren't you done working? You like those machines better than you like me!"

Straker turned to see Tachina, Lazarus' former concubine, sashay over to Murdock from the doorway. She wrapped herself around him like an anaconda and pressed her plump lips to his cheek.

Murdock blushed and said, "Later, honey. I'm finishing up with Captain Straker just now."

Tachina turned her artfully made-up face toward Straker. "Oh, hello, Captain. I didn't see you standing there."

Straker nodded stiffly. "Good to see you making friends, Miss Tachina."

Redwolf chuckled from behind him.

"Oh, I'm good at making friends." She blinked slowly at him, her overlong eyelashes seeming to reach for him. "We should get together sometime."

Straker opened his mouth to protest, but Tachina went on before he could speak.

"You know," she said, "Frankie and his *woman*, you and your *girl*, sharing a meal, some wine, some *fun*."

Straker felt as if Tachina were targeting him with waves of sexual energy. He had no idea how she did it, how she could be molded to the other man's body yet still manage to act available to Straker. Murdock was such a nerd, he probably had no idea.

What was her game? If he had to guess, she was intent on attaching herself to the highest-status male she could find, climbing the ladder of power. She'd probably made a play for Captain Gibson, but Straker knew the man was married with a family back on a Mutuality planet, a family he hoped someday to rescue. Now she was making it clear she'd ditch Murdock for Straker if he wished.

"Maybe sometime Miss," he said, "but I'm extremely busy for now."

Never gonna happen, he told himself. He could only imagine how Engels would react. She hadn't completely recovered her beauty from before the Hok injections, or the torture scars. The improvement had halted, leaving her skin mottled and rough. Comparing herself to Tachina would make her feel even worse about it.

That reminded him of the main reason he'd come to talk to Murdock. "Miss Tachina, I have one more thing to discuss with Frank, and then I'll send him home to you, I promise. Half an hour, no more."

Tachina pouted, but left with a flounce clearly designed to keep the men's eyeballs glued to her posterior until she was out of sight.

"Gods, what a woman," said Murdock reverently.

"That she is." Straker lifted an eyebrow. "Enjoy her while you can."

"What… what's that supposed to mean?"

"Forget it," Straker said, deciding not to dash the man's happiness before the inevitable ending. "You know, just a saying. Seize the day and all that. But speaking of women, I have a special project for you."

"More work?" Murdock complained.

"Yes, sorry. You can assign a tech if you're not the right expert, but I need the best work and no mistakes."

Murdock straightened and rubbed his hands. "Sure, boss. You can count on me. What's the job?"

Straker explained it to him with Murdock growing more concerned with each word he spoke.

∗ ∗ ∗

Once done with Murdock, Straker found his way to the nearby docking port hangar. There was one at each end of Freiheit. By placing them at the ends, near the habitat's axis, they minimized the apparent motion of the entrances, making it easier for ships to enter and exit.

In the big space he saw *Lockstep, Liberator,* and the seven surviving attack ships. Thick cables snaked from the vessels to plug into a large humming machine, some kind of power distributor, to augment the habitat's single auxiliary reactor.

Revenge was nowhere to be seen. She had docked externally, as she had no landing surfaces or struts. The Ruxin ship had never been designed to set down on anything solid. Straker doubted Murdock had run a power tap to her. The systems were almost certainly incompatible without major modification.

Zaxby had suggested putting Revenge down in the lake, but Straker vetoed that idea. The Ruxins were weird enough without them disturbing the civilians by living in the middle of the hab's main recreation area. That said, the octopoids did swim in the lake during the day, and the locals were starting to get used to them.

Engels waved at Straker from *Liberator*'s open hatch. Technicians welded crysteel patches over some of the worst damage, and others had one of the ship's six lasers dismantled on the deck. One woman in a suspended harness was finishing up painting over the corvette's old numerical designation.

Straker jumped up easily to the hatch in the low gravity and embraced Engels, kissing her soundly. "You happy with '*Liberator*'? Now's the time to choose a new name for your ship, before the paint dries."

"Absolutely," Engels said as she led him into the cramped wardroom of the compact ship.

"I like it too. But even if I didn't, she's your ship, not mine."

"I may be the ship's captain, but you're the admiral, Derek."

Straker shrugged. "I'm thinking maybe 'Commodore' is more appropriate. Calling myself 'General' is pretentious, not to mention it would seem like I'm trying to imitate DeChang."

"Fine by me." Engels drew two mugs of caff and sat. "How's the mechsuit situation?"

Straker sat across from her and accepted a cup. "No problems. We should be able to put out one unit a month."

"So few?"

"Mechsuits are complex things, and this is a small factory, only ever designed to make replacement parts. The machinery can turn out any piece, but only one thing at a time. Then we need to fit each and test it, and–"

Engels held up hand. "I get it."

A knock came at the wardroom's open door. It was a tech, one of Murdock's people. Several more nerds could be seen behind her.

"Sir, ma'am?" the tech said. "Where's the autodoc?"

Engels pointed aft. "This ship's not big enough to get lost in. Second door on the left. What's going on?"

Straker waved the techs onward. "Carry on." He turned to Engels. "I ordered the autodoc removed and installed in the clinic. It's the most advanced piece of medical technology we have. We can get a lot more use out of it there."

"Okay, I can see that. Hate not to have it aboard in a fight, though. Daniels wouldn't have survived his laser burns without it."

"We'll try to get you another one. The Ruxins have an industrial base a hundred times bigger than ours. We just need to persuade them to adapt some of their production to our needs."

"You really think they'll welcome us?"

Straker spread his arms. "Why not? I'm the War Male. I commanded the ship in its first action."

"*Her*, Derek, remember? Ships are *her*."

"Why is that, anyway?"

She reached for his hand. "Because they need a lot of care, but if you give it to them, they'll never let you down."

Straker smiled. "I thought it was because they could be bitches."

"That too."

"Okay, I'll try to remember to call it *her*. Makes as much sense as calling Zaxby *him*. Anyway, Zaxby and I trained her crew. If the Ruxins rebuild a fleet to liberate their homeworld, those squids will form the basis of their naval personnel. Plus, we'll share our technology with them. They're eighty years out of date, remember? And I don't see them piloting mechsuits, so we humans will keep a lock on heavy ground combat. They'll see how working together helps both species."

Engels shook her head. "I don't think it'll be as easy as you think, but I agree it has to be done."

Straker squeezed her hand and stood, finishing his caff. "Hey, it's been good to spend some time with you, but I have a dozen other things to do."

"Remember to delegate," she reminded him.

"No problem—especially things I don't want to do. I wish I could delegate the trials, though."

Engels walked him out of the ship. "You need to be there for those. At least the capital cases. They have to be seen as fair, and it's part of your role to dispense justice."

"I know, but it's such a chore now that the battles are over."

"They're not over," she said, "just on hold. Unless you want to give up your dream of liberating the galaxy?"

Straker snorted. "The galaxy? I'll settle for the Mutuality and the Hundred Worlds."

Engels cocked her head. "I'm not sure whether you're dreaming too large or too small, Derek. It's a big universe."

Straker kissed her one more time. "Don't go all brainiac on me now. I had enough of them today already. See you at dinner." He leaped to the deck, waved, and strode off, a bounce in his step.

That bounce disappeared as his old handtab beeped. It was reminding him of the beginning of the trials.

Outside the same makeshift brig, still filled with Unmutual prisoners, he'd parked his mechsuit, a reminder of the hanging of Master Sergeant Yates. A rope with a noose had been thrown over the outstretched arm.

More than one of the people gathered there stared at that ominous symbol of justice—local citizens, guards, and those with faces pressed to the barred windows awaiting trial.

And that's what it needed to be, Straker knew. Not retribution, not revenge, but *justice*. It had to be seen as fair, even merciful, giving the accused every chance to avoid the grim reaper's scythe—but it had to be there as the ultimate end of those who committed the most heinous of crimes.

Straker nodded at Mayor Weinberg and took his seat. This time he would preside as the commander-in-chief, but he'd only intervene if things got out of hand. Those controlling the process were seven judges, chosen from among the whole of the community and Straker's cohort, those with judiciary experience. Others with skill in the law would act as attorneys for the prosecution and defense.

The judges would determine guilt or innocence, and decide on sentences ranging from flogging to hard labor to hanging. Straker had insisted there be no long-term incarceration, no "life sentences." The goal was to rehabilitate and integrate, not create a permanent drain on the resources of the community. If the judges didn't think an offender stood a chance of rehabilitation, he or she would be executed.

Fourteen trials had been completed by the time Straker declared the weary day over with. All but two had admitted their crimes and apologized publicly for their disgusting actions. This was a condition of their sentencing.

Nine had been flogged publicly, brutally whipped until they bled profusely from the cuts of the fiber strands, with everyone looking on. Some broke down and pleaded for mercy, but there was none to be had... not until the requisite number of strokes had been applied.

Many among the populace turned away, sickened. This, too, was something Straker wanted, something he'd discussed with Engels and Loco and Weinberg and others of his inner circle. The common people had to understand what their representatives did in their name. They needed to see that justice, while necessary, had its ugly side, and couldn't be shoved behind closed doors for someone else to take care of.

Once these nine had received their floggings, they were taken to the habitat's tiny hospital and given minimal treatment—disinfectants and antibiotics only, no pain medications. As soon as possible, they'd be released to positions in Straker's Breakers as common soldiers, remaining under strict military discipline until the chain of command determined they could be trusted.

Three others, in addition to being flogged, were sentenced to periods of hard labor ranging from one to six years. They would work out their punishments in the mines or the farm fields, giving something back to the community as scant recompense for the misery they'd inflicted.

Of the two remaining, one had been acquitted. The other had been stubbornly contemptuous of those who judged him. He'd been sentenced to hang.

The hanging ended the day. The miscreant was not given any final words or any particular dignity.

Once the man had stopped dancing in the air, Straker stood, reciting a short speech he'd memorized. "Let this criminal's body be tossed into underspace, there to drift forever, forgotten by all, remembered by none, with nothing to mark his grave or his passing. So shall be the fate of all who commit capital crimes here on Freiheit or anywhere I command." He picked up the gavel in front of him and struck it on the handmade wooden table. "These trials are adjourned for the day. We resume at noon tomorrow."

Chapter 45

Aboard Freiheit.

Three days later, after all the trials were done and justice dispensed, Straker met with his inner circle. This group consisted of the leaders and key personnel from among his subordinates. Fresh bread and butter, cheese and fruit adorned the conference room table, along with hot caff. It wasn't the exquisite cuisine he remembered from his Hundred Worlds days, but it sure beat shipboard nutrition paste.

Once everyone had a chance to stuff some food in their faces and gulp caff, Straker rapped his knuckles on the table.

"Thanks for coming," he boomed, "and thanks for all your hard work so far. Report around the room. Afterward, we can work on solutions to whatever issues arise."

"Sure, *Commodore* Straker," Loco said with a grin. Straker noted with irritation his boots were already on the table. "Congrats on your promotion. Now I can be a captain, maybe even a commander?"

"Changing ranks to fit our new situation..." Straker said. "Not a bad proposal."

Loco looked startled. "It wasn't my idea. I thought–"

"No need to be bashful about it," Straker said loudly. Some in the group laughed, as Loco had never been bashful a moment in his life. Straker looked at Engels, who shrugged.

"Might as well make it official," she said. "With this many people, we need an expanded chain of command with enough room for many levels of officers. All in favor of officially making Straker a commodore?"

Everyone in the room spoke in assent, and applause broke out.

"Thanks, all," Straker said. "Loco, Engels, Gibson, you're getting new ranks as well. Zaxby and Loco are lieutenants, naval-style. Engels and Gibson are commanders. I always thought having one structure for Fleet and one for ground forces was stupid anyway."

Loco perked up immediately. "What's my new pay scale? Do I get my own concubine issued?"

Straker glared. "No concubines. If you can't get enough action with your boyish charm, tough shit."

Loco pouted ostentatiously.

Straker pulled out his handtab and looked at his notes. "Enlisted ranks will be based on ground troop conventions, as follows: Private, Corporal, Sergeant, Master Sergeant, with the courtesy titles of Spear and Chief, depending on position. Officers will be naval: Ensign, Lieutenant, Commander, and Commodore, with the courtesy title of Captain for ship bosses. Anyone got a problem with that?"

No one spoke up against the decree.

"Loco, since you opened your mouth first, you get to start the reports."

Loco nodded and sat forward. "I've organized the ground forces into a regiment, with companies, platoons and squads. I've requisitioned a couple of warehouses as barracks for the single soldiers, and there are empty residences where paired couples can live among the civilians. I'm working with the mayor to find jobs for the rank and file when they're not performing military duties. Only the noncoms and officers will be full-time. The rest will be a semi-militia, highly trained and well equipped, to be mobilized as needed. That's as far as I've gotten."

"What about equipment?" Straker asked.

"Mostly just small arms," Loco replied. "We're short of grenades, crew-served weapons, rocket launchers, battlesuits, and we have no armored vehicles. If not for the Sledgehammer and the Foehammer, we'd be completely sucking wind."

"Thanks. Mayor Weinberg?"

The mayor looked over the top of her reading glasses. "I've reconstituted the community council and I've promised elections within a year. We'll have to figure out a system of money and taxation, job and work allocation, and a number of revisions to laws. Fortunately, as WG604 we were already fairly autonomous. Since being, um, *liberated...* and then liberated again into Freiheit Station, we have been winging it, but I'm confident things will shake out." She cocked her head with a wry expression.

"Great..." Straker said, looking around at the rest of them. "Zaxby?"

"My young fellow Ruxins are enjoying their R&R. They are not used to so much freedom from crowding or such a pleasant aquatic recreational area. Did you know that over the two centuries this habitat has been in existence, the lake has developed its own ecosystem, and one of the species of freshwater mollusks there is quite tasty? I have had to insist they do not overindulge. Also—"

"Uh yeah, Zaxby..." Straker said. "How about a status report? Any engineering issues? Anything practical, anyway?"

"Always focusing on the practical, Commodore Straker... Can't you simply enjoy life as it comes?"

Straker narrowed his eyes. "Not with so much to do and so many to mourn, no."

Zaxby made a sighing noise. "Very well. The vessel will need a thorough refit in dry dock. We did the best we could in the original refurbishment, but many parts are old and need to be renewed completely. We expended most of the fusion warheads, and fissionables to trigger the detonations were in short supply among my people when we left. You will have to insist on prioritization of finding and processing uranium isotopes, or we will have an Archer without enough float mines. Once these issues are handled, *Revenge* should be combat-effective again."

Straker stroked his chin. "How about the possibility of building more sneaky ships, or heavier warships? Corvettes, maybe?"

"My people's industrial capacity is not infinite. War materiel is expensive and does not make for good long-term economic policy. Premier Freenix was just beginning to build and colonize more asteroid habitats. This is the work of years, and she will not want to divert resources for further battles."

Straker nodded. "Fair enough. I'll twist her arm—or, tentacle—as much as I can, but we might have to find ships elsewhere."

Loco laughed. "So we'll be freebooters after all."

"Maybe so. Now, Zaxby, what about Freiheit?"

Murdock stage-coughed, and Zaxby slid his eyes to him. "I will defer to my supervisor on that issue," he said.

"You guys getting along now?" Straker asked.

The human and the Ruxin eyed one another. "We're working together okay," Murdock admitted. "But I spend more time reining in the Ruxins than getting them moving, unlike the rest of my people," he said. "They want to tinker with everything."

"We've improved the efficiency of many systems," Zaxby said sharply.

"By using nonstandard methods and techniques I can't replicate or maintain," Murdock replied. "But... as long as we can keep some of the Ruxins here as civil engineers, we'll do all right."

"Aha!" Zaxby exclaimed. "So, you admit the value of the Ruxin contribution?"

"Sure, if you'll admit you'd rather live among humans than go back to being a neutered drone in your overcrowded squid-pile."

Zaxby squirmed. "I cede your point, and I hope Commodore Straker will argue for keeping me and my fellows here to assist you."

"You just don't want to go back to being a small fish in a big pond!" Loco crowed. "You like being a big shot."

"Of course, *Lieutenant* Paloco. Which reminds me, Commodore. What about *my* promotion? Have I not earned an increase in status?"

Straker smiled. "You have, *Lieutenant* Zaxby. You're junior to Loco, though, and don't let it go to your big fat head. I can always demote you, remember."

"I could hardly forget. My memory, like the rest of my physiology, is excellent."

"Moving on..." Engels said.

"Yes," said Straker. "Continue, Mister Murdock."

"Sidespace systems are fragile. Wherever we emerge, that's where we'll be for a while. More critically, we need power generators, or we need a star nearby. Without power, we can't repair as much, mine as much, build as much. Or grow as much, for that matter. We need to be able to run the luminary generators at least eight hours per day or the crops won't yield properly. That's my number one issue."

"I'll make that my number one issue with Freenix, then," said Straker. "Heiser?"

The big noncom stood. "With Lieutenant Paloco's guidance, I've appointed noncommissioned officers and drafted a tentative training plan. We could use a lot more equipment, but for now, we'll make do. You will be there at tomorrow's memorial service, sir? I'm setting up an honor guard."

Straker nodded. "Of course I'll be there."

Heiser let out his breath. "Thank you, sir. The Ritter brothers would especially appreciate it."

Straker raised an eyebrow. "Really? Why?"

"Ah, well, given that Bernhard didn't make it…"

"What? What happened?" asked Straker.

"Two Unmutuals hiding in the tunnels. They shot and killed him. His men returned the favor, but…"

"Damn. I hadn't heard. And after the real fighting was over. What a waste."

Engels leaned forward and interrupted harshly, "You *didn't* just say that, *Commodore* Straker."

Straker stared at her, lifting his eyebrows. "What? No?"

She shook her head. "No, you *didn't* say anything about his honorable sacrifice being a *waste*. Understand, sir?"

"I only meant–"

Engels spoke slowly, her words heavy with meaning. "I know what you meant, sir, but it's critical that the commander-in-chief makes it clear that *every* death has meaning and purpose, that it serves the greater good. People don't want to believe their comrades and friends died for nothing."

Straker held up a hand. "Got it, got it. Thank you, Commander Engels. And all of you, never be afraid to tell me something I need to hear, like that." He tapped his handtab. "I guess I need to work on my eulogy." He turned his eyes to the next man at the table. "Commander Gibson?"

"*Lockstep* is fine, my crew is fine. Giving assistance where we can, mostly repairing *Liberator*," Gibson said. "We'll hold up our end and do what needs doing, but now that we've had a chance to breathe, my people are already asking me about when we can go rescue our families."

"As soon as we can, Commander Gibson," said Straker. "You have my word. But you have to know, given the paranoid nature of Mutualist society, they might already have been sent to re-education camps."

"Or worse." Gibson, middle-aged and weary, looked positively bleak. "We knew that might happen when we killed the Lazarus. I killed him, I mean… but we'd long ago agreed that if we had a chance to defect to some better society, we would."

"And we're damn glad you did." Straker waited a moment, and when Gibson gestured toward Engels, he shifted his eyes. "Commander?"

Engels laced her fingers in front of her and hunched her shoulders. "We came through the battle as well as could be expected. No deaths, several injuries. And I really think we need to get some research going on this Hok biotech. If we could adapt it, get only certain benefits, like the strength and fast healing, it would help a lot." She rubbed her face. "And lose the effect on skin."

Zaxby waved a tentacle. "I suggest looking to my people for this possibility. Premier Freenix might grasp at the chance of acquiring such knowledge, and she likely has many skilled biologists available. But Commodore Straker needs to raise the issue, not me. I am viewed as tainted by my long association with humans."

"Bummer, dude," Loco said. "Maybe when we liberate your homeworld they'll see you as a hero."

"I'm not holding my breath. Not that I need to hold my breath, as I have both gills and lungs, but–"

Engels interrupted, "I've identified seven humans as attack ship pilots or pilot-candidates. We can't afford to leave firepower parked in the hangar. And speaking of firepower, we need to upgun those things. They have single-shot missile tubes but no missiles, and they can handle a larger beam weapon than they currently have. I've got a few ideas for improving *Liberator* as well."

"We'll do the best we can, but resources will be tight for a while," Straker said.

He turned to the last person at the table, Chief Gurung, who said, "Sir, I am working on a naval crew training regimen. We have many volunteers. Perhaps they see the positions as more desirable than infantry."

"Anything's better than being a grunt," Loco mumbled.

"For the individual, maybe," Straker said, "but we need grunts too. What else?"

"That's all I have," Gurung said.

Straker stood. "Anything more for me? If not, carry on. I have an appointment." He left quickly, allowing his subordinates to remain to coordinate among themselves. He'd found that if he stuck around too long, he impeded them in their work rather than helping. Besides, he had something important to do.

At the tiny habitat hospital he visited the wounded and sick. Some kind of flu seemed to be going around, no doubt a product of mixing humans from several different sources. Medic First Class Campos, the closest thing to a doctor they had, assured him various minor diseases should run their courses over time, finding new hosts and stabilizing as the populace built immunities.

Once done with the visiting duties, he slipped into the room with the autodoc. Campos followed him in and sat at a small desk that held the machine's detachable control panel. One of Murdock's technicians closed up an access port and began putting away her tools.

"Is it ready?" Straker asked.

"Yes, sir," Campos said, repeatedly smoothing her hair behind her ears.

"Nervous?"

"A little, sir."

"What could go wrong?" Straker demanded. "It's not like it'll chop my arm off... right?"

"Oh, no, sir! The worst that could happen is failure... and some pain."

Straker smiled. "Good. Let's give it a try."

"Get in, then, sir," she said, opening the coffin-like machine's clear crysglass lid. "You'll have to take off your, ah, trousers. We'll try a patch of your left leg first, if that's all right with you."

When he came out of the autodoc two hours later, the skin on his leg hurt like hell. The machine turned off his nerves with an electronic field while he was inside, but he'd refused painkillers afterward, reserving the scarce medicine for people who really needed it.

The results seemed promising, though, and he felt happy. Why this one small victory should cheer him up so much in the face of so much death and disruption, he had no idea, but it did.

"We'll make adjustments and try it again later today, if you please, sir," said Campos.

"I'll come by after lunch. You keep working. Great job."

Campos face lit up. She was a plain-looking girl when working earnestly, but when she smiled like that, she became quite attractive. Straker hoped Loco treated her well. In fact, he made a note to himself to give Loco a stern warning. It wouldn't do for one of the senior officers to play the field and break hearts all over the tiny community. He needed to set a good example.

Then Straker laughed. You're turning into quite the patriarch, he said to himself, shaking your finger and telling everyone to stay in line or else. But the alternative was letting things slowly drift and fall apart, maybe even turn rotten like Ramirez's command had. Once corruption set in, it would be hard to root out. Better to start firm and loosen later.

He grabbed a quick lunch and took a walk around the circumference of the hab's interior along one of the crosswise paths. He still couldn't get used to the fact that he could start at one place and walk in one direction until he returned, less than a kilometer later, to the exact same spot.

By the time he returned to the hospital and Campos examined his leg, it showed much smoother to the eye and the touch.

"The mottling and roughness disfiguring that patch of skin are much reduced," Campos said. "It will be a slow, steady process, though, to avoid scarring. We'll let the 'doc scan you and we'll revise the protocol even more." She clapped the machine with her palm. "Hop in again, sir."

Two more sessions improved the procedure enough that Straker was confident it could be tried on someone else. When he went home that evening to Carla, he could hardly contain his good cheer, but refused to tell her why he was so happy, even after she laughingly demanded the information after a bout of athletic lovemaking—in the dark, he insisted, to hide the autodoc's work.

The next morning he led her by the hand to the hospital and, in the bright light of the autodoc chamber, showed her his left leg, now looking like ordinary human skin. The difference was dramatic alongside his untreated right leg.

"That's amazing," Carla said, running her hand over the smoothed skin.

"Keep doing that and we may have to send the others away," Straker said with a grin.

"Down, boy," she told him. Then, as if in sudden realization, Carla lifted her hand to her face. "Oh… Great Cosmos… I might…"

"Yes," Campos said with a grin. "We can fix your face!"

"It's not perfect," said Straker, "But I think with a little makeup you'll look…"

"Normal?" Carla said.

"I was going to say *better than ever.*"

Engels threw her arms around his neck and kissed him. "This means a lot to me."

He smiled hopefully. "You hardly need any improvements, but if it makes you feel better, I'm happy."

It was the right thing to say, and she embraced him enthusiastically.

✳ ✳ ✳

The honor guard was just arriving at the cemetery when Straker and Engels got there after changing into their dress uniforms. The two senior officers spent the next hour greeting people, shaking hands and hugging a few civilians, even kissing a couple of babies while speaking their condolences.

Straker hadn't known most of the dead personally, but he had a list of names and did his level best to make all the family and friends know he cared. Forty-seven simple fiber caskets would be lowered into the ground today, under a suitably dim and somber lighting that simulated an overcast sky.

When the proper time came in the mass ceremony, after the community chaplain had spoken his words of comfort, Straker took the podium. He gazed out over the crowd of several hundred—as many as could do it took time off from duties for this observance.

"I'm not much of a public speaker," he began, "and I don't know much about where our souls might go when we die. But in the Regiment—my old mechsuit regiment, that is—when a comrade-in-arms was struck down by the enemy, the chaplain recited words like these, and we all echoed them."

He looked down at his handtab, at the modified version of a mechsuiter's funeral benediction, and read. "Ashes to ashes, dust to dust. Unknowable Creator, into your hands we commend the bodies and spirits of our friends and comrades. As they were worthy, resurrect them on the Final Day, that they may serve honorably in your Celestial Realm once more. Amen."

Straker raised his eyes to the onlookers. He didn't know for sure that what he'd said was even true, but these people needed hope, not doubt. "I believed those words then, and I believe them now. Death is not the end. But even if it were, I wouldn't do anything differently. I'm going to do my very best to lead you, to lead everyone, down a road that will liberate the oppressed people of the Mutuality, and anyone else we find who suffers under tyrants. Nobody should live beneath the boot-heel of a system that crushes their humanity with torture and threats to their families. This I promise you."

He walked off the low dais to more applause and cheering than seemed appropriate for a funeral, but he hoped the people would remember his words and pass them on to their neighbors. He stood at attention next to Engels, Loco, Zaxby, Heiser, the Ritter brothers and others, saluting crisply as the honor guard fired blanks into the air and a bugler sent a sad and ancient melody floating above the gathering.

When the shots and the music had ended, when the final caskets had been lowered into their graves, Loco and Carla turned instinctively toward him.

"What now, boss?" Loco asked.

"Now?" Straker clapped his best friend on the back with one hand and hugged Engels with the other, staring past them at the slowly brightening habitat. "Now the war of liberation really begins."

The End

About the Authors

David VanDyke is a Hugo Award finalist, and the bestselling author of the Plague Wars and Stellar Conquest series, which have sold more than 300,000 copies to date. He is co-author of B.V. Larson's million-selling Star Force Series, Books 10, 11 and 12. He also writes P. I. mysteries under the pen name D. D. VanDyke. He's a retired U.S. military officer, veteran of two branches of the armed forces, and has served in several combat zones. He lives with his wife and dogs near Tucson, Arizona.

B. V. Larson is the author of more than fifty books with over two million copies sold. His fiction regularly tops the bestseller charts. He writes in several genres, but most of his work is Science Fiction. Many of his titles have been professionally produced as audiobooks and print as well as ebook form. Eight of them have been translated into other languages and distributed by major publishers in foreign countries. He writes college textbooks in addition to fiction, and his three-book series on computer science is currently in its sixth edition.

CASTALIA HOUSE

MILITARY SCIENCE FICTION
The Eden Plague by David VanDyke
Reaper's Run by David VanDyke
Skull's Shadows by David VanDyke
There Will Be War Volumes I and II ed. Jerry Pournelle
Riding the Red Horse Volume 1 ed. Tom Kratman and Vox Day

SCIENCE FICTION
The End of the World as We Knew It by Nick Cole
CTRL-ALT REVOLT! by Nick Cole
Somewhither by John C. Wright
Back From the Dead by Rolf Nelson
Victoria: A Novel of Fourth Generation War by Thomas Hobbes

NON-FICTION
MAGA Mindset: Making YOU and America Great Again by Mike Cernovich
SJWs Always Lie by Vox Day
Cuckservative by John Red Eagle and Vox Day
Equality: The Impossible Quest by Martin van Creveld
A History of Strategy by Martin van Creveld
4th Generation Warfare Handbook
        by William S. Lind and LtCol Gregory A. Thiele, USMC
Compost Everything by David the Good
Grow or Die by David the Good

FICTION
Brings the Lightning by Peter Grant
The Missionaries by Owen Stanley

FANTASY
The Green Knight's Squire by John C. Wright
Iron Chamber of Memory by John C. Wright

AUDIOBOOKS
A History of Strategy narrated by Jon Mollison
Cuckservative narrated by Thomas Landon
Four Generations of Modern War narrated by William S. Lind
Grow or Die narrated by David the Good
Extreme Composting narrated by David the Good
A Magic Broken narrated by Nick Afka Thomas

CPSIA information can be obtained
at www.ICGtesting.com
Printed in the USA
BVOW03s0456190617
486870BV00006B/164/P

9 789527 065334